THE
PERSONA
PROTOCOL

By Andy McDermott and available from Headline

ANDY McDERMOTT

THE PERSONA PROTOCOL

headline

First published in 2013 by
HEADLINE PUBLISHING GROUP

1

Cataloguing in Publication Data is available from the British Library

Hardback ISBN 978 0 7553 8068 8
Trade paperback ISBN 978 0 7553 8069 5

Typeset in Aldine 401 by Avon DataSet Ltd,
Bidford-on-Avon, Warwickshire

Printed and bound in Great Britain by
Clays Ltd, St Ives plc

Headline's policy is to use papers that are natural, renewable and
recyclable products and made from wood grown in sustainable forests.
The logging and manufacturing processes are expected to conform
to the environmental regulations of the country of origin.

HEADLINE PUBLISHING GROUP
An Hachette UK Company
338 Euston Road
London NW1 3BH

www.headline.co.uk
www.hachette.co.uk

For my family and friends

1

Being Giorgi Toradze

Peshawar, Pakistan

The voices in Adam Gray's head were being controlling, as always.

'There's an intersection on your left, thirty metres ahead,' said Holly Jo Voss through the tiny transceiver implanted in the American's right ear. 'Go down it.'

'Okay,' he said under his breath, lips ventriloquist-still. He raised the brim of his heavy black umbrella to check the street. The torrential downpour had scoured the thoroughfare of its populace, those few Pakistanis not taking shelter scurrying along with coats shrugged up over their heads. A narrow side road was visible through the spray where Holly Jo had said. 'I see it. How far to the rendezvous?'

'Less than sixty metres, at the far end.'

'Anyone waiting for me?'

Another voice came through the 'earwig': male, young, cocky. 'I see two assholes chilling on the corner,' Kyle Falconetti told him. Somewhere above, a compact remotely controlled quadrotor was tracking Adam's progress through the city. Even without the rain, he doubted he could have spotted the little drone; it was designed to be stealthy, and the New Jersey native was a skilled pilot. 'Either they don't got the brains to come in out of the rain, or they're your new buddies.'

This was it: first contact with the targets. He swelled his chest with borrowed confidence as he rounded the corner, shifting the weight of the large, heavy black case in his right hand. 'Here we go.'

Let's do the deal, said a third voice.

This one was not in his ear.

Giorgi Toradze: age forty, Georgian, a former mercenary who had discovered more profit in selling weapons to those who wanted to fight wars than participating in the conflicts himself. The case contained samples of his deadly trade. However, the arms dealer was small fry, of limited interest to American intelligence.

The same was not true of his potential clients.

Toradze had been intercepted en route to Pakistan. Adam had replaced him, his dark hair dyed fully black and a fake moustache painstakingly applied, contact lenses turning his grey eyes blue. He was slightly taller and in much better physical shape than the Georgian, and a full decade younger, but with an overcoat concealing his build and Toradze's gold jewellery on conspicuous display, he would superficially match the description the Pakistanis had been given.

The deception would instantly collapse if any of them had previously met the real arms dealer. But Toradze knew that was unlikely.

And everything Toradze knew, now Adam did too.

He made his way along the side street, rain pattering loudly off his umbrella's strong fabric. Ahead, a man leaned against a wall.

Early twenties, scraggly beard, a grubby sky-blue nylon jacket open despite the deluge. Right hand held pressed against his chest, fingertips edging under the zipper as he saw the approaching figure.

Look at this cretin. Could he make it any more obvious that he's got a gun?

Toradze's assessment, but Adam shared it. The man waiting for him was doubtless a recent recruit to the terrorist group, eager to prove his worth. Adam looked him in the eye as he got closer, challenging without being aggressive.

The Pakistani met his gaze with a twitch of belligerence. In the highlands of the country's north-western provinces, where his organisation operated in the open, such provocation would have met with an angry, even violent response. But here in the city he had to tread carefully. He regarded Adam for another moment, then said a single word in Pashto over one shoulder.

A second man, a few years older, came round the corner. He looked the new arrival up and down, comparing what he saw with what he had been told to expect. Black hair, moustache, about a hundred and eighty centimetres tall. Gold watch.

Toradze had specifically mentioned the Rolex in his self-description, being very proud of the ostentatious timepiece. Adam made sure it was clearly visible on his wrist as he lifted the umbrella higher. 'Is there a dentist near here?' he said, the English heavy with Toradze's native accent.

The second of the pair replied. 'Do you have a toothache?'

It was a simple pass code. Adam gave the agreed response. 'I have a delivery.'

The man nodded. 'You are Toradze?'

Adam gave him a cheery smile. 'Call me Giorgi. And you?'

'Umar. This is Marwat.'

'Good to meet you. Okay, I think we better get out of this rain! Let's go, hey?'

'This way.' Umar set off down the street, Adam following. Marwat took up the rear, right hand still poised across his chest.

'They're moving,' said Kyle. One of the large flat-screen monitors before him showed the three men walking down the road, viewed from overhead. The drone he controlled was hovering some eighty metres up, well clear of the surrounding buildings. He adjusted a dial and the view zoomed out to provide a wider view of the street maze. 'Heading north.'

'Don't lose them.' Tony Carpenter, the team's field commander, was watching the scene on his own monitor.

'Wasn't planning on doing, brah,' Kyle replied, with a little sarcasm. He nudged a joystick to send the UAV after its targets.

The fair-haired man ignored the mild insubordination. He was used to Kyle, and there were more important concerns. He regarded the aerial view intently, then looked across at another of the room's occupants. 'Holly Jo, check his tracker. We might lose line of sight.'

The willowy blonde tapped a command into her computer. A few seconds later, a hollow green square was superimposed on the street scene – directly over the black dodecagon of the umbrella. As Adam moved, so did the vivid symbol. 'Tracker is on, good signal.'

'Great.' Tony spoke into his headset. 'John, he's made contact and is on his way to the meet. We'll give you its location the second we have it.'

John Baxter, a former captain in the US Marines, was waiting in a van a few streets from the rendezvous point with a small team of armed men. 'Remember, the kill option is still available once we know where these bastards are.'

'Syed is more valuable to us alive than dead,' said Tony, reminding Baxter of the mission's objective – and who was in charge. On the monitor, the three figures were still heading for what might prove a very dangerous destination. 'If the plan works,' he added quietly.

'It'll work.' The fourth person in the dirty room was also one of the main reasons it was so cramped. Dr Roger Albion was a hulking bear of a man, college quarterback build still solid despite his last game being forty years earlier. 'Adam's not just imitating Toradze – he *is* Toradze. You of all people should know that. He can do this.'

'I hope so.' The umbrella disappeared from sight as the trio turned into a narrow alley, the green square still moving. 'For his sake.'

Adam followed Umar through the urban labyrinth. The deluge was beginning to ease off, some braver souls emerging from shelter. 'So, is it much further, hey?' he said. 'If I'd known we were going to walk in the rain, I would have paid for a taxi!'

'It is not far,' said Umar. He gestured ahead. 'Up there.'

The building he indicated was a disorderly five-storey block of brick and concrete. Adam assessed it. One door at the front, probably another to an alley at the back. Flat roof, the railings along its edge suggesting it was easily accessible. The building to its left was higher, hard to climb, but to the right was a lower rooftop that could act as an escape route.

Toradze had his own opinions. *What a dump!* The Georgian did not foresee trouble, feeling nothing but confidence – and greed. *They want what I'm selling. They* need *what I'm selling. Make the deal, make the money – then I can leave this craphole.*

They reached the building. Beside the entrance was a bank of doorbells, small signs listing the occupants in a mixture of Urdu,

Pashto and English. Umar thumbed one button. Adam read the sign: DR K. R. FARUQUE, DDS. 'So we really are seeing a dentist, hey?' he said with a laugh. 'Does Dr Faruque give you boys a discount?' The crooked-toothed Umar responded with an irritable look.

Holly Jo spoke inside Adam's ear. 'Dr Faruque, got it. I'll get Levon to confirm the address.'

Seconds passed, then a click came from an intercom. A man spoke in tinny and hollow Pashto, to which Umar replied tersely with his name. Another pause, then a buzzer rasped. He pushed open the door. 'In here.'

Adam stopped in the doorway, shaking water off his umbrella before straining to pull the folding spokes closed. The mechanism finally clicked, the device now reduced to a foot-long baton. He slipped it into a coat pocket. Marwat made an annoyed sound at being forced to wait outside.

Tony's voice came through the earwig. 'We've got the address. Sending John's team there now.'

Adam didn't reply, instead following Umar up a narrow flight of stairs to the third floor. A door of scuffed dark wood bore the words DENTAL PRACTICE in flaking gold leaf. Umar rapped on it: two quick knocks, a pause, then two slower ones. The door opened a crack, someone peering suspiciously at the three men on the landing, then moving back to let them enter.

The room beyond was a combined reception area and waiting room. Adam immediately saw that none of the five men inside were there for a check-up. The openly displayed guns – some pointed at him – were a giveaway.

This is it. Play the part. *Be* the part.

He let Toradze's persona come to the fore as he took in the terrorist group, the sum of the Georgian's past experiences shaping his thoughts. Though there was some fear, it was mostly masked by dismissive arrogance. *God, what a stink. Don't these pigs use soap? And look at this idiot, holding his pistol sideways like he's an American gangsta. Amateurs. But as long as they pay . . .*

His eyes moved to the reception desk. An AK-47 assault rifle lay upon it. *Like an icon on the Holy Table.* The gun's owner sat behind, watching him intently. Older than his companions, though not by much – early thirties, but aged further by the weathering of conflict. A grey-streaked beard reaching down to his chest, dark-rimmed eyes set in a blocky, unsmiling face.

Adam recognised him immediately. Malik Syed, leader of an al-Qaeda terrorist cell. Fanatic. Killer.

Target.

Umar and Marwat quickly frisked him. Wallet, passport, phone, the umbrella. A SIG-Sauer P228 handgun and spare magazine. He waited for them to finish their search and return his possessions before speaking to the man behind the desk. 'You must be Syed,' he said almost casually. The arms dealer would have appeared unfazed by the guns; he had to be the same. He switched the heavy case to his left hand, holding out his right. 'It is good to meet you.'

Syed made no effort to extend his own hand. 'You are Toradze?'

'Giorgi, please! Yes, I am.' Adam cocked an eyebrow. 'You were expecting someone else?'

The dark eyes narrowed. 'You are younger than I thought.'

'Only than I look. I take care of my appearance.'

One of the other men whispered something in Pashto, which aroused muted chuckles from his companions. 'I think he said "Just like a woman",' said Holly Jo, affronted.

'It helps me *get* the women,' Adam told the joker, his smile taking on a lecherous tinge. 'Especially the virgins, hey? You can have yours in the afterlife; I'll take mine now!'

The young man seemed both surprised that the visitor had

understood him and offended at being mocked, but a stern look from Syed told him to contain his anger. 'You have brought the merchandise?' asked the terrorist leader.

Adam turned back to him. 'I have. If you still want to see it.'

'I do . . . Giorgi.' Syed stood, finally raising his right hand.

'I knew we would be friends,' said Adam with a grin as he shook it. 'Okay! You want to take a look?'

Syed nodded, sliding the AK-47 aside to clear a space on the desk. Adam hoisted the case on to it and clicked the tumblers on the combination lock before opening the lid. His audience instinctively leaned forward for a better view.

The case was filled with impact-resistant foam rubber. Set into it were three squat olive-green cylinders with conical noses, long metal tubes extending from their bases. Adam carefully lifted one out. 'This is a Russian PG-7VX rocket-propelled grenade,' he announced, Toradze's persona automatically launching into a sales pitch. 'A triple-stage HEAT warhead, so new it is still technically experimental. Not even the Russian army has them yet. It works with a standard RPG-7 launcher – which I think you are all familiar with, hey?' he added with another grin. 'But it has almost twice the power of a normal anti-tank round. It will blast through nine hundred and sixty millimetres of armour . . . even the reactive kind.'

It took a moment for the Pakistanis to absorb the full significance of that, but when they did, they were duly impressed. 'That is right,' he went on. 'One of these can penetrate the side of an American Abrams tank! And it doesn't matter if it is using slat armour to deflect RPGs.' He indicated the rocket's nose. 'There is a small shaped charge designed to shatter slat armour before the rest of the warhead hits it. It will still get through. You don't need dozens of rounds to take out a target with these. One hit, one kill.'

He paused, the excited expressions telling him that his pitch had been successful. *That was good. That was damn good. Just look at them. They'll pay whatever I want . . .*

Sudden disgust filled him. Syed and his group wanted to use the warheads to kill Americans and their allies, to spread their extremism through terror and murder. And he was helping them do it . . .

Calm down. Remember the mission. Play the part. Be the part.

Be Toradze.

I am *Toradze.*

If his brief crisis of conscience had shown on his face, none of the others noticed. Syed finally tore his gaze from the rocket. 'How many do you have?'

'At the moment, only ten. But I will be able to get another fifty in the next two weeks, and maybe as many as three hundred in the month after that.'

Caution tempered the terrorist's anticipation. 'If they are still experimental, how can you get so many?'

'I said they are *technically* still experimental. But that only means they have not yet been approved for field use by the Russian army. They are in full production ready for export sales – and I have a pipeline into the factory.'

Syed nodded. 'And . . . the price?'

Be bold, be firm. They want *them. I can tell.*

'Per warhead? Two thousand US dollars.'

The Pakistani visibly flinched. 'Two *thousand* dollars?' he erupted. 'But we can buy anti-tank rockets for only two *hundred* dollars!'

Adam had anticipated the objection. 'Rockets that bounce off tanks. Rockets that cannot even break through the slat armour on a Stryker. Malik, my friend . . .' He gave Syed a broad smile. 'An

Abrams tank costs over six million dollars. You can kill that tank for just two thousand. It is a bargain.' *He's considering it. Keep pushing.* 'And if you want proof that they really work, then the three warheads here? They are yours, for nothing. My free sample.'

Syed considered the offer. 'Will they work?' he said eventually. 'Are they as good as you say?'

'I will bet my reputation on it,' Adam said proudly.

The terrorist leader stared at the warhead. *He's hooked. I've got him.* 'Okay. I will accept your . . . gift. If they work, how soon will you be able to deliver—'

The door buzzer sounded.

The other terrorists raised their guns in alarm. Suspicious eyes glared at Adam. But Syed waved a hand for them to remain still. He thumbed the intercom button and spoke in Pashto.

'Muhammad,' came the reply. Syed buzzed him in. His men lowered their guns. The terse response was probably a form of code, Adam decided, remembering that Umar had done the same. Saying anything more than their name would warn those inside that the new arrival was there under duress.

Syed turned back to his visitor. 'How soon will you be able to get us more rockets?'

'As I said, I can have fifty in two weeks. I will need a down payment – half the money in advance. Then all I need to know is where and when to deliver them.'

'One hundred thousand American dollars? It is a lot of money.'

Adam shrugged. 'It is a lot of firepower. But you can test that for yourself, hey?' He put the rocket back in the case. 'If you get three hits, you will get three kills. I guarantee it.'

For the first time, Syed's expression became something other than grim mistrust, the corners of his mouth crinkling upwards with malevolent anticipation. 'I look forward to it.'

'I thought you would.' *Got him. I've got him! Champagne to celebrate, once I'm out of this backwards alcohol-free country!* The part of him that was Toradze revelled in his success . . . while the rest struggled to conceal his loathing at his actions. Syed's group now had three devastating anti-tank weapons; while they would never receive any more, no matter how events played out – Toradze's contact at the weapons factory would soon be arrested – it was still three too many. The men in Washington who had authorised the mission had deemed the risk worth it. Adam didn't necessarily agree.

But his opinions were irrelevant. He had a job to do. Follow orders. Complete the mission.

Syed picked up one of the rockets, admiring it. 'After we test them, what then?'

'I will come back to Pakistan to collect my down payment,' Adam replied. 'Then we will arrange delivery.'

Syed nodded, then looked round at a knock on the door. Two quick, a pause, then two slower taps. Guns were raised again. Marwat, nearest the entrance, opened the door slightly to check who was outside, then let him in.

Cold fear surged through Adam's body as he recognised the newcomer.

The young man's name was Muhammad Khattak. He had met the arms dealer before. And he would know at a glance that the person standing alone in a room full of terrorists was not the real Giorgi Toradze.

2

Identity Crisis

Puzzlement grew on Khattak's face as he stared at Adam. He had expected to see somebody else, and at any moment would expose the supposed arms dealer as an impostor—

'Ah-ha, Muhammad Khattak!' said Adam with a broad smile. 'I did not expect to see you here. I thought you were fighting in Kurram?'

Khattak was baffled. He looked between the American and Syed. 'But – who are . . .'

Adam's grin widened. 'Oh, come on, Muhammad. I know it has been a few years since we met in Drosh, but even with the plastic surgery I don't look *that* different, do I?'

'Plastic surgery?' snapped Syed. He put the rocket back in the case, one hand moving towards the AK-47. 'Muhammad, what is going on?'

Khattak's confusion faded, replaced by worry – and anger. 'I don't . . . This – this is not Toradze!'

The room exploded into commotion. Two men rushed to the window, checking the street below, while Umar hurried to cover the door to the landing.

Every other man aimed his weapon at the interloper.

'Adam!' said Holly Jo urgently. 'Baxter's team can reach you in less than two minutes. If you need backup, tell us.'

Adam remained silent. Syed picked up his AK, flicking off the safety with a loud click. He gave the agent a cold stare. 'Tell me. Who are you?'

'I am Giorgi Toradze,' Adam replied, tempering defiance with exasperation at being doubted. He looked back at Khattak. 'Muhammad, it is me. Really! I had plastic surgery because my face was becoming a little too well-known. Look, see?' He brought his hand up, pointing at his neck behind the right side of his jaw.

Khattak moved for a closer look, Syed also leaning forward to see. Below Adam's ear, down the line of his jawbone, was a thin scar. It was a remnant of the earwig's implantation, but the terrorists couldn't possibly suspect that – he hoped.

'It was expensive,' Adam went on, 'but it kept me out of prison. I had a nose job, my teeth straightened. I even lost weight! But – you really don't recognise me? *Azim*, I can't believe you don't know me from my eyes!'

The Pakistani was startled by Adam's use of the nickname. He looked more closely at the other man's face. The real Toradze had quite distinctive eyes of an intense blue; the contact lenses were a good simulation.

Doubt appeared in Khattak's own eyes . . .

'It really is me, Muhammad,' Adam pressed on. 'I will prove it. Ask me anything about when we met.'

Khattak frowned. 'If you are a spy, you would have interrogated Toradze to find out what he knew about me.'

Adam laughed. *The boy is as stupid as when I met him!* '*Azim*, when I met you four years ago, you had only just become a man! How long had you been with Yusef's group? A few months? Do not take this badly, but you were not important enough for a spy to know about! The reason *I* remember you is because . . . you made me laugh.'

Khattak's doubt increased. 'How? *How* did I make you laugh?'

Toradze's memory came to Adam's mind as easily as if it were his own. Despite the guns pointing at him, he smiled. 'When I arrived and met Yusef, you were standing behind him, holding a Kalashnikov. You looked so proud of it – you were a warrior, with your first weapon! But when he turned round to go into the next room, you stepped back, bumped against the door frame . . .' The smile widened. 'And your gun's magazine fell out and hit your foot.'

Khattak actually appeared embarrassed, before uncertainty returned. 'What else? Where did we meet?'

'A house on the edge of Drosh. There was only one little window in the back room, and all you could see outside was a chicken coop. The whole place stank of birdshit!'

Syed asked a question in Pashto, Khattak nodding as he answered. 'He asked if that was right,' said Holly Jo.

The leader pursed his lips, then lowered the AK – though he didn't put it down. 'It seems you are telling the truth,' he said to Adam.

'I have changed my face, but not who I am. And Muhammad knows that Giorgi Toradze always delivers what he promises, hey? It is how I stay in business – and how I stay alive.'

The Kalashnikov was finally returned to the desktop, the other weapons lowering. Adam concealed his relief behind Toradze's more casual acceptance of the situation: *of course they believe me. I am Giorgi Toradze!* However, Khattak still seemed troubled. A potential problem?

For now, Adam's main concern was the mission. There was still something he needed to do – beyond simply getting out of the building alive.

'If you are happy when you test these,' he said, gesturing at the case, 'then will you agree to my price? Two thousand dollars for each warhead.'

'It is still a lot of money,' said Syed.

'Yes, I know. But my contact in the factory is taking risks to obtain them for me – he demands to be well paid.'

'And you demand your profit too.'

'Of course! I am a businessman, after all.'

'Then you know the importance of haggling. One thousand dollars each.'

Adam shook his head. 'I would make a loss at that price. My contact is not the only person I have to pay. They have to be transported, there are officials to bribe . . .'

'One thousand two hundred.'

'I am also taking risks. No, two thousand is a good price.'

Syed struggled to hide the anger in his voice. 'One thousand *five* hundred.'

'Ah-ha! Now we are getting somewhere.' Adam patted one of the rockets. 'Malik, my friend, you are a hard man – but also a fair man. I think we can make a deal that suits us both. Say for . . . eighteen hundred?'

'One thousand six hundred.'

'Seven hundred. My final offer.' There was sudden steel in Adam's voice, his expression hardening.

The terrorist leader drew in a slow breath. 'Very well. One thousand seven hundred dollars.'

'Excellent!' Adam clapped his hands together – and as he did, he pushed one of the rings on his left hand around so that its setting pointed outwards from his palm, a small dark square on the gold. 'We are both happy – it is good business, hey? Now, we shake on it.' He held out his right hand to Syed again.

Syed hesitated, then took it. Adam gripped hard as he shook, preventing the Pakistani from pulling away, and placed his left hand firmly on Syed's sleeve. 'A good deal, a very good deal,' the American agent said with enthusiasm. 'You won't regret this.'

'I had better not,' Syed replied quietly, the threat unmistakable. Adam finally released his hand. 'I will contact you again in . . . one week? After we have tested these.' He closed the case.

'I will be waiting for your call.' Adam raised his left hand to rub an imaginary speck from the corner of his eye, surreptitiously checking the ring. The little grey square was gone. 'Until then, have fun, hey?'

Syed regarded him with disdain. 'One week,' he repeated, before issuing a Pashto command. The other members of his group prepared to move out. Adam was about to do the same when Syed raised a hand. 'And Giorgi?'

'Yes?' A sudden adrenalin surge. Was this a betrayal?

The leader indicated the case. 'The combination?'

'Ah, how did I forget?' Relieved, he showed Syed the tumblers. 'It is easy to remember. One, two, three . . . five.'

'Five?' said Syed dubiously.

'Who would think to try that? Four ones, four nines, then one-two-three-four – everyone tries those, but after that they are lost. Nobody has ever got into my luggage with that combination!'

'Perhaps they did, and you did not know.'

'Oh, I would know. Trust me.' He gave Syed a conspiratorial smirk. 'But now, it is time to get my other luggage from the hotel and go to the airport. There is a lot to do. I will talk to you in one week. Until then, *nakhvamdis!*'

Adam followed Marwat and Umar out and down the stairs, the other members of the cell coming after him. Syed had delegated the task of carrying the case to another man. Was there still some way to prevent the terrorists from using the improved warheads?

He forced himself to dismiss the idea. Syed was the mission's sole objective. As much as he wanted to somehow sabotage the rockets, that wasn't why he was here.

Umar opened the door to the street, warily checking outside before stepping through. He and Marwat didn't go far, waiting by the neighbouring shopfront. 'We see you,' said Holly Jo with relief as Adam emerged after them. 'Baxter's in the van, fifty metres to your left.'

He glanced in that direction. It was still raining, but only lightly. The street was much busier than before. On the far side was an anonymous blue Mercedes van, dirty and dented. He ignored it and headed right. 'The tracer's on Syed,' he whispered.

'Testing . . . okay, we have it.'

'Good work,' said Tony. 'You had us worried when that other guy showed up.'

'Well bluffed. Remind me never to play poker against you,' added Albion.

On the pretext of checking for traffic as he crossed the street, Adam looked back. All the terrorists had now left the building, splitting up. Standard practice for such a cell; dispersing individually made it harder for observers to track everybody.

Except . . . not everyone was going their own way. Khattak was the last to leave, and he had called back Umar and Marwat.

The gazes of all three followed Adam.

'I think I'm going to have company,' he said. A few seconds later, he was proved right as the trio started after him. 'Khattak and two other guys.'

'We can't give you eyes,' Holly Jo warned. 'The UAV's tracking Syed.' The terrorist leader had disappeared down a narrow alley.

'You need to lose them,' Tony warned. 'You can't lead them to the rendezvous.'

'I'll do what I can,' Adam replied. 'Just make sure you get Syed.'

'We'll bag him. See you soon.'

The Mercedes grumbled past as Adam reached a junction. He rounded the corner on to a side street.

A surreptitious glance back as he turned. The three men were still moving purposefully after him.

Tony stared at a high-resolution satellite photograph of Peshawar on the screen. The tiny tracer Adam had stuck to Syed's sleeve while shaking his hand now revealed its position as a red diamond; the van was a green circle. Directing the latter to intercept the former should be a simple task.

In theory.

He knew from experience, however, that no satellite overview could beat personal knowledge. 'Imran,' he said into his headset, 'he's going east. Do you know that part of town?'

'I know the *whole* town.' The van's driver was Imran Lak, a Peshawar native – and also a CIA asset. 'I'll catch him.'

'He's just come out of the alley,' reported Kyle. The view from the drone's camera slowly but constantly shifted as he followed the terrorist from above. 'Crossing the street . . . now going north.'

The green circle had only just turned east. A tag floated above the symbol, showing the distance in metres between the two subjects. It was gradually increasing. 'He's getting away from you,' said Tony into the mike. A statement of fact, not reproach – yet. 'Turn north as soon as you can. We can't lose this guy.'

Lak looked ahead, trying to see past the overloaded truck in front of the van. There were alleys between the buildings, but none was wide enough for the Mercedes. The nearest road he could take was at least two hundred metres away.

He sounded an impatient blast on the horn, pulling out to overtake but finding a couple of cars coming the other way. Frustrated, he swung back behind the truck.

'You're losing him,' said an American voice behind him. 'Come on, get this thing moving!'

Lak flicked a look over his shoulder. The darkened rear cabin was lit by the pale glow of laptop screens, four burly men huddled over them. 'I can't drive through walls,' he complained.

John Baxter was in no mood for excuses. 'If we miss this guy, we might as well have spent the day playing with our dicks,' he said, Alabama accent strong. 'Catch up with him!'

Lak frowned, but said nothing. The cars passed. He pulled out again, dropping down through the gears and accelerating past the truck.

'He's turning again,' Kyle warned. 'Heading east.'

The street Syed had entered was crowded, pedestrians milling about as vehicles slowly bullied their way through the throng. 'What's this?' Tony asked. 'Kyle, show me the street ahead. Careful, though – don't lose sight of him. And switch on the auto-tracking.'

'He's still got the tracer on him.'

'Yeah, but it might get brushed off if he bumps into someone, and we'd end up following the wrong guy.'

Kyle entered commands. A pulsating blue outline appeared around the red diamond. The computer had locked on to Syed's figure, identifying it by colour and shape; as long as the terrorist leader was partially visible to the drone, even in a crowd, the system would track him – and predict his movements and reacquire him if contact were briefly lost.

The camera tilted upwards to show the busy street ahead. In front of the shops, numerous small stalls were strewn along the sides of the long road, seeds sown in a furrow. 'Imran, he's at an outdoor market,' said Tony. 'He probably thinks he can lose any tails in the crowd.'

'I know the place,' came the reply. 'There's a street where we can cut across and get ahead of him.'

Kyle angled the camera back down to regard Syed from directly overhead. Even at the UAV's altitude, it was easy to see the terrorist turning his head every few metres to check if anybody was following him. 'You're lookin' the wrong way, assfag,' Kyle said with a smirk. Holly Jo made a faint *tsk* sound.

'Let's keep the language professional,' chided Tony. Everything that happened in the operations centre was being recorded. 'John, is your team ready?'

'Soon as you give the word,' Baxter answered.

'Okay.' The distance between the green circle and the red diamond on the overview was rapidly shrinking. 'Get ready.'

Lak swerved around a three-wheeled autorickshaw, giving its driver a blast on the horn before looking ahead. The road the Mercedes was now on ran parallel to the market street. 'How far away is he?'

Baxter's laptop displayed the same overhead view of the city as Tony's. 'Three hundred metres,' he reported. 'Two fifty.'

Lak accelerated, spray gushing from the van's wheels as it jolted through puddles. He spotted the side road. They would emerge on the market street in front of Syed, but not by much. 'The turn's coming up,' he called to the men in the back.

'He's eighty metres ahead,' said Baxter. 'Fifty, twenty . . . okay, we just passed him.'

'Hold on!' Lak braked sharply, the Mercedes squealing in complaint as he made the turn. The side street was short, but busy, a few stalls that had overflowed from the main thoroughfare at its far end. He sounded the horn again. Disgruntled shoppers cleared a path.

'Jesus, he's less than twenty metres away,' Baxter muttered. If

Syed decided to take the side road, they would have a tough job turning back around to follow.

But he was on the other side of the street, still moving through the market. 'Here he comes,' said the Alabaman. 'Go right, go right!' Lak turned again, forcing a taxi to an irate stop as he pulled out across its path and brought the van on to the crowded street. 'Okay, we're in front of him.'

Lak surveyed the street. Although there was strictly speaking only room for one lane of traffic in each direction, in places there were three or even four rows of vehicles as autorickshaws and scooters forced themselves into any available gap. 'Which side of the road is he on?'

'The left.'

'Okay. Ready with the distraction?'

Baxter looked to one of his team, a beefy, mustachioed man named Perez, who nodded in reply. The laptop now showed that Syed was twenty-five metres behind the slowly moving van. 'Ready, get ready . . .' The gap opened up slightly. 'Okay, go!'

Lak brought the van to a sudden halt, a scooter's horn providing a shrill rebuke from behind. Perez slid open the side door and hopped out. He rounded the back of the Mercedes and jogged across the street, one hand raised to ward off an autorickshaw coming in the other direction. The van set off again.

Even though his target was now less than fifteen metres away, Perez didn't turn his head, keeping his gaze ahead as if transfixed by the stacks of cheap plastic goods on one of the stalls. His hand slipped into a pocket, finding a roll of cigarette-sized metal cylinders.

He went to the stall's side, pretending to examine a set of brightly coloured bowls as he took out the roll. The stallholder was haggling with a woman, not looking at him. A flick of his hand, and the cylinders were tossed into a doorway. The woman's eyes twitched round at the faint clatter as they landed, but Perez had already moved on.

Syed was now level with him on the other side of the street. The American kept pace. The terrorist leader was about fifty metres from the van, which had stopped again beside a telephone pole. Perez crossed diagonally back across the hectic thoroughfare, slotting in behind his target. His hand went into his other jacket pocket. 'Just give the word,' he muttered into his Bluetooth headset.

Kyle zoomed in. None of the people in the operations centre needed the coloured symbols to pick out the players any more, watching unblinkingly as Syed drew closer to the van.

'Stand by,' Tony told Perez. Ten metres, the distance shrinking by the second.

Baxter and his two other men, Spence and Ware, stood inside the van, poised at the rear doors. The windows were covered with a tinted film to prevent onlookers from seeing in; the view outside was darkened, but still clear enough to reveal Syed approaching.

'Set?' Baxter asked. Both men nodded. One slowly pushed down the door handle, releasing the catch.

Baxter hefted the stubby stun baton in his right hand, thumb poised on its trigger.

'Ready . . .' said Tony.
    Five metres. Four—
    '*Go!*'

Perez thumbed the button on the radio-control unit in his pocket.

The detonators he had thrown into the doorway exploded one after another, cracking like gunfire. The woman screamed, the stallholder leaping away in fright and knocking his merchandise to the ground.

People spun in shock and fear at the noise. Terrorists, the army, criminals – any of them could send stray bullets into the crowd. Where was the shooter?

For a moment, all eyes were looking in the same direction.

Including Syed's.

He was two metres from the van when the device went off, whirling to find the source of the – gunfire? No, the sound wasn't right. Just fireworks—

It took his mind only a fraction of a second to reach that conclusion, but by then it was too late.

The van's rear doors swept open. The first two men jumped out to flank him. Baxter, a step behind, pressed the stun baton against the back of his neck. A harsh buzz – and over a million volts flooded through Syed's body.

The cell leader slumped as if his bones had liquefied, eyes rolled up into his head. Ware and Spence caught him, swinging his nerveless body around and hauling it into the van. Baxter was already back inside; Perez followed, slamming the doors behind him.

Lak set the Mercedes moving as the last detonator fired. The entire procedure had taken a fraction under seven seconds. A few people on the street were left vaguely aware that *something* had happened behind the van – but in the confusion, all attention on the sound of shots, nobody could remember what the man who had been there just moments before even looked like.

The van turned down a side street and sped away.

3

A Game of Leapfrog

'We got him!'

Adam could tell from the excitement in Holly Jo's voice that Syed's capture had gone exactly to plan. Baxter's team would now be bringing their prisoner to the operations centre.

That was his destination too. But first . . .

'I'm still being tailed,' he said, ostensibly into his phone. He had used the device's glass screen as an impromptu mirror, seeing Khattak, Marwat and Umar about thirty metres behind. 'How soon can Kyle get eyes on me?' While his accent was now clearly American, it was still strongly tinged with Toradze's Georgian tones.

'About four minutes. The drone's still over the capture point.'

Another quick glance at the screen, as if checking an app. Khattak gestured to one side. Umar angled away, heading for an alley. Marwat split off in the other direction. *Ah, the idiot boy is not so stupid after all!* Rudimentary spycraft; Khattak was sending the two other men to cover the parallel streets. If Adam changed direction, there would be someone ready to pick up his trail.

'Adam, we need you here fast,' said Tony. 'The longer this takes, the more chance Syed will suspect something happened to him.'

'I'll be there as soon as I can.' He pretended to end a call, taking one final look at the dark reflection before pocketing the phone. Khattak was closing, and judging from his determined expression he had decided that his doubts were justified. 'Holly Jo, I need an evasion route.' He increased his pace.

'Okay, hold on . . .' Seconds ticked by as Holly Jo brought up the satellite photo and overlaid his position, the tracker implanted in his body giving his position to the metre. 'Okay. Running parallel on your right is a main road. On the left everything's a bit more, I dunno, slummy. The streets are narrower and more crooked.'

'I'm going left. Give me directions once I'm round the corner.' He reached an intersection. The buildings to the left were smaller and lower, jumbled beneath a web of electricity cables. A sidelong glance back at Khattak as he rounded the corner. His pursuer was now talking on his own phone, no doubt warning Marwat that their target was coming his way. Another call would follow to Umar, telling him to leapfrog the streets covered by the other two men so Adam once again had someone following on each side.

Rudimentary spycraft – but effective. The technique had a weak point, though. Khattak was not in real-time contact with his comrades, but would have to keep making phone calls to relay Adam's movements. That would cost him time, and if the calls could be disrupted . . .

'Holly Jo,' Adam said, 'link Levon in. The guys following me are using cell phones – can he hack into the network and cut them off?'

'One second.' It took slightly longer, the connection to Levon James in Washington affected by the delay of a satellite transmission. 'Okay, he's on.'

'Adam, I heard you,' said the baritone voice. 'Even if I bring in

NSA, I'm not sure how much I can do – Pakistan's got six or seven cell companies, and I don't know which they're using. I can probably hack in and pin them down, but it'll take a few minutes.'

When the hefty African-American said he could 'probably' hack into something, that was a modest way of saying 'almost certainly', Adam knew – but time was the more important issue here. 'Do what you can.'

He reached a T-junction. A truck struggling to make the tight turn had forced other vehicles to stop, arousing horns and gesticulating hands. Adam looked left as he crossed the road – spotting Marwat, phone to his ear. The young man hurriedly looked down at the ground in a feeble attempt to hide his face. Adam continued on as if he hadn't noticed.

A larger, older building amongst the huddled cinderblock houses. A high archway led inside, the carved words PEEL CLOTH EXCHANGE, EST. 1897 visible in the pollution-blackened stone above. A remnant of British colonial rule – and still doing business, judging by the people coming and going.

'Go straight ahead, then right,' said Holly Jo, but Adam was already veering left towards the archway. He would stand more chance of losing his tails in a crowd.

He reached the entrance. A long arcade ran through the building, busy shops and stalls on each side. It had once had a glazed ceiling, but most of the glass panels had been damaged over time, opaque – but cheaper – replacements of wood and corrugated metal taking their place. The effect put him in mind of a sparsely worded crossword puzzle. The electric lights hanging from the roof fell far short of making up for the lost illumination, the interior shadowed and gloomy.

Marwat crossed the street to follow him. The truck finally negotiated the junction, pulling away to reveal Khattak at the intersection. No sign of Umar, but Khattak had probably told him to run to the other side of the hall.

Adam entered the building. Chatter in several languages echoed through the tiled space, deals being struck, prices argued over. The hall had maintained its original function even after well over a century, most of the stalls selling clothing or fabrics, everything from sheets of raw cotton to swathes of bright silk.

He picked a path through the arcade. The shoppers were almost exclusively women; he drew a few curious looks. At the far end was a second archway, grey daylight beyond. *Run for it. If Umar has made it to the other side of the building, I can take him. He is only one man.*

Toradze's choice of action: Adam ignored it. An arms dealer shaking off a tail could be accepted; such people liked privacy, even from their clients. An arms dealer attacking one of said clients would be harder to dismiss.

Nevertheless, he continued through the crowd. A clothing stall had a large mirror for customers to check potential purchases on themselves. Adam moved towards it, finding the angle that let him look back at the entrance. Marwat was already inside the building. Khattak had just reached the arch.

He slowed, letting his hunters close the gap. Halfway through the arcade. He stayed close to the stalls along one side of the long room. Most were oversized tables, but some were handcarts that could be wheeled back into the shops behind them at the end of the day.

He approached one barrow with a single set of large wheels at its centre, propped up at one end on cardboard boxes and at the other by a length of two-by-four. The stall was laden with bolts of fabric, multicoloured pashminas hanging down from a rail above them. The stallholder was cheerfully haggling with several women at once.

Adam curved round the little crowd to the cart's side as if examining the merchandise – then with a sharp kick knocked away the wooden prop, pushing a hand down hard on the corner of the stall as he ducked behind it.

The cart tipped on its end with a crash. Pashminas flapped like frightened birds, the women jumping back with squeals and cries. Ripples ran outwards through the crowd as people jostled each other.

Bent low, Adam scurried along the shopfronts back the way he had come.

Khattak and Umar had been unsighted by the disturbance. The latter hopped on his toes, trying to spot Adam over the reeling crowd. Khattak's head snapped from side to side as he looked between both archways.

Adam lost track of them, head still bowed as he returned to the entrance. He slipped outside, not straightening to his full height until he was out of Khattak's line of sight.

He ran across the street, following the directions Holly Jo had given him. The turning was just ahead. He looked back as he reached it.

Khattak emerged from the hall—

Adam rounded the corner. He didn't know if Khattak had seen him or not.

Which meant he had to assume that he had.

He kept running. 'What's the route, Holly Jo?'

'Keep going,' said the voice in his ear. 'Take the second street on the left.'

'How long before Baxter reaches you?'

'Two minutes.'

'I'll be there.' He swept around surprised pedestrians. The heavy umbrella in his coat pocket thumped against his side. Past the first turning. A look back. No sign of Khattak.

28

Yet.

He angled across the narrow road towards the next intersection. The building on its far corner was a small shop. He made the turn, catching the dimly reflected scene in its window.

Another running figure was behind him.

'I'm still being followed,' he warned. 'I'm coming straight to you. Be ready – everyone has to be inside when I arrive.'

'They will be,' Tony assured him. 'Have you got enough of a lead on this guy to get out of sight yourself?'

Adam pushed himself harder, feet pounding over the dirty road. 'I will soon.'

Baxter listened to Tony, then spoke to Lak. 'Our man's got a hostile following him – we need to get there before he does. Step it up!'

'I'm going as fast as I can,' Lak shot back. He took a turn at speed, crashing down through the gears as the van's back wheels slid out on the wet surface. One of the men in the rear blurted an obscenity. 'We're nearly there.'

Baxter turned back to his team. 'Get ready to move him.' Syed lay on the van's floor. He was still unconscious, but bound with plastic zip-ties. The stun baton's effects would soon wear off.

'Two more turns,' Lak called. The Mercedes raced down a narrow lane between closely packed apartment blocks. Traffic was very light; few people in this part of Peshawar could afford a car. 'Hold on.'

He braked hard, taking the van around the corner at a slightly more controlled rate. The new street was even narrower, work-shops interspersed amongst the housing. 'Okay, we're almost there! Last turn!'

The final corner was much tighter. The front bumper scraped against concrete in his haste. But he made it through, giving the

Mercedes one last burst of speed before skidding to a halt in a small muddy square.

The rear doors burst open, Syed's limp form carried by three of the men as they hustled out. Baxter followed, looking down the street leading from the square's far side.

Adam hared around its corner, coat flapping.

'Move, move!' Baxter snapped. A door in the building beside the van opened. Tony hurriedly waved the group inside. Syed was bundled through, Baxter squeezing past the mission leader in the tight hallway.

Adam reached the square proper. Smoke wafted from the van's open window as Lak hurriedly lit a cigarette and took several drags on it.

Adam shot through the haze, shoes slithering on the dirt as he reached the opening and darted inside. Tony shut the door—

Khattak ran round the corner.

Panting, he rushed into the little square – then stopped in angry confusion. He had been at most twenty seconds behind the other man, but now there was no sign of him, and there was no way he could have reached the square's only other exit already. He surveyed his surroundings. Light industrial buildings, all closed. A grubby white Ford van was parked in a corner of the square behind him, another vehicle ahead. A man was reading a newspaper in the cab, but he wasn't Toradze.

There was no obvious escape route the arms dealer could have taken. Khattak checked behind the white van. Nobody there, or inside it. Frustrated, he hurried towards the Mercedes.

'He's coming towards me,' Lak reported quietly. He pretended not to have registered the other man's approach until Khattak rapped on the van's side. 'What?'

'Did a man just run past you? A foreigner?'

Lak took the cigarette from his mouth. 'Yes. I didn't see where he went, though – I wasn't really looking. That way, I think.' He gestured vaguely over one shoulder.

Khattak scowled, then peered past him to check that his quarry was not hiding in the back of the van before jogging away. Lak watched him in the wing mirror. The terrorist crossed to the other side of the square to investigate the concrete stairs leading up the side of one building, but found the metal gate at their bottom locked. He spun in sheer exasperation, then took out his phone and continued down the narrow street.

'He's left the square,' said Lak. 'But I don't think he's going far.'

'Watch him,' Tony ordered. 'If everything works here, we'll be ready to move Syed in a few minutes. We can't let this guy see us.'

'Roger.' Lak sat back, eyes still fixed on Khattak's image in the mirror as the terrorist made a call.

4

Change of Mind

Adam and Tony followed Baxter's team into the makeshift operations centre, the high-tech equipment incongruous against the peeling paint of what had once been the owner's office. The former Marine clicked his fingers, and Syed was dumped on the floor.

'Careful,' chided Albion. 'We can't let him get *too* banged-up.'

'The cover story'll explain away a few bruises,' said Tony with dark humour. 'Are you ready?'

Albion nodded towards two metal cases, one large, one small. 'I need to calculate the dose.' He took out a notebook bound in black leather. 'Mr Baxter, can you and your men help me weigh our friend, please?'

There was an electronic scale on the floor beside the cases. Baxter's men hauled Syed to his feet – producing a groggy moan. Holly Jo gave him a worried look. 'He's waking up.'

'Thought he'd be out for longer,' said Tony.

Albion shook his head. 'It won't make any difference.' Syed was manoeuvred on to the scale. He mumbled something, trying to move, only to find his limbs restrained. 'Okay, let go for a moment, see if he can stand up on his own . . . excellent. One

32

hundred sixty-four pounds.' Albion noted the figure, then produced a tape measure and quickly ran it up Syed's body. 'And five feet ten inches. Just one more to get . . .'

He wound the tape around Syed's head at forehead height, pulling it tight. The Pakistani's eyes opened. Alarmed – and angry – he struggled against the ties, almost falling off the scales in the process.

Two of Baxter's men grabbed him. 'Okay, put him back down, please,' said Albion. 'Face-up, and hold him in place. I need to check his overall condition.'

Syed was lowered back to the floor, far from gently. 'Americans!' he croaked. 'You – you bastards!' A string of curses followed.

'Yes, yes,' said Albion, unconcerned. He knelt and shone a penlight torch over the prisoner's face. 'A bit scrambled from the shock, obviously, but the eyes look fairly clear, no broken blood vessels. Dark rims around them, but coloration looks healthy, so . . .' He made more notes, muttering to himself. 'Now, if I can just see your gums?'

'I won't give you anything, you shit-eating dog!' Syed snarled.

Albion swept the spot of light over his mouth. 'Thank you. I'd suggest a breath mint, but otherwise . . .' More writing, then he stood. 'All right, gentlemen, hold him there, please.'

Lak's voice came through the team's headsets. 'Two more men are approaching me.'

Kyle looked up from his console. 'Tony! The drone's back. I've got eyes outside.'

Tony and Adam regarded the screens. 'There's Khattak,' said Adam, spying a figure at the intersection. 'And those are Umar and Marwat.' The other two men jogged through the square. They passed Lak's van to meet their comrade.

Tony's face tightened. 'We can't move Syed if they're hanging around.'

Albion snapped his notebook shut. 'Okay, I've got the dosage.'

'Do it,' said Tony. 'Adam?'

Adam found room alongside Syed in the limited floor space, lying down. The Pakistani glared at him. 'Muhammad was right! You are not Toradze! You bastard, you shit! You son of a *whore*! I will cut off your balls and feed them to you!'

Baxter raised a booted foot as if to stamp on Syed's head. 'Can I shut this clown up?'

'He'll be quiet enough in a minute,' said Albion amiably as he opened the larger case. Inside was a piece of equipment resembling a laptop computer, but with a much bulkier base. He raised the screen. The machine came to life, fans whining as the display lit up. Diagnostic tests flashed on it, replaced after several seconds by a simple statement: PERSONA READY.

Albion took something from a pocket in the case's lid: a skullcap, a mesh of thick black nylon dotted with dozens of coin-sized grey electrodes. Wires ran from each one, joining up at the cap's back to form a thick umbilicus.

Syed stared at it. 'What is this? What are you doing?' He tried in vain to break free. *'What are you doing?'*

'Just stay calm,' said Albion as he pulled the cap down over Syed's skull. The terrorist resisted, but one of the men forced his head up so the doctor could tug it into place. A strap was fastened under his chin and secured tightly with Velcro. Albion fussed with the electrodes, nudging them into alignment, then took a second skullcap from the case.

This one he placed on Adam. It took him longer to secure it, positioning the electrodes with more care. Finally he opened the smaller case. He took out a jet injector, a glass vial containing a colourless liquid already loaded, and gently pushed the blunt stainless-steel nozzle against Adam's neck. 'Are you ready?'

'Yes.'

Albion's finger tightened on the trigger. There was a sharp *phut*, then he withdrew the injector, leaving a faint pink mark.

Adam flinched at the sharp pain as the drug was blasted through the pores of his skin. But the brief discomfort that had briefly registered on his face quickly faded . . .

Followed by all other expression, leaving him blank as a mask. His eyes defocused. Albion watched him closely, every few seconds glancing at the sweeping hand of his watch.

Even with his head restrained, Syed observed what was happening with a mix of fascination and fear. 'What are you doing to him?' he said, with more trepidation than before. 'What are you going to do to *me*?'

Albion ignored him, still counting off time. Thirty seconds. He held a hand above Adam's face, waving his fingers from side to side. Adam blinked, eyes tracking the movement.

Albion leaned closer. 'Adam, can you hear me?'

'Yes, I hear you.'

'I'm going to do a memory check. I want you to tell me . . . the name of Giorgi Toradze's best friend when he was a child.'

For a moment there was no reaction, then a slight frown creased Adam's brow. 'I . . . I don't remember.' His accent was now a neutral American, all traces of the Georgian's inflection gone.

'What about the name of the first girl Toradze fell in love with?'

Another frown. 'I don't remember.'

Albion gave him a reassuring smile. 'Okay, that's good. Toradze's persona has been wiped. I'll give Syed the Hyper-thymexine.'

The terrorist thrashed and screamed, but could not get free, his captors pushing down with painful force. Albion took out a second jet injector, this one with a red stripe around its body. He inserted a vial of a faintly amber liquid and turned a dial marked in millilitres to a particular number.

'What is that?' Syed shrieked, staring at it in horror. 'What are you doing?'

'Just relax,' said Albion, bringing the injector to the terrorist's neck. The Pakistani tried to twist away, but had nowhere to go. 'You're going to have a brainstorm.'

He pulled the trigger.

Syed screamed, face contorting as if he had been burned – then the sound faded to a gurgle in his throat as every muscle in his body tensed, tendons straining under his skin.

Albion tapped a key on the black-cased machine. The words on the display changed. ACTIVE: PERSONA TRANSFER IN PROGRESS. Columns of rapidly changing numbers scrolled up a window on one side of the screen. An oval object appeared beside it; a stylised graphic of a human brain, seen from above. It shimmered, each pixel subtly shifting in hue.

The changes suddenly became anything but subtle.

Syed's eyes went wide, pupils constricting and flicking from side to side with unnatural speed. Adam also reacted, fingers clenching. His eyes began to flicker just like Syed's – as if in time to their movements.

Albion watched the screen. The graphic was now flaring, swathes of colour sweeping across it. The scrolling numbers moved ever faster, barely legible, but he took in enough from them to nod in satisfaction. 'The transfer looks good,' he announced.

'How much longer?' Tony asked.

'The usual amount of time. Two or three minutes.'

Tony turned to Kyle. 'What are our friends outside doing?'

'They're checking the next street,' Kyle answered. The three men being watched by the hovering drone had split up, a blue symbol generated by the automatic tracking software highlighting each. Khattak was still at the intersection looking back at the square, seeming unwilling to accept that his quarry had left it. One of his companions was heading right along the road, while the other skirted the buildings to the left, checking for unlocked doors.

Tony jabbed a finger at Khattak. 'As long as this guy's still watching, we can't take Syed out of here.'

'What's he gonna do, just stand there staring at the van?' said Baxter. 'He'll move.'

'He'll have to, otherwise—' Tony broke off, finger moving to the leftmost blue symbol as the man within it moved out of sight behind a building. 'Where's this guy going? Kyle, get him back in view.'

Kyle was already working the controls. 'I can't get an angle on him. I think he's gone inside.'

'Damn. Keep watching, we need to find him – but zoom back out. We can't lose track of the other guys either.'

Kyle did so. The computer reacquired Marwat. Khattak had not moved from the intersection – but he had at least turned away from the square. 'He looks pissed. I think he's gonna leave soon.'

'Let's hope so.' Tony turned back to the strange tableau on the floor. 'Roger?'

'Not long now,' Albion replied. He checked the screen again. The colour changes on the graphic gradually slowed. He watched the scrolling figures as they too reduced in speed, then tapped commands on the keyboard. CALCULATING LATENCY ESTIMATES. A new set of numbers appeared.

They were to Albion's satisfaction. 'That should do it,' he announced, turning back to Adam and unfastening the skullcap's strap. 'Can you hear me?'

Adam blinked several times, then sat up sharply. 'Roger! Did it . . .' His voice had changed again, a new and different accent discernible even in a mere three words.

'Let's find out, shall we?' Albion looked the younger man straight in the eye. 'What is your name?'

The reply was immediate. 'Malik Syed.'

5

No Reception

The others watched in fascination as Albion continued to ask questions. 'Your date of birth?'

'The eighth of March 1982.'

'Place of birth?'

'Mushtarzi.'

'Where is that?'

'It is a small town about ten kilometres south-west of Peshawar.'

'Okay. Your mother's name?'

'Hadeel.'

'When is her birthday?'

'The fifteenth of September.'

'What is your most guilty secret?'

Adam hesitated, shamefaced, before answering. 'I . . . I watch pornography. Western pornography. There is a man in Islamabad who sells me DVDs. They are . . . they are foul, whores debasing themselves, but I cannot stop myself.'

'So he watches some good old American porno,' said Kyle. 'Nothing wrong with that!'

Holly Jo gave him a tired look of disgust. 'Knock it off, Kyle,' said Tony firmly. 'And find that other guy.' There were still only two blue symbols on the screen. 'Roger, is he ready?'

Albion asked Adam a few more questions, all purely factual queries about Syed's past. The answers were prompt, without hesitancy. 'I think the transfer's fine.'

'What about you, Adam? How do you feel?'

Adam stood, brushing dust from the dirty floor off his coat. His accent was not the only thing that had changed; even his body language was subtly different. Toradze's rolling swagger had gone, replaced by hunched wariness. He regarded the Americans around him almost with suspicion. 'I'm fine. I'm ready for questioning.' He gazed down at Syed, who was now still and staring blankly upwards, mouth agape. 'Or he is. We are.'

Holly Jo shifted uncomfortably. 'It's too weird when you do that. You sound just like him.'

'I think like him, too.' Adam's intense stare did nothing to ease her discomfort.

'Hopefully not *too* much like him,' said Tony. 'Okay, we've got what we need. Time to put Syed back where we found him.'

'We should just kill the son of a bitch,' rumbled Baxter. 'Now that we know everything he knows,' a glance at Adam, 'we'd be doing the world a favour.'

'If Syed's group doesn't realise they've been compromised, they'll carry on with their current operations – which we'll soon know all about. We can take out the entire cell in one go.' Tony looked at his watch. 'Eleven minutes since we bagged him. John, turn his watch back . . . eight minutes.'

'Kind of a long gap,' said Holly Jo, as Baxter crouched and lifted Syed's left wrist.

'We'll have to live with it. Roger, the amnestetic.'

Albion replaced the injector's vial with one containing a paler liquid. 'I assume you want the blackout to start before he was captured?' Tony nodded. 'Five millilitres of Mnemexal should do it.'

The big man waited for Baxter to adjust the watch, then injected the terrorist's neck. Syed's eyes closed and he went limp.

'How long before he wakes up?' asked Perez.

'Ten minutes or so, but you'll have adequate warning.'

'Get those ties off him and take him back to the van,' Tony ordered. 'Kyle, is the square clear?'

'A couple of people went through, but I don't think they were Syed's guys,' Kyle reported. 'Neither of the two I can see have line of sight on the square.'

'What about the third one?'

'He hasn't come back out.'

Tony examined the screen. The surrounding structures directly abutted each other. The missing man could be anywhere inside. 'The clock's ticking – we've got to move him now. We'll keep the op centre running until you've made the drop. Roger, go with John and keep an eye on Syed.'

Albion removed the skullcap from the terrorist. He gestured at the machine. 'What about the PERSONA?'

'I'll pack everything up.'

Adam plucked the tiny tracker from Syed's sleeve. 'I'll open the front door.' He left the room. Baxter and his men picked up Syed and followed, Albion behind them.

Tony looked back at the images from the drone. Khattak and Marwat were checking the nearby buildings.

The third terrorist was still nowhere to be seen.

Adam opened the door and looked out cautiously into the little square. Nobody was in sight. A chatter came from the van as Lak restarted the engine. 'Where are the bad guys?' he said.

'Two of them are still on the next road,' Tony replied via the earwig. 'Can you see the third one?'

He surveyed his surroundings. The rain had picked up again, but other than that there was no movement. 'Nobody in sight.'

'Okay. Go if you're sure.'

Another check of the exits from the square. Still no sign of Umar. 'Looks clear.' Baxter strode past him to the back of the Mercedes and pulled the doors wide.

The three other men from the snatch team pressed close together to hide Syed's slack form between them. They quickly climbed into the van. Adam stayed in the doorway, but it was not wide enough for the oversized Albion to squeeze past him. He stepped outside to let the bigger man through.

'Sorry,' said Albion, smiling. 'Guess I could stand to lose a couple of pounds.'

Adam made no comment. His gaze followed the doctor as he passed.

Movement through the rain, a face behind a second-floor window. *Umar—*

Adam threw himself back through the doorway as gunshots echoed across the square. One bullet struck the wall behind him.

Another hit Albion.

Blood spurted from a hole in his lower back. He fell to the wet mud, too shocked even to scream.

Baxter and his team were already reacting to the attack with highly trained efficiency, dropping Syed and drawing their own weapons. Perez and Ware jumped from the Mercedes as Baxter and Spence stood at its open rear doors. All four had their pistols up, firing as one.

Umar had pulled back, but that did not save him. The wall around the window was wood and plaster – giving no protection against the hail of .45 calibre rounds from the team's handguns.

A chunk of his forehead exploded away from his skull amid a spray of brain matter.

'Shots fired!' roared Baxter, free hand pressed to his earpiece. *'Man down!'*

Adam stared at the motionless figure on the ground. Part of him felt a sudden, malicious glee: *an American is dead!* It wasn't even exultation that a specific target had been hit – the death of *any* American would have received the same response. He angrily drove the thought back, jumping up and rushing outside.

Perez was already checking Albion's neck for a pulse. 'He's still alive!'

'Get him back inside!' Tony ordered.

But Adam spoke over him. 'Baxter! Get Syed to the drop point! We've got to complete the mission.' He looked past the bullet-pocked building towards the road. Khattak had heard the shots and raced back to the intersection to investigate.

Their eyes met.

Khattak shouted a warning to Marwat, then ran, disappearing from view.

Adam made an instant decision. He drew his own gun and sprinted after the fleeing terrorist. Marwat flashed through the intersection ahead, following Khattak.

'Adam, what are you doing?' Holly Jo said in concern.

Tony's voice was far harder. 'Get back here! Roger needs medical help!'

'We can use the emergency persona—'

Adam cut her off. 'We'd have to wipe Syed's. And if you don't get him to the drop point before he wakes up, Roger will have been shot for nothing.' He reached the intersection and rounded the corner. The two men were still running from him. Khattak took something from his clothing.

Not a gun; a phone.

'Levon!' Adam shouted as he ran. 'The cell network – shut it down! Khattak's going to warn the others!'

The satellite delay meant that Levon took a moment to respond. 'What? I can't— Adam, I haven't got that much access yet!'

'Anything you can do to jam his phone, *anything*!' Khattak was struggling to enter a number from memory as he ran, his group's contacts too risky to commit to a SIM card – but it still would not take him long to thumb in eleven digits.

Tony spoke. 'Levon, can you give us a map of the local cell towers?'

'Yes, but—'

'Do it, quick! Kyle, find the nearest cell tower – and use the UAV's self-destruct to take it out.'

'Seriously?' said Kyle, surprised – and thrilled. 'Awesome!'

'Is Syed moving yet?' Adam asked.

Holly Jo gave him the answer. 'The van just left. But what about Roger?'

'Either you can stabilise him, or you can't.' He didn't know if the coldness of the statement was from Syed's persona or his own.

He was closing on Marwat, but not quickly enough, the young man's fear fuelling him. Beyond him, Khattak was forced to lower the phone to keep his balance as he wove between people coming the other way, but he brought it back up the moment he cleared them, his thumb finding another digit on the keypad.

In the office, Perez and Ware began first aid on Albion's wound. Tony reluctantly looked away to Kyle's screens. 'Levon, where's that damn map?'

'It's coming, it's coming!' came the frantic reply. 'Okay, it's on stream seven . . . now!'

Holly Jo overlaid the incoming data on the satellite image of Peshawar. Dozens of dots popped up. She zoomed in on those around the green symbol marking Adam's position. 'Kyle, I'm sending the nearest towers to you.'

'Got 'em,' Kyle replied. 'Okay, closest one is . . . rooftop, a hundred and twenty metres west of the drone.' He glanced at Tony for confirmation.

'Take it out,' Tony snapped.

'All *right*!' He took the UAV's controls, re-angling its camera so that instead of looking down it showed the view ahead, and swung the drone round on a new course. 'Can't believe you're finally letting me do this . . .'

The little aircraft dropped towards the rooftops. 'There,' said Tony, pointing. A six-storey building was home to a skeletal tower.

'I see it.' The phone mast grew rapidly as Kyle swept the drone in on its kamikaze run, aiming for the crown of antennae. But instead of crashing, he slowed the quadrotor sharply just before impact. It was built of lightweight materials, so simply ramming it into a target would have done little more than glancing damage.

The self-destruct unit would deliver far more. The explosive running through the UAV's fuselage was intended not merely to wreck the machine but to completely obliterate it, preventing its sophisticated camera and computer systems from falling into the wrong hands.

Kyle flipped up a protective cover on the control console to reveal a red button. He stabbed it down, hard. 'Bickety-*boom*!'

The feed from the drone's camera went blank.

Khattak entered the final digit. He clamped the phone to his ear, looking back as he raced into an alley. Marwat was not far behind him; Toradze was catching up fast.

A voice from the other end of the crackling line. 'Hello?'

'Nasir, it's Muhammad!' Khattak gasped. 'Tor—' He broke off as a loud bang came from somewhere nearby, echoing off buildings. A grenade? 'Toradze is working with the Americans! They've captured Syed!'

There was no answer. 'Nasir? Nasir, can you hear me?' Still only silence; even the crackle had gone. He looked at the phone's screen. NO NETWORK. But he was in the middle of the city!

The explosion. Toradze's associates must have destroyed the nearest phone mast, cutting him off.

But they would only have taken such drastic measures if they had been unable to shut down the entire network. If he got close enough to another mast, he could get a connection. The towers were dotted all over Peshawar – surely one couldn't be far . . .

A rooftop! If he were clear of the surrounding buildings, he would get a better signal. Khattak reached the end of the alley, emerging on a street. He looked up.

An apartment block across the road stood five floors high, taller than its neighbours. Rain-soaked washing hung heavily from a line on its roof. There was a way up there. He swerved around a passing autorickshaw and ran for the building's entrance. 'Don't let him get to the roof!' he called back to Marwat.

'The cell tower's down,' Holly Jo told Adam. 'We cut off his call.'

Adam didn't reply. It wouldn't take Khattak long to get into range of another mast.

Marwat angled right as he ran out from the alley's far end, following Khattak. Adam was only seconds behind, gaining on the two men. He had the SIG in his hand, but knew that the chances of hitting a running target while he himself was sprinting were practically zero, even with his training. Instead, he rushed into the open—

To see a car coming at him.

The battered Nissan was barely doing twenty miles per hour, but still slithered on the wet road, ill-maintained brakes shrilling. Adam banged both hands down on its hood to absorb some of the impact, taking a painful blow to his hip. He staggered before regaining his balance and continuing after Marwat. The driver yelled angrily as he ran past.

The collision had cost him several seconds. Khattak had disappeared into a building. Marwat went through its entrance.

A woman cried out. His gun had been seen. He ignored the spreading alarm and ran to the entrance.

A small lobby area floored in dirty red tile. He heard the rapid thud of footsteps from the narrow wooden staircase.

They'll set an ambush on the stairs . . .

Adam's own assessment of the situation was the same as Syed's. But he had to make the ascent to stop Khattak from warning the rest of the terrorist cell. He ran up the stairs, gun at the ready.

When would the attack come? Marwat would be waiting – but on which floor?

The stairwell was confined, dark. He pounded up it, the umbrella's handle scraping against the wall. Nobody on the first landing. He could still hear hurrying feet above as Khattak headed for the roof.

He continued upwards. Was Marwat waiting for him on the next landing, or the one after?

This one—

The Pakistani lunged into view, pointing his gun down the stairs – but Adam was prepared and had his own weapon raised. He fired just as Marwat saw the danger and jerked back. The bullet narrowly missed and hit a wall, scattering scabs of shattered plaster.

He reached the landing. Marwat's pistol came up—

Adam swept his own gun arm across Marwat's chest to knock the muzzle away as the terrorist pulled the trigger. The shot was painfully loud in the confined space. The American drove his shoulder against the other man's sternum, slamming him back against the wall.

With his right arm holding his opponent's gun at bay, Adam couldn't get a shot with the SIG. Instead he drove his left fist into Marwat's stomach. Two punches, three. The terrorist gasped in pain.

Adam shifted his weight, about to drive his elbow into the other man's groin—

Marwat threw himself forward.

The impact made Adam stumble. As he fought to stay upright, Marwat charged, forcing him across the landing.

They crashed against a door. It burst open, the lock splintering from the frame. Adam tripped as he reeled into the room. Both men fell, the American taking the brunt as he collided with a small table. It collapsed beneath him. Marwat landed heavily on top of him, knocking the breath from Adam's lungs . . .

And the gun from his hand.

Marwat immediately saw his advantage. He pushed himself off Adam.

Adam swept his hand over the floor to search for the P228. He found no metal, only wood—

The crouching terrorist brought up his gun – only to screech in pain as one of the broken table's legs smashed against his wrist like a baseball bat. The shot went wide. Before he could recover, Adam's heel hit his knee. He tumbled on to his back.

Adam threw the makeshift club at him and rolled to search for his gun. It had ended up a few feet away. He scrambled for it.

Marwat sat up, enraged. He saw his adversary moving and took aim—

Adam was faster, snatching up the SIG and twisting to fire in a single fluid motion. The bullet hit Marwat in the right side of his chest, a rope of dark blood gushing out as he fell backwards.

'Adam!' It took him a moment to register Holly Jo's voice in his ear over the adrenalin surge. 'Are you okay?'

He got to his feet. 'I'm fine. One terrorist down. Tag this location – Imran's people need to get a clean-up team here to remove the body. Third-floor apartment, on the left.'

He went to the door. Marwat lay by it, bloodied hands pressed against the bullet hole. The terrorist groaned, looking up as Adam approached . . .

The SIG roared twice.

Wet starbursts of red and grey exploded across the floor from the exit wounds in Marwat's skull. Adam stepped over the corpse and returned to the landing, resuming his run up the stairs.

He would have compromised the mission if he had been left alive. Again, Adam and Syed shared the same cold, pragmatic view on the termination. But there was something else; part of it regret at the death of a comrade in the war against the infidels, another part . . .

An almost visceral joy in taking a life.

That was Syed. It was all Syed.

It had to be.

More floors passed, sounds of concern and confusion coming from the apartments as the residents reacted to the shots. On the top landing, a woman peered out timorously through her door, only to slam it shut as Adam rushed past.

The last set of stairs led to the roof. Daylight from above – the door at the top was ajar.

He ran towards it.

6

The Only Way Is Down

Khattak had also heard the shots. He didn't know if Marwat or Toradze had fired last, but was taking no chances, his gun covering the stairs as he held up his phone, trying to get a signal. There had to be another mast in range, there *had* to be . . .

He reached the roof's edge, the ground several vertiginous floors below. Still no network. He glanced at the stairwell. No movement. Back at the phone—

An icon appeared. He had reception! Only one bar, but that was all he needed. He redialled the last number.

Adam stopped just before the top of the stairs. He peeked through the doorway. The residents obviously considered the rooftop as much a part of their living space as their apartments. It was strung with washing lines, padlocked wooden boxes stacked beneath a makeshift shelter of corrugated metal.

But Khattak was out of sight.

With the drone destroyed, Adam had no extra eyes to help him. It was him versus the terrorist, and the other man had the advantage: there was only one place from where his pursuer could appear.

But he heard a voice, somewhere to the left. *Khattak.* Syed recognised it instantly. *He will be warning Nasir about the Americans!*

Adam rushed up the last steps and out on to the roof.

He spun to the left, gun raised in a two-handed grip. Khattak was at the edge of the roof, pistol pointed straight at him – but the mere act of speech had slowed his reactions. Only by a fraction of a second, but enough for Adam to drop and roll sideways. The bullet seared past him.

He jumped up to return fire as Khattak ran along the roof's edge. Sodden washing on the lines blocked Adam's line of sight. He aimed at where he thought the other man would be and pulled the trigger, but hit nothing except wet cloth.

There was a chimney-like brick structure near the rooftop's corner. Khattak darted behind it, pressing his back against the wall. He returned the phone to his ear. 'Nasir, I'm being—' Three beeps interrupted him: a dropped call. The chimney had been enough to block the weak connection. 'No!'

Adam heard the cry of dismay, immediately guessing its cause. He ducked past the washing and advanced on the chimney—

Khattak burst out from behind the brickwork at a sprint – and leapt off the roof.

Adam didn't have time to fire before the other man fell out of view. A thump and a pained yell reached him. He ran to see where Khattak had gone.

Another apartment block, a storey lower, came into view below. The two buildings were separated by an alley about twelve feet wide. The Pakistani had made a hard landing on the roof, which was even more cluttered than the one he had just left. He scrambled behind a pigeon loft.

Adam knew he had to follow. But he would be vulnerable in mid-air, more so immediately after landing. Easy prey for the terrorist.

Unless—

He backed up, then made a running leap across the gap . . .

And opened fire in mid-air, unleashing every remaining round in the SIG at the wooden loft – not with any expectation of hitting Khattak, but to force him to stay in cover.

The trigger clicked, the gun's slide locking back. Empty. The roof rushed at him—

The impact sent a hammer-blow of pain through his legs. He rolled. The umbrella in his coat pocket dug hard into his side as he came to a stop and looked up.

Khattak was just a metre away, having ducked as bullets tore through the pigeon loft. He blinked in surprise at the sight of the American.

No time to reload. Adam dropped the P228 and sprang at him, tackling the Pakistani back against the wooden structure. Birds flapped in panic inside their cages. Khattak staggered, his gun clattering away across the roof.

But he was far from incapacitated, delivering a vicious kick to Adam's stomach. The American lurched back. Khattak straightened and reached into his jacket.

He pulled out a knife.

Adam stared at the nasty little blade. It was only about four inches long, but it was serrated, sharp, strong.

And Khattak knows how to use it.

Syed's memories provided proof. The terrorist was well-practised with a knife, both for fighting and for his own personal pleasure. More than one man had been tortured with it, finally meeting a bloody end at Khattak's hands while his leader watched approvingly. The image of flesh peeling away from bone as easily as the skin of an orange flashed through Adam's mind.

Khattak read the wariness on the American's face. His mouth twisted into a cruel smile as he swept the blade in a series of swift, measured movements, a cobra swaying before the strike. He stepped closer.

Adam kept his gaze fixed on the knife. Syed's knowledge of his comrade was betraying him. Khattak would be overconfident—

The blade thrust at his face.

He jerked back. Another stab forced him to sidestep. Khattak advanced, jabbing the knife. Adam dodged each time, but realised that the Pakistani was trying to corner him. He had to fight back or be trapped.

Weight in his coat. The umbrella.

He snatched it out, wielding it like a truncheon. Khattak let out a mocking laugh. He lunged, the knife aimed at the American's chest—

Adam whipped up the umbrella. The terrorist yelped in startled pain as it cracked against his hand. Hard. The flimsy-looking cylinder was solid as a cosh.

It was no ordinary umbrella.

Anger drove him to attack again, the knife slashing at Adam's throat. The umbrella blurred to intercept with another heavy thud. Khattak gasped through bared teeth.

Adam watched him closely, reading his face, his body movements. Khattak was still angry, but now cautious too, knowing that his advantage had shrunk. Another stab – but this stopped short, a feint, changing direction as Adam moved to block. The blade's tip sliced through his sleeve . . . and the skin beneath.

This time it was Adam who let out an involuntary gasp. The cut was not deep, but it burned like a thin line of acid.

Khattak's malevolent smile returned. Adam suppressed Syed's anger, controlling his own.

Another stab—

Adam batted his arm away – then slammed the umbrella against the side of Khattak's head.

The Pakistani lurched back. Before he could recover, Adam hit him twice more, rapid yet brutal blows to his face.

Khattak retreated, expression now fearful. Adam kept pace as the pair circled. The terrorist made an experimental jab at him, but it was easily deflected. 'Who are you?' demanded Khattak. 'Who are you *really*?'

Adam had no answer. He continued circling, waiting for the next strike . . .

Khattak made his attack – but not the one Adam expected.

He didn't stab with the knife. Instead he roared and rushed at the American, the blade leading his charge like a rhino's horn.

Adam delivered a fierce hit to his head with the umbrella, but not hard enough to fell him. He twisted to dodge the knife.

He was only partly successful. It ripped through his coat, slashing across his chest. Khattak ploughed into him, knocking him backwards. They crashed against the pigeon loft. Cages broke open, terrified birds blinding Adam in a swirl of flapping wings. His foot caught something and he fell. He sensed as much as saw Khattak through the maelstrom and kicked as hard as he could. The Pakistani stumbled away from him.

Adam used his arm to shield his eyes from the whirling pigeons. The empty SIG was a few feet away.

He still had a spare magazine.

He scrabbled for the gun. He grabbed it, about to drop the umbrella and take out the new mag . . .

Khattak had retrieved his own pistol.

The wood and wire of the pigeon loft would not stop a bullet, and the cover of the stairwell was too far to reach in time. But the roof's edge was just a few strides away.

The agent ran for it. Khattak turned, gun raised—

Adam plunged off the roof as the terrorist fired, the bullet whipping above his head.

Khattak stared in amazement before a brief, disbelieving 'Hah!' escaped his mouth. Toradze, or whatever his real name was, had just committed suicide. Even if the four-storey fall hadn't killed him, the landing would have broken his legs, leaving him a helpless and immobile target below.

He swaggered to the edge and looked down.

The other man was on the ground. But he was neither dead nor crippled. He was standing, the open umbrella a discarded black flower at his feet as he slapped a new magazine into his SIG-Sauer and took aim—

The bullet went through Khattak's right eye, punching out of the top of his skull in a spray of blood and fragmented bone.

He collapsed, toppling forwards and falling. His body hit the ground with a horrific crunch, limbs splayed at unnatural angles. Blood oozed out from his head.

A good shot. A good kill.

Adam returned his gun to his coat, then dragged the broken corpse against a wall beside a pile of trash, using a flattened cardboard box to conceal it as much as possible. 'Holly Jo?'

Her reply was hesitant. 'Are you okay?'

'Yes.' He glanced down at his chest. There was blood on his shirt, but not enough to concern him. 'Tag this location. There's another body for Imran's people to clean up. It's next to a pile of garbage under some cardboard. Tell Tony that you can start packing up your gear. I'll make my own way to the airport. Out.'

Before Holly Jo could say anything else, he tapped a spot behind his right ear. There was a small bulge beneath the skin – a control for the implanted radio. The touch switched it off. He fastened his coat to conceal the blood and picked up the umbrella. The shaft was made from kevlar and steel, the spokes ultra-strong carbon fibre able to support his weight on parachute-grade nylon. The device, which could slow a person enough to survive a thirty-foot fall unharmed, had inevitably acquired the nickname 'Mary Poppins'.

Adam's landing from a greater height had not been painless, but training had taught him how to roll to absorb most of the impact. He raised the umbrella over his head, then set off down the back street, limping slightly. Behind him, the rain slowly washed the splattered blood into the gutter.

'Hey, hello? Can you hear me?'

Malik Syed slowly opened his eyes to see people looking down at him with concern. The closest, a man, patted his cheek a few times. 'Can you hear me? Are you okay?'

'He's waking up,' said a woman behind him, relieved.

Hands helped him to his feet. Syed looked around in bewilderment, his neck aching. Where was he? An alleyway – he had been lying amongst plastic sacks of garbage at its end. 'What . . . what happened?'

'I think you were mugged,' the man said. 'I saw someone run out of here and came to see what was going on.'

Syed hurriedly checked his pockets. His phone had gone, as had his wallet. The latter was only a minor inconvenience, as the identity card in it was a fake and he could easily get hold of a replacement as well as more money, but the phone was more of a worry. While he didn't keep the numbers of any of his al-Qaeda contacts in its memory, it still held a record of its most recent calls, which the authorities might be able to use against the group. 'Did you see who did it?'

'I didn't get a good look, but he was just a kid. Sixteen, maybe seventeen. He had a spanner or something in his hand – he must have hit you with it and pulled you down here.'

That was, oddly, a relief; it was unlikely that the police or counterterrorism agents would use street urchins to do their dirty work. He checked the rest of his belongings. His mugger had left his watch, a cheap Casio. Several minutes had passed since he last remembered checking the time . . .

What *was* the last thing he remembered? Thanking his benefactors, he stepped out on to the street. He wasn't far from the market. He had gone through it to shake off anyone who might have been following him, but then . . . nothing. He frowned.

'Are you okay?' the man asked again. 'Are you hurt?'

'I'll be all right.' He squinted down the road, mentally trying to retrace his steps, but the memory would not come.

'He might have hit you on the head,' said the man. 'Maybe you should see a doctor.'

'I'm fine,' Syed said irritably. He turned in the other direction and strode away. He was already dismissing the incident as bad luck, falling victim to an opportunistic thief, rather than anything sinister. If Pakistani or American intelligence agents had been behind the attack, he would be on his way to a torture cell by now.

The other onlookers dispersed, leaving the man alone. He watched until Syed was out of sight. The earpiece that had been in his pocket while he 'helped' the terrorist was returned to his ear. 'Tony, it looks like Syed bought it,' reported Lak. 'He doesn't remember what happened. Now,' a sigh, 'where are these bodies we need to clean up?'

7

The Schizoid Man

Pakistan had been left far behind as the private jet crossed over the Kazakhstani border into Russian airspace, heading north on a trans-polar route back to the United States.

Adam had been undergoing a debriefing – at times, almost an interrogation. Malik Syed was only a relatively small cog in the terrorist organisation, and as such his knowledge of its overall activities was limited, but even so there was urgency to the questioning. Part of this was due to the desire of the American agents to obtain the most vital information as quickly as possible. Lives, after all, could be at stake.

The other part was a matter of neurochemistry. The process that had transferred Syed's memories into Adam's mind was only temporary.

Tony was conducting the debriefing in a small cabin at the rear of the jet, Holly Jo recording everything. The field commander had a long list of questions: names of contacts, meeting places, phone numbers, email addresses, past operations, future targets. Adam's answers often led to tangential but equally valuable queries, stretching out the process. They were almost four hours in, and barely halfway down the list.

And getting an answer was not always straightforward.

'Who gave Numan Aaqib's location to Syed?' Tony asked. Five weeks earlier, the safe house where a double agent who had infiltrated an al-Qaeda cell was being debriefed had been attacked. The informer and four agents from Pakistani and US intelligence were all killed. The safe house was supposed to be top secret; there was almost certainly a mole within the Pakistani government.

'I won't—' Adam began, defiant anger in his voice before he regained control. More calmly, he spoke again. 'I don't know the name of the mole, but Syed was given the address by . . .' He stopped again, faint twitches of his facial muscles betraying the internal conflict as he forced out the information. 'By Mohammed Qasid.'

Holly Jo typed the name into her laptop. A file appeared on its screen after a few seconds, the machine connected via satellite link to the US intelligence network's enormous database. 'Qasid,' she read. 'He's . . . wow. He's one of Muqaddim al-Rais's lieutenants.'

'Al-Rais?' exclaimed Tony, surprised. 'You mean Syed's only two steps removed from the head of the organisation? No way we got *that* lucky on the first go.' He looked back at Adam. 'Did Syed ever meet al-Rais?'

The younger man shook his head. 'No. And he only met Qasid once – he came with Syed's usual contact.'

'Sloppy security,' Holly Jo commented. 'A cell leader at Syed's level shouldn't ever have come into direct contact with somebody that high up the chain.'

'Bad for them, good for us,' said Tony. 'Who did Syed normally deal with?'

'A man called . . .' Again, it took a moment for the name to emerge, the other persona within him not wanting to give up the secret. 'Hanif Fathi.'

Another, much shorter file came up in response to Holly Jo's request. 'Not much on him, not even a photo. The Pakistanis might be able to give us more.'

A sour note entered Tony's voice. 'Assuming they haven't been completely infiltrated by al-Qaeda sympathisers. Okay, go back to Qasid. Did he tell Syed anything else we can use? Names, future plans?'

Adam thought about it. 'Nothing specific, they didn't spend much time together, but . . . there was something. A code name. Qasid called it "Operation Lamplighter".'

'Lamplighter?' Holly Jo echoed as she entered the name into the laptop. A list of possible meanings appeared. 'None of the hits look relevant.'

'Does Syed know what it is?' Tony asked Adam.

He shook his head. 'Just that it's something major – al-Rais is handling it personally. Qasid only mentioned it in passing.'

'No indication of dates or possible targets?'

'No.'

'Something else for Langley and Fort Meade to listen out for, then,' said Tony. 'If it's important to al-Rais, it's twice as important to us. All right, so about Fathi—'

He was interrupted by a knock on the cabin door. It opened before he could reply, Kyle leaning in. 'Morgan wants to talk to you.'

'We're kind of in the middle of a debriefing,' said Holly Jo.

'He says it's important. Wants everybody there. Like, now.'

Tony checked his watch. 'Okay, we'll take a break. A short one.'

The trio followed Kyle back through the main cabin. Midway along it was a bed, on which lay Albion. The big man was asleep, one of the plane's flight crew – also a trained nurse – looking up as they approached. 'How is he?' Tony said quietly.

'Stable at the moment,' she replied. 'I've done as much as I can. But he would have been far better off if he'd been taken to the US consulate. They have full medical facilities—'

'This is a black operation,' Tony reminded her sternly. 'We couldn't risk linking it to US civilian agencies.'

'Yes, sir. Sorry, sir.'

His tone softened. 'No need to apologise. I'm not wild about the situation myself.'

'I sure as hell bet the Doc isn't, either,' Kyle added.

Holly Jo was more rueful. 'Or Mr Morgan.'

'We'll find out soon,' said Tony.

The group continued up the cabin. At its forward end was a small conference table. Baxter and his team were already seated at it. A large screen on the bulkhead displayed a live teleconference link. The screen was divided in two; Levon was on one side, his thick round glasses crooked as he rubbed sleepily at one eye.

The other half held the image of Martin Morgan, Tony's superior. Late forties, black, wearing a pair of slim silver-framed glasses that blended almost perfectly into his greying sideburns and hair.

And not in a good mood. 'Do you know what time it is here in DC?' he asked, before the late arrivals had even taken their seats.

'I'm guessing around six a.m.,' said Tony.

'That's right. Which means that three hours ago, I was getting a preliminary report on the Persona Project's first full mission with its new lead agent. Which means that *one* hour ago, I was getting my ass chewed off by the Admiral for waking him up to tell him there had been complications. Although that wasn't how he described them. His terms were a lot more colourful. The main one started with the word "cluster".'

Kyle smirked. Morgan's glower deepened. 'Something amusing you, Mr Falconetti?'

The smirk hurriedly vanished. 'Uh, no, sir.'

'Damn right it shouldn't be. What the hell was going on over there? Shots fired, three people dead, the CIA's local assets working in overdrive to clean up after you. You were meant to achieve your objective using stealth and subtlety, not this James Bond bullshit!'

'With all due respect, sir,' said Baxter, 'the hostiles fired on us first. We were defending ourselves.'

'And we *did* achieve the objective,' Tony pointed out. 'We successfully implanted Syed's persona into Adam – we're in the middle of debriefing him,' he added, with emphasis, 'and then put Syed back on the street without his realising what had happened.'

'And when he finds out that three of his people have mysteriously vanished, then what?' demanded Morgan.

To everyone's surprise, Adam answered – almost in Syed's voice. 'He will be suspicious, but will accept it as a natural risk of fighting the holy war. He has lost other members of his cell before. In Pakistan, people do sometimes just . . . disappear.'

Morgan was faintly unsettled, as if he were being briefed by the terrorist himself. 'Even three at once?'

'It is the price of jihad. And there are many more to take their place.'

'Well, that's reassuring to know,' Kyle muttered sarcastically.

'As you can see,' said Tony, 'Adam's got Syed's knowledge on tap. So, if you're going to chew us out, wait until we get back to DC so we can keep extracting it while we still have time. Once we've done that, *then* you and the Admiral can decide if the Persona Project is a success or a failure.'

'Right now, the Persona Project is dead in the water, Tony,' Morgan snapped. 'I don't know if you've forgotten, but there's more to it than just Adam. And the other man it depends upon took a bullet to the back!'

Tony glanced back towards Albion's bed. 'I hadn't forgotten.'

'Good. Then I hope you also haven't forgotten that he's the only person who knows how to calculate the drug doses so they don't kill the subjects. Without him, we don't *have* a project. And his chances of going back into the field any time soon don't look good.'

'He's currently stable.'

'Stable isn't the same as healthy.' He looked down at something below the camera's field of view. 'I see from the mission transcripts that Ms Voss suggested using the pre-recorded emergency persona so that Adam could perform field surgery on Roger. That might have improved his chances – why didn't you consider it?'

'That was my decision,' said Adam before Tony could reply. 'Doing that would have erased Syed's persona, and let his men escape. It would have cost us the mission.'

'Not doing it might have cost us the entire project,' Morgan countered. 'Why wasn't Syed's persona recorded during transfer?'

'We needed to get Syed back into play as fast as possible,' explained Tony. 'All the encoding and compression needed to record a persona would have taken too long. Also,' he added, before his superior could respond, 'doing that would have meant imprinting Adam with the same persona twice. You know we can't risk the potential side effects.'

Morgan was annoyed at being challenged, but acquiesced. 'Okay. But I want recording of subjects' personas to be standard operating procedure from now on unless absolutely necessary.'

'Understood.'

'That is, assuming there's ever another mission. We can't do anything without Roger to administer the drugs.'

'There might . . . be a solution to that problem.'

Everyone looked round at the weak voice. Albion was awake

and trying to lift his head, despite the efforts of his nurse to keep him still. 'Roger, you should be trying to rest,' said Tony.

'Rest is for babies and the idle,' Albion replied, forcing a thin smile. 'No, I've been listening; to some of it, anyway. I'm not sure what drugs this young lady's given me, but they make me . . . drift in and out. They are . . . rather good, though.'

'I guess I haven't given you enough,' the nurse complained. 'Please, lie down.'

'In a minute. Look, Martin, I know someone who . . . might be able to stand in for me – to be my locum tenens, so to speak.'

Morgan's expression turned probing. 'I thought determining the drug doses was too complicated for anyone but you?'

'She has the necessary training to . . . assess the subject's condition and make the appropriate calculations.' Albion's head sagged on to the pillow, to the nurse's relief. 'I'm sure I can . . . teach her.'

'I'll consider it,' said Morgan. 'But right now, you need to get some re— some sleep.'

'I'll see that he does, sir,' said the nurse. Albion made a 'Bah!' sound, but settled back into the bed.

Tony looked back up at Morgan's image. 'Are we done for now, Martin? Because I need to get back to the debrief. We've already found a connection between Syed and Muqaddim al-Rais—'

'Al-Rais?' Morgan interrupted. Baxter also reacted with surprise at the name. The Saudi was the most wanted terrorist in the world, the current leader of al-Qaeda – which ten months earlier had taken revenge for the loss of its previous commander, Mahjub Najjar, by detonating a massive car bomb in the Pakistani capital Islamabad. The explosion had not only killed over a hundred people, but also assassinated its primary target: the US Secretary of State, Sandra Easton. 'How strong a connection? Anything that would give us his location?'

'No – at least, not yet. But we do know that he's personally overseeing something. "Operation Lamplighter" is what Syed says it's called.'

'It doesn't ring any bells,' said Morgan. 'But I'll pass it straight up to the Admiral so we can get the entire USIC on it. Anything that gives us a shot at al-Rais . . .'

'I'd be happy to take the shot personally against that son of a bitch, sir,' said Baxter.

'I'm sure we all would. All right, Tony, get back to work on Syed. The rest of your chewing-out can keep until you get back to Washington.' His image disappeared.

'So, uh, are we done, Tony?' Levon asked drowsily from the other half of the screen. 'Not that I don't mind being dragged out of bed to be shouted at by the boss, but I'd kinda like to get back to sleep now.'

'We'll see you tomorrow. Today. Whatever damn day it is in DC,' Tony told him. Levon grinned, then the screen went dark. 'Okay, Adam, Holly Jo – let's get back to it.'

'Whoa, a three-way,' said Kyle, smirking at Holly Jo as she stood.

She sighed and gestured towards the emergency exit. 'Can I kick him out of that hatch?'

Tony smiled. 'If you take care of the paperwork.' He led the way back down the cabin, pausing as he reached Albion. 'Roger, is this friend of yours really good enough to take your place?'

'Oh, nobody's good enough to do *that*,' Albion whispered, with a feeble smile. 'But she has the right background in medicine and psychology, and has . . . a good handle on people. I think she'll be able to fill in until I'm back on my feet.'

'You make sure that doesn't take too long, okay?'

'Get well soon, Roger,' Holly Jo added.

Adam, behind her, said nothing, staring down at Albion in

silence. For a brief moment his eyes widened, taking on the intensity – and anger – of Syed's gaze . . . but then it faded.

Only Tony had noticed. 'I think we need to finish the debriefing,' he said quietly.

Adam looked at him, face now blank. 'I think you're right.'

The following hours saw the jet pass over the Arctic wastes of Greenland and Canada, cruising above Quebec and New York State before beginning its descent towards the eastern seaboard. The debriefing was finally concluded. Every secret Syed knew about the terrorist organisation's operations and members had been exposed, the Pakistani's memories picked clean.

Now it was time for another kind of cleansing.

Adam emerged from a washroom, drawing a double-take from Holly Jo. 'Wow. I almost didn't recognise you,' she said, only half joking.

Toradze's moustache was gone, the black dye rinsed out to return Adam's hair to its natural dark brown. Even his eyes had changed, the piercing blue of the Georgian's gaze a softer grey now that the contact lenses had been removed. The expensive clothing had also been replaced by an unremarkable shirt and slacks, the gold jewellery returned to an evidence bag.

Shorn of the arms dealer's distinguishing marks, what remained was . . . *anonymous*. Had random onlookers been asked to describe Adam Gray after glimpsing him in a crowd, that would have been the recurring word. He was handsome enough in a way that could charitably have been described as 'generic', none of his features particularly distinctive. Even his background was hard to determine; most of the hypothetical onlookers would have thought him Caucasian, but the more observant might have picked out other traits. Some Hispanic ancestry? Persian, perhaps, or Arabic? It was impossible to be sure.

'It's an improvement,' said Tony, looking up. The other team members were in various states of sleep throughout the cabin. 'Welcome back.'

'Not quite yet.' Adam held up the case containing Albion's medical equipment. 'There's one more thing to do.'

'You don't want to let it happen naturally?' Holly Jo asked. 'You look exhausted – you've been awake for nearly twenty-four hours. You really need some sleep.'

'I want Syed's persona wiped.' There was a tinge of disgust to his otherwise flat voice. 'Now.'

Tony looked towards Albion. 'Will it be safe without Roger to work out the amount?'

'It's a standard dose.'

Tony hesitated, then took the case. 'If you're sure.'

'I'm sure. I don't want this guy's thoughts in my head any more.'

The two men went to the rear cabin. Adam sat and tugged down his shirt collar as Tony took out the jet injector. 'Is this set?'

'Yes. Do it.'

Tony cautiously placed the nozzle against Adam's neck and pulled the trigger. Adam flinched, then leaned back in his seat and closed his eyes.

Tony waited, counting thirty seconds on his watch. 'Adam? You okay?'

'Yes.' He slowly opened his eyes. 'Do a memory check. I want to be sure he's gone.'

'Okay. Let's see . . . what year did Syed go on the Hajj?'

'That was . . . 2005.' Adam caught Tony's dismay. 'No, it's okay – that came up during the debriefing, remember? When you asked how he first met Fathi. If we pulled it out of his memory, now I remember it too.'

'Sorry.'

'No problem. Ask something else.'

'How about . . . the name of Syed's first imam when he was a kid.'

Adam thought for a few seconds. 'No idea.'

'How old was he when he first fired a gun?'

Another pause. 'Nothing.'

'He's gone?'

'Yes.'

'Thank God. You must be relieved to be rid of that bastard.'

Another emotionless 'Yes.' Adam rubbed the mark on his neck, then stood. 'How long before we land?'

'About thirty minutes. I need to go straight to STS once I've seen Roger to the hospital; I imagine Morgan's got a boot with my ass's name on it. Harper too, I expect. You should go home, though. You could use some sleep.'

'So could you.'

'I didn't get shot at. You deserve the morning off for that, at least. Never say I'm not a generous boss.' He grinned.

Adam didn't respond to the joke. 'Okay. I'll be at STS by noon.' He returned to the main cabin.

'See you there,' Tony said with a sigh.

Washington DC, United States

After the plane touched down, Albion was taken away by an ambulance, Tony going with him. The rest of the team dispersed. Holly Jo offered to share a taxi with Adam, but he declined.

He returned to his apartment. The living room was plain, even spartan. White walls with no pictures, comfortable but utilitarian black Ikea furniture, a desk in one corner with an Apple laptop upon it. No ornamentation of any kind. There was no television. Or a stereo, even a radio. The entire place was devoid of personal touches, anything that might give a hint about its occupant's private life.

It did not occur to Adam that there was anything unusual about this.

He entered the bedroom, unpacking his baggage and putting everything in its proper place, then pulled the curtains to shut out the morning light. He undressed and was about to get into the bed when he hesitated. The moment passed and he climbed in, switching off the lights. Despite his tiredness, it took some time before he finally fell asleep.

He knew what was waiting for him.

The dream was one he had experienced too many times before. He ran down a street; where he was, he didn't know. Something terrible had happened. People fled the other way, screaming and crying, frightened faces flashing past as he battled against the tide.

But there was one face ahead that was not moving. He reached it, kneeling down. It stared up at him. The eyes were wide but lifeless, unmoving, surrounded by dirt and blood.

The dead man's face was his own.

Adam jerked awake, breathing rapidly. The breaths slowed. He looked at the glowing figures of the clock beside the bed. Barely an hour had passed. He closed his eyes again, but knew that the same dream would find him once more.

8

Day of Change

Reading, England

This was the most important day of Bianca Childs' life, yet the only thing she could think about was her sore feet.

The pain was her own stupid fault. No, actually, it was James's fault for insisting that everybody 'dress smartly for the investors. Yes, even you, Bianca.' Laughter all round, though hers was decidedly forced.

That said, turning up at the lab to discover she was the only woman not in high heels had produced some weird kind of peer pressure, compelling her to make a rapid drive from the science park to fix the anomaly. In hindsight, though, spending just ten pounds on the first pair of black stilettos that fitted, from a place calling itself Megasave Shoe Warehouse, had been asking for trouble.

So now she was in a rented function room at a hotel, trying not to fidget as James concluded the presentation that could make her career . . . or see the whole company knocked back to square one. Or even zero. Of the several research projects Luminica

Bioscience had sunk its dwindling capital into, Thymirase was the one with a chance to be a breakout success. And she had been its primary architect; her ideas, her two years of solid work, had led to the lab team piecing together the complex chains of molecules that would become a miracle drug.

If it worked. Computer simulations said it should, and initial tests on animals – something Bianca was never happy with, but which James had decided were a necessary evil considering Thymirase's potential – had produced the expected results. But testing on humans was another thing entirely, and Luminica didn't have the financial resources either to engage in full-scale trials, or to deal with potential lawsuits if things went wrong.

Enter the investors.

Six people: four men, two women. They represented a venture capital group specialising in medical research, here today to decide whether they would put money into Thymirase. If they did, and the drug did everything Bianca believed it would, the licensing fees from the patents could potentially be worth *billions*. The investors would take the lion's share, and as the company's founder James Harding would claim a hefty chunk of the remainder, but all of Luminica's fourteen employees were assured of a piece of the action. In a best-case scenario, Bianca's slice would be worth . . .

She didn't even want to think of the number in case doing so jinxed the deal. Anyway, it was too much – more than she could possibly need in several lifetimes. Even if she made sure that the people she cared about were provided for in perpetuity, the amount left over would still be obscene. There would be a lot of charities receiving unexpected – and large – donations.

God, her feet hurt. She tried to force a state of Zen calm upon herself to overcome it, with limited success, as James clicked on his final PowerPoint slide. It would soon be time for her to add her own contribution to the presentation. She tried to judge the investors' feelings. Were they going to buy in? The mere fact that they were here at all was a good omen, but she had friends in other pharmaceutical start-ups who had come so close to a life-changing deal . . . only for everything to collapse at the last moment.

She had a good feeling about *this* deal, though. The body language of the six expensively dressed visitors – none had bought *their* shoes for a tenner – was veiled, but they couldn't disguise their interest. All were subtly leaning forward, necks craning as if trying to get closer to something delicious. Hungry Hungry Venture Capitalists. The thought brought an involuntary giggle, which she hurriedly tried to hide behind a fake cough.

But there undeniably was a hunger there. One man watched James with literally calculating attention, head bobbing milli-metrically as if he were working a mental abacus. The others displayed similar subtle signs of their keenness.

Nothing had been signed yet, though. They still had to be convinced to take the final step . . .

James gestured in her direction, the VIPs' heads turning as one. 'So with that in mind, I'd like to introduce the person whose insight and dedication has led to the development of Thymirase: Dr Bianca Childs.'

This is it. 'Thank you, James. Thank you,' she said as she stood to polite applause. 'But Thymirase was really a team effort – it wouldn't have happened without the help of my incredibly talented colleagues. Some of whom are much better at public speaking than me, so thank you again, James, for making me face my fears!' The joke got a small amount of laughter.

'So, what I was supposed to talk about now,' she went on, 'were the technical details of Thymirase – how it affects the protein kinases that build connections between neurons, the neurochemical boost this gives to a patient's recall, and so on. But James has already done a very good job in his presentation of explaining what the drug will do to help sufferers of Alzheimer's, so rather than repeat what's already been said, I'd like to talk about something else instead.' She let James sweat for a moment, imagining his thoughts: *oh God, please don't let the crazy hippie woman scare off the investors!* 'The reasons *why* I started the research that created Thymirase.'

James appeared relieved, if not entirely secure. Her audience, meanwhile, seemed intrigued. Even the most number-crunching capitalist could still appreciate a human interest story.

Bianca composed herself, trying to assemble what was essentially a huge ad lib. The last time she had done anything similar was an attempt at a performance piece while at university; she hoped this would be better received. She had tied back her long frizzy dark hair, but a strand had managed to work loose and drop down annoyingly over one eye, so she flicked it away before beginning.

'All long-term debilitating diseases have tragic costs,' she said, 'both in the purely financial sense of treatment and care, and personally for the sufferer and their family. But Alzheimer's is especially cruel, because not only is it currently incurable, but it destroys what makes a person unique – what makes them *them*. If our personalities are defined by our experiences, by our memories, then Alzheimer's literally kills who you are, one thought at a time. It's painful for the sufferer when there's still enough of them left to realise how much of their . . . *soul*, for want of a better word, has been eaten away. And it's agonising for their families, because they see someone they love being destroyed a little bit more each day, and there's absolutely nothing they can do to stop it. I know how that feels, because I've watched it happen. Twice.'

She paused to draw breath and lick her drying lips. James was still on tenterhooks, not sure if she was helping or hindering. The investors, however, all watched with interest. Reassured, she continued.

'I've never talked about this much, because it's still painful, even after the time that's passed,' she confessed. 'But when I was fifteen, my grandmother died after suffering from Alzheimer's for several years. Seeing her reduced to a . . . a helpless shadow of herself was horrible, and what made it worse was that my mother was a nurse – she spent every day helping people, but there was nothing she could do to help her own mother. That was what started me on a medical career path – I wanted to do something *more* to help people like my grandmother.

'And then,' she went on, 'five years later, when I was at university, my grandfather – on my father's side – also died from Alzheimer's. And it was just as painful to watch as it had been before.' Her throat suddenly felt raspy; she swallowed. 'And again I felt . . . helpless. There was nothing I could do about it. After his funeral I decided that there *should* be something I could do. There had to be a way to help people who were dying from this horrible disease. So I made up my mind: I was going to find one. And now, ten years later, my greatest hope in the world is that . . . that Thymirase might be it.'

She blinked, startled to realise that she had begun to tear up. Reliving the past had been more affecting, more painful than she had expected. She was about to say something else when she was interrupted by another surprise. The investors were applauding her. Not in a Hollywood way, jumping to their feet with tears in their own eyes, but still out of more than mere politeness.

Cheeks flushing with sudden embarrassment, she offered stumbling thanks before sitting back down. 'Well, thank you, Bianca,' said James with an approving – and relieved – nod. He turned to the investors, 'I think that shows the kind of drive and determination that everybody working on Thymirase shares. Luminica Bioscience isn't just about money – what we do is also from a personal desire to make the world better.'

Bianca wanted to tell him to stop the hard sell before he spoiled things, but fortunately it was now clear that the presentation was concluded. Hands were shaken, pleasantries exchanged, then those not directly involved in the business side of the deal decamped to let the money start talking. As Bianca headed for the exit, James quickly whispered: 'Good story. I think it helped.'

'I meant everything I said,' she whispered back, mildly affronted. But he had already moved on. She huffed, then left the room.

She was looking forward to taking off her awful shoes, letting her hair down and discussing the presentation with her friends, but instead she found two people – a raven-haired woman in a sharply cut trouser suit and a fair-haired man in his mid-thirties – waiting for her in the hallway. 'Dr Childs?' said the former.

'Yes?'

She held up an identity card. The name beneath her photo was Emma Sergeant, but Bianca's eyes snapped to the turquoise logo in the card's corner: the lion and unicorn of the royal coat of arms, symbol of the British government, with SECRET INTELLIGENCE SERVICE written beside it. 'MI6' was appended in a thinner grey typeface. 'May we have a word, please? In private.'

Bianca almost laughed. 'Is this a joke?' Why would MI6 possibly want to talk to her?

'It's no joke,' said the man. He had an American accent. 'It's very important. We need to speak to you about Dr Roger Albion.'

'Roger? I haven't seen him for, I don't know, three or four yea—' She stopped as a horrible fear struck her. 'Is he all right? Has something happened to him?'

Her colleagues were still looking on curiously. 'Can we talk in private, please,' said Sergeant, more as a command than a request.

'Er, okay.' Bianca gave a helpless shrug as she moved with the two visitors out of earshot. 'What's going on? What's happened to Roger?'

'You do know him, then?' said the man.

'Yes, he was my professor when I was doing my doctorate. And my friend, too. Is he okay?'

'I'm afraid he's in hospital.'

'What happened to him?'

He lowered his voice. 'He was shot.'

'Shot!' Bianca cried. 'Oh my God!'

'He's in a stable condition, but he's had to undergo surgery, and is very weak. He's asked to see you.'

'How did he get shot?' Bianca demanded, before coming up with another, more immediate question: 'Who *are* you?'

The man took out his own ID card. 'My name's Tony Carpenter. I work for the Central Intelligence Agency.'

'The CIA?' Now she was completely lost. 'What's Roger got to do with the CIA?'

'He was helping us with an operation. The reason we asked our British partners,' he nodded at Sergeant, 'to find you is that Roger thinks you can help us too.'

'How? What kind of operation?'

'I can't discuss that here, I'm afraid. But it's a matter of national security. We have a jet waiting; we can talk about it on the flight.'

'On the flight? Wait a minute,' said Bianca, now feeling as if the ground had opened up under her feet and sent her tumbling down the rabbit hole. 'I can't just jet off to the States at the drop of a hat. I'm in the middle of something; I need to be here to answer questions for our investors . . .'

'We'll take care of everything with Mr Harding,' said Sergeant impatiently.

'And,' added Tony, 'I'm very confident that the venture group is going to buy into Luminica to secure the Thymirase research and patents, even without you here. Just a feeling.'

'How do you know about . . . oh. Right. CIA. MI6.' She gave the pair a disapproving frown. 'I'm pretty sure there are laws against that.'

Sergeant looked to be struggling not to roll her eyes. 'Dr Childs, we can't force you to go, but we – that is, Her Majesty's Government – think it's very important that you do. As Mr Carpenter said, it's a national security issue. Lives could depend on it.'

'I don't understand how, though,' Bianca protested. 'Roger's in pharmaceutical research; he's a neurochemist, like me. He helps develop medicines. How does that affect national security?'

'The best person to explain that is Roger himself,' said Tony. 'He specifically asked to see you, and said you're the only person capable of duplicating his work.'

'Me?' That came as a surprise; he was a friend, yes, but she'd had no idea he rated her so highly.

And what *was* his work? What could he be working on that was so important to the CIA and MI6? She had to admit, she was now curious . . .

'How long will this take?' she asked. 'I mean, after I've seen Roger – you just mentioned duplicating his work. Do you want me to carry on with it?'

'Right now?' said Tony. 'I can't give you an answer. It depends what Roger has to say. But we can have you back in England tomorrow, if that's what you want.'

She looked back towards the function room. 'It's just . . . the timing . . .'

'As I said, we'll talk to Mr Harding,' Sergeant told her. 'I'm sure he'll be understanding.' She sounded vaguely threatening.

'Okay, so if I say yes, what happens?'

'We'll stop by your home so you can pick up your passport and clothes, your toothbrush, anything else you need,' said Tony. 'Then we'll drive to the airport and the plane will take us to DC.'

'Just like that? No queuing, no having my shoes scanned for bombs and my nail clippers confiscated?'

'It's a US government jet, and it's been sent here specifically to fly you to the States.'

'Huh. Well, I guess I've got to go, then. It'd be an awful waste of jet fuel if I didn't.'

'The US taxpayers appreciate it,' Tony said, with a light edge of sarcasm.

'I was more concerned about the polar bears, but . . .' She was still in two minds, but foremost in both was the thought of her former teacher and mentor. Whatever had happened to him was clearly serious, and he had specifically requested to see her. Without Albion's tutelage she wouldn't be where she was today. She owed him a lot; certainly enough to visit him in hospital. That the American government thought the meeting important enough to put a private jet at her disposal added an almost irresistible layer of intrigue.

'Okay, I'll go,' she said. 'But please let me tell James myself. I can't just disappear without a word.'

'All right,' said Sergeant, with evident reluctance. 'We'll both go and talk to him now.'

Tony took out a phone. 'I'll get the ball rolling while you do that.'

Bianca and Sergeant returned to the function room, leaving him to make his call. Just as Bianca reached to open the door, Sergeant put a hand on her arm. 'There's one thing, Dr Childs.

SIS is doing this as a favour to our American friends – professional courtesy, so to speak. But . . .' She glanced back as if to check that the CIA man wasn't eavesdropping. 'They're being very tight-lipped about what your friend Dr Albion was actually working on. Counterterrorism, they say, which is why it's a national security issue – but they won't say in what area. And if they won't give us the full story, it affects *our* ability to fight terrorism.'

Bianca knew there was something else coming. 'So, you want . . .'

'We just want you to keep your eyes and ears open while you're over there. Discreetly, of course.'

'Of course,' Bianca said cuttingly as she knocked on the door, wondering what she was about to let herself in for.

9

Friends Reunited

Washington DC, United States

'Bianca!' said Albion. He tried to sit up, but grimaced at a stab of pain. 'Great to see you again. Glad you could make it.'

'I could hardly say no,' she said, leaning down gingerly to embrace him. Despite his size, he seemed worryingly small and weak in the hospital bed. Tony, who had brought her to the room, stood back and waited.

'You're looking well. And you've done something to your hair, I think?'

'I tried a new tint. Kind of a—'

'Oh no, I didn't mean coloured. I meant *combed*.'

'You cheeky old sod!' she said, but with a smile.

'Sorry, I couldn't resist. But no, you look great. So, how are you? You were going to join Jimmy Harding's start-up. How's that working out?'

'Pretty well,' she said, not wanting to jinx anything. She still hadn't heard any news from James about the deal, good or bad.

'Yes, I've been there over two years. We've had some promising results.'

'I'm not surprised, knowing you. So, you're here. Tony, would you mind if I talked to Bianca in private? Don't worry, I won't give away any state secrets.'

Tony nodded. 'Dr Childs, I'll be outside when you're done. Talk to you later, Roger.'

Albion waited until he had left the room before speaking again. 'Decent guy, just . . . a bit of a straight arrow,' he opined. 'Worryingly few vices. Anyway, take a seat.' He pushed a button to elevate the head of the bed as Bianca pulled up a chair. 'I imagine you're ever so slightly curious about what's going on.'

'Nooo, I hadn't given it the slightest thought the whole time the CIA was flying me to Washington in a private jet.'

Albion chuckled. 'It's amazing how much money the US government is willing to throw around to get something they want. I'd be up in arms at the waste of taxpayer dollars,' he dropped his voice, mock-conspiratorially, 'if I didn't have an extremely good accountant making sure I pay as few of them as possible.'

'Don't tell me you've joined the one per cent, Roger!'

'There's always going to be a top one per cent; it's simple math. Better to be in it than not.' He cocked his head, seeing her look of disapproval. 'Oh, sorry. I forgot you're a commie.'

'Hardly. But right now, you Americans think that anyone to the left of Margaret Thatcher is a communist,' she retorted, prodding his arm. 'People over here start screaming "Socialism!" about policies that even the most right-wing government in Europe would consider a bit extreme. I don't know if it's funny or scary.'

'When it comes to American politics, it's both. It's always both. But,' he went on, becoming serious, 'this isn't so much politics as realpolitik. You've got questions. I'll answer them – although there are some things I can't tell you just yet. Even though I imagine Tony asked you to sign three hundred pages of forms just to get limited security clearance.'

Bianca pulled a face. 'He did, and I almost didn't sign them, to be honest. They made it sound as if I'd be sent to Guantanamo Bay if I breathed a single word.' She narrowed her eyes. 'And you can't tell me things "yet"? It seems like you're expecting me to be around for a while.'

'We'll see how it goes. But I guarantee you'll be interested. So, ask.'

'Okay. The obvious first: what the hell happened to you?'

'I took a trip to Pakistan, where I got a nine-millimetre bullet to the back.'

'Oh my God!'

'Yeah, that was basically my reaction, but with more "aaaargh". I won't bore you with the literally gory details, but suffice it to say that the next time I eat solid food, which won't be for a while yet,' he waved a hand at the intravenous drip beside the bed, 'it'll have a slightly shorter journey through and out. Somewhere around here, there's a jar with about a foot of my small intestine in it.'

'Jesus,' Bianca said. 'Was there any other damage?'

'No, I was, air quotes, lucky. Part of my deal with my employers was that I get danger money for working abroad – and also a paid medical plan. Just as well, in hindsight.'

'I can't believe how . . . how relaxed you seem about it.'

'Well, the first reason is that what's done is done, so there's no point having hysterics. The second reason is that I'm drugged to the eyeballs! They've got me on quite a cocktail. A good buzz, actually. Reminds me of my college days.'

'When did all this happen?'

'Yesterday. Or was it two days ago? It's confusing enough with the time zones, even if I didn't feel like I'd just had a damn good toke.'

'Roger,' she chided. 'What about Jill, and the kids? Have they come to see you?'

He shook his head. 'I haven't spoken to either of the kids in over a year. And Jill, well . . .'

She noticed a band of paler skin on the ring finger of his left hand. 'Oh, Roger! Not again!'

'Don't give me that look! I'd already been divorced three times, so the odds of wife number four faring any better weren't good. Besides, I enjoy looking for the next ex-Mrs Albion. It's a lot more fun than the actual marriage.'

'You are a terrible human being,' Bianca told him mockingly. 'But what were you doing in Pakistan?'

The jocular look disappeared. 'I've been working on something for US intelligence. I can't tell you anything else until you get full security clearance, but suffice it to say that something I developed is key to it.'

'A drug?'

'Yes. Well, more than one, but they're related in function. The reason I was out in the field rather than sitting in a nice clean safe lab is that the doses have to be very precise. They depend not only on the subject's size and weight, body characteristics and so on, but also on an assessment of their physical condition. It's too complicated to be left to a chart – someone with medical knowledge has to make a determination before deciding the dose.' Albion glanced towards the door, dropping his voice to a whisper. 'At least . . . that's what I told them.'

She leaned closer. 'What do you mean?'

'I mean, any chimp with an iPhone app could work out the right dose. The reason I said it's incredibly complicated and only

83

I could do it was that the moment they found out I wasn't indispensable, they would have fired my ass.'

'What! You . . .' She brought her voice back down to a strained whisper. 'You lied to the CIA?'

'Technically they're not the CIA, but I'll let them explain that. But yes, I bent the truth a little.'

'A *little*! Are you out of your mind? They would have sent you to prison if they'd found out. And even though they didn't, it's not like you're any better off. You got *shot*!'

Even through the drugs, Albion was annoyed by her criticism. 'Yes, I know, it didn't exactly turn out as I'd hoped. But I had over two years working for a *very* generous client. We're talking black budget here – it's like a bottomless well of cash. But if I'd said, "Okay guys, here are the formulas and my little black book telling you everything you need to work out the dosages," then it would all have gone, just like that. Poof! No more money – not even patent royalties. There was no way I was going to give that up willingly.'

Bianca's tone became scathing. 'And look where it got you. Stuck in a bed with your gut in a jar.'

'I don't need a lecture from you, Miss Childs!' he snapped, before calming. 'Sorry, I'm sorry. Yes, I know all this is entirely my own dumb fault. But I've just been through yet another divorce, for God's sake. I need the money, and if I gave up this opportunity, then what? Go back into academia for peanuts? Become a dancing monkey for big pharma, doing work-for-hire to develop new kinds of impotence treatments?' His evident disgust at the prospect passed, his eyes becoming beseeching. 'Bianca, I'm too old to do what you did and risk joining a start-up. I *needed* this. I'm sixty-two – if I can keep this job going for another couple of years, I can retire without having to worry about clipping coupons just to afford to eat.'

'Everything's about money with you, isn't it, Roger?'

'Yes – but at least I'm shameless and consistent about it.' The joke thawed her, a little. 'You've known exactly what I'm like ever since we met. After all, the reason I was teaching in England in the first place was a nice fat research grant. Oh, I miss those days.'

'Teaching in England?'

'No, when pharma companies threw money around without demanding specific results to a timetable. Damn bankers crashing the economy, they ruined everything! But,' he added, 'I'll admit I miss working in England too. Country pubs, I liked them. And big fries with vinegar splashed all over them.'

'They're called chips,' Bianca corrected in a teasing tone.

'Whatever. But I met some good people there, too. Good friends. Like you.'

She knew him well enough to spot the approaching hard sell. 'So what is it you want from this particular good friend?'

'Oh! I'm cut to the quick!' he said, in mock offence. 'How could you possibly think, yadda yadda. No, you're quite right – I want you to help me keep this job.'

'The job that got you shot.'

'I'll admit, as perks go that's not quite up there with free dental. But . . . there's something else.' A cloud crossed his face. 'I'm sixty-two – and my mother's eighty-five.'

'Rosemary?' She had only met Albion's mother once, but it had been enough to see where he had got his vitality and gift of the gab. 'How is she?'

'Not good. She's going to have to go into a care home, which she'll detest – but the early symptoms have started to manifest.'

She didn't need to ask to know that the symptoms were those of dementia. 'Oh God. Roger, I'm sorry.'

'Yeah.' He sighed. 'I can't help wondering if the human brain just wasn't meant to last. If you think about it, we've added twenty or thirty years to the average life span over the past couple of centuries …' Another rueful breath. 'But yes, she's going to need care. And since this is America and not some communist utopia like Britain,' a faint smile, 'that care does not come cheap.'

'You're doing this for her?'

'I'm not the dashing mercenary rogue I like to portray myself as, Bianca,' he said. 'Well, not *entirely*. But yes, I might not have found a cure for Alzheimer's – I'll have to leave that to you – but I can at least make sure that my mother is treated with the respect and dignity she deserves. And I'd like you to help me.'

'So what do you want me to do?'

'To stand in for me until I'm back on my feet.'

A long silence. 'In the job that, to reiterate, got you shot.'

'Hopefully they've learned a lesson in workplace safety from that! But think of it as an opportunity. I understand things are looking very good at Jimmy's company right now—'

She made an exasperated sound. 'Does *everybody* know about that?'

'The term "intelligence community" isn't *entirely* ironic. But I know how these things work – the live tests have to be approved and set up, due diligence, legal and patent paperwork, et cetera, et cetera. You won't be doing any lab work of actual importance for a couple of months. They can spare you – especially if the US government says how grateful it would be for your services, and maybe offers compensation in return for your temporary loan. No drug company is going to turn down a quid pro quo from Uncle Sam. It's good business sense.'

'And what would this job actually entail?'

'Just what I said before. You assess the subject, calculate the drug dose, then administer it.' He lowered his voice again. 'And make it look beyond the ken of mere mortals, obviously. Bamboozle everyone with medibabble. It's what I do.'

'Did.'

'And will do again, I hope. But it's straightforward enough – I'll teach you. And you get to travel; I visited some very interesting places, and got shot in almost none of them.'

Bianca pursed her lips, considering it. 'These drugs of yours – what *are* they?'

'They're called Neutharsine, Hyperthymexine and Mnemexal. Can't tell you what they actually *do* yet, I'm afraid – classified. Although I'm sure you can make educated guesses from the corrupted Latin in the names. But they're an offshoot of the development I did on Netronal, if you remember that.'

'Of course I remember; I helped you with some of the lab work when I was a postgrad.' She paused, puzzled. 'Wait – I thought Netronal didn't get picked up?'

'No, but the new drugs built off my old research.'

'So they're related to memory formation?'

'Again, I can't say anything just yet. But please, Bianca, it's not exaggerating to say that my future – and my mother's – depends on my keeping this job. All I'm asking is that you act as my substitute for a few weeks. You might not even be needed; it depends if they carry out any operations. The whole thing could end up as nothing more than a paid vacation, and Washington's a fascinating place to visit. I know you'd like the National Gallery of Art.'

Another pause for thought. 'I'm not going to commit to anything until I know more about what I'm supposed to be doing,' she said. 'But . . . I'll at least find out what that is before I make a decision.'

Albion tried to cover his disappointment. 'Well, that's as much as I could hope for right now, I suppose.'

She took his hand. 'Roger, I mean it – I'll see what they have to say. And, you know . . . I really don't want you or Rosemary to starve.' A smile, her first for a while. 'But whatever happens, I want you to get better, okay?'

'Believe me, it's at the top of my to-do list.'

Bianca kissed his cheek. 'All right. I'll tell you what I decide before I go back to England. See you again soon.'

'Bye, Bianca. And thank you for coming.'

'Thank *you* for an intriguing proposition.'

'Don't thank me just yet,' he said quietly after she left the room.

10

The Admiral

'So, what do you think of Washington?'

Bianca pulled her gaze away from the streets outside the government-issue black SUV to look at Tony. 'Roger said it was interesting. He was right.' The ride had taken her past the Capitol and what she recognised from an addiction to *The X-Files* in her youth as the FBI building, even giving her a brief view of the White House before continuing north-west into the city's business district.

'Yeah, it's quite a place.'

Now that she was over her initial surprise and bewilderment at the whole situation, she had been able to give her companion a more thorough assessment. Tony was handsome and well-built, a wily intelligence behind his pale blue eyes – which met hers as he glanced away from the road. She realised he was also appraising her, making her feel briefly and foolishly self-conscious, wondering if she was being rated as highly on his internal scale as he was on hers.

As if sensing this, he smiled in reassurance. 'We're almost there.' He indicated a building ahead.

Their destination was a modern but mundane office block,

standing apart from its equally ordinary neighbours on a tree-lined street. A large sign read HELMONT DATA SYSTEMS, INC. She peered up at the building as the SUV drove into an underground parking area beneath it.

'Something wrong?' asked Tony.

'No, I just assumed we'd be going to CIA headquarters.'

'Helmont exclusively does contract work for the US government, including the CIA,' he replied, as if that explained everything. The SUV went down to the first subterranean level, stopping near an elevator.

They got out and went to the lift. A uniformed guard was waiting for them. Tony showed him his ID, then produced several pages of closely printed text. One of the many frightening security agreements Bianca had signed on the plane, she saw, recognising her own signature on the last page. The man scrutinised it, then nodded. Tony inserted his card into a reader beside the elevator; a green light came on, and the doors opened. 'After you,' he said.

Bianca entered, immediately noticing security cameras mounted prominently in each corner of the ceiling. 'It's a good thing cameras don't really steal your soul,' she said, trying to cover her sudden nervousness. 'You've got plenty of them!'

He grinned. 'I dunno, that might explain a lot about people who work their whole lives in Washington.' The joke eased her tension, slightly.

Tony pushed the button marked '5'. The elevator began its ascent. 'The bottom floors actually are used by Helmont,' he said. 'They do a lot of low-level but still classified data-processing, so nobody thinks twice about the security measures. The upper floors are ours, though.'

'The CIA?' she asked.

'Not quite. This project's actually run by the Special Technology Section – STS.'

'I'm glad it's not called the Special Technology Division!'

It took him a moment to get the joke, which produced a crooked grin. 'It's connected to the CIA and other US intelligence agencies, without being controlled by them. The org chart for the US intelligence community is . . . complicated. To say the least.'

'But your ID said you were with the CIA.'

'I am. On paper, anyway. STS is a black agency – it doesn't officially exist. Like I said, it's complicated.'

A chime announced that they had arrived at the fifth floor. The doors opened.

Bianca was almost disappointed. She had half expected some kind of elaborate control room illuminated by stylish blue lights, the sort of place where James Bond or Jack Bauer would feel at home. Instead, she stepped out into what looked like a perfectly ordinary business, corridors leading off to various offices.

'Good afternoon, Mr Carpenter,' said a woman seated behind a reception desk. 'Mr Morgan is waiting for you with the Admiral and Dr Kiddrick in briefing room B.'

'Thanks. When did the Admiral arrive?'

'About fifteen minutes ago.'

Tony's expression suggested he had just tasted something bitter. 'Should be fun,' he said, half to himself. 'Okay, Dr Childs. Follow me, please.' He led the way down a hallway and opened a door. 'After you.'

The room was anodyne, the view of the linden trees through the windows masked by a heavy tint applied to the glass. A very large flat-screen TV occupied one wall. Three men sat at a long conference table, rising as she entered – one of them somewhat belatedly.

'Dr Childs,' said Tony, 'I'd like you to meet Martin Morgan, the project director' – a stern, middle-aged black man with glasses and greying hair – 'Dr Nathaniel Kiddrick, senior scientific adviser' – the gangling slow-stander; late fifties, with unsettlingly wide eyes beneath a domed forehead, sporting the kind of tough-guy-wannabe moustache that could only be carried off successfully by a cop or soldier – 'and Admiral Gordon Harper, Director of National Intelligence.'

Bianca shook Morgan's hand, then Kiddrick's before greeting Harper. Despite being introduced as an admiral, the white-haired man wore a suit rather than a uniform. His hand almost swallowed hers in a brief but steely grip. Unlike Kiddrick with his silly moustache, he didn't need to try to be intimidating. Even though he was well into his sixties, he was still over six feet tall and clearly did far more exercise than the occasional round of tennis or golf. He had the hard, no-nonsense air of someone used to being obeyed immediately at all times, and who would not hesitate to take sanctions against anyone failing to fall into line.

'Dr Childs,' said Harper, voice as curt as she had imagined. 'Take a seat.' She did so, the men following suit. 'Since you're a Brit, I don't expect you to know what my position as DNI entails. It means I'm in overall charge of USIC, the US intelligence community – CIA, NSA, FBI, Homeland Security, a dozen other agencies – and that I report directly to the President of the United States.' He gave Tony an irate glare. 'It also means that my time is extremely important.'

Tony looked uncomfortable, but met Harper's gaze. 'Sorry, sir.'

'So, I'll keep this brief. I know that you just spoke to Dr Albion, and that he asked you to help us by temporarily taking his place on this project.'

'Yes, that's right. But he didn't tell me what the project actually *was*.'

His flinty stare warned her that he neither anticipated nor appreciated being interrupted. 'Well, I'll give you the précis.

The Persona Project is a black-budget operation run by STS. The technology it has developed allows the memories of one person to be read, recorded and downloaded into the brain of another.'

It took Bianca a moment to process the statement, and when she did, it produced a short, disbelieving laugh. 'What? Oh, come on. That's not possible.'

If Harper disliked being interrupted, his displeasure at being contradicted was even greater. 'Dr Childs,' he said, interlocking his fingers and putting both hands on the table with an audible thud, 'not only is it possible, it is being used to protect the security of the United States – and its allies – right now. The results it has obtained are valuable enough that Dr Albion's injury denies us the use of an important intelligence-gathering asset. And that is something I am not prepared to allow.

'Dr Albion says you are the only person capable of continuing in his role. Without information to the contrary, I have no choice but to believe that.' He gave Morgan and Kiddrick momentary glances, Bianca realising that he was waiting – even hoping – for either man to provide such information. But neither replied. 'That being the case, I will do whatever it takes to make this happen. I'll start by offering a carrot: we'll pay you whatever you want, within reason, to take over from Dr Albion until he's fit enough to return to duty.'

Bianca was taken aback by the bluntness of the offer. 'Ah, that's very . . . generous. But I've got responsibilities back in England – my company's in the middle of making a major deal, and I'm a key part of it. If I walk out on them, even if it's only for a month or two, it could affect the deal, cost my friends their jobs—'

'I know about the deal,' Harper interrupted. He slid a sheet of paper from a folder. 'You know what else could affect it?

Thymirase being denied approval by the Food and Drug Administration for sale or use in the United States. I guessed from your file,' he tapped the page, 'that the carrot wouldn't do much for you, since money isn't your motivation.'

'Wait – how did you get a file on me?' Bianca demanded.

But Harper continued, his words rolling over hers like a juggernaut. 'So here's the stick. If you don't agree to help us, your investors will be officially informed, within the hour, that the FDA will never grant approval for Thymirase. Without access to the US market, no drug company will ever buy the rights or fund further research. Your company's deal will be dead in the water.'

Bianca was so outraged she struggled to speak. 'You – you can't do that! That's blackmail, that's illegal. You can't *do* that!'

'Yes I can,' was his cold reply. 'In this business, if you have no choice, you have to make sure the other guy has even less. Right now, if we want the Persona Project to continue – and we do – we have no choice but to bring you aboard.'

'And I have no choice but to be press-ganged?'

'That's about the size of it.' He pushed the paper back into the folder. 'I'm not happy about it either. Under normal circumstances, a foreign national, even from a close ally, would never have been allowed near STS. Especially not one with your political leanings. But we need you. And we're going to get you. I take it we have your agreement?'

Bianca shook with fury, made all the more intense by the humiliation of being rendered helpless. She had no doubts whatsoever that Harper would carry out his threat; if he did so, she would return to England to find that Thymirase was dead, taking the entire company down with it. The careers of fifteen people would be wrecked, and the two years she had spent working on the drug wasted.

As Harper had said: no choice.

'Do we have your agreement?' Harper repeated, more forcefully. She nodded, unable to speak. 'Good. Martin, you deal with the specifics. Dr Kiddrick can explain the technical side. In the meantime, I have a meeting at the White House.' He collected his documents and placed them in a briefcase before leaving without a further word.

Morgan looked apologetic. 'Ah . . . sorry, Dr Childs. I didn't realise the Admiral was going to be quite so . . .'

'Unpleasant?' she almost spat.

'Hard-headed. But we can talk money – and I'll arrange accommodation, a car . . .'

'Whatever.' She clenched her fists under the table, trying to stop them from trembling. 'Well, I'm in, you've got me – you might as well tell me all your secrets now. Since I'm apparently the only person in the world who can help you use them.'

'Apparently, indeed,' said Kiddrick. His nasal accent, allied with his suddenly condescending manner – which had manifested the moment Harper left the room – did nothing to endear him to Bianca. He picked up a remote control and used it to switch on the big screen. 'I'll give you the basics for now, since I'm guessing you're not in the mood for a detailed lecture.'

'You guessed right,' she replied, scathing.

A slide appeared on the screen, the logo of the Special Technology Section – an elaborate circular seal with a circle of stars enclosing circuit patterns forming a stylised American eagle – overlaid with text. THE PERSONA PROJECT: A PRESENTATION BY DR NATHANIEL KIDDRICK, JR. Kiddrick's name, she noticed even in her angry state, was larger than the other words.

'Persona, in this instance,' Kiddrick began, clearly enjoying the sound of his own voice before a captive audience, 'has a triple meaning. It's the code name for this STS project, of course, but the obvious meaning also applies – the persona of a human being. Their character, personality, memories, all the things that make them an individual—'

'Dr Kiddrick,' Morgan cut in. 'I think Dr Childs is well aware of that definition of the word.'

Kiddrick's already wide eyes bugged even further to deliver an irate glare, but he composed himself, skipping forward in some mental script. 'The third definition, though, is an acronym. PERSONA – Portable Electroencephalographic Recording and Stimulation of Neural Activity.' He clicked the remote, the text on the screen replaced by an illustration of a piece of technology resembling a laptop. 'This is the PERSONA device. It is, in essence, a memory recorder. Designed by myself,' he added with pride.

In any other situation Bianca would have dismissed the idea as a hoax, but a private jet trip to the States was an awful long way to go for a prank. 'How does it work?'

'To put it simply, the device records a subject's brain impulses three-dimensionally in real time using an advanced array of electrodes' – a click of the remote, and the black box gave way to a graphic of a head wearing a cap dotted with circular objects – 'which it then processes and sends to a receiver.' *Click*, and another head appeared, animated arrows running from the first to the second.

'Wait, wait,' said Bianca. 'So you're claiming that reading a person's memories and transferring them into somebody else's mind is as simple as copying a file from one computer to another?'

'I'm not claiming that at all,' Kiddrick replied. 'It's *far* from simple. I'm just saying that for ease of explanation.'

'Well, I do have a PhD in neurochemistry, so I know a *little* about how the brain works. You don't have to give me the *Sesame Street* version.'

Kiddrick frowned. 'If you insist.' He clicked repeatedly on the remote. Slides flashed by, stopping on one showing a series of images taken by a CT scanner: 'slices' of a brain's activity.

It was instantly obvious to Bianca that the brain in question belonged to no ordinary patient. 'Has something been implanted?' Fine white lines ran through the tissue, a tiny sphere at the end of each.

'Yes – they act as amplifiers, taking the signals from the agent's own electrode array via induction and redistributing them throughout the synaptic pathways. Essentially, they're recreating the engrams of the subject's brain by overlaying them on to the equivalent areas of our agent's.'

That raised many questions in Bianca's mind, but she asked the biggest one first. 'But isn't that just a fancier form of electroshock therapy? It's more targeted, yes, but the end result will be the same – it'll scramble the synapses, not neatly plop new memories into them. And what about the memories that are already there?'

'That's where Dr Albion's work comes in,' said Morgan.

Bianca looked questioningly at Kiddrick. 'Yes, yes, Roger played a role,' he said, as if the admission were being wrung from him in court.

'A role?' she said. 'You make it sound as though he was just your lab assistant or something.'

'Roger is the Persona Project's *other* senior scientific adviser,' Tony clarified. 'They worked together to make it possible.'

'The drugs Roger developed were important, yes, but the concept behind PERSONA and all the basic research required to make it a reality were mine,' said Kiddrick sniffily. 'But in answer to your question, the drugs in essence wipe the targeted synapses' – a sweeping motion with one hand to illustrate – 'and make them ready to receive the new data.'

Bianca was horrified. 'You're *wiping* people's memories?'

'It's more like temporarily suppressing them. As you know, the brain doesn't work like a computer by storing one byte of information in a single place – it's more of a distributed network. Memories are reassembled through protein synthesis in a particular group of neurons when the brain specifically calls for them, but until then they're kept in the cloud, you might say. One of Roger's drugs, Neutharsine, modifies the recall process – basically tricking the brain into accepting the imprinted memories as its own. But the effect wears off quickly.'

'How quickly?'

'The longest we've ever seen an imprinted persona last is just over twenty-four hours. And sleep seems to act as a natural reset button before then. Once the agent goes to sleep, everything that's been imprinted is washed away.'

The list of answers Bianca wanted – factual as well as ethical – kept growing. 'You said that's one of Roger's drugs. What do the others do?'

'The primary one, Hyperthymexine, is used on the subject. It's a recall *enhancer*, putting the protein synthesis process into overdrive. A brainstorm, we call it; the subject remembers everything they've ever experienced, all at once. The electrical signals this produces are picked up by the PERSONA device and transmitted via the electrode net to our agent.'

'That sounds incredibly dangerous. Wouldn't triggering that much synaptic activity at once carry risks? Overheating and tissue damage, or blood pressure issues, potential haemorrhage—'

'Nothing so far that we've seen,' Kiddrick interrupted.

'And what about mental side effects? It sounds like you've got the perfect recipe for a psychotic break.'

The scientist was growing increasingly irritated at being challenged. 'Obviously we've thought of that,' he snapped. 'We use another drug called Mnemexal, a variant of the protein inhibitor we use to prepare the agent for the process, to completely erase the subject's short-term memory. It's no different from dentists using midazolam to repress a patient's memory of a procedure,' he added, seeing that Bianca was about to raise another objection. 'If they can't remember the pain, then effectively it never happened.'

'That's one interpretation,' she said, voice cutting.

'It's an interpretation that fits the facts. The point is, PERSONA *works*. We can put one person's memories – more than that, their entire *personality* – into the mind of another. Our agent can literally become anyone, know everything they know, use every skill they possess.'

'Reveal all of their secrets,' Tony added. 'That's what the Persona Project is ultimately about. It's an intelligence-gathering tool that we can use to protect the lives of American citizens – that we *are* using. The mission Roger was on when he was shot gave us inside information on al-Qaeda that would have been impossible to obtain by any other means.'

The truth was dawning for Bianca, and she didn't like it. 'When you say "subjects", I take it they're not exactly volunteers.'

'You heard what the Admiral said,' Morgan replied. 'We will use whatever means necessary to protect this country and its allies.'

'And it's not as if we're *torturing* them,' said Kiddrick, his tone almost mocking. 'Would you prefer that? Once we've transferred their persona into our agent, we wipe their short-term memory and put them back where we found them. They don't even know anything's happened to them.'

Bianca matched his derision. 'Until you send a drone to blow up their house.'

'But this way, we know for certain that we've got the *right* house,' countered Morgan. 'There's no guesswork, no interpretation of scraps of information from multiple sources. What we have is direct from the source, and one hundred per cent accurate.'

'As accurate as human memory gets, you mean. And you'd be surprised just how shaky that can be.' She remembered another question of her own. 'This agent you keep talking about – I take it he's the one with the implanted electrodes.'

'He is.' Morgan stood. 'And now, you're going to meet him.'

11

Who Is Adam Gray?

Despite still being livid about her treatment by Harper, and appalled by Kiddrick's ethics, Bianca couldn't help but be impressed by the large room to which Morgan took her. Now *this* was worthy of Bond or Bauer! The moodily lit chamber brought to mind NASA's mission control, banks of workstations facing a wall of large screens.

However, there were currently no missions to control. Most of the displays were either blank or displaying the STS logo on a screensaver background. There were enough workstations to accommodate thirty or forty people, with space for more towards the rear of the room, but only about half were currently active. Whatever work was going on appeared to be bureaucratic or system maintenance rather than high-pressure espionage.

'This is the Bullpen,' Morgan announced. 'Its official name is the Project Operational Command and Control Centre, but nobody much likes the acronym.'

'It's not as good as PERSONA, no,' said Bianca.

'That was more of a backronym, really. You can thank Dr Albion for it. But this is where we oversee missions when our people are out in the field.'

'It's impressive,' she had to admit. 'Looks expensive, too.'

'It wasn't built just for the Persona Project, if that's what you're thinking. It's an existing facility that Persona has been assigned. We don't like to throw money away on black projects, whatever the public perception may be.' He led Bianca, Tony and Kiddrick through the room. 'Here, I'll introduce you to the team.'

Of the twenty or so people present, most were clustered around one particular workstation. An enthusiastic male voice was the focus of their attention. 'Levon must have a new puzzle,' Morgan said.

Kiddrick was not impressed. 'Don't your people have anything better to do?'

Tony gave him a half-smile. 'You're only saying that because you can't solve them.' They stopped at the edge of the group to listen.

Bianca peered through the crowd. The speaker was an overweight young black man with a shaved head, eyes darting behind Coke-bottle glasses as he swivelled his chair to make sure everyone was taking in his words. 'So, that's the assignment. The diamond will be taken out of the vault by its owner in exactly twenty-four hours. You have to get that diamond. Question is . . .' a broad smile, 'how are you going to do it?'

'Bribe the guards,' Tony suggested.

The question master – Bianca assumed this to be Levon – shook his head. 'The guards are very loyal to their employer. It would cost more to bribe them than the diamond is worth.'

Another man, older and rougher-looking, had an alternative approach. 'Tactical assault. Eliminate the guards and blow the safe, then withdraw before local law enforcement arrives. Five minutes after the alarm's set off, you said. That should easily be enough time.'

'Wow, bloodthirsty,' said a slender woman with long blond hair, shaking her head.

'Uh-uh,' said Levon to the man. 'You've got selective hearing, Mr Baxter! Like I said, it'll take at least an hour to force your way into the safe by any means you have available.'

Baxter wasn't giving up on his idea. 'A shaped charge would do it.'

'My puzzle, my rules. You've got to work inside the limitations of the scenario. That's kinda the whole point. Doesn't matter what you use – explosives, drills, lasers, whatever – it'll take sixty minutes to break that safe. I set the hard limits; now you gotta figure out ways around them.'

A dismissive grunt. 'Sounds like some sort of unrealistic *Mission: Impossible* crap. Count me out of this one.'

'I'll take your place if you like, John,' said Morgan. 'Make sure you copy me in on the rules, Levon. What was the solution to the last one, by the way?'

'The power lines,' said a tanned twenty-something man with a heavily gelled haircut. 'Take out the substation in the town to cut off the juice, then climb along the lines to get over the perimeter defences. Simple.'

'Yeah, Kyle, so simple you didn't think of it until two days after Tony,' said Levon. 'And a day after Holly Jo. And—'

Kyle waved his hands dismissively. 'Yeah, yeah. The point is, that was the right answer. And I got it. Just like I'm going to get this one.'

'Not before me,' said the blonde. 'And I'm going to beat Tony this time as well. A huge diamond? That is *so* mine.'

'Just don't spend too much time thinking about it while you're on duty,' said Morgan. The undertone of *fun's over, now get back to work* was faint, but firm. It had the desired effect; the group began to disperse. 'Not all of you – there's someone I want the chief specialists to meet.' He waited until only six people remained. 'This is Dr Bianca Childs. She's agreed to stand in for Roger until he's fit to return to work.'

'"Agreed" is rather a simplistic way of putting it,' said Bianca.

Baxter was instantly suspicious on hearing her voice. 'She's not an American? Isn't that going to be a security issue, sir?'

'For the moment, Dr Childs has been granted limited security clearance on the authority of the Director of National Intelligence,' Morgan replied. 'In due course, she'll receive whatever she needs to carry out her role.' Baxter didn't seem entirely mollified, but nodded. 'Dr Childs, these are the senior members of the Persona Project.'

He made the introductions. The slender blonde in expensive stilettos was Holly Jo Voss, communications specialist. John Baxter, tactical commander; Bianca assumed from his general demeanour that he was a soldier. The puzzle-setting Levon James – his desk cluttered with Transformer toys – was the information and systems specialist, or as he jokingly put it, 'chief hacker'. Smug hair-model Kyle had the improbable surname Falconetti and the title of surveillance controller; his job – as far as Bianca could tell from his boastful but vague description – was some sort of pilot.

There was another man, standing behind the others. Until Morgan gestured him forward she had barely registered his presence. Brown hair, dark grey eyes, far from unattractive but . . .

Normally she thought she was good at reading people, but this man was giving nothing away. His expression was neutral, body language unrevealing. But it didn't seem a deliberate attempt to shield his true self.

It was almost as if he had nothing to shield.

'This is our lead agent,' said Morgan. 'At the moment, also our *only* agent, but . . . well, we'll see. Dr Childs, this is Adam Gray.'

The agent needed only a moment to perform his own assessment, she saw. No wasted time, just a clinical, almost machine-like sweep of his gaze over her. 'Hello,' he said.

'Hi.' They shook hands. Again, she could draw no conclusions about him. This grip was neither clammy like Kiddrick's, nor as domineering as Harper's. Firm, cool . . . blank. It told her nothing.

He released her hand. She expected him to say something else, but he stayed silent.

'Okay,' said Morgan. 'Adam, Tony, I'd like Dr Childs to see a demonstration of PERSONA. Dr Kiddrick?'

Kiddrick led the way out of the Bullpen. The group headed through several security doors to a lab, what resembled an operating table in the centre with a pair of curved benches near its head. Computer workstations occupied the room's far end, a large metal cabinet between them.

'I'll set everything up,' said Kiddrick.

Adam lay on the table as the scientist opened the cabinet. The upper shelves were filled with row after row of what Bianca at first thought were DVD cases before realising they were somewhat larger, while below them were racks containing glass bottles and phials of various sizes. The drugs Roger had developed?

'Need a hand?' Tony asked as Kiddrick fumbled with the two weighty metal cases he had taken from the bottom shelf.

'No, I've got it,' Kiddrick muttered. He clomped back to the benches, putting one case on each side of the operating table. The first one he opened contained the piece of equipment from Kiddrick's slide show – though Bianca noticed it was somewhat bulkier and less sleek than its illustration, with an almost jury-rigged appearance; a prototype rather than a production model. The other contained a similar device, but thicker still and with a prominent slot set into its front. 'Who do you want to use for the demonstration?'

'Who aren't we likely to need?' asked Morgan. 'We don't want to waste someone who might be useful in the future.'

Kiddrick took the second device from its case. 'What about, ah . . . Wilmar, he'll do. Conrad Wilmar.'

'Do we have any video of him?' said Morgan. 'It would help to show Dr Childs how effective PERSONA is.'

'There should be a recording on the server,' said Tony, going to one of the computers.

'Now, Dr Childs,' Kiddrick said, 'I'll explain the procedure in more detail when the time comes to train you on it. For now, this,' he indicated the first machine, which he had just connected to its companion with a fat length of cable, 'is the PERSONA device itself, which handles the reading, transfer and imprinting of the subject's synaptic patterns into the agent. Adam, I mean.' Bianca glanced at the man in question, who was staring silently up at the overhead light cluster. 'The other device is the recorder.' His tone became critical. 'It's a separate unit because it was only intended to be used in lab conditions, but that plan went by the wayside.'

'It gives us more flexibility,' insisted Morgan.

'Well, if it breaks, don't blame me; I advised against it. Still, at least I don't have to haul the whole system around. It's rather heavy.' The mocking look he gave Bianca suggested he expected that to be her responsibility.

'I found the video of Wilmar,' said Tony from the workstation.

'Good,' Morgan said. 'Dr Childs, take a look at this, please.'

She went with him to the computer while Kiddrick continued to fuss with his equipment. 'What am I looking for?'

'Just get a handle on his personality,' Tony told her. He clicked the mouse, and a video began playing.

Conrad Wilmar, it turned out, was a middle-aged man with large glasses and crinkled, receding red hair. 'No, no, that's fine,' he said to someone off-camera. 'Okay, so, what do you need me to do? Are you going to ask me questions, or . . . ?'

'No,' said Albion's voice. 'Just tell us about yourself and your area of expertise.' Bianca recognised the background as the lab in which she was standing.

'Sure, sure, no problem,' Wilmar replied. He had squirrelly, fidgety mannerisms, as if his brain were working slightly faster than his body could handle and was dumping its excess energy straight into his nervous system. He looked directly into the lens. 'You want me to start? Okay, my name is Conrad Wilmar, and I'm a professor of biochemistry at Carnegie Mellon. I'm currently working with DARPA, the Defense Advanced Resear— Hey, is it okay for me to be talking about this?' He looked towards his interviewer. 'I know we've all got proper clearance, but I don't want to take any chances, y'know?'

'It's fine,' said Albion.

'Okay, right. So, what was I saying? Oh, yeah. I'm working with DARPA to develop battlefield treatments and inoculants against biological weapons. Specifically, against weaponised strains of *Bacillus anthracis* and *Neisseria meningitidis*, which if anyone is ever mad enough to employ bioweapons in warfare are likely to be among the prime threats . . .'

Wilmar kept speaking, but Bianca had already drawn some conclusions about his personality. Very smart, jittery and seeming socially inept on the surface – but with an inner confidence emerging upon moving on to his specialist subject. An alpha nerd, then; someone who could seem nervous and bumbling when out of their usual element . . . but anyone underestimating them did so at their own risk. She knew the type. She had worked with quite a few of them.

'Okay,' said Kiddrick. Bianca looked round to see him fitting Adam with the complex skullcap of electrodes from the slideshow, a cable running from it to the PERSONA device. 'Tony, can you find Wilmar's disk?'

Tony went to the cabinet and ran his finger along the cases. 'Vulich, Wagner, Wall, Warner . . . here we are.' He slipped the box out from its companions.

Bianca regarded it dubiously. 'So, how big are these disks if they can supposedly record the complete memories of a human brain? You'd need more than just a blank CD.'

He opened the case to show her. Inside was a flat, dark grey slab of plastic, about an inch thick. 'It's not really a disk – we just call them that because it's easier than saying . . . God, I can't even remember the full name. High-Capacity Rapid Access Multiplexing Static Memory Module? Something like that.'

She tried to pronounce the acronym. 'Hurk . . . huckramsumm?'

Tony grinned. 'Yeah, that's why we stick to "disk". Anyway, it's basically a very, very big and fast flash drive.'

'I still don't see how any kind of computer memory would be big enough to record a person's entire memories, though. The brain has billions of neurons – *trillions* of synapses. Storing them all would be like trying to fit the entire Internet on an iPod.'

'On a normal, direct transfer, it's just a matter of having enough bandwidth to push the data through,' Kiddrick explained patronisingly as he finished securing the skullcap. 'Which we do. Recording takes longer, though, because it has to encode and compress everything to fit on the module. To continue your iPod analogy, it's like shrinking a raw audio file down to an MP3. It sounds the same, but takes up far less space.'

'I know some audiophiles who'd argue at extremely tedious length about it sounding the same,' said Bianca. 'And doesn't an MP3 lose some of the data when it's compressed?'

'The brain interpolates the missing information and fills in the gaps.'

'That doesn't sound a good idea when you're talking about memories. People already have enough holes in their recollection as it is.'

'Well,' said Kiddrick, stepping back, 'you'll see for yourself in a minute. Everything's ready. Tony, can I have that disk?'

Tony brought it to him, Bianca and Morgan joining them at the table. Kiddrick opened the PERSONA's screen and waited for the machine to start up, then carefully inserted the disk into the recorder's slot. He checked some figures in another window, then returned to the cabinet. 'The drug we use to prime the agent to accept a new persona is called Neutharsine. Roger's name; I'm not keen on it myself. It's the protein inhibitor I mentioned.' He returned with a jet injector, carefully loading a small vial of liquid. 'It suppresses certain parts of the target brain's memory, and it's also used after a mission to erase the implanted persona.'

Bianca looked down at Adam. He was still staring silently up at the lights, unmoving. 'Are you sure there aren't any long-term side effects?' she felt compelled to ask. 'Especially if you're giving him repeated doses.'

Kiddrick shot a look at Tony – whether seeking his permission to speak or warning him not to say anything, Bianca couldn't tell – before replying. 'There are side effects, yes, but they're minor and easily managed. Now, watch this.' He moved to the head of the operating table and positioned the injector against Adam's neck. 'Ready?'

'Yes,' said Adam, without emotion.

Kiddrick pulled the trigger. Adam grimaced, then relaxed. Bianca watched him closely. Though it was hard to imagine how, he seemed to become even *more* expressionless, as if the little personality that he had expressed was draining away.

After half a minute, Kiddrick clicked his fingers above Adam's face. The agent's gaze instantly locked on to them. 'Okay, Adam. Does everything feel normal?'

'Yes.'

'Good.' He examined the PERSONA's screen, seeing a ready message. 'Okay. Here we go.'

He typed in a command. New windows appeared, one displaying a simplified graphic of a brain. Coloured patterns drifted across it – then flared into brilliant, manic life.

Adam's whole body spasmed. Bianca jerked back in surprise, before leaning in for a closer look. His eyes were flickering rapidly from side to side. She also saw that his hands had twisted into gnarled fists. 'Is he in pain?' she asked, concerned.

She expected Kiddrick to answer, but Tony spoke first. 'No. It's not exactly pleasant, but it doesn't hurt.'

'Okay, the transfer is in progress,' said Kiddrick, looking up from the machine. 'It'll take six or seven minutes. That's longer than a direct transfer would take, because it has to decompress the data.'

Bianca kept watching Adam. His eye movements, she realised, mirrored the unconscious flicks of a person recalling memories – but at a far greater speed. 'You know, I have real trouble reducing the sum total of a person's self to just "data".'

'Would you prefer if I called it the "soul"?' Kiddrick replied sarcastically.

They waited for the device to do its work. The whirlwind of colours on the graphic eventually dimmed and slowed. Kiddrick peered at some numbers on the screen, then nodded. 'Okay, it's done. Now, Dr Childs.' He gestured theatrically at Adam. 'I'd like you to meet . . . Conrad Wilmar.'

Adam sat up, blinking. His gaze hopped to each person around the table. 'Okay, ah . . . yeah, I can do without the whole staring thing, thanks.'

Bianca was no expert in American accents, but even from those few words she could tell that Adam's had changed. It *did* sound like Wilmar's, but she wasn't prepared to accept that alone as proof that the PERSONA process genuinely worked.

'The memory check?' Tony prompted.

'Yes, yes.' Kiddrick signalled for Adam to face him. 'Okay. What's your full name?'

'Conrad Mathias Wilmar,' said Adam, peering quizzically back at him.

'What was your date of birth?'

'June twelfth, 1959. At twelve minutes past six. So, six twelve on six twelve.' A lopsided grin at the quirky coincidence.

'Where were you born?'

'Bridgeport, Connecticut.'

'Your mother's maiden name?'

'Schumacher.'

Kiddrick nodded, then an oily little smirk crept on to his face. 'Now . . . what's your most guilty secret? The one that you'd least want anyone else to ever know?'

'I . . .' Adam's expression suddenly turned to one of shame, even alarm. 'I, I mean he, he . . . I've been unfaithful to my wife. There's another woman, Meg, I've been seeing. We work together.'

To Bianca, it felt as though each word was being forced out of him at gunpoint, so clear was his reluctance to make the admission. She looked at the others, to find that the three men were regarding Adam with anything from mild curiosity – Tony – to Kiddrick's outright amusement. 'Wait a minute,' the latter said. 'Not Meg Garner, surely?'

Adam nodded frantically. 'Yeah, yeah.'

Kiddrick chuckled. 'Well, that should be fun next time I go down to Carnegie Mellon!' Adam's face expressed utter dismay.

'Wait a minute,' protested Bianca. 'You just got Adam – Conrad – whichever, to confess his biggest secret, and you're treating it all as a big laugh? I mean, he's . . .' She stopped, unsure exactly what to say. *Did* she mean Adam, or Conrad? Who was the man in front of her?

'Everything we learn using the PERSONA process remains top secret,' Morgan said. 'For reasons of national security. Nothing we discover can be used in a court of law, because we don't officially exist.'

If he had been trying to reassure her, it had almost entirely the opposite effect. 'That implies you're operating outside the law.' Morgan said nothing.

'Ah, we have a bleeding heart in our midst,' said Kiddrick. 'I suppose you're going to say we should *reach out* to terrorists,' an airy wave of one hand, 'and try to empathise with their issues – rather than putting Hellfire missiles through their windows.'

'I suppose you're going to say we should bomb them because "they hate us for our freedoms", or something equally idiotic,' she shot back. Morgan was less than impressed, but Tony seemed to have a more nuanced outlook, giving her a small smile.

'We're not here to argue about politics,' Morgan said impatiently. 'Dr Childs, what do you think of PERSONA? The results, I mean – not the ethics.'

'Damn, and I was just about to start a ten-minute rant about that,' she replied, before turning back to Adam. 'It's still hard to believe. I mean, I can't imagine why you *would*, but you might just be acting.' If he was, she had to admit, he was delivering an Oscar-worthy performance. His anguish at exposing Wilmar's affair had appeared utterly genuine and heartfelt.

'It's not an act,' said Kiddrick. 'To all intents and purposes, right now Adam Gray *is* Conrad Wilmar. Whatever Wilmar knows, he does. That's one reason I picked Wilmar's persona for this test. He doesn't work in quite the same field as you, but there's some crossover. Agent briefings don't go so far as to give them a doctorate in biochemistry, so test him for yourself.'

'If he's now Conrad Wilmar, then where's Adam Gray?'

'Oh, I'm still Adam,' said Adam, swinging himself off the table and standing up. 'It's not as if I've, y'know, disappeared? Or been subsumed, anything like that. I'm still me, I'm always in control. It's just that now there's this whole temporary other me in here too.' His hands flicked excitedly in time with his words, as if trying to fan them towards her more quickly. 'So, yeah, test me. What do you want to know?'

He certainly had Wilmar's mannerisms and rat-a-tat speech pattern. 'Okay,' Bianca said hesitantly. 'You said you were working on treatments for biological weapons?'

'Yeah, that's right.'

'Specifically, meningitis?'

He nodded. 'We've encountered a strain of *N. meningitidis* that's a lot more virulent than normal, and resistant to the standard vaccines. Nasty little SOB! Not sure where it came from, but we've got our suspicions. *Da, comrades!*' He tapped the side of his nose.

'What's the effect on the brain?'

'What you'd expect; swelling of the meninges, particularly concentrated in the pia mater. It has a tendency to spread to the spinal pia too, but only once the initial infection is firmly established.'

'What's the treatment?'

'Straight in with empirics, of course, backed up by an adjuvant course of corticosteroids. The doses need to be higher than normal, but at this stage we're just trying to stabilise things.' His speech quickened. 'Then we've got a suite of new antibiotics that we can tailor to the exact results of the CSF test – I can't tell you the specific compositions, though. You don't have clearance. Sorry.' He seemed genuinely apologetic.

'That's okay.' What he had told her was accurate enough, rattled out without hesitation, but Kiddrick clearly wanted to test *her* as much as she was supposed to test Adam. She drew on her own memories to devise something particularly probing. 'There was a paper that came out about two years ago, on the effects of new-generation cephalosporins on brain chemistry, particularly enzyme—'

'Oh, yeah, yeah!' Adam interrupted, with great enthusiasm. 'Hartmann and Yun's paper. Yes, I read it. Helped a lot with the transpeptidation issues of our new drugs. Smart guys.'

'Yeah, they are.' Bianca was startled that not only had he heard of a decidedly esoteric scientific paper, but also that he had correctly – and instantly – identified its authors based on only a most general description. That was definitely beyond anything she could imagine his having been briefed on.

Kiddrick regarded her smugly. 'Convinced?'

'I'd have to say . . . yes,' she admitted.

'Good. Adam, there's nothing else we should know about Wilmar, is there? He's not selling secrets to the Chinese or plotting to release anthrax on the New York subway?'

Adam shook his head. 'Nothing like that. Jeez, suspicious much?'

'It's best to be sure while we have the opportunity,' said Morgan. 'Okay, Dr Kiddrick, bring him back to normal.'

Kiddrick picked up the injector again and told Adam to return to the operating table. Another hiss from the gun, and Adam closed his eyes. Bianca watched in fascination as Wilmar's twitchiness seemed to dissolve, returning him to the same blank, unrevealing state as before.

'How much will he remember?' she asked.

'From Wilmar? Only anything he specifically recalled from the implanted persona,' Kiddrick answered. 'Other than that, nothing.'

'We'll check, though,' said Tony. 'Adam – what pets did Conrad Wilmar have as a kid? What were they called?'

Adam sat up. 'He had . . .' He trailed off. 'I don't know.'

'The name of his high school?'

'I don't know.'

'But he still remembers things like the day Wilmar was born?' said Bianca.

'Six twelve, six twelve,' Adam cut in before she could continue.

'Yes, like that. How does that happen?'

Kiddrick began to remove the skullcap. 'The same way any memory is kept. Short-term to long-term transfer, if you go by the Atkinson–Shiffrin model.'

'I'm more of a Baddeley theorist myself, but I understand what you mean. If he brings something out of the persona's memory, it stays in his?'

'Exactly.' He tugged the cap free. 'All right, Adam, you can get down now.'

Adam climbed off the table. Unlike when he had hopped down as Wilmar, his movements were smooth, precise, with no wasted energy. He stood, watching the others impassively.

Bianca had a question. 'Adam?'

'Yes?'

'You remember things from Wilmar's memories – but do you actually remember what it was like to *be* him?'

A fleeting look of incomprehension. 'What do you mean?'

'Do you remember his feelings? The enthusiasm when he – I mean, you, were talking about his work, or the . . . the *shame* when you told us about his affair?'

'Meg Garner,' Kiddrick said quietly, chuckling again. 'Who would have thought?'

Bianca shot him a dirty look before returning her attention to Adam, trying to judge what was going on behind his mask. But she could pick up nothing conclusive. 'No, I don't,' he said at last.

'Well, anyway,' said Kiddrick, 'now you've seen that PERSONA works as advertised, you'll need to know how to operate the device in the field. We'll start the lessons tomorrow, at nine sharp.'

'I think we need to give Dr Childs some time to acclimatise first,' said Tony, politely but firmly. 'Considering that she's just flown here from England with, what, one change of clothes?'

'Yeah, afraid so,' she replied. 'I was rather under the impression that I'd be flying back home tomorrow.'

Tony smiled. 'I'm sure our budget can stretch to a trip to Macy's, at the very least. Can't it, Martin?'

Morgan was less amused. 'As I said earlier, Dr Childs, we'll set you up with everything you need while you're here. We'll take care of everything regarding your absence from Luminica as well.'

'That's work – what about personal matters?' Tony asked. 'Have you even told your family and friends about this yet?' One eyebrow rose slightly. 'Boyfriend?'

'No, I haven't had a chance to talk to anyone,' she complained. 'My parents'll think I've gone mad when I say I've suddenly gone to the States for no reason I can tell them about. And no, I don't have a boyfriend.' The eyebrow rose higher. She tried to hide a smile, feeling her cheeks flush a little at his suggestive attention.

'It'll all be taken care of,' Morgan reiterated. 'Okay, we still have some more points to cover, so Dr Childs, if you'll come with me?'

'Good to have you aboard,' said Tony as Morgan led her to the door.

'Thanks.' She gave him a small smile in reply, then glanced back at Adam.

His face was completely void of expression.

12

The Cube

'You really are an utter shit, Roger,' said Bianca. 'What the hell have you dragged me into?' Her tone was humorous, but it had enough of an edge to make it clear she was still angry about the situation.

Albion laughed. 'Oh, come on, Bianca. What's life without a little adventure?'

'Your last little adventure ended with you getting shot.'

'If life were completely safe, it would be very dull. Besides, I've struck up quite a rapport with one of the doctors here. I think that once the whole tedious doctor–patient relationship issue is out of the way when I'm healed, I might see if she's interested in becoming my next ex-wife.'

She shook her head, amused. 'You never change, do you?' The amusement turned dark. 'And speaking of ethics . . .'

Albion sighed. 'Yes, I wondered how soon you'd bring that up.' He looked at a wall clock. 'Fifty-three minutes! Longer than I'd expected.'

Bianca pulled her chair closer to the bed, frowning. 'Seriously, though. From what Tony and Morgan told me, Persona's mission seems to be to fly around the world, kidnap people, steal their innermost secrets and then use them so that the CIA can pick targets for its robot death-planes.'

'The targets are terrorists and other deeply unpleasant people. We're doing the world a favour.'

'I don't want to sound like an absolute pinko hippie—'

'Too late for that!'

'—but terrorist *suspects* have rights, like anyone else – and one of them is "innocent until proven guilty".'

'Things change in war.'

'You're not a soldier. And I didn't notice anyone else at STS wearing a uniform either. Not even so-called "Admiral" Harper.'

Albion cocked his head to one side. 'Be careful when dealing with him, Bianca. Very careful. He's not someone you want to make an enemy of. As the saying goes, you wouldn't like him when he's angry.'

'I don't like him *now*!'

'Well, that makes two of us. But really, try to avoid pissing him off. Just grit your teeth and stand in for me, and think about all that money waiting when you get back to England. As for *how* you stand in for me, we'd better get back to your training.'

'What training?' she protested, holding up a notebook. 'It only took you fifty-three minutes to explain everything!'

'Not that part of the training – I meant the part where you make it look as complicated as possible. If it seems too easy, they might figure out that they don't need me any more and kick me out.'

She smiled. 'Don't tempt me. Besides, I'm surprised they haven't considered hooking *you* up to the machine so Adam can load up your persona and work out the doses himself.'

'I'm sure they *have* considered it. But fortunately – for me, at least – it wouldn't be practical. We have a policy that a persona can only be imprinted on him once.'

'Why?'

'We found out the hard way that it causes . . . complications. So we don't do it any more.'

'What kind of complications?'

'Severe headaches, confusion – and worse. When you only have one active agent, it's not worth the risk of compromising his readiness.'

'Are there plans to recruit more?'

'People haven't been lining up to volunteer.' He adopted a gung-ho voice. '"Gee, I sure do want to undergo experimental brain surgery so I can think like a terrorist!" I'm not sure how it would be worded on the recruitment posters.'

'So why did Adam volunteer?'

'I have no idea.'

She was surprised. 'Really?'

'I know that he *did* volunteer, but he came to us – well, was presented to us, more accurately – from outside, about ten months ago. Harper had something to do with it. I think Adam used to be with SOCOM – Special Operations Command. Special Forces, in other words.'

'You think? You don't know?'

He shifted in the bed, his discomfort more mental than physical. 'Adam is rather the elephant in the room at the Persona Project. There's an unofficial policy of, shall we say, limited fraternisation. The team members are discouraged from getting too close to him on a personal level.'

Bianca made a face. 'How does anyone have the right to decide who gets to be his friend?'

'It's a US government black project. Rights don't enter into things. They can order you to wear different-coloured underwear depending on the day of the week, if they choose.'

'You've worked with him pretty closely, though. You must be able to tell me something more about him. And by something, I mean *anything*. Seriously! The man is a literal walking enigma.'

'Yes, I know. But there's nothing more I can tell you.'

'Because you don't know, or you're not allowed to?'

A wry smile. 'Perceptive as ever. Let's just say I have to wear a particular colour of metaphorical underwear on that subject.'

'Orders from on high, eh? From Morgan?' Albion's eyes briefly flicked upwards. 'Higher? Harper?'

'No comment.' His smile widened. 'But knowing you as well as I do, that won't stop you from trying to find out for yourself, will it?'

'Am I that transparent?'

'Positively see-through. But then, you are British – very pale-skinned from never getting any sun.'

She laughed. 'Well, I doubt I'll be in the States long enough to bring out my bikini, so I won't be getting a tan. But . . .' She became more serious. 'I don't want to find out more about Adam just to spite The Man. There's something . . . well, *wrong*. Not with him, but *about* him, if that makes any sense. Nobody's that unreadable – nobody who's still able to function, anyway. But Adam's so blank I'd consider it a form of catatonic stupor if it wasn't for the rather obvious fact that he's fully active and lucid.'

Albion's demeanour suggested that he knew considerably more about the subject, but was not going to share it with her. 'And you think you can help him?'

'If I can.'

'You haven't changed much since you were my student,' he said. 'Too tenacious for your own good.'

'You can't achieve anything if you don't stick at it.'

'Just make sure you don't get completely stuck. Anyway!' He changed position again. 'Time to polish up another of your student skills, and do some acting. I still need you to help keep my job!'

★ ★ ★

After another couple of hours at the hospital, Bianca returned to STS, driving the Ford Fusion that had been provided for her. The sedan was larger than her own car, and driving on the 'wrong' side of the road in Washington's traffic did not make the trip a comfortable experience. But the satnav, once she puzzled it out, at least meant that she didn't get lost.

Tony was waiting for her in the fifth-floor lobby. 'Hi there.'

'Hi,' she replied. 'You look like you were expecting me.'

'I had the security system beep me when you used your ID to get into the elevator.' She had been issued with the card shortly before leaving the previous evening. 'Thought I'd welcome you, it being your first proper day on the job.'

'I can't exactly say I'm thrilled to be here,' she said, before softening a little. 'Nothing personal.'

'No offence taken. How's the car?'

'It's nice. A bit too big with just me in it, though. Feels like I'm wasting petrol. Or gas, I suppose I should say.'

'STS is picking up the tab, so don't worry about it. And the hotel?'

'It's fine. It's . . . a hotel.' She shrugged.

'We'll set you up with an apartment soon. You don't want to be living out of a suitcase the whole time you're here.'

'However long that is.'

'So how is Roger, since that depends on him?'

'Well, he's started making divorce plans, so that's hopefully a sign of improvement.'

Tony laughed. 'Sounds like he's getting back to his old self.' They walked down a hallway.

'How long have you known him?' she asked.

'More than two years. Since I came on to the Persona Project.'

'Two years? I thought Adam only joined ten months ago.'

'There was a lot of work needed to set things up. Let's face it, what we do here sounds like science fiction – it's complicated. And sometimes things didn't go as planned.'

'But everything's working fine now?'

'Yeah. Well, until Roger got shot.' They reached a set of security doors. Tony was about to use his card to open them, before smiling. 'After you.'

Bianca put her own card in the slot, getting a green light. 'That's a relief. I'd hate to get a red light when I was running for the loo.'

They went through. 'You've got access to pretty much the whole floor,' he said. 'Everywhere except data storage and the weapons and equipment room.'

'What, you've got your own Q Branch full of guns and spy gadgets?'

'So we can mobilise quickly if we need to. It's easier to have most everything we might need on site, rather than rounding it up from a dozen different places.'

'What about the rest of the building? You said yesterday that STS has everything above the company downstairs. Is Persona only on this floor?'

'Yeah. The floor below us is STS bureaucracy; it handles paperwork for operations here and at other STS facilities. The floor above's like this one, with another Bullpen – projects can be assigned there if need be. There's nothing active upstairs at the moment, though. Or if there is,' he added drily, 'it's so secret nobody's told me about it. Then there's a machine floor above that with air-con, water tanks, that sort of thing. The building's actually designed to be self-sufficient, by the way – if there's a biological or chemical attack, it can be sealed up with its own air and water supplies for a few days. There are generators down in the basement.'

'I hope I don't get a demonstration of that while I'm here!'

'Me too. But it's best to be prepared.' They arrived at the Bullpen's entrance. Tony used his card to enter.

As on the previous day, there was little going on. Bianca recognised some of the people she had been introduced to – Holly Jo, Levon, Kyle – at their workstations. 'Hey, brah,' said Kyle, swivelling to face them as they approached. 'Dr Childs.'

'Hi, Kyle,' Tony replied. He looked round. 'Where's Adam?'

'In the Cube.'

'The Cube?' Bianca asked.

Kyle nodded towards a door on one side of the chamber. 'Adam's personal chill-out room. He meditates in there, or something. Me, I prefer playing Xbox in the break room. They won't let us hook up to Xbox Live for security reasons, though, which kinda sucks. Oh, hey, Tony,' he added, sitting upright with sudden excitement. 'I just got off the phone with Brad. He's got the new UAVs ready to test, says his guys figured out a way to increase speed without costing too much battery life. I'm going over later to play with 'em.'

'Let me know how they perform,' Tony said as he headed for the Cube, Bianca following. 'And don't forget to fill out the assessment documentation this time!'

'Yeah, brah,' Kyle replied with a dismissive wave.

'What's this "brah" thing?' Bianca asked.

'It's like calling someone "bro", but more annoying. It's what all the hip young kids are saying today, so I'm told.'

'You hardly look any older than him.'

'I'm flattered! No, he's only twenty-four, twenty-five, something like that. Actually, most of the project staff are pretty young – the ones in the Bullpen, anyway. They make me feel like a kindergarten teacher.'

She made a minor show of examining his handsome features. 'I'd say you were about . . . thirty-five.'

'Okay, I'm slightly less flattered than I was a moment ago. Only a little, though.'

They shared a smile as they reached the door. Tony knocked. 'Adam? You in there?'

'Yes,' came the reply. They entered.

The Cube didn't quite live up to its name, being rectangular in plan. It did fit the bill as a meditation room, however. The walls and ceiling were plain white, lit by soft recessed spotlights, while the carpet was a neutral cream. A low leather couch, similar to a psychiatrist's, occupied the centre.

Adam, however, was seated on one of the matching chairs at the room's far end. If he had been meditating, his pose showed no evidence of it; it looked to Bianca more as if he had simply been staring into space. His eyes fixed upon the new arrivals. 'Tony. Dr Childs.'

'You can call me Bianca, you know,' she said. 'Both of you. Now that we're working together.'

'Bianca, then. What can I do for you?'

'We need to introduce Doc— I mean, Bianca,' Tony gave her a sidelong grin, 'to the exciting world of international espionage – or, as we call it, reading directives and filling out forms.' The joke was only mildly funny, but still enough to produce a smile from Bianca. Adam's expression – or lack thereof – remained unchanged, however. 'I want to bring her up to speed on what we do and how we do it. Gently, though. I think there might be some culture shock.'

Adam nodded. 'When?'

Tony checked his watch. 'It's coming up on lunchtime, so there's no point doing anything until after then. How about we meet at two, in briefing A?'

'Okay. I'll see you both then.'

That was clearly the end of the conversation. Bianca and Tony exited. 'So, is that what Adam does when he's not on a mission?' she asked facetiously as they crossed the Bullpen. 'Sits in a plain room staring at the wall? I mean, he didn't even have a newspaper to read.'

Tony was defensive. 'He does a lot more than that. Assessing intelligence reports, briefings, physical training, weapons training – anything that can make him even better at his job. The personas he uses are only a boost to his abilities; he still has to be a top-flight agent in his own right. The Cube's just where he goes for some peace and quiet. But,' he said, in a more apologetic tone, 'if he asked for anything else in there, we'd give it to him. He just hasn't asked.'

'Oh. Sorry, by the way. I didn't mean to be rude. I know he must be your friend.'

'Yeah. I suppose . . .' For a moment, it didn't seem as if Tony was actually sure. 'Anyway, as I said, it's close to lunchtime. How about I treat you to something from one of DC's fine range of franchised sandwich shops?'

Bianca laughed. 'How could I refuse?'

Kyle leaned over Holly Jo's workstation, watching Bianca and Tony as they left the room. 'So, guys – what do you think?'

Levon padded over from his nearby desk. 'About Dr Childs?'

'No, brah, about the Fed's new fund rate. Of course about her, dumbass!'

'I just think there's something weird about the whole thing,' said Holly Jo. 'All the times they've told us that the PERSONA tech has to be kept ultra-secret, even from other parts of STS, no leaks . . . and then they bring in a foreigner out of nowhere?'

'She's supposed to be some old student of Roger's,' said Levon.

'Supposed to be? Or actually is and you hacked into her file to see for yourself, and are just saying "supposed to be" to cover your butt?'

Levon put up his hands in a protestation of innocence. 'She's supposed to be, that's all I'm saying.'

Kyle leaned closer. 'Next time you hack in, can you look at my personnel assessment and see if I'm up for a raise?'

The hands went up again. 'I ain't doin' nothing!'

'So what do you think?' Holly Jo asked Kyle.

He stroked his chin. 'Well . . . I wouldn't kick her out of bed.'

'Oh, for God's sake,' she sighed.

'What? I wouldn't! Sure, she dresses kinda frumpy, and her hair's a mess, but you know what they say – it's the quiet ones who get wildest in bed. She's got a sort of sexy librarian thing going on. And, y'know, chicks with English accents – always kind of hot.'

Levon shook his head. 'Man, one of these days you are going to come into work and find a sixteen-page sexual harassment lawsuit on your desk.'

'Only sixteen?' said Holly Jo. Kyle made a dismissive *pffft!* noise. 'But seriously, you guys – what happens if Roger doesn't come back for six months? Or ever? Is there even still a project without him? Would we all lose our jobs?'

Levon looked round as Adam emerged from the Cube. 'I don't think it's Roger's health we should be worrying about. If there's one person the project depends on . . .'

Kyle shook his head. 'Adam can take care of himself. Come on, he took out a bunch of terrorists single-handed and jumped off a friggin' *building*, and there was hardly a scratch on him. That's some Jason Bourne shit, right there. Dude's a badass!'

'I don't think Levon meant Adam's *physical* health,' Holly Jo said as the trio watched the blank-faced man cross the room.

13

Chasing the Tail

Bianca spent the afternoon learning more about how the Persona Project – and Adam – operated. Some of what she discovered shocked her: not least that Adam was, technically, a cyborg. With a two-way radio implanted inside one ear, powered by a kinetic battery beneath the skin at the base of his spine that used his body's own movements to recharge itself, he certainly fitted the dictionary definition.

However, whatever startling revelations there were about Adam Gray the agent, she still had no handle on Adam Gray the man. He remained as opaque as the first moment they'd met. His answers to all of her questions were precise, factual . . . and devoid of anything resembling an emotive viewpoint.

After a few hours, her attention began to slip. 'Okay, I think we should take a break,' said Tony. 'You look like you need some coffee.'

She shook her head. 'Oh God, no. If I have too much caffeine in the afternoon, I can never get to sleep.'

'Something else, then. We've got a selection in the break room. Even tea – maybe that'll help you feel more at home?'

'You know, not all Brits are obsessed with tea,' she mock-chided. 'Just like we don't all talk like Dick Van Dyke and have bad teeth.'

Tony was caught off guard. 'Sorry, I didn't mean . . .'

She let him off the hook. 'But *I* like tea.'

'Great. We'll pick up in twenty minutes, then.'

They left the briefing room. Bianca followed Tony, but Adam went to the Bullpen. Bianca glanced back as he entered. Was he going to talk to one of the analysts, or . . .

'I'll catch up,' she told Tony as they passed one of the bathrooms. He nodded and continued on his way. She went into the ladies' room, waited until she was sure he would be out of sight, then returned to the door of the Bullpen.

Her card opened it. She went inside. No sign of Adam. The nearest person she knew by name was Holly Jo. 'Hi. I'm looking for Adam – did he just come in here?'

'Yes, he went into the Cube.' The Specialist wagged a manicured finger towards the door.

'Okay, thanks.' Bianca crossed the chamber, Holly Jo watching her with curiosity.

She stopped outside the Cube's entrance, considered what she was about to say, then knocked. After a few seconds she got a reply, and entered.

This time Adam was on the couch. He sat upright. 'Bianca, hi. What can I do for you?'

His greeting was so similar in tone and cadence to that of a few hours earlier that it could have been a recording. 'Oh, nothing – just a social call,' she said. 'I thought that since we'll be working together, it might be helpful if we got to know each other better.'

He didn't recoil in horror at the prospect, but neither did he display any enthusiasm. 'What do you want to know?'

'Just a bit more about you, really. I mean *you* you, not agent you.'

That finally brought a glimmer of emotion to his face, though it wasn't one she had expected. He seemed mildly bewildered by the very idea. 'Really?'

'Yes, sure. What are you like when you're not being someone else? I'd like to know.'

'Well, I'm . . .' He hesitated. 'I can't—'

The door flew open, Kiddrick rushing in. He had the manic aggression of someone who expected to discover their spouse in flagrante. 'What's going on?'

'What do you mean, what's going on?' said Bianca, surprised.

'I mean, what are you doing in here with Adam?'

'I'm . . . talking to him? Like I have been for the past three hours.'

'He comes in here for privacy and quiet,' Kiddrick snapped. 'Not for chit-chat! When he's in here, it's because he wants to get away from the stresses of his work. You should respect that, and stay out of here.'

'Are you his dad or something?' said Bianca, riled by his attitude.

His eyes bulged even wider than usual. '*What* did you say?'

'I said, are you his dad? Are we in your house? Because you seem to be setting ground rules for everyone.'

He drew himself to his full height. 'Now look here! I created the Persona Project, and when I tell you to do something—'

'Is there a problem?' said Tony, entering.

Kiddrick spun to face him. 'She's talking to Adam!'

He nodded calmly. 'Okay. And you're angry about that because . . . ?'

'Because she shouldn't be! The Cube is supposed to be a refuge, a sanctum – you of all people should—'

Another person appeared. 'This room doesn't sound much like a sanctum to me,' said Morgan. 'What's going on?'

Kiddrick spoke first, jabbing a finger at Bianca. 'She—'

'Dr Childs,' Morgan interjected. 'What's all this about?'

'I just wanted to ask Adam something,' she replied, taking brief pleasure in Kiddrick's fury at being cut off. 'The next thing that happened was that Dr Kiddrick burst in here like the Tasmanian Devil.'

Kiddrick glared at her, then turned to Morgan. 'You know why I—'

He was interrupted again. 'All right,' said Morgan. 'Dr Kiddrick, calm down – we can discuss this in my office. Dr Childs, I know that you're new both to STS and the entire working ethos of an intelligence agency, but you have to realise that this is not a social club.'

'It wasn't as if I was asking him out on a date,' she protested.

'I'm sure you weren't. But please, in future, if Adam is in here, then respect his privacy. Okay, Dr Kiddrick?'

Still seething, Kiddrick stomped past him back out into the Bullpen. Morgan gestured for Bianca and Tony to follow. They did, Bianca looking back at Adam. His gaze met hers, still seeming perturbed by her interest.

Outside, the commotion had drawn an audience. 'All right, show's over,' said Morgan as he closed the door. Heads reluctantly turned back to monitors. 'And where are you going?'

Tony was guiding Bianca to an exit. 'Getting back to what we were doing, Martin. Adam and I were taking a break from briefing Dr Childs. She's British, she can't function for long without tea.'

Morgan made an amused sound. 'All right. But don't take too long about it.'

They headed for the break room. Bianca shook her head. 'Talk about overreacting.'

'I'm sorry, I should have warned you,' said Tony. 'Kiddrick doesn't like Adam . . . well, he calls it "fraternising" with anyone.'

'Roger mentioned it,' she said, remembering her earlier conversation. 'So where exactly do I stand with Kiddrick? Is he my boss?'

A small laugh. 'He likes to think he's *everyone's* boss. But no, he's not. He and Roger both report directly to Martin, but they're equal in . . . not rank, exactly, but position. They're outside the operational chain of command, though.'

'So if I'm standing in for Roger, does that mean I've got equal status to Kiddrick?'

'As far as I'm concerned, yes.'

'Good! I'll remember that the next time he goes off on one at me.'

Tony laughed again. 'That should be fun to watch. Okay, let's get your tea.'

The long day over, Bianca returned to her car. The Fusion was not all the agency had provided; although her own phone was compatible with the US network, she had still been given another, Tony explaining that it had 'NSA-grade security'. However, that was of less interest to her than having the American government pay for her international calls.

So, she first rang her parents to assure them she was perfectly fine and her sudden decampment to the other side of the Atlantic was nothing to worry about; then James Harding to say much the same for business rather than personal reassurance. The good news there was that the deal had gone through, the investors finally signing earlier that day. Harper's threat had remained unused. Her absence would not even be an immediate issue – as Albion had said, everything was now in the hands of lawyers and bankers.

'But,' said James, 'you *will* be back here when everything gets moving again, won't you? You are rather important to Thymirase's development, after all.'

There was definite concern behind his understatement. Bianca couldn't do much to alleviate it. 'Believe me, I'll be back the second Roger is on his feet. When that'll be, though . . . I don't know. A few weeks. Maybe.'

'Hopefully not much longer. Are you seriously telling me there's literally not a single person in the whole of the States who could take over for him?'

'Apparently not,' she replied, deciding he wouldn't like the truth even if she could tell him.

'Oh. Great. Still, whatever it is you're up to is obviously important, considering I had MI6 talk to me yesterday and somebody from the US embassy today. So make sure you claim for everything you can think of on your expenses, all right?'

'They're paying for this call, for a start . . .' She trailed off on seeing someone crossing the parking garage.

Adam. He went to a car, a Fusion like hers only dark blue instead of silver, and got in.

A wild impulse took control. 'Anyway, sorry, but I've got to go,' she hurriedly told James. 'I'll talk to you soon, okay? Bye.' Before he could reply, she had disconnected.

Okay, mystery man, she thought. *I'm going to find out something about you today, even if it's only where you live.*

Adam set off. She started her own car and cautiously followed.

While she didn't know anything about the techniques of spying, it struck her that staying six feet behind his rear bumper would give her away, so she paused at the top of the ramp to let a couple of other cars pass before pulling out after him. It was now dark, which made her even more nervous about the mirrored road rules. But the traffic was not moving especially quickly, so she decided that if she just went with the flow she would probably be okay.

Adam was still two cars ahead as they stopped at traffic lights.

If her bearings were correct, he was heading east. Green lights, and they set off again. He changed lanes to turn left. Nervously, she indicated and edged into the adjoining lane to follow, getting an irate honk from the car behind. There was now only one car separating them as they made the turn.

She maintained the gap as her quarry continued through Washington, making a couple more turns. Before long, she was completely lost. The satnav was no help, since she didn't know where Adam was heading. All she could do was keep after him.

A smile came to her lips. This was, in a strange kind of way, fun. Under the circumstances, playing the spy felt oddly appropriate.

They left central DC on a main road, heading . . . north-east? She wasn't sure. The office buildings gave way to a lower sprawl. Adam kept going, minutes passing. Her girlish enthusiasm started to fade. For all she knew, he lived fifty miles away. Perhaps this hadn't been such a great idea after all . . .

Adam suddenly switched lanes, cutting sharply to the right. Horns sounded. Bianca was not sure how to follow – there was no space in the lane beside her. She braked, indicating right and creeping over. One car refused to let her in, but she held her ground. To her relief, the vehicle behind it slowed to give her space. She waved in thanks and pulled into the gap.

Adam was now out of direct sight, two or three cars between the two Fords. What was he doing? There was a junction ahead, a side road leading right. Was that where he was headed? She kept going—

A brief shrill of tyres and the growl of a fast-revving engine told her that he had made his move. His Fusion was almost lost in the dark, only the flash of reflected street lights and the red scowl of its tail lights giving it away. Had he chosen its colour for exactly that reason?

It took several frustrating seconds before she reached the intersection and could turn after him. He was clearly speeding, the red lights pulling away fast. Bianca accelerated, the smile returning. She enjoyed putting her foot down; the six penalty points on her licence back home were testament to that.

Her surroundings appeared to be mostly commercial buildings; warehouse-like retail outlets and industrial units. Nothing residential, so Adam didn't live here.

Had he seen her? Was he trying to shake off his tail?

She kept accelerating, closing the gap. A glance at the speedometer told her she was doing over fifty, and she was pretty sure the limit was thirty. A pang of fear; American cops had guns. Her foot moved to the brake . . .

Adam beat her to it. His Fusion's rear lights flared as it made a hard left turn. Its tyres squealed again.

He was definitely trying to lose her. More doubts – she was chasing a genuine *secret agent*, for God's sake! But she still braked and threw the car into the turn after him. Fright pumped through her heart as her Fusion's rear end slid wide, but she wrestled it back into line.

The new road was less well-lit, lined with darkened warehouses. Adam was already turning again, sweeping right into a narrower side street. She lost sight of him, but could still hear the wail of his tyres. *In for a penny*, she thought, following—

His car had vanished.

Bianca flinched, genuinely startled. There was no sign of the other Ford. But that was impossible . . .

Headlights glared blindingly in the mirrors.

He was *behind* her. But how—

Her car shook as Adam's hit it. The impact was not hard, but still enough to make it swerve to the left . . .

The front wheel hit the kerb before she could straighten out.

'Shit!' she wailed as the steering wheel bucked in her hands. The Fusion leapt up over the sidewalk. Chain-link fence flashed through her headlights – then there was a flat *bang!* and another jolt that threw her sideways.

The stricken Ford juddered to a stop. Dazed and shaken, Bianca sat up. The car's front wing was buried in the fence.

Her door was yanked open. She looked round in fright—

A fist froze inches from her face. She shrieked.

'Bianca!' said Adam, sounding as shocked as she felt. 'What are you doing?'

'What am *I* doing?' she cried. 'Jesus Christ! What are *you* doing? You just rammed me off the road!'

He looked at the damage, then back at her. 'Are you okay?'

'I don't know, I . . .' She experimentally moved her limbs. All were still attached. 'I think so.'

'Good. Here.' He extended a hand to her. She shot him a mistrustful look, then let him help her out.

'Oh God,' she said as she saw what had happened to the Fusion. Between the paving and the fence was rough ground, soil and gravel and strewn garbage – and broken glass. The front tyre had run over a smashed bottle and instantly punctured. What remained of it was wrapped loosely around the wheel rim like a rubber lei. 'They give me a car, and less than twenty-four hours later, it's wrecked. That'll make me popular.'

'Yeah. Uh . . . sorry,' he said sheepishly. 'I'll call STS to pick it up and fix it. I'll explain that it was my fault.'

'Well, yes!' she exclaimed. 'Why did you ram into me?'

'Why were you following me?'

'Because I . . .' She tried to find an answer. 'I don't really know, okay? I suppose I just wanted to find out more about you. *Anything* about you.'

'Why?'

'Because I don't like being told "no"? Especially not by idiots like Kiddrick. I don't know!' She threw up her hands. 'But what about you, suddenly turning into Mad Max?' She looked back at the corner, seeing a darkened loading dock set into the warehouse wall. He must have hidden inside it, but she couldn't imagine how he could possibly have made such a tight turn at the speed he had been going. 'How did you get behind me like that?'

'Evasive driving,' he said. 'Useful when you want to get rid of a tail.'

'You have a very odd definition of "evasive". I always take it to mean *not* hitting other cars.' She gave the damaged wheel another mournful look, then turned back to him. 'Wait, how long did it take before you realised I was following you?'

'About three blocks. You're not very good at it. Are you sure you're okay?' He sounded genuinely concerned.

'Yeah, I'm fine. Just shaken up.'

'Okay, good.' He took out his phone. 'I'll call STS.'

'About that,' Bianca said. 'Maybe it would be better if you didn't say exactly what happened?'

For the first time since they had met, his face showed a hint of a smile. It suited him. 'I'll just tell them you had an . . . incident.'

'Thanks.'

'No problem.' He made the call, being told that someone would collect the wounded car within twenty minutes, then pocketed the phone. 'I'd better give you a ride. This doesn't look like a very good neighbourhood to be waiting for a cab. Where are you staying?'

'Oh, a hotel. The, ah . . . the Beauregard.'

'I don't know it, sorry. You have the address?'

'Yes.'

'Great. You got everything from your car?'

She collected her bag, on Adam's suggestion leaving the car

key on the driver's seat to make life easier for the mechanics, then got into his vehicle. He entered the hotel into the satnav and turned back the way they had come. Near the junction, Bianca saw curving tyre marks freshly scorched on to the road surface. Whatever Adam had done to get behind her clearly involved some sort of controlled skid, but she still could not figure out exactly how he'd managed it.

They returned to the main road. Adam headed back towards central Washington. 'So,' said Bianca when the silence became overpowering, 'I've found out *something* about you.'

'What?'

'You're not very chatty.'

Another little smile. 'No, not really.'

'But like I said at STS, I think it'd help us work together if I got to know you better.'

'Makes sense.'

'So . . .' He didn't respond to the prompt. She changed tack. 'Roger said you used to be a soldier – Special Forces?'

'I'm afraid I can't discuss that.'

'Oh. But you volunteered to join Persona after you left?'

'I can't discuss that. I'm sorry.'

'Right.' She sighed, frustrated by the diktats of security. 'Okay, so what about you personally? I don't know much about American accents – I can recognise N'Yawk and yee-hah Deep South, but that's about it, so I can't tell where you're from originally.' Silence. He might be a spy, but taking hints was obviously not in his training. 'So, where *are* you from originally?'

'Sorry, I can't discuss that.'

She regarded him with incredulity. 'Seriously? You can't even tell me where you grew up?'

'I can't . . .' He looked confused, as if only just realising what he had said.

'Adam?'

His expression hardened – though his eyes still betrayed uncertainty. 'I don't think we should discuss this any further. Sorry.'

'Okay,' she said, making her bewilderment clear with each syllable.

'Your hotel's only a few minutes from here. I'll drop you off, and see you at STS tomorrow.'

'Fine.' It only took one syllable to show her disapproval.

He gave her an apologetic look, then continued driving. They soon reached the hotel. Bianca got out. 'See you tomorrow, then.'

'Yeah,' he replied. 'Oh, and . . . sorry about the car.'

'Thanks,' she said, unsure what to make of him. She watched as he pulled away, then went into the hotel.

Bianca jerked awake as her phone rang. Its screen said 6:03. Who the hell was calling her so early in the morning? Someone in England who hadn't grasped the concept of time zones? 'Mmyeah?'

'Bianca?'

It took her a moment to identify the voice. 'Tony?'

'Yes, it's me.'

'Why – what is it?' she complained. 'It's only six in the morning.'

'We need you to come into STS, right away.' If he had also only recently been stirred from sleep, his voice gave no sign; he sounded alert and focused. 'We have a mission.'

14

The Russian Connection

All the Bullpen's screens were alight with information, every workstation occupied by hurriedly roused staff . . . but nobody was looking at the monitors. Instead, all eyes were on the person who had just entered the control room.

Bianca didn't recognise him. 'Who's that?' she quietly asked Tony as the tall, thin man in an expensive suit shook hands with Morgan.

'Alan Sternberg,' he replied. Her blank look prompted him to elaborate. 'The National Security Adviser.'

'I thought that was Harper?'

'He's the Director of National Intelligence.'

'Ah, I see.' A beat. 'No, I don't. What's the difference?'

'Political, mostly. The DNI has to be approved by Congress, so there's always a lot of horse trading to get someone both sides agree on. The National Security Adviser doesn't need approval, though. The President can appoint anyone he wants. And Sternberg just so happens to be the President's old friend – and campaign manager.'

'So who's the top dog?'

'In theory, Harper, as he's got congressional authority. In practice . . . well, being the President's golf buddy gives you a lot of sway.'

Another tall man entered the Bullpen. This one Bianca recognised: Harper. He seemed discomfited to find Sternberg already there, but quickly covered it and marched over to join him and Morgan. 'Do they have different agendas, then?' she asked.

Tony chuckled. 'Oh yeah. Harper came from the Department of Defense, which controls the NSA, NRO, DIA and half a dozen other three-letter intelligence acronyms. But Sternberg is ex-CIA – and the CIA *isn't* controlled by the Pentagon. It's probably fair to say they hate each other almost as much as al-Qaeda.'

'The CIA and the Pentagon, or Sternberg and Harper?'

'Yes to both.' A wry smile. 'The Pentagon would love to take full control of the CIA – and the other independent agencies like STS, for that matter. It's not likely to happen, though. Certainly not while Sternberg has the President's ear.'

Harper and Sternberg concluded their chilly greetings, then had a brief exchange with Morgan before the black man turned to address his audience. 'All right, everyone.' The murmur of conversation ended. 'As most of you know, we discovered on the mission in Pakistan that Malik Syed had been in direct contact with one of Muqaddim al-Rais's lieutenants. At that meeting, Syed heard that al-Rais was planning something big. He didn't know what – he wasn't told anything more than a code name. But after using PERSONA to obtain information from Syed, we discovered that code name: Operation Lamplighter.'

Bianca had been groggy from her early wake-up call, but the name of Muqaddim al-Rais caught her full attention. She didn't need to be a spy to know the name of the world's most wanted terrorist. Any residual sleepiness was now gone. She listened intently as Morgan continued.

'We passed that code name to other agencies in the USIC to see if anything came up. Last night, something did. NSA got an ECHELON hit on Operation Lamplighter from this man.' He indicated a grainy photo, blown up to fill a block of the screens behind him. 'His name is Ruslan Pavel Zykov. He's a Russian arms dealer.'

Bianca stared at the image. It had been taken using a telephoto lens, looking down from on high at the subject as he climbed into the back of an SUV. The group of beefy men shielding him suggested that he preferred to be in public view as little as possible. He appeared to be in his forties, with bristling black hair and a broad, pugnacious face, a chunky gold necklace around his neck.

'The code name came up in a phone conversation between Zykov and a man called Hadrami, whom we strongly believe has a direct connection to al-Rais,' said Tony, moving to stand beside Morgan. 'The full transcript is in your file packets, but to summarise: Zykov is acting as a middleman between Hadrami's client – presumably al-Rais – and an unknown party, who has possession of something vital to Operation Lamplighter. Whatever it is, a price has been agreed to buy it. Seven million US dollars.'

That produced a stir around the room. 'So it's more than a crate of RPGs, then,' said Holly Jo.

'It looks that way,' Morgan replied. 'For that kind of money, we're talking high-end anti-aircraft systems, NBC materials, armoured vehicles or gunships – the works.'

'NBC?' Bianca whispered to Levon, whose workstation she was standing beside.

'Nuclear, Biological, Chemical,' he told her. 'Germ warfare, dirty bombs . . . nasty stuff.'

'Oh. Great.' She felt a sudden chill.

'Whatever it is,' Morgan went on, 'if al-Rais wants it, it's not to make the world a better place. Now, other agencies will be working on this from their own angles, but since it was STS that learned about Lamplighter in the first place, we're being given the chance to follow up on it and prove the Persona Project's worth.' He looked over at Harper and Sternberg, who were standing with their respective aides between them like human barricades. 'So, as of now, our mission is: find out what Operation Lamplighter is, and stop it. Start thinking, people.'

'Snatch team,' said Baxter, who was standing near the front of the audience. 'We go in and grab Zykov like we did Syed.'

'If it were that easy, you'd already be on a plane to do it,' said Morgan, shaking his head. 'Zykov isn't a small-timer like Toradze. He's . . . connected. He's former FSB, and still has close links to the Russian secret service – and also the Russian government. At very high levels. As you can see from the photo, he's also paranoid enough to have constant protection from bodyguards, most of whom are also former FSB. His dacha outside Moscow is like a fortress. Grabbing him by force would be tough – and if anything went wrong, it would cause a serious diplomatic incident between Russia and the US.'

Sternberg spoke. Even though his voice was quiet and calm, it dominated everyone's attention. 'The President has made it clear that cannot be allowed to happen. Any operation in Russia will be under condition of maximum deniability.'

'Sounds like we're being disavowed,' Kyle muttered to Levon.

Levon nodded. 'Your mission, which you don't have a choice about accepting . . .'

'There may be a way to catch him outside Russia, though,' Tony told the room. 'According to his file, he's a serious gambler. He's often dropped half a million dollars or more on poker games. And usually won.'

Kyle whistled appreciatively. 'Dude's a real player.'

'NSA also went through all Zykov's other communications and found that two days from now, he's going to be in Macau. There's a regular high-stakes VIP game at the Imperial Casino there – quarter of a million dollars minimum buy-in. And he's buying in. That's where he'll be vulnerable. Macau is Chinese territory, and he won't be able to call on the kind of backup he can in Russia.'

Sternberg cleared his throat. 'Deniability of operations extends to China just as much as to Russia. The State Department is not willing to jeopardise the current round of trade talks.'

'For God's sake, Alan,' growled Harper. 'How the hell are we supposed to operate if State keeps sticking its nose in? We're at the sharp end here.'

'I'm aware of that, Gordon, but State had to patch up the tears the sharp end made in our relationship with the Pakistanis after the last STS mission. They don't want to have to do it again with Russia or China. And that's direct from the President. State's still in shock after Sandra Easton's assassination – and the international situation is already tense enough without American agents causing a diplomatic incident.'

Morgan was unhappy with the development, but had no choice but to take it on board. 'So, we need a deniable plan, then. Suggestions?'

Levon raised a hand. 'Are we talking a straightforward grab, like Mr Baxter wants, or do we need this guy to stay oblivious?'

'The latter would be better,' said Morgan. 'If Zykov's contacts realise we got to him, they might go underground, and take Lamplighter with them. If al-Rais is willing to pay seven million dollars for it, he'll be able to find another middleman to replace Zykov. And we might not know who that middleman is until it's too late.'

Bianca hesitated before speaking, feeling extremely self-conscious and out of place. 'Ah . . . what else do you know about this Zykov?' All eyes turned to her. 'You said he was paranoid – was that based on any specific assessment, or just because he's got six guys with no necks surrounding him?'

Kiddrick was about twelve feet from her, but his mutter of 'So now we're listening to the hired help?' was perfectly audible. Others also voiced similar feelings, though more quietly.

Tony stared them down. 'Dr Childs makes a good point. He is paranoid, yes – because people really *are* out to get him. He has friends in high places, but he's also made a lot of enemies. His file – and criminal record – says he's prone to violence. He's even attacked close friends because they did something to make him mad.'

'Sounds like a nice guy,' Bianca said sarcastically. 'But could you use that against him? Do something that makes him mad enough to drop his guard?'

'Something like taking him for a quarter-million dollars at poker?' Everyone looked round as Adam spoke. He was standing unobtrusively at the edge of the group.

Tony grinned. 'Something like that, yes. If we use the persona of a world-class card sharp . . .'

'I'm sure we've got someone suitable,' said Morgan. 'All right! We know the person, we know the place. What we need now is a plan. Get on it. I want first proposals by eleven a.m., and we'll take things from there.'

The assembly broke up, everyone dispersing with purpose. As Morgan departed with Harper and Sternberg, Tony came over to Bianca. 'Good call.'

She felt a little embarrassed at the praise. 'It was fairly obvious – someone else would have said it if I hadn't.'

'But you said it first. Looks like Roger was right – you really are the perfect choice to take his place.'

'I wouldn't go that far. But thanks for backing me up.'

'No problem.' He smiled at her, then addressed his colleagues. 'Okay, I want everyone to divide up into working groups. We need as much information as we can find on Zykov, Hadrami, known associates, and the Imperial Casino in Macau, plus any local assets we might have. We have less than forty-eight hours to work out how to crack this guy, and seventeen of them will be taken up by flying there. So get those brains started, people!'

For the second time in a few days, Bianca found herself aboard a private jet.

This aircraft was considerably larger than the one that had brought her to Washington; she didn't know the type, but she had been aboard similarly sized airliners on regular commercial flights. It seemed excessive, since the team going to Macau only comprised thirteen people including herself, but she assumed that STS had simply requisitioned the first available US government jet.

It gave her room to stretch out, though. A general plan had been worked out in Washington, and was now being fine-tuned en route, Levon and others offering contributions from the other end of a satellite link with the Bullpen. Tactics were not her concern, however, so she was taking a break from the discussion in the VIP section at the front of the cabin.

She looked out of a porthole. Nothing was visible beyond except blue, the empty sky and the Pacific mirror images against the pale line of the horizon. A shift of focus, and she caught her own reflection in the window. 'What the hell am I doing here?' she whispered.

It was not the first time recently that she had asked herself the question.

Someone opened the dividing curtain. She looked round. 'Hey,' said Tony, coming to her seat.

'Hi. What's up?'

'Work, I'm afraid. We have a plan. We're about to present it to Martin.'

Bianca stood and followed him out. Most of the team were seated at a large table, others overflowing on to the rows of standard aircraft seats behind it. There was a space at the table for her. She took it, then looked up at the screen on the bulkhead.

It was divided into three windows, the faces of Morgan, Levon and Kiddrick occupying them. Morgan finished talking to some-one off-camera and tapped a button to unmute his microphone. 'Okay. Let's have it.'

Tony took his own seat between Bianca and Adam. 'Right. We know that Zykov is staying in one of the Imperial's penthouses, and Levon got the plans from the French firm of architects who designed the place.'

Levon beamed on his screen. 'Right down to the position of the last faucet. There might be a lot of security in the casino, but there was hardly any on the architects' servers!'

'The penthouses have private elevator access and twenty-four-hour concierges, as well as full CCTV coverage of the hallways outside,' Tony went on. 'The chances of entering unseen that way are almost zero. We thought about getting into his penthouse from the roof, but it'd be tricky – especially for Dr Childs.'

Bianca blinked in surprise. 'What?'

'Wherever we grab Zykov, you need to be there, remember?' said Tony. 'You have to administer the drugs. And we figured that you probably wouldn't want to climb along the edge of a fiftieth-storey rooftop.'

'While carrying about twenty pounds of PERSONA gear,' Kiddrick added with sardonic pleasure.

'So the penthouse was out. But,' Tony said, nodding at Baxter, 'John came up with an alternative that we think will work.'

'It follows on from what Dr Childs suggested,' Baxter began. 'We make Zykov mad as hell by having Adam clean him out, and get in his face about it. Really gloat, maybe even drop a hint that he was cheating.'

'Which he will be, of course,' said Holly Jo. 'Every edge we can give Adam, he'll have.'

'Even Zykov won't be dumb enough to do anything in the casino itself – there are cameras covering every square inch, and probably a couple hundred security guards. If he gets arrested, he won't be able to complete the deal with al-Rais. But if we can get him *outside* the casino . . .'

'That gives us freer rein to operate,' finished Morgan, nodding. 'What are you thinking?'

Tony took over the explanation once more. 'The Imperial is brand new; it only opened this year. It's in a part of Macau called Cotai, which is reclaimed land between two of the other islands. The whole area is still being developed – right now, some parts of it are actually empty. Our thinking is that if we can get Zykov riled enough to follow Adam out of the casino to somewhere with nobody around, we can catch him there.'

'How?' asked Morgan.

'We can't just mug him, like we did with Syed,' said Baxter. 'We have to deal with his bodyguards at the same time. We've got to take them all out simultaneously.'

Bianca was shocked. 'Wait, you mean – *kill* them?'

'That'd be kind of a giveaway to Zykov that something untoward was going on,' Kiddrick sniped. 'Of course not.'

'He means knock them out,' Tony assured her. 'There are various fast-acting drugs we can use. It means setting things up very carefully – we can't just shoot tranquilliser darts at them.

But if we play things right, Zykov will have to follow Adam from the casino in a cab. And we can make sure he gets into one of ours. Billy,' he glanced at the team's technician, a skinny, taciturn young man who was typing on a laptop with intense concentration, 'has worked out a way to rig the cab so that all the passengers will be unconscious just a couple of seconds after the collision. He's sending the details on to our people in Macau. They should have started fitting it by the time we land.'

'So, a staged car crash?' Morgan asked.

'Yeah. There are risks, but we've done it before. Like in Rio.'

Adam spoke for the first time. 'How did it go?'

'Fine,' said Tony. 'The target suffered some minor scrapes, but he bought the story that he'd been knocked out. It gave us enough time to get his persona.'

Bianca suddenly realised the comment's implication: the Persona Project had been carrying out missions before Adam joined it. So he wasn't its first agent?

'If you're sure you can make it work, then yes, do it,' said Morgan. 'So how are you going to make sure Zykov gets mad enough to follow Adam? Can you actually beat him?'

'We think so,' said Tony. 'The persona Adam will be using is a top-flight card player. He knows every trick in the book – and some that aren't.'

'He's a cheat?'

'He spent three months in a Nevada prison for it.'

Kyle was unimpressed. 'So maybe he's not that good.'

'He was sold out by his accomplice – nobody caught him during the game itself,' Tony reassured him.

'And we can help Adam out as well,' said Levon. 'I've got a program that counts cards. It won't be perfect, 'cause the casino switches decks every few games, but it'll still give him an edge. If we rig him with a camera so we can see the other cards in play, the computer can calculate what the other players might have in their hands. Then Holly Jo tells Adam that through the earwig.'

'It's still not a guarantee that you'll win, though,' Bianca pointed out. 'I read Zykov's file – as well as being just a really unpleasant guy, I'd say that he has intermittent explosive disorder. It means he sometimes has a disproportionately angry response if he's provoked,' she added by way of explanation. 'It's often linked with other disorders like pathological gambling, and he fits the bill for that as well. But it *doesn't* mean that he's going to explode with rage whenever he gets a bad hand, or start sweating uncontrollably if he's bluffing. His responses might be very subtle. I mean, he usually wins, so he's probably got a very good poker face.'

'He'll have everybody at STS watching that face,' countered Kiddrick. 'The slightest tell, and we'll see it.'

Tony looked doubtful. 'Maybe not. The Imperial's VIP rooms have metal detectors at the entrance, according to the architects' plans. With that much money at stake, they don't want anybody sneaking in gadgets to help them cheat. The only camera we'd be able to get in there without tripping an alarm would be a skittle.'

'Excuse me?' said Bianca.

'A skittle – it's our nickname for a micro-video camera and transmitter. It's about the size of a Skittle; you know, the candy.'

'Oh, right. Wow, that's tiny.'

'Yeah. But because it's so small, the picture quality isn't great. It should be able to read cards on the table, but I don't know about spotting tiny changes of expression on somebody sitting on the far side.'

'We need more eyes in there,' suggested Morgan. 'Someone who can watch the other players as well.'

Tony nodded. 'We've got enough contingency cash to cover a second player.'

Kyle immediately stuck his hand up. 'I volunteer!'

'Point one,' said Holly Jo, 'you're not exactly an expert at picking up subtle changes in people's emotions. Point two, nobody would ever believe you were worth a quarter of a million dollars.'

'Hey!' he protested.

'Besides,' said Tony, 'we need you tracking Adam and Zykov with the UAV once they leave the hotel. No, it would have to be someone else. Someone with . . .' he turned slowly to Bianca, 'a background in psychology. How are your poker skills?'

'What?' she said, almost laughing before realising that he was serious. 'Wait a minute! I'm only supposed to be here to work out the drug dosages, and now you want me to be an *agent*? Forget it!'

'No, it could work,' said Morgan. 'Everyone else on the team will have an active role, either during the poker game or in capturing Zykov. But you don't need to do anything until we actually have him. Someone else at that table working with Adam increases our chances of taking Zykov to the cleaners.'

'Think of it as a night on the town – with two hundred and fifty k, on us,' Tony added. 'All you'll have to do is make sure you lose to Adam. It might even be fun.'

'I was thinking more that all that money could do an awful lot of good for society,' replied Bianca. 'Rather than risking it ending up in the pocket of some arms-dealing scumbag.'

'It *will* be doing good,' said Morgan, with a firmness that warned Bianca the decision had been made, no matter her opinion. 'It'll be helping to prevent the world's most dangerous terrorist from committing a major attack. I think that's worth an evening of your time, don't you?'

She couldn't come up with any objections that didn't sound selfish and petty. 'You seriously want to give me a quarter of a million dollars and have me lose it all at poker?' she asked instead. 'How do you know I won't just run off into the night with it?'

'Because that wouldn't be like you,' said Adam. The quiet comment surprised everyone, not least Bianca.

'Okay, then,' Morgan said. 'Unless someone comes up with anything better by the time you land, that's the plan. Clean Zykov out, get him mad, set up a car crash, get what's in his head. Tony, give me an update on the operational details in . . . six hours.'

'Will do,' said Tony.

'All right. Good luck, everybody.'

He disconnected, his third of the screen going blank. Kiddrick followed suit almost immediately. 'If you guys need anything, let me know,' said Levon. 'I'll get to work on this card-counting program.'

Holly Jo raised an eyebrow. 'I thought you said you already had it.'

'Well, I've got it in my head – I've got to *write* it, obviously! Don't worry, it's just calculating probabilities. Ain't no big thing. Catch you later.'

He disappeared from the screen. Tony looked at the others round the table. 'Everyone knows what they're doing? Good. Let's grab this guy.'

The meeting broke up, its members dispersing into smaller groups. Bianca watched Adam as he stood. Since the incident with her car more than a day before, he had revealed no more of the brief glimpses of an actual personality behind the expressionless face – until his comment about *her* personality. It suggested that he was not as disinterested as he appeared . . . but now the blinds had come down again. If he was thinking about anything other than the mission, it didn't show.

'Bianca?' said Tony, gesturing towards the forward compartment.

She nodded and went with him. She hesitated at the dividing curtain, looking back at Adam.

'Something wrong?' Tony asked.

'I'm not sure,' she said, still regarding Adam before finally turning away. 'When you were talking about setting up the car crash, you said you'd done it before, to get a copy of someone's persona, but Adam didn't know anything about it.'

'No, he wouldn't have.' He motioned for her to take a seat, waiting politely until she was down before sitting beside her.

'So Adam isn't the Persona Project's first agent?'

'There was someone else before him.' A pause. 'Me.'

She was surprised. 'You?'

He turned his head and used his thumb and forefinger to part his hair in a particular spot, revealing a small scar. 'I've still got the electrode filaments inside my skull; they decided it was too risky to take them out. So in theory, I could still use the PERSONA device to take on someone else's personality. In practice, though . . .'

'What?'

He chewed on his lower lip, reluctant. 'It's a long story.'

'It's a long flight.' They were still more than eight hours from Macau.

'Okay. Just keep it to yourself. Not everybody out there,' a nod towards the other cabin, 'knows the whole story, and some of it I'd prefer to keep that way. Not for security reasons, just . . . personal ones.'

'I won't say a word,' she promised.

'Thanks.' He smiled briefly. 'So, before I became the Persona Project's head of field operations, I was its first field agent. In other words, I was the guinea pig.'

'How short a straw did you draw to get that assignment?'

'Actually, I volunteered. I used to be US Army – 1st Special Forces Operational Detachment Delta,' he said proudly, before clarifying to the uncomprehending Englishwoman, 'Delta Force. Like the British SAS.'

Again, she was surprised. 'Really? You don't look like . . .'

One side of his mouth creased into a sardonic grin. 'A grunt?'

'I was going to say "some sort of grim-faced super-soldier", actually. Aren't they all supposed to have macho names like Flint or Stone, or Gristle?'

'What's wrong with Carpenter?' he said, in mock offence. 'There have been some badass carpenters in history. One had a whole book written about him. Two thousand years ago, or thereabouts.'

'No besmirchment of your good name intended. I meant, you don't look . . . I don't know, like a strip of old leather that's been chewed by the dog. That's the mental picture I have of those guys. Like John Baxter.'

Tony burst into laughter. 'Oh, that's fantastic!' he said. 'But you're right, he kinda does, doesn't he?'

'Don't tell him I said that,' she added hurriedly.

'If you can keep a secret, so can I. Anyway, yes, I volunteered.' He became more sober. 'The reason was simple enough – I'd seen too many of my friends die in places like Afghanistan. All we were doing was picking off low-level soldiers. I wanted to go after the *leaders*. Persona gave me that chance.'

Bianca had been fervently opposed to the wars in the Middle East, but she couldn't help feeling sympathy for him. The deaths that had altered the course of her life had been from long-term, debilitating diseases; they were horrible to witness, but one knew roughly when the end would come. To see people your own age, friends and comrades, violently cut down without warning was something else entirely. 'So you took the risk?'

'Yeah. Roger and Kiddrick were there from the start; they made it possible, after all. Martin was brought in from the CIA to oversee things and make sure they didn't kill each other. The two of them don't exactly get on. Kiddrick thinks he's the brains of the operation, and that Roger's just a glorified pharmacist.'

'Yes, I got that impression,' she said, smiling.

'But the theory was all there, and it was time to see if it worked in practice. So I had the procedure, and . . . it did. All those disks in the lab at STS? Most were recorded as tests for the system; they got volunteers from all kinds of potentially useful backgrounds – like our card player – by telling them it was a psychological research experiment. Measuring their brainwaves in response to certain stimuli, that sort of thing.'

Bianca's sense of ethics was jabbing at her again. 'Nobody told them they were having their minds copied for someone else to read? All their secrets, everything?'

'No. They didn't even remember the actual process, because Roger blanked their short-term memories after the transfer.'

'Did he now.'

'It doesn't sound like you approve.'

'I can't say that I do, particularly,' she told him. 'So you had all these personas. Were they useful? Did everything work?'

'Perfectly. At first. Some of the personas gave me specialist knowledge that helped me carry out missions. Languages, local lands and people, how to fly a chopper – all sorts of things.'

She asked the question that had been on her mind since the demonstration at STS. 'What . . . what did it *feel* like? Having someone else's memories?'

Tony considered it. 'Odd,' he finally said. 'In a lot of ways it seemed totally natural – drawing on a person's memories or skills was just like recalling my own. It's automatic, unconscious; it just happens. It only got weird if I actively thought about how they weren't *my* memories. So I tried not to do that too often.'

'I can imagine it must have been bizarre, having someone else's thoughts in your head. A whole different personality, even – like when Adam started behaving like Conrad Wilmar.'

'Actually, Adam shows that a lot more strongly than I did – acting like the other person, I mean.'

'Why?'

'Different personality, updated procedure, I guess. But,' he went on, with a renewed intensity that suggested he wanted to leave that line of enquiry behind, 'the missions we ran were all successful. PERSONA worked, and provided intel that would have been impossible to get any other way. And then . . . we had the big one. The mission where we caught Mahjub Najjar.'

'Where you caught—' She broke off as the full implications of what he had just said hit her. 'The al-Qaeda leader? But I thought he was killed by a drone! It was all over the news. I mean, you even had your president gloating about it.'

'I wouldn't call it gloating,' Tony said sharply. 'It was a cover-up. We'd just captured the world's most wanted terrorist. More to the point, we had a way to find out everything that he knew. Every planned attack, the names and locations of all his cell leaders, how he was moving al-Qaeda's money around the world . . . every single secret that was in his head, we could put into mine. We knew it all. But if we'd announced that he'd been captured, his second-in-command – Muqaddim al-Rais – would have changed all the plans on the first day he took control. So we told the world he'd been killed. Dead men can't be interrogated.'

'Only now they can,' Bianca realised. 'If you've made a recording of his persona . . .'

'Yeah. Once I was imprinted, I knew everything Najjar did – and could tell it all to our people.'

'So that's what PERSONA is really all about? Interrogation without torture?'

'Torture doesn't work. Not on people like Najjar. But this way we didn't even need to lay a finger on him. I did all the talking.'

The limitations of the PERSONA process came to her mind. 'For twenty-four hours.'

'Twenty-four hours *at a time*. Najjar's persona disappeared every time I went to sleep. The next morning, it would be re-imprinted so the interrogation could carry on where it left off.' His expression darkened at a painful memory. 'Until . . .'

'Something went wrong,' Bianca realised.

'Yeah.' He stared out of the porthole at infinity. 'Like I said, I was the guinea pig. And PERSONA was experimental. It turned out that repeating the process over and over has side effects.'

'What kind of side effects?'

He shifted in the seat, reluctant to speak. 'First it was headaches. They weren't much to begin with, but they turned into full-on skull-splitters. Then I started having periods of confusion, blackouts, and finally . . .' Another lengthy pause. 'Finally, I had a breakdown.'

'Oh God,' Bianca said softly. 'I'm sorry.'

'I was hospitalised for a week, and was out of commission for nearly another month. When they finally tried to imprint Najjar's persona again, it was . . . agonising, like my mind was rejecting it. Almost an immune response. They stopped the procedure, but I knew that was it. It was over.'

She leaned closer to him. 'Did they . . . did they try again?'

'Yeah, with a different persona. They waited a few days, but it was the same result. Still,' he said, sitting upright with strained lightness, 'that's science, I guess! You learn as much from the failures as the successes.'

She knew that he counted himself as one of the former. 'But you came back to the project.'

'The technique worked and had incredible potential, so it was obvious they were going to try again. I decided to stay, so I could help them work out the . . . kinks.' That last was said somewhat acerbically. 'And be sure that whoever they got to replace me didn't suffer the same problems. The first thing I did was make them put in a rule that a persona could only be imprinted once. That way, it'd eliminate one of the possible causes of what happened to me. As for the other . . .'

'That the problem might be cumulative?'

'Exactly. Maybe there's a limit on the number of times the process can be used before the brain says enough. We just don't know.'

Bianca looked back at the divider. 'So what about Adam? Has he shown any signs of problems?'

'Not yet. He went through tests and what you could call warm-up missions before the first full operation in Pakistan, but that's all. He hasn't been imprinted as much as I was. So far, everything seems normal.' A pause. 'With the process, anyway.'

She knew what he meant. 'But about Adam himself . . . ?'

He straightened. 'I'm not going to go there. What he was like before he joined the project, I don't know – and it's his business, not mine.'

'But you know that he's not . . . well, *normal.*'

'Like I said, I'm not going to go there.'

Bianca took the hint. 'So what happened to Najjar?' she asked instead.

'He's out of circulation.'

'Dead?'

'I'm afraid I can't discuss that.'

'You know, it's not the first time I've heard that line recently.'

He gave her a wry smile. 'That doesn't surprise me. So, anyway,' he said, getting back to business, 'let's talk about how you're going to throw away a quarter of a million dollars.'

15

The Gambler

Macau, China

Like Las Vegas, Macau – a former Portuguese colony now returned to, but not fully assimilated by, the People's Republic of China – was a city dominated by one thing: gambling. The relentless growth of the pastime, fuelled by increasingly affluent Chinese tourists making the trip from the mainland to wager their new wealth, had led to a full two square miles of new land being reclaimed from the sea – not to accommodate the people of one of the most densely populated places on earth, but to provide space for ever-larger casinos.

The Imperial was one of this new wave, a combined gambling emporium and hotel rising fifty storeys into the sky. It was styled to resemble, at least superficially, a traditional Chinese pagoda. A steeply pitched roof outlined in red neon curved upwards from the tower's top, a garish hat with the word IMPERIAL blazing along each of its long sides. Even in daylight more neon was visible streaking down the tower itself, the structure visually jostling for attention amongst its equally glitzy neighbours.

'So there's no word in Macau for "subtle", I see,' said Bianca as she peered out of the window at the building. The team had set up temporary stall in another hotel not far away. 'Zykov's in the penthouse?'

'Yes,' said Holly Jo. 'He checked in about three hours ago. He's in the one on the right-hand corner.'

Bianca looked more closely. She could pick out windows beneath the illuminated crown, a balcony offering the occupants a spectacular view across the islands. She could also tell that the edges of the roof jutted out quite a distance from the tower itself. 'Tony was right. I really wouldn't want to climb along there.'

A knock at the door. 'Can I come in?' called a voice.

'Yes, I'm decent.'

She turned as Tony entered the bedroom, a cellophane clothing bag draped over one arm. 'I come bearing – wow, that's a different look.'

'I know.' Holly Jo, in addition to her technical and linguistic skills, had revealed that she was also quite the stylist. Tying it back was normally the limit of what Bianca would do with her hair, but it had now been straightened and held up in a loose, stylish twist. 'It's so different I wasn't even sure if I liked it, but I think it's starting to grow on me.'

'Just wait until I do your make-up,' said Holly Jo.

'Don't make me look too tarty, okay?'

'I don't think that'll happen,' Tony said, smiling. 'I've got the dress. And the shoes.' He raised his arm to show off both the garment in question and a shoebox.

Bianca regarded the former dubiously. 'It's very . . . red.'

'Ooh, let me see,' said Holly Jo, hopping up to pluck at the cellophane. 'Is that a Moschino?'

'Only a knock-off, I'm afraid,' Tony replied.

She put a hand on one hip in disapproval. 'You're giving her a quarter of a million dollars to gamble away, but you won't spring for a genuine dress for her to wear while she's doing it?'

'This is a mission, not a fashion show. Anyway, I doubt anyone'll be looking too closely at the quality of the stitching.'

Holly Jo shook her head. 'The women will be,' she chided, before taking the shoebox from him. 'Louboutins!' she squealed, seeing the red soles inside. Then her excitement abruptly faded. 'Oh. Let me guess, more knock-offs?' Tony shrugged helplessly. 'You are *so* cheap.'

'Hey, you try justifying a pair of thousand-dollar shoes to Harper.'

'Just give me the chance and I will!'

Bianca took the box from Holly Jo. 'High heels aren't really my thing,' she said, examining the vertiginous court shoes.

'High heels are *everyone's* thing,' Holly Jo insisted, turning a foot to show off her own. 'You just haven't found the right ones.'

'Anyway, foot fetishism aside,' said Tony, putting the dress on the bed, 'it's time. Adam's waiting in the other bedroom.'

'Okay,' Bianca said, hesitant. She knew what she was supposed to do; Kiddrick's tutorials had been thorough, whatever she thought of him personally. But the original plan for her to practise using one of the recorded personalities at STS had been abandoned in the rush to reach Zykov. This would be her first time imprinting Adam for real. 'Well . . . let's give it a try.'

She went with Tony through the suite's main room, where Kyle was stretched out on a sofa watching TV. Behind him, at a table, Billy Kerschner was working on a piece of equipment through an illuminated magnifier. Also in the room was a stocky Chinese man called Lau, whom Tony had introduced as one of the CIA's local contacts. She nodded to them as she passed, then entered the other bedroom.

The PERSONA device and its recording unit had been set up on a desk. Adam sat beside it, staring at the window. He looked round as Tony and Bianca came in. 'Are we ready?'

'Yes,' Tony told him. 'Okay, Bianca. Trial by fire.'

'I wish you'd found a less scary way to say that,' she complained as she took the skullcap from the case. 'Right, let's see if I remember how to put this on . . .'

'The open part goes at the front,' Tony joked.

She shot a sarcastic smile over her shoulder, then turned back to Adam. As she gently tugged the cap into place and positioned the clusters of electrodes, she realised he was watching her expression, his eyes tracking hers. But there was no sense that he was doing so out of any desire to form an emotional connection; it seemed purely analytical. Data-gathering.

She secured the strap under his chin. 'Okay, that's done. I hope.'

The disk had already been inserted into the recorder; she opened the screen on the main unit and started it up. It ran through its initial self-tests, informing her that it was ready for use.

She took the gas injector from the medical case. A quick glance at Tony, who gave her a look of reassurance, then she leaned over Adam. 'Are you ready?' A brief flick of his eyes sufficed as affirmation. 'Okay. Here we go . . .'

She pressed the injector to his neck and pulled the trigger.

Adam drew in a sharp breath through his nostrils. Bianca couldn't help but cringe at having caused his discomfort, but nevertheless began to count off the passing seconds. Ten, twenty. Any faint vestiges of expression that had been on his face evaporated away.

Thirty seconds. 'Adam? Are you all right?'

His gaze locked on to hers, clear and blank. 'Yes.'

'Good, okay. Well. This is it, then.'

She turned to the PERSONA and entered a command.

The screen came to life as the transfer began. Adam jerked as if he had received an electric shock. Bianca knew what to expect this time, but was still worried. Despite Tony's assurances, which she now knew were from first-hand experience, the process still looked painful. His fists were balled tight, tendons straining.

Nothing to do now but wait for the machine to do its work. She pulled up a chair, eyes on her patient as he took in the memories and experiences of another man. *Was* it more than just data? Had something of the other subject's 'soul' actually been copied? She didn't know, and wasn't sure if the philosophical implications of the answer were something she *wanted* to know.

Tony stood beside her. 'It's going fine,' he said. '*You're* doing fine.'

'Thanks.' But she was still filled with concern.

Minutes passed. Then the activity on the screen slowed. The rapid flutter of Adam's eyes returned to normal.

Tony reached into a case and took out a piece of paper. 'Cheat sheet,' he whispered. 'To check his memory.'

Bianca nodded, still watching Adam. His eyes closed and he took in a long, slow breath, a look of pleasurable relaxation spreading across his features. 'Adam?'

His eyes slowly opened again. The look he gave her was sleepy, and she might even have taken it for dumb docility – if not for the hint of a far sharper intelligence hiding behind it. 'Hey, Bianca,' he said, voice languid. 'Tony, hi.'

'We need to do the memory check,' Tony told him.

'Sure, sure.' Another relaxed breath, then he shuffled his feet on the carpet as if settling them into a comfortable pair of slippers. 'Ask away.'

'Your full name?'

'Peter William Vanwall.'

Tony checked the sheet, nodding. 'Your date of birth?'

'September twenty-first, 1951.'

'Place of birth?'

'Wilmette, Illinois.'

'Mother's maiden name.'

'O'Connor.'

'The guilty secret that you would never admit to anyone.'

A pause, then a sly smirk slowly oozed across Adam's face. 'Well, I wouldn't say that I'd never admit it to *anyone*, since my gambling buddies all know – hell, some of them have even been in the room. But I'd really rather you didn't tell my wife that I've paid for a few, ah, sexual encounters. Okay, more than a few.' He looked Bianca up and down, taking in her undisguised expression of distaste. 'Jeez, Bianca, don't get your panties in a knot. She lost interest in sex years ago. Besides, what happens in Vegas stays in Vegas, right?'

'Except for STDs,' she said, annoyed – before the realisation struck her that she was being repelled by the behaviour of somebody who wasn't even there. She was talking to *Adam Gray*, not Peter Vanwall. Peter Vanwall was thousands of miles away. She didn't even know what he looked like.

Tony put down the paper. 'Everything seems okay. The big question now is: can you beat Zykov at poker?'

'Hell, yes,' drawled Adam, standing. 'Unless they're actually cheating, I can take on just about anyone in the whole world. And since we'll be cheating as well, I figure that puts us over the odds.'

'Is that Vanwall boasting about how good he is, Adam,' said Bianca, 'or is it you assessing his chances based on what you know about him?'

'A bit of both,' he replied. The smirk had gone, though a faint but seemingly permanent upward turn remained at the corners of his mouth, as if he had worked out the punchline to the joke that was life but was keeping it to himself. 'Vanwall is as good as he says – as good as he thinks, anyway. He genuinely believes he's a world-class player.'

'Don't all gamblers? I used to play the occasional card game at university, and I thought I was pretty good compared to my friends. But I'm sure I would have been cleaned out in five minutes if I'd taken on a serious player.'

'I'm confident.'

'You, or Vanwall?'

'Both.'

'I hope you're right,' Tony said to him. 'You *and* Vanwall. Because if we can't get Zykov's persona, we won't have any leads on al-Rais or Lamplighter.'

'I'll beat him,' said Adam. He was more serious now, but Vanwall's lackadaisical smugness was still present. 'You just make sure everyone else is set to catch him.'

'We will be. Speaking of which, it's your turn to get ready, Bianca. I'll turn you over to Holly Jo.'

'God knows what I'm going to end up looking like,' she said as she headed for the door.

Adam watched her go, paying particular attention to the sway of her hips. 'I'm looking forward to finding out.'

Bianca looked at herself in the mirror. 'Well, that's . . . rather good, actually.'

'I'm glad to hear it,' said Holly Jo, leaning over her shoulder to fuss a powder brush over her cheek. 'So? Happy?'

'Yes, thanks.' The combination of the new hairstyle and the slightly overdone but still elegant make-up was leagues removed from her everyday look, but she couldn't deny that it was perfectly suited to her character for the evening: the wealthy English dilettante splurging money on a new thrill. PERSONA wasn't the only way to take on a new identity.

'Cool. Okay, get your dress and shoes on, then Billy should have some special jewellery for you.'

Bianca regarded her newly applied false nails. 'Can you give me a hand with the zip? I don't want to break these.'

'No problem. Step into it?'

She did so, Holly Jo helping her slide the bright scarlet dress over her legs and body. As the American started to pull up the zipper, the door opened and Kyle rushed in. 'Hey, we need to— Saaay,' he said, tone swinging instantly from urgent to smarmy. 'Two girls playing dress-up. Nice.'

'Kyle!' Holly Jo yelped. 'First, knock. And second, shut up!'

'For God's sake!' Bianca added, blushing. 'Five seconds earlier and you would have caught me in my underwear!'

'Oh, you shouldn't have said that,' said Holly Jo, with a disgusted sigh. 'Now he's thinking about it. What do you want?'

He filed away the mental image for future reference before becoming more professional. 'We need to get moving. One of Lau's guys at the casino said they're about to start taking buy-ins for the game.'

'Already?' said Bianca. 'I thought that wasn't until six o'clock.'

'I guess they can't wait to get their hands on the money. Anyway, we've got to get over there before all the places are taken. It's first come, first served.'

He backed out, giving Bianca another quick look before closing the door. 'That jerk,' Holly Jo muttered, pulling the zipper all the way up. 'Okay?'

'Yes.' Bianca fidgeted with the dress, then hurriedly put on her shoes. They may have been knock-offs of a designer brand, but they were still a much better fit than the pair she had worn for the Luminica presentation – God, only four days before. Her life had undergone a drastic change in a very short time, she realised as she caught her reflection in the mirror. Red dress, high heels, glam look . . . and about to throw away a quarter of a million dollars as part of a plot hatched by a team of international spies. 'This should be a movie,' she said quietly, hardly able to believe it.

'You look the part,' Holly Jo assured her. 'Ready?'

'Yes. I think. I hope!'

The two women went back into the suite's main room. Its occupants had been joined by Baxter and one of his men, the leader of the tactical team talking to Tony. 'When our truck gets within twenty feet of the cab, the transponder activates the rigs under the passenger seats and Zykov and his guys all get a needle in the ass. By the time they feel it, the truck will have hit the car. Five seconds after that, they're out . . .' Baxter trailed off as he realised that Tony's attention had wandered, and turned to see why. 'Damn,' he said as he saw Bianca.

'All right, guys, knock it off,' said Holly Jo. 'It's not as if you've never seen a woman before.'

'Not one as stunning as this,' said Adam, grinning broadly. He swaggered across the room to the pair. 'Not that there was anything wrong with the way you were before, but right now you look like a million dollars.'

'Only a quarter of a million,' Bianca reminded him. She stopped, teetering for a moment on her towering shoes. 'Oh! Bloody heels.'

'They look great,' Adam said, giving her legs an admiring look. 'But they'd also look good kicked off at the foot of a bed.'

She couldn't help blushing, the overbearing Vanwall persona so different from Adam's usual self. 'Well, er, they will be,' she managed to say. His smile took on a more lascivious curl. '*My* bed, after we're done tonight. And I go straight to sleep.'

The unctuous smirk faded, but didn't disappear. 'It's gonna be a long night. Who knows what'll happen?'

'What'll happen,' said Tony firmly, with more than a hint of disapproval, 'is that we complete the mission and get the hell out of here. Okay, the taxi is rigged. Adam, it's up to you to get Zykov out of the casino and into that cab. Make sure that he's mad enough to come after you to get his money back. We'll handle the rest. Bianca, Billy's got some equipment for you.'

From his use of the word 'equipment', she half expected to see a selection of guns and lasers laid out on the table for her, but instead found a pair of large gold earrings and two small plastic cases, similar to the kind used to hold memory cards. 'These aren't just to make me look pretty, I assume.'

'No, no, these are something special,' said Billy. He picked up one of the earrings, cradling it in his palm. 'There's a skittle camera inside it. It points forward, so it'll see more or less what you see. It'll set off the metal detector, but then it's a piece of metal, so they'd expect it to, right? There was enough room for an extra battery, so it should work for about six hours. Hopefully the game'll be done by then.'

'That'd be a long game,' Bianca agreed. 'What about Adam, though? Won't the metal detector pick up his earwig and the power pack and everything?'

Billy shook his head. 'They're mostly conductive polymers rather than metal. A lot harder to pick up. And speaking of earwigs, I've got one for you.' He put down the earring and tapped one of the plastic cases.

Bianca looked more closely. Inside was a silver sliver the size of a grain of rice. 'You're going to drop that in my ear?' she said with dismay.

'Oh, don't worry – I'll glue it in.'

That actually sounded worse, but she still sat – with considerable trepidation – so he could do the deed. 'What's in the other box?' she asked, as he delicately picked up the earwig with a pair of angled tweezers and dipped each end into a small drop of clear adhesive.

'It's a microtransmitter,' Billy said. 'Okay, stay very still . . .' She held her breath as he lowered the earwig into her right ear.

'So you can tell us if you think Zykov or any of the other players are bluffing without having to speak,' Tony elaborated. 'We'll glue it under your fingernail – a fake one, not your real one,' he quickly added. 'It doesn't do much, just sends a bleep if you apply pressure to it. But that'll be enough for you to give us a code. One bleep if they've got a genuine hand, two bleeps if they're bluffing. If you're not sure, don't send anything. Holly Jo will pass your signal on to Adam via *his* earwig.'

To Bianca's relief, Billy withdrew the tweezers. 'Okay, it's secure. Holly Jo, can you check that it's working?'

Holly Jo had already donned a headset and crossed the room to her laptop. 'Okay, Bianca, I'm sending . . . now. Testing, testing, can you hear me?'

The last was said in a whisper, but Bianca heard it – tinny, but perfectly clear – as if it were coming from inside her skull. She flinched. 'Oh! That was really, really weird.'

Another telepathic whisper. 'But you can hear me okay?'

'Yes. It's as if you're right next to me. Well, closer. You're literally a voice in my head.'

'Don't worry,' said Adam. 'You'll get used to it.' Tony nodded in agreement.

Billy took her left hand and placed the transmitter under the false nail of her little finger. 'Holly Jo? The bleeper's in place. Bianca, if you can just very lightly press your nail against the table . . .'

She did so. 'It's working,' Holly Jo called.

'Great,' said Tony. 'Okay, Bianca, we've got some extra jewellery so you look the full part, and then you and Adam need to get moving.'

'Don't worry,' said Adam as she stood. 'These guys'll be watching out for you the whole time. Just be cool, have a good time . . . and lose all your money.'

Enough of the real agent came through the sleepy, smarmy Vanwall persona to make her feel that she genuinely was in safe hands. 'Okay,' she said. 'And you just make sure that you win it all back.'

Vanwall returned. 'Oh, I will. Be sure of it.'

16

When the Chips Are Down

By the time she reached the casino, Bianca's unease had returned. Merely knowing that she was carrying a valise containing a quarter of a million dollars in cash had been stressful enough – had a random bag-snatcher picked her as a target, he would have found the risk more than worth it – but now she was being escorted by an obsequious casino employee to one of the Imperial's VIP rooms, carrying that amount in high-value poker chips. Her mission: lose it all, while helping another player cheat. She had seen enough Martin Scorsese films to assume that the casino would not take it lightly if they were discovered . . . to say nothing of how the other players would react.

They reached the metal detector, another casino worker standing beside it. He gestured for her to go through. As she had expected, an alarm went off, though it was more a quiet trill than a clamour of bells. The attendant ran a wand over her. The jewellery inevitably provoked another electronic warble, but he was unconcerned, seeming more suspicious that she might have some device concealed in her hair. When his check revealed nothing, he gave her body a more cursory examination – the dress was snug enough to make hiding anything under it a tricky proposition – before nodding to her guide and respectfully stepping back.

She set off again, rounding a corner to enter the VIP room itself.

The mission's target was already there.

She recognised Ruslan Zykov immediately from the surveillance photograph. What it hadn't revealed about the Russian was how short he was. Zykov was only about five foot five – and something about his stance, an imbalance she knew from her own high heels, suggested that he had resorted to lifts in his shoes to bring him up to that. If he was sensitive about his height, that went some way to explaining his temper.

Zykov had permanent frown lines creased into his forehead, despite presently smiling – with condescension – as he spoke to an Asian man. He also clearly worked out a lot, compensating for the vertical with the horizontal. His barrel chest and thick arms stood out even under his tuxedo.

Dangerous, she thought. She would have had the same instinctive opinion if she'd known nothing about him beforehand.

She took in the room. Softly lit, lavishly if tackily decorated. There was a bar at one end with tables from where the players' companions could watch the game. About a dozen people, expensively dressed men and women, were already there. Two of the men appeared to be drinking only water rather than anything alcoholic, and were watching Zykov closely. His bodyguards? According to Tony, he had arrived at the Imperial with four companions: all male, all large. This pair matched that description.

Dominating the room was the poker table, an elongated oval of green baize rimmed with darkly varnished hardwood. Nine chairs were arranged round it. One for the casino's dealer, the other for the players.

And she was one of them. The game was a regular event at the Imperial. There was no need for an invitation, or even a recommendation by an existing player. To buy in, all you needed was enough money. Tonight, that amount was two hundred and fifty thousand US dollars.

Eight players. Two million on the table. Zykov thought he was good enough to take it all.

Adam had to be better.

'Madam?' said her escort, directing her to the table.

Zykov caught the new arrival in his peripheral vision – then did a double-take to get a better look at her. His smile became genuine, if predatory. He said something dismissive to the other man, then turned to face Bianca. '*Dobryi vecher,*' he said, following it with, 'Good evening.'

'Good evening,' Bianca replied, giving him a bright smile.

'Ah! English, yes?'

'Yes, I am. And you are . . . Russian?'

'That is right, yes.' He eyed her stack of chips. 'So, you are playing against me tonight?'

'I am. I hope you won't clean me out *too* quickly!'

He laughed, then regarded her with a sly grin. 'Now, are you trying to give me a false sense of security by acting innocent?'

'Oh, no, no,' she said, remembering her own persona for the evening. 'I'm just here to have some fun.'

'It is an expensive way to have fun, hmm?'

'I can afford it.'

'Well, then I think we shall both have fun tonight!'

'I'm sure we will. By the way, my name is Bianca. And you are?'

'Ruslan,' he said proudly.

'Ruslan the Russian. That should be easy to remember!'

Another smile. 'You will not forget me any time soon.'

'I'm sure I won't.'

A voice in her ear, a whisper so as not to startle her. 'Bianca, it's Holly Jo. Adam's just gone through the metal detector.'

'Okay,' she automatically replied – before realising her mistake and hurriedly adding, 'So, where are you sitting?'

Zykov waved a hand at the stacked chips in one of the table's places. 'Here.'

'Do we pick our own seats, or—' She broke off as she saw Adam enter the room.

Even in a sharply pressed dinner jacket, there still seemed something vaguely crumpled and disreputable about him, Vanwall's languid arrogance soaking through like a thin sheen of oil. He was living his part; now she had to do the same with hers. 'Oh no,' she said, trying to sound disgusted.

'Do you know him?' Zykov asked.

'Yes. I'm afraid so.' She and Adam had devised a little act during the short journey to the casino. 'I've played him before, in London. He *beat* me.'

The Russian picked up on the subtext, as she had hoped. 'It does not sound like you think he did so fairly.'

Before she could say anything more, Adam spotted her and, with a big fake smile, strode over. 'Well, looky who it is! This is a surprise, Bianca.'

'Not a pleasant one,' she replied, voice icy.

'Aw, don't be a sore loser. Besides, a rich girl like you, it's just a drop in the bucket.' He nodded towards her chips. 'Looking forward to taking those from you tonight. Now, where are you sitting?'

'Why don't you pick a seat first, then I'll decide?'

He smirked, then pointed at the place facing Zykov's. 'That looks lucky.'

Bianca put her chips down beside the Russian's. 'This looks luckier.'

'Don't count on it. Have a good evening – for as long as it lasts.' He dropped his chips in messy piles at his seat, then headed for the bar.

Zykov watched him, eyes narrowed. 'You think he cheated you?'

'I'm absolutely positive. But I couldn't prove it.'

A glance towards the two muscular men. 'If he cheats tonight, he will regret it.' So they *were* his bodyguards. Two in here – which meant the other two were probably somewhere close by in the casino.

She smiled at him. 'I like the cut of your jib, Ruslan.'

It took him a moment to work out her meaning, but when he did, he was pleased. 'I think we are both going to have a good evening tonight.'

'It'll be interesting, I'm sure.' That was something she couldn't deny.

Two million dollars. And I'm going to take it all.

Adam's poker face matched Peter Vanwall's: a near-permanent hint of arch smugness, each card, good or bad, regarded with the same heavy-eyed smirk. It was a technique honed over many years by the Illinois card sharp, and it had served its user well. Stoic unreadability was one thing, but Vanwall had found early in his career that infuriating his opponents with nothing more than the curl of his lips was better. Pissed-off players made mistakes.

And Zykov was pissed off.

The Russian was trying to hide it, but his anger was rising with each lost hand. Bianca thought she had spotted telltale hints of when he was bluffing early on, silently relaying them to the team outside the casino with nothing more than gentle pressure on a fingernail. Holly Jo relayed her assessments back to Adam through his earwig, and it had only taken a few games for him to spot the pattern.

It wasn't so much a distinct tell – no nervous tics or beads of sweat here – as a shift in Zykov's entire demeanour. On a weak hand, he seemed to *shrink*, his squat, muscular frame drawing protectively inwards. It was very subtle, but once noticed it became impossible to miss.

Would he have picked up on it without Vanwall's persona in his mind? The gambler had taken on every kind of player imaginable in his long career, thousands of different faces blending together into twenty or so types. The raccoon, skulking at the edge of the action and only darting in with a big bet when it felt completely safe. The pigeon, pecking at everything on the table. The shark. The spider. The owl. Everyone was an animal.

Almost everyone. Bianca was the exception. The fact that she was deliberately playing to lose made her hard to assess. A cat, maybe, carefully stalking until the right moment? He wasn't sure.

But Zykov was definitely a bear, appropriately enough. He relied on sheer force of presence, slamming down big bets at the earliest opportunity in an attempt to scare off the competition. And if anyone dared to challenge him, they would frequently find that he was not bluffing.

Only now, Adam could tell when he was.

Most of the time. That remaining uncertainty made the game dangerous, even with help to tip the odds in his favour.

'Okay, Adam,' said Levon inside his ear, 'there's a twenty-four per cent chance that Zykov has a hearts flush. Be careful.'

He hadn't needed Levon's program to know that, based on the cards already played, but the precise odds helped him assess the risk. If Zykov's hole card was a heart, then the Russian had won this game. His own hand was three of a kind, sevens. He surveyed the table. Three players had already dropped out of the betting. Bianca also had a potential three of a kind, but only fours. The Indian, Nair, might have a straight, but with the weakness of his bets it was unlikely. Cau, the Chinese, possibly had two pair, but was also reluctant to keep up with the betting.

Zykov's bet. Was the hidden card a heart?

The Russian pondered his hand, then slowly slid a stack of chips away from his others. Ten thousand dollars. Calling the last bet . . .

And raising it. Another ten thousand in neatly ordered chips joined the first pile. 'Raise ten,' he said.

Nair threw in, as did Cau. Adam's turn. Was Zykov bluffing? *Yes.*

He was sure of it. The Russian had almost imperceptibly raised his defences.

Almost imperceptibly.

Bianca made the tiniest movement with her little finger, pressing the tip of her fingernail against the table. Twice. Two bleeps would have just come through Holly Jo's headset, passing on the Englishwoman's belief that Zykov was bluffing. In a moment Holly Jo would relay that to him through the earwig.

But he didn't need that help any more. He could now tame the bear for himself.

'Bianca thinks he's bluffing,' Holly Jo told him redundantly.

Adam looked back up at Zykov, allowing his smirk to fade slightly. Satisfaction in his opponent's eyes. Then it returned in full force. 'I think I'll see your ten,' he said, nudging chips into the pot, 'and raise you . . . twenty.' A flick of his forefinger, and another stack clinked across the baize.

The Russian's stony poker face cracked. His lips tightened, eyes narrowing in anger. Then he managed – with evident effort – to bring himself back under control.

Bianca's bet. In a normal game, Adam could tell that she would have dropped out. But she was playing to lose. 'Call,' she said with reluctance, thirty thousand of her own joining the pot.

Back to Zykov. 'Call,' he growled.

Showdown. Adam had been the last to raise, so went first. He turned over his hole card. Seven. Three of a kind. Bianca had the option to 'muck' her hand, simply giving up without turning over her hole card, but instead opted to give Levon's card-counting program more data. Jack of diamonds. One pair of fours, that was all.

Zykov's turn. The reveal of Bianca's card increased the probability that his hole card was a heart. Had Adam misjudged him? He watched, tension rising, as the arms dealer put his fingers on the last card . . .

And with a barely contained snarl of anger shoved it away, unturned, with the rest. Without a fifth heart, all he had was a king high. Worthless.

Adam grinned at him. 'Well now,' he said, sweeping the pot across the table to join the rest of his chips, 'looks like I just bought myself a new Porsche. Thanks, everyone.'

The other players glowered at him, while Zykov was positively seething. 'There is still a lot to play for,' he said through his teeth.

'There sure is.' Adam cracked his knuckles. 'Let's get on with it, shall we?'

Play continued. Before long, players started to drop out. Nair was first to leave, going all in with a bluff that he held a full house – but Adam already knew via Holly Jo that Bianca held one of the two cards he needed, the tiny camera in her earring having revealed her hole card to the team. His own hole card was the other. The Indian ended up with nothing but two pair, losing everything to Adam.

Another Chinese player, Hong, departed next, followed by a rotund South African called Lumbano. Five players remaining, then four as Cau finally threw in the towel. Bianca stayed, having the benefit of Levon's program herself, and trying to make sure that if she lost any large bets, they were to her secret partner.

Zykov; a taciturn Korean named Pak; Bianca; Adam. Adam already had over a million dollars in chips before him, more than half the total buy-in. Zykov had the next-largest reserve, arranged in neat towers as if trying to build a protective wall. Bianca's stacks were shrinking quickly, and Pak was almost out of money; on the next game he dropped out, having no choice but to go all in with three of a kind. Unluckily for him, Zykov had a straight, and that was the end of the Korean's night.

Adam and Bianca had both folded early on, recognising that Zykov was not bluffing about having a strong hand. 'Well, this is cosy, isn't it?' said Adam. 'Just the three of us. Of course, three's a crowd, so . . .' He waved a dismissive hand at Bianca's shrunken reserves. 'You might as well just slide that across to me right now, Bianca. Save some time.'

'The night isn't over yet,' she snapped back.

'Try to make it soon, though,' said Tony through the earwig. 'Everything's set up for the crash – John and his team are in position, and Lau's got the truck ready. Adam, step things up – it's time to get Zykov mad.'

Adam let his ever-present smile widen, looking directly at Zykov as the dealer shuffled the pack. 'You know, little buddy, I think this next round's going to be a good one. It's almost like I can see your cards.'

Zykov stiffened, then quietly spoke to the dealer. The current set of cards was removed from the table, replaced by a fresh pack – which on the Russian's suspicious glower was swapped for still another cellophane-wrapped deck. Adam smirked again. The seed planted by Bianca, that the American was somehow cheating, had just been given fresh water.

The game resumed. This time, it was clear from as early as the third street that Zykov had three of a kind, despite his best efforts to cloak his confidence. Bianca folded rather than risk losing any more money to him, while Adam stayed in until the showdown. He had been right, Zykov's three tens easily crushing his meagre pair of eights. 'You did not see my cards *that* time, did you?' the Russian gloated.

'I'm still ahead,' Adam replied. 'But if you're so confident, how about we make this next one more interesting? Double the ante, maybe?'

Zykov shrugged. Bianca was less happy. 'But that's ten thousand dollars to open,' she protested.

Now it was Adam's turn to shrug. 'Funny, what was it you called that much money the last time we played? "Chicken feed", wasn't it? Mind you, that was before I took it all from you.'

'All right,' she said, pouting, 'ten thousand it is.'

New cards were dealt. Thirty thousand dollars went straight into the pot on the ante, which Bianca raised by another ten thousand on her bet. 'Her hole card is the ten of clubs,' reported Holly Jo after Bianca had checked her hand. Her first face-up card was the jack of diamonds. There was potential for a straight, then, but it was more likely that the best she could hope for was two pair or three of a kind.

Adam's own hand was nothing notable; a king and a six, different suits. Nevertheless, he called Bianca's bet. So did Zykov, his visible card a nine. Still plenty to play for.

With fewer players, and therefore fewer face-up cards, Levon's program had far less data to work with. The game now became as much about reading the players as the table. Adam watched Zykov closely as the next cards were dealt. Good hand, or bad? It was hard to judge. The Russian now had a nine and an eight visible, but didn't seem either pleased or angered by his hand. If

180

his hole card were a ten or a seven, he had an outside chance at getting a straight.

Adam received another king. That beat Bianca's hand so far, but he gave nothing away on his face. Bianca had been dealt a second jack. She had the highest visible hand, so controlled the bet. 'All right,' she said, smiling. 'I bet . . . twenty-five.' She assembled a large stack of chips and thrust it into the pot.

She wanted the others to think she had three jacks. Adam pretended to mull over his next move, then: 'Raise ten.' He added his own bet. Zykov called, leaving Bianca with no choice but to do the same to stay in play. 'I don't think you've got anything there. Just a feeling.' He put a smug emphasis on that last.

Bianca frowned at him. 'We'll see.'

Fourth street. Bianca was dealt the two of spades; Adam the eight of clubs; Zykov the three of diamonds. Bianca still had the best visible hand and bet another twenty-five. Adam again raised by ten. Zykov, with veiled reluctance, called. He probably only had one pair at best. Bianca hesitated, then: 'I raise twenty.'

'Well now, things are warming up, aren't they?' Adam drawled. He tapped a chip on the top of one of his ragged stacks, then looked across the table at her reserves. Her remaining chips had dwindled to a meagre handful. 'Okay, I'll call . . . and raise *fifty*.'

Zykov raised his eyebrows, but called the bet, apparently keen to see how things would play out. Bianca, meanwhile, visibly blanched. Playing to lose didn't make the actual *act* of losing any easier to swallow. 'All right,' she said after a moment. 'All right. I go . . . all in.' She shoved all her chips to the centre of the table.

She was still playing her bluff of three jacks. Under normal circumstances, Vanwall would have become more cautious: there was a chance she was not bluffing.

But Adam knew she was. 'Okay,' he said, with a laconic smile. 'Let's see how this plays out.'

Fifth street: the last card. Bianca's was the four of clubs. Adam got the five of diamonds. Two kings beat two jacks; he had won. Part of him felt an immense surge of cruel pleasure. *Crushed the bitch! That'll teach her not to put out.*

He pushed the feeling down, both because he didn't want to give anything away, and out of distaste for his own – no, Vanwall's – thoughts. Instead, he waited for Zykov to be dealt his final card. Four of hearts. One pair at most, and the minuscule sag of the Russian's shoulders confirmed it.

Since Bianca had gone all in, Adam now had the bet. 'Well, looks like you might have three of a kind there,' he said to Bianca. Her only answer was a sly smile. 'But you know what? I don't think you do. Another fifty.'

Zykov mucked his cards. 'Fold,' he growled.

There was nothing else Bianca could do but go to the showdown. Adam turned over his hole card. 'One pair, kings,' he announced. He broadened his smirk to the widest, most arrogant extent it could go. 'So, let's see that trey.'

Breathing heavily, she slapped her hands down on the table. 'You bloody cheat,' she said. 'You bloody *cheat!*'

'Oh, now don't be a sore loser, Bianca,' he said as he raked in his winnings.

'No, no, you cheated!' she cried, jumping to her feet. 'There's no possible way you could have thought you were going to win, unless you already knew what my first card was. You *must* have cheated!'

'Hey, now settle down, little lady,' Adam said in the most patronising tone he could muster. 'You'd better not throw accusations like that around unless you're prepared to back them up.'

'I *am* accusing you of cheating! You did it in London, and now you've done it again. You've got something on you – a computer, or an earpiece or something.' She turned to the dealer. 'He's cheating, I know it! Can't you search him?'

The dealer looked most unhappy at the prospect, but Adam simply held out his arms in a broad shrug. 'I've got nothing to hide. If she wants to make a fool of herself, that's fine by me.'

Zykov regarded Adam with a calculating expression. 'Somehow, I do not think they will find anything, but . . . if he is willing, I can wait.'

The dealer reluctantly spoke to another member of the casino staff, who trotted out of the room, returning soon afterwards with the man who had been running the metal detector. The wand was in his hand. Still smirking, Adam stood and allowed the device to be run over his body. It trilled several times, but each time Adam removed the cause – his watch, a phone, a set of keys – and the second pass was negative. The wand finally came down to Adam's waist, warbling as it hovered over his belt buckle. 'Now, I've been hoping all evening that you'd ask me to take off my pants,' he said to Bianca with a lecherous grin.

'There is nothing else on him, madam,' said the dealer. 'I think it would be best if you were to leave now. Quietly.'

'All right, I'm going,' she snapped. The attendant raised a hand as if about to take her by the arm, but she jerked away. 'You *are* cheating, I know you are,' she told Adam as she walked out.

Making sure that Zykov could see, Adam silently mouthed a reply: *you'll never know how*. The intense stare he found locked on to him when he looked back at his sole remaining opponent told him that the Russian had some ability to lip-read.

Insouciant smirk returning, he sat back down. 'Okay, my little comrade,' he said to the affronted Zykov. 'Let's play some *real* cards.'

17

All In

Bianca emerged into the slot-machine clamour of the main casino, feeling exhilarated . . . but also exhausted. Even though losing all her money was part of the plan, she had felt outraged at seeing her last chips swept away – and the smugness of Adam's persona as he took them provoked a spark of actual anger.

Now, though, her part in the little play was done. 'Okay, Holly Jo?' she whispered. 'I'm out of the room. What do I do now?'

'Tony's coming to meet you,' came the reply.

She spotted him approaching. 'Well?' she said when Tony reached her. 'What did you think of my performance?'

'For someone who didn't even want to do it, you certainly threw yourself into the part,' he replied.

'I was in the drama club at university. We did *The Tempest* – I was Miranda.' She adopted an exaggeratedly thespian voice. 'I suppose the call of the craft never leaves you, dahling.'

'You did a great job,' Tony told her, grinning. 'Once Adam cleans out Zykov, I'm sure we'll hook him. I was watching him through your earring camera – he was getting pretty furious when he lost some of those games.'

'I can't say I'm surprised. Adam was making *me* mad. So what now?'

'Adam knows he's in the endgame now, so I don't think this'll take much longer. Once he leaves, if Zykov goes after him the van'll pick us up so we can follow him. All the PERSONA gear is loaded and ready for you.'

'*If* Zykov follows him.' That was still the wild card. She looked back towards the VIP room, wondering what was happening within.

Adam looked at the chips on the table. He had around two thirds of the total: over one point three million dollars. That put Zykov at a disadvantage, but not a crippling one. With strategic betting, the Russian could draw the contest out for some time.

More to the point, he could still win it. With Bianca gone, not only did that deprive Adam of his clandestine partner, but also the tiny camera in her earring. No more computerised help with the odds.

It was all up to him. He had to rely on Vanwall's poker skills . . . and his own ability to read Zykov's bluffs.

'So, little buddy,' he said. 'You want to step this up?'

Zykov regarded him coldly. 'What do you mean?'

'How about we raise the ante to, say . . . fifty thousand? Speed things up. I want to be out celebrating taking all your money before all the hottest girls are gone!'

'You will have nothing to celebrate tonight.' The arms dealer's glance towards his bodyguards made it clear that would be the case whether Adam won or lost.

Adam gave him a toothy grin. 'We'll see about that. So, fifty thousand?'

'Fifty thousand.'

Both men pushed their chips into the pot. The dealer put

down the first cards. Adam's face-up card was the ace of diamonds, Zykov's the king of clubs. The house rule was that aces were high, so Adam had the opening bet. He checked his hole card. Queen of spades. Potential for a straight, but it was unlikely. Only one game had been won with a hand that high – and it had been Zykov's.

What was the Russian's hole card? Adam watched Zykov closely as he thumbed back one corner of his own hidden card. No visible reaction. That meant nothing at this early stage of the game.

The dealer waited for him to bet. 'Okay, then,' said Adam, 'let's make this fun. Fifty thousand.'

Zykov glowered, but matched the bet. *He knows I'm trying to bleed him dry.* Adam's larger pool of chips gave him the advantage. Even if the Russian folded on the first two cards, he would still be fifty thousand dollars down because of the increased ante. And if he played on, Adam could raise the bets to a point that would force him to go all in. If he lost then, he lost everything.

If he lost. If Zykov won, his position would be strengthened. He might even regain the advantage.

Can't let that happen.

Next card. Four of hearts. Worthless. Zykov got the king of diamonds. *Crap.* That gave him one pair . . . or possibly three of a kind? The Russian seemed confident.

Zykov's bet. He gave Adam an unpleasant smile. 'Sixty thousand.'

A single pair was a weak hand, but at the moment it was all Zykov needed to win. *Fold, or play on?* The best Adam could hope for was three of a kind – which his opponent might already have.

Was Zykov bluffing? He was definitely tense, but with over a hundred thousand dollars already on the table, that was hardly surprising. Adam searched Vanwall's memories for advice. Names and faces and hands of cards flashed through his mind: times when the gambler had tried to force an adversary to go all in. It was a risky strategy. Sensible players would fold and keep some chips in reserve rather than potentially lose everything . . . unless they were sure they had a winning hand.

But nobody playing for these stakes was exactly sensible. *Risk big. Win big.*

'Sixty . . . and raise you sixty.'

Zykov stared at Adam as he shoved the chips to join the crowd already at the table's centre. Both men were now doing the same thing, trying to spot a bluff. Seeing who would crack first.

'Call.'

If Zykov was bluffing, he was doing a better job of concealing it than before. But nor did he seem as openly confident as he had on previous strong hands. The rising stakes had focused his mind, forcing him to suppress his emotions.

Those emotions would explode back out if he lost, Adam was sure. That would make him easier to lure into the trap outside.

But first, he had to be beaten. And even with all Vanwall's experience, the American still didn't know if that was going to happen.

Cards. The four of spades joined Adam's hand. One pair, at least – but it was still lower than Zykov's two kings. Nevertheless, he faked a small nod of approval. If he could convince Zykov that his hole card was an ace, he might still be able to bluff him into folding.

Three of hearts for the Russian. A small smile appeared on his lips. 'One hundred thousand dollars.' Several imposing stacks of chips slid across the table.

Not many spectators remained in the bar area, most having left when the players they were accompanying had been eliminated, but the size of the bet still provoked sounds of surprise and awe. If Adam called the bet, there would be over six hundred thousand dollars on the table. If he folded, he had just lost two hundred and twenty thousand dollars and put both players back on more or less level pegging.

And he still wasn't sure if Zykov was bluffing. The Russian obviously wanted him to think he had three kings. But even if he didn't, his two kings would still beat the pair of fours.

Adam regarded Zykov for a long moment. He appeared confident – but since he held the best hand based on the visible cards, that wasn't surprising. Third king or not, right now he would still win a showdown.

Was he bluffing?

There had to be a giveaway, a tell. The Russian had been unable to conceal his feelings, positive or negative, earlier in the evening. There was no way he could have suddenly locked himself down now, not with so much at stake. He was smiling, but that meant nothing. Look *past* the smile, see what was behind it. True confidence, or just bravado?

The two men's eyes were locked. Both trying to judge the other. A mental duel, seeing who would flinch first . . .

Just for a moment, Zykov's eyes revealed . . . *concern.*

The Russian quickly covered it up by speaking. 'Well? Are you going to bet?'

Adam said nothing. He didn't know what had caused the tiny flicker of worry, but something about it, an almost indefinable shift in the short man's . . . *aura*, was the word Vanwall rather surprisingly chose, convinced him that it was involuntary. Genuine.

He was bluffing.

Make him angry. Attack.

Adam leaned forward, a maddening smirk growing. 'You know, little comrade?' Zykov frowned at the insult. 'I don't believe you've got a third king there.' He pointed at the other man's hole card. 'And I'm so confident of that, I'm willing to bet everything I have on it. All in.' To audible gasps from the bar, he shoved all his remaining chips into the pot.

Without the video feed from Bianca's camera the other team members had been quiet, but the gamble drew a reaction even blind. 'Uh, Adam,' said Holly Jo. 'I really, *really* hope you've got a winning hand.'

So do I. He waited for Zykov's reaction. If the Russian believed his bluff, he would have no choice but to fold and take a hit of three hundred and twenty thousand dollars – half his remaining chips. That would make him extremely vulnerable to another round of high betting in the next game . . .

There was not going to be a next game.

'All in,' said the Russian. He pushed all his precisely stacked chips into the centre. They toppled, cascading down across the rest of the pot.

Two million dollars. All hanging on the final cards.

Adam battled to hide his tension. If he was wrong, if Zykov really did have a third king, there was no possible way he could beat it. The best hand he could get was three of a kind, fours – which would not beat three kings. Even if Zykov was bluffing, he would need a four, a queen or an ace to beat the two kings. The odds of that were now less than one chance in five. And that was without even considering Zykov's last card, which might be a second three, or match his hole card . . .

I'm a gambler. So gamble.

He grinned at the dealer, affecting nonchalance. 'Okay, then. Deal.'

Risk big, win big . . .

The dealer turned over Adam's last card.

The queen of diamonds.

Ho-lee shit! Vanwall cried inside him. The gamble had paid off. Two pair, queens and fours. He still had a chance.

If he had been right about Zykov's bluff.

The final card. Adam held his breath. The dealer turned it over.

Nine of diamonds.

He looked up from the card at Zykov. The Russian was, for once, completely stone-faced. Adam didn't know if he had won or not.

Showdown.

Technically Zykov should have turned over his hole card first, but at this stage of the game it no longer mattered. Adam flipped his to reveal the queen of spades. 'Two pair. Let's see what you got.'

Even without a third king, Zykov could still win. If he had a three or a nine, his two pair – kings high – would beat Adam's queens. The Russian reached for his hole card . . .

Even before he touched it, Adam knew he had won. Zykov's hand shook. Not with nerves, or dismay at losing. With *fury*. The volcanic temper he had been fighting to hold inside all evening was about to erupt.

He slapped the card down. The six of spades.

Useless. *'Mudilo!'*

Twist the knife. Make him mad.

Adam began to laugh, slowly and mockingly. 'Two. Million. Dollars,' he said, beaming at Zykov. 'Thank you very much, little comrade.'

The Russian seethed like a pressure cooker. 'If you call me that again . . .'

'Oh, don't you be another bad loser like Bianca! Just face it, I beat you.' He let the smugness return. 'And you'll never know how.'

Zykov reacted as if stung. 'I will find out,' he said in a low, threatening voice.

'No. You won't.' Still smirking, Adam turned to the dealer. 'Can you swap me those for something bigger?' he asked, gesturing at his winnings. 'I don't want to drop any.'

The dealer raked in the loose chips, in return sliding him two larger plaques worth one million dollars each. 'Thank you so much,' said Adam. He clacked the plaques together. 'Hey, my friend, do you hear that? That's the sound of *money*. Your money – or, whoops, it was. Now it's *aaaall* mine.'

'Spend it fast,' said Zykov, standing. 'You never know when your luck will run out. It could be very, very soon.'

'Not tonight, comrade. Not tonight.' Adam got up, noticing in his peripheral vision that one of Zykov's bodyguards was talking on his phone. To the other two goons, most likely – he was summoning the troops.

Time to get moving.

Adam left the VIP room and entered the main casino floor. He spotted Tony and Bianca not far away, but didn't acknowledge them. Instead, he pretended to get his bearings, glimpsing Zykov and the two bodyguards steaming out of the room behind him, then slipped the plaques into his jacket and headed for the exit.

'There goes Adam,' said Bianca. Holly Jo had already told her he had won. She stood, about to follow him.

'Not yet,' said Tony sharply. He was several feet away, idly feeding coins into a slot machine. 'Wait until Zykov's gone.'

The Russian and his bodyguards emerged from the VIP area. Another two hulks joined them. 'There are more of them! What if they catch Adam?'

'They won't.'

The group started after the American. Zykov, inside the

human cordon, was barely visible behind his much larger companions. His gaze was fixed on the man disappearing with two million dollars . . .

Then something made him look to one side. His eyes met Bianca's. He stopped.

'Oh God,' she whispered.

Tony gave her a sidelong glance. 'What?'

'Zykov's seen me! What do I do?'

'Stay calm. Do nothing.'

The Russian briefly spoke to his men, then changed direction. 'He's coming this way!'

Tony pretended to fumble money from a pocket, turning slightly to see Zykov and two of his bodyguards approaching. The others were back on Adam's tail. 'Ignore me, you don't know me. Just stay in character. Holly Jo, patch Bianca's earwig through to me so I can hear them.' He walked away.

'Ah, Bianca!' said Zykov as he reached her, now all smiles and pushy charm. 'What are you doing here?'

'I was . . . sulking,' Bianca improvised. He didn't seem to fully understand, so she elaborated: 'I was in a bad mood about losing, so I wanted to cool off before I did something stupid. And then,' she added truthfully, 'I realised my feet hurt, so I had to sit down.' She waggled a high heel.

'Louboutins,' said Zykov approvingly. 'Very nice, but I can see they would hurt after a time!'

'So is the game over?'

He frowned. 'Yes, the game is over.'

'Ah. I take it you ended up in the same boat as me.'

'I did, yes.' He fired an angry look after Adam. 'He did the same to me that he did to you.'

'He cheated?'

'Somehow, yes. I am sure of it.'

'I knew it! But you still don't know how he did it?'

'No. But I will. He picked the wrong man to cheat. But enough about him!' His face brightened again. 'Would you join me for a drink? We can both drown our sorrows, as you say.'

She was about to give him a polite refusal when Tony's voice sounded in her ear, making her flinch in surprise. She covered it by scratching her neck. 'Go with him,' said the American. 'If he's not following Adam, we need a new plan. Keep him occupied for as long as you can.'

'Well, I was rather thinking of calling it a night,' she told Zykov. 'Losing a quarter of a million dollars to a cheat does rather dampen one's enthusiasm! But . . . I think I could be persuaded to have one drink.'

He grinned. 'Good! Although I should warn you – as a Russian, I never stop at just one.'

'I *could* go as far as two, I suppose . . . All right, why not? Where shall we go? The bar?'

His chest swelled with braggadocio. 'My penthouse suite, of course!'

Bianca pretended to be impressed, despite becoming more nervous by the moment. 'You have a penthouse? Somebody told me this place has fifty floors – you must have a terrific view.'

'It is very nice, yes.' He was looking directly at her chest. 'I have champagne, caviar, everything we need for a good time. Come, this way.'

It was all but a command. Behind Zykov and his men she glimpsed Tony, a phone to his head. 'Go with him,' he said through the earwig. 'We'll watch out for you, and get Adam up there as soon as we can.'

'Okay,' she said, replying to both men. She smiled at Zykov, hiding her worry. 'Lead on.'

18

High Society

Adam emerged from the casino into the humid Macau night. Taxis and minibuses were collecting and disgorging tourists and gamblers. 'What's the situation?'

'Not great,' said Holly Jo. 'Bianca's going with Zykov and two of his guys. The other two—'

'They're following you,' Tony cut in. 'I'm behind them. Pick me up in the van.'

Adam headed along the sidewalk, away from the scrum outside the casino's entrance. 'Where's the cab?'

'Coming your way,' said Kyle. 'The UAV's airborne – I see you. The cab'll be with you in thirty seconds.'

Adam didn't make any attempt to look for the drone; in the dark, it would be invisible. Instead he glanced back, seeing the two bodyguards. Tony came through a revolving door behind them. With so many people and surveillance cameras nearby, it was unlikely that Zykov's goons would take any action against him here. Instead, they would follow him to somewhere more suited for a mugging. That had been the plan all along, but now the details would have to change.

'Is the rigged cab still in play?' he asked.

'Yes,' said Holly Jo. 'It's coming in behind the first one.'

'Good. Have it ready to pick up my tails.'

'You still want to knock them out?'

'Only if we have to. I'll try to lose them another way.' He saw two taxis approaching. While they had the same black bodywork and cream roof as many of the other cabs around the casino, the lead one had two bright blue LEDs shining from its radiator grille. The customisation was minor enough not to draw attention, but it told him at a glance that he had the right car.

'The guys behind you are getting closer,' Kyle warned.

Adam raised his arm to flag down the taxi. It pulled over. He opened the door and quickly got inside. 'Go,' he ordered. The driver set off before the door was fully closed. The two bodyguards broke into a run to catch up, but were too late. Adam pretended not to have noticed them. He moved across the rear seat and glanced in the mirror, seeing one of the men step out into the road to stop the next cab.

The rigged taxi. It would only take one command for the pair to be knocked out . . . but without Zykov there was no point. In fact, it would only make the arms dealer suspicious.

'Change of plan, Fa,' he told the driver. 'I need you to take the guys following me on a long tour of the islands. But I've got to get back to the casino.'

Fa checked his mirror. The second cab had set off after them. 'We're not far enough ahead for you to get out without being seen.'

'I won't need you to stop.' Adam looked at the street ahead. With Cotai being newly developed, it was laid out in large blocks to accommodate the giant casinos and hotels. Finding somewhere to exit the cab unseen might be easier said than done. And the longer it took him to shake off his pursuers, the more danger Bianca was in. Zykov had undoubtedly invited her to his penthouse with more in mind than sharing a commiserative drink. 'Holly Jo?'

'Yes?'

'Tell the other driver to fall back. I need room to manoeuvre.'

'Okay. And Adam, Bianca's just gone into Zykov's suite. You need to get back to the casino.'

Vanwall's sarcasm permeated his voice. 'There's no place I'd rather be.'

There were any number of places Bianca would rather have been than the penthouse of an explosively tempered arms dealer with a history of violence. But she kept that to herself, instead deciding to appear impressed as Zykov led her past the concierge at a desk facing the private elevator and into the suite itself.

As it turned out, she didn't need to fake it. The lounge was expansive and opulent; a bit overdone and showy for her tastes, though far more restrained than the VIP room in the casino. But it was the view that caught her attention. One entire wall was glass, opening on to a balcony that overlooked the former colony. The islands were ablaze with light, shining against the backdrop of the dark sea.

'That's an amazing view,' she said, genuinely awed by the sight.

Zykov spoke in Russian to one of his bodyguards, who nodded and headed for another room, then opened the door to the balcony. 'Take a better look.'

A brief pang of fear struck her – what if Zykov had realised she was working with Adam, and intended to throw her off the roof? But there was no overt menace in his attitude, and whatever services the concierge provided for penthouse clientele, she doubted that they stretched to covering up murders.

Still, she followed him outside with apprehension. 'What do

you think of it now?' Zykov asked, sweeping an arm across the vista as if it belonged to him.

Without the reflections on the glass, it was even more stunning, a pulsating jewel box of neon. 'I can see why you paid extra for a balcony,' she said. A moment of vertigo caught her as she looked over the edge. 'Ooh. That's a *long* way down.'

'I am good with heights,' said Zykov, unconcerned. 'I was a paratrooper.'

'Really? How . . . fascinating.'

'I have many stories. I will tell you some – the ones suitable for a woman to hear, anyway!' He laughed. 'But first, a drink.' The bodyguard came on to the balcony, bearing two glasses and a silver ice bucket containing a bottle of champagne. The other man, Bianca noticed, had left the lounge – but she doubted he had gone far, ready to respond to the whims of his boss.

Zykov took the glasses as the bodyguard uncorked the bottle. The *pop!* made Bianca flinch; the anticipation of sudden noises put her on edge at the best of times, and this sounded uncomfortably like a gunshot. The Russian filled the glasses, then handed one to her. 'Here.'

'Thank you,' she said. 'Although I'm not sure if being cheated out of a quarter of a million dollars is really something we should be celebrating.'

'Then we shall celebrate something else. The future, perhaps?'

'That sounds good to me.' They clinked their glasses. 'To the future.'

'The future!' Zykov echoed, draining his champagne in a single swig. He eyed her. 'I think it will be good. For both of us.'

'I'm sure it will be,' she replied, concealing her growing nervousness.

Adam looked over his shoulder. The second cab was about a

hundred yards behind. It had fallen further back for a while, but the bodyguards had obviously demanded that their driver pick up the pace.

Fa's taxi approached an intersection. On the right, a half-built casino rose skeletally into the night sky, tall barriers cutting the construction site off from the sidewalk. There were very few people about; the area was still under development. 'Go right here,' Adam ordered, sliding over to that side. 'Keep going once you're round the corner – don't slow down. Get them to follow you for as long as you can.'

The driver made the turn. Adam half pulled the door handle until he felt the latch release, then held it in place. As the other cab slowed to follow, it was briefly blocked from sight by the barriers on the corner—

He pulled the lever and dived out of the car.

Even with his arms crossed tightly across his chest and his head bowed to shield it as much as possible, Adam still hit the pavement hard. Pain flared in his left shoulder. He rolled, tumbling diagonally across the sidewalk and hitting the wooden barrier with a bang.

He flattened himself along the foot of the fence, burying his face in his arms. Fa's cab pulled away, and he heard the second taxi take the corner. He had to hope that the bodyguards' attention was on the vehicle ahead and not the shadows at the roadside . . .

It drove past. Adam lifted his head. His pursuers' cab was following the first. No brake lights, no sudden turns. They hadn't seen him.

Wincing at the ache in his shoulder, he stood. 'Holly Jo, I'm out. Where's the van?'

'Almost there,' she replied. 'We'll pick you up at the corner.'

Checking again that the second cab was still heading away from him, he trotted back down the street to the intersection, seeing an anonymous white van approach. It pulled over, and he hurried to the back. The rear door opened. 'You okay?' Tony asked as he helped Adam inside.

'Yeah.' The back of the van had been turned into a mobile operations centre, albeit a very cramped one. Kyle and Holly Jo sat in staggered positions, the various components of their portable workstations secured to racks on the cabin walls. Tony had a similar arrangement for his own system. 'What about Bianca?'

'She's fine, so far,' Holly Jo reported.

'Good. Kyle, where's the drone?'

Kyle indicated one of his monitors. It showed an aerial view of the intersection, the van stationary at the roadside. 'Right overhead.'

'Get it back to the casino. We need eyes on Zykov's penthouse.'

'On it.' The intersection swept off the screen as the UAV turned and ascended.

The van set off. 'How are you going to get in there?' Holly Jo asked.

Adam gave her one of Vanwall's sardonic smiles. 'That's a good question.'

Tony spoke into his headset. 'Levon, we need those hotel floor plans. The routes we considered to reach the penthouse – bring them back up.'

Levon's voice came through the comm system. 'You do remember that all those routes looked incredibly dangerous, right?'

'It'd crossed my mind,' said Adam.

'Juuuust checking.'

Adam regarded the cases containing the PERSONA equipment. 'There's no way I'll be able to get across the roof carrying those. I need a backpack – something that leaves my hands free.'

Holly Jo peered under her console. 'There's a laptop bag here that should be big enough. It's only got a shoulder strap, though.'

'Nothing better?' Tony asked, getting head shakes in response. 'Okay, it'll have to do. Pass it down.'

Adam opened the cases. It was not so much the dimensions of the PERSONA device and its recorder unit that would be a problem as their weight – and fragility. The large, solid cases had plenty of high-impact foam padding inside them. A laptop bag, however big, would have almost nothing. 'It'd make things easier if I didn't take the recorder.'

'Martin's orders,' said Tony. 'We need a backup of Zykov's persona in case anything goes wrong.'

'That would mean imprinting it into Adam twice,' Holly Jo objected.

Adam chuckled sarcastically. 'If anything goes wrong fifty floors up, the only thing I'll be imprinting will be the sidewalk.' He took the bag from Tony and opened it. It was big enough to hold both parts of the PERSONA system . . . just. The smaller medical case was another matter. 'Kyle, that strap holding your laptop in place. Toss it over.'

Kyle unhooked the black nylon band and threw it down the cabin. 'Hope we don't hit any bumps, brah,' he said, awkwardly wedging the laptop in position with his knees.

Adam looped the strap through the medical case's handle and secured it with a tight knot. He slung it over his shoulder to check the length. 'Not very stylish,' said Holly Jo.

'It'll have to do. How long till we reach the casino?'

Tony checked a screen displaying a map of Macau. 'Three minutes.'

'Okay. What's Bianca doing?'

★ ★ ★

Despite the night's warmth, the blustery wind fifty storeys up had forced Bianca and Zykov back inside the penthouse. 'Sit, sit,' said the Russian, gesturing at a plush sofa. She did so, only to be taken aback as he plopped down right beside her, one arm along the back of the sofa behind her.

It took every ounce of willpower to prevent her sudden rabbit-in-headlights feeling from showing. Instead, she took a sip of champagne, switching her glass to the hand closest to him so her arm would act as a subtle psychological barrier. 'Mmm, this is lovely,' she said, holding the elegant flute up to the light. 'What label is it?'

Zykov shrugged. 'French. I don't know. But yes, it is nice.' His hand dropped down to touch her shoulder.

'So, ah,' she said hurriedly, 'you were a paratrooper, then? That sounds very exciting. You know, I'm genuinely interested in what it must be like to be a soldier. My father was one, so I suppose that accounts for my fascination!' He was actually a teacher, and would be horrified at the prospect, but she offered him a brief mental apology before pressing on. 'I've heard that Russian military training is very tough. Is that true?'

Zykov seemed torn between annoyance at the conversational diversion and flattered by her interest. He finally smiled, accepting the latter – for now. 'It is, yes. We are tough in Russia – toughest in the world. We have to be, it is a very tough country! We hear stories about what hard men the British and the Americans are with their SAS and their Delta Force. Ha! Even an ordinary private in the Russian army is stronger!'

'Bianca,' Holly Jo said quietly through the almost forgotten earwig while Zykov spoke. 'Adam is coming into the casino now. Keep Zykov occupied for as long as you can.'

'You're doing great,' Tony added. 'Oh, and what he just said about Delta? Totally not true.'

Bianca smiled at his remark, realising too late that the Russian had taken it as directed at him. 'I will show you how strong I am, if you like,' he said, leering.

She felt panic rising, again struggling to keep her true feelings hidden. 'I'm sure you're very strong,' she said. 'You look as if you work out a lot.'

Zykov's conflict between lust and ego was harder-fought this time, but again came out in favour of the latter – just. 'Yes,' he said, his wandering hand now taking a firmer hold on her shoulder, 'I do. I lift weights, I run . . .'

'I think Bianca *really* wants you to get up there as fast as you can,' Holly Jo told Adam as he approached the elevators. The laptop bag, stuffed to bursting point with the PERSONA hardware, thumped against his hip with every step, and the makeshift strap on the medical case was uncomfortably short. His discomfort was made worse by the numerous items now inside his jacket.

'Is she in trouble?' he replied, pretending to talk into his phone.

'Not yet, but Zykov's making moves on her. And I don't think he'll take no for an answer much longer.'

'I'm at the elevators now.' To one side, two lifts stood apart from the others, a uniformed Imperial employee standing in attendance – or rather, on guard. Access to the private elevators to the fiftieth floor was strictly controlled.

That wasn't where he was going – yet. He waited for a regular elevator to arrive, then entered, pushing the button for the forty-ninth floor. 'Levon, what have you got?'

'I found you a way up to the roof,' came the reply from STS. 'The central section of the penthouse level is mostly machinery – air-con, elevator winches, things like that. There's a maintenance access on forty-nine that leads up there, and from there you can reach a service area with a hatch to the roof.'

The elevator began its ascent. 'How far to Zykov's penthouse?'

'Well, that's the thing.' Levon sounded less than happy. 'You know that sign on the roof that says "Imperial" in big neon letters?'

'Yes?'

'And you know how that's in the *middle* of the roof, and the penthouses are on the *corners*?'

'Levon . . .'

'The hatch opens right behind the centre of the sign, okay?' Levon explained. 'You've got to go halfway along the top of the damn building. And when you get to the penthouse, you've still got to climb down from the overhang. It's nearly twenty feet to the balcony – and over *eight hundred* straight down!'

Tony was marginally more reassuring. 'Kyle's got the UAV in position. It looks like there's a beam on the underside of the roof you'll be able to use.'

'Looks like?' said Adam dubiously.

'The plans say it's a structural support. Let's hope they didn't change anything.'

'Yeah, let's hope!' The elevator continued to climb. 'Okay, I'm almost there. Which way to this maintenance room?'

'Turn left,' Holly Jo told him as the ascent slowed, then stopped. Adam stepped out. The corridor was a creamy white with a deep scarlet carpet, woven with the repeating pattern of a Chinese dragon. A security camera was mounted high on the wall directly opposite the elevator doors. He went left. 'Take the next corner,' she said as he approached a junction. Another camera watched the intersection. He rounded the turn. 'Okay, the door is just on your left.'

He gave it a quick glance as he passed. A sign saying 'No Entry' in several languages; a keycard lock. He had a computerised keycard in his pocket that could hack it, but it would take at least twenty seconds to find the right code, during which time he would be in full view of the security camera. He kept walking. 'Levon, can you do anything about the cameras?'

'From DC?' came the distinctly sarcastic reply. 'They're on a local system – you know, a *closed circuit*? They're not hooked up to the Internet, man.'

'No need to twist your panties, I was just asking.' At the corridor's far end was another camera – but, he realised, its offset position relative to the one behind him meant there was a blind spot in the security coverage. Only small, a narrow triangle against one wall . . .

It was enough.

A fire extinguisher was clipped to the wall. He yanked it free as he passed and pulled out the safety tab before squeezing the handle to set it off. Water gushed out. He sprayed the wall and carpet for several strides, then dropped the canister just before the end of the blind spot. 'Holly Jo, can you patch my phone through to the front desk?'

'Sure I can, but why—'

'Put me through.' He tapped her number into his phone and waited. Seconds passed, subtle changes in the background hiss telling him that the call was being rerouted – then it rang.

A brief wait, then: 'Imperial Casino and Hotel, how may I help you?'

'Uh, hi,' said Adam, exaggerating Vanwall's accent to make himself sound like a clueless tourist, 'I'm staying here, I'm on the forty-ninth floor? Uh, someone's set off a fire extinguisher. There's water everywhere, it's a real mess.'

'Can you tell me the number of the nearest room, please?'

He had memorised it with a quick glance. 'Yeah, sure. It's outside room forty-nine fifteen.'

'Thank you, sir. We'll send someone to clean it up right away. We're sorry for any inconvenience.'

'No problem. Bye.' He disconnected. 'Okay, let's see how quick their maids are.'

He stopped near the end of the corridor, pretending to be involved in a phone conversation for the benefit of the camera. It didn't take long before someone arrived to assess the problem. It wasn't a maid, but a man in grey overalls. He rounded the far end of the hallway, shook his head in disapproval on seeing the fallen extinguisher, then plodded over to pick it up.

Adam started towards him. The maintenance worker's keycard was hanging from a reel on his tool belt. Keeping the card on a short, self-retracting cord was supposed to make it impossible to lose or steal, but there were ways around the latter. He put a hand in one pocket, feeling cold metal.

The man lifted the extinguisher and turned to return it to its place. Adam walked up behind him and with a swift, precise motion swept his hand at his belt. A moment's hard pressure on the multitool's clippers and *snick*, the cord was cut, the flat sound covered by an 'Excuse me.' He caught the card before it had time to fall more than an inch and strode past without looking back. If the man had realised what had happened, a shout would come at any moment . . .

The only sound that reached him was the clunk of the extinguisher being pushed back into its clips. Adam approached the door to the maintenance room, the card ready. *Now* he glanced back. The man was still occupied with his task.

Adam angled towards the door, sliding the card into the slot with a marksman's precision. Green light and a clack from the lock. He quickly opened the door and went through, the laptop bag scuffing against the frame. Unless someone had been looking directly at the camera feed at that exact moment, his illicit entrance would have been too fast to be noticed. He paused as the door swung shut, listening for a response from the hotel worker . . .

Nothing. He hadn't been seen.

'Levon, I'm inside the maintenance area,' he said. The room was utilitarian, unpainted cinderblock and drywall. Cabinets and shelves contained cleaning products and racks of replacement fittings: light bulbs, lamps, faucets, even televisions.

'Okay, the way to the roof is straight ahead,' Levon told him, but he was already moving; there was nowhere else to go. He passed more cabinets and stacked boxes, reaching a narrow metal staircase that zigzagged upwards. He ascended, footsteps echoing.

The room above was only dimly lit. Large pieces of machinery lurked in the shadows, a loud electrical hum coming from somewhere nearby. 'Where's the hatch?'

'Head right from the top of the stairs,' said Levon. He turned to see a narrow passage, and went along it. The hum grew louder as he neared a short set of steps. 'The hatch is at the end.'

'I see it.' It was set into the steeply angled roof. He climbed the steps. The hatch was padlocked, but a few seconds' work with one of his tools took care of that. He swung it open.

He was right behind the illuminated IMPERIAL sign, the glare from its thousands of powerful bulbs dazzling even indirectly. Macau spread out vertiginously before him.

And he was suddenly gripped by fear, a cold terror paralysing him. His hand clamped around the edge of the hatch. The city far below seemed to roll, as if the towering casino had turned to rubber.

He forced out words. 'We've got a problem.'

'What is it?' Holly Jo asked.

'It turns out Vanwall . . . is afraid of heights.'

19

It's Tough at the Top

Bianca was running out of things to say. Zykov had oozed closer, his hand caressing her shoulder, making his intentions absolutely clear.

And he was getting impatient. 'Bah, enough about that,' he said, waving away her latest attempt to draw him into a hopefully very long story about his military career. 'Forget the past, eh? What is done is done. What counts is what we do next, eh?'

'Well, what I'd like to do next is . . .' She quickly finished her drink. 'Use the bathroom, I'm afraid!' She shrugged his hand off her arm and stood. 'Sorry, but sometimes nature's call does come first.'

The look in Zykov's eye frightened her for a moment. Her resistance was angering him. 'In there,' he said in a brusque tone, waving towards a door.

'Back soon.' Wishing that she had thought to take off her shoes, she went through it – finding to her alarm that she had just entered Zykov's bedroom, his king-sized bed dominating the space. Another glass wall to the balcony overlooked the island city.

A door led to a bathroom. She thumped it shut behind her, turning the lock with a firm *clack* and leaning back against the polished wood. 'Holly Jo!'

'Yes?'

'*Where the hell is Adam?*'

'Why the hell didn't this come up before?' said Tony.

Even through the earwig, Adam had trouble hearing him over the gusting wind. He forced his hand off the hatch to cover his ear and blot out part of the noise. 'It didn't register until I saw the drop.' A vision of a similarly high vantage point – though inverted – leapt vividly from his adopted persona's memories. 'Vanwall once crossed the wrong people in Vegas, and they hung him upside down off the roof of the Sands!'

'You're not Vanwall,' Tony reminded him. 'You're Adam Gray, and you're *not* afraid of heights. Push him back down and get across that roof.'

'Easier said than done.' He reluctantly stepped through the hatch, revealing more of the vista below. His sense of vertigo returned.

Not my sense. His. I don't have vertigo. I've . . .

He wasn't sure *how* he was so certain, only that he *was* certain. The more he tried to recall why, the greater the feeling that something was missing from his mind.

Not missing. *Taken—*

'I know you can do it,' said Tony, bringing his focus back to more immediate concerns. 'Ignore Vanwall. He's just an imprint, and he's done his job. You don't need him any more.'

Another step. The wind caught the bags he was carrying, their straps digging into his shoulders as they shifted. The neon cityscape swayed beneath him. Despite the wind in his face, he felt as if there was no air.

This isn't me! I'm not afraid. Ignore his fear. It's his, not mine. I can do this.

Adam drew in several breaths, filling his lungs. He took in the view again, picking out points of interest: a flashing sign on another casino, cars weaving ant-like through an intersection. They remained steady.

I'm not afraid.

Tony spoke again. 'You've got to get to Bianca, and soon. Zykov's getting impatient. She needs your help.'

I'm in control.

'I'm going,' he said firmly, moving fully out on to the roof. He stepped over skeins of electrical cables and headed for the Russian's penthouse. The sign jutted out from the roof's edge on a gantry. There was just enough room for him to put one foot in front of the other behind it; once he cleared the last letter, he would have a little more space – but nothing to hold on to if he slipped. The tiled roof curved steeply upwards, offering no handholds.

He nudged the heavy laptop bag behind his back for better balance. The medical case bumped against it. He kept going, picking his way past more letters. I, A, L, and he was in the open.

Vanwall's terror resurfaced as he looked straight down over the edge for the first time. Eight hundred feet, neon hyperspace streaks pointing the way to earth. *Not my fear.* Another deep breath. He brought up his arms to balance himself. One foot in front of the other. He looked ahead. The corner of the roof projected outwards in an oversized parody of a traditional pagoda. He could see part of the penthouse's balcony beneath it.

One foot, then the other. The distance slowly closed. He kept his eyes fixed on his destination. *Keep moving.* A stronger gust caught him, making him wobble, arms see-sawing before he regained his balance. The laptop bag swung behind his back, twenty pounds of bulky electronics acting like a pendulum. Even with the gambler's fear suppressed, the seconds before he stabilised were terrifying.

'Adam, I can see you on the UAV's cameras,' said Holly Jo, concerned. 'Are you okay?'

'Yeah,' he replied. 'Just some wind.'

'That's always a problem when you eat Chinese,' Kyle cut in.

'Kyle, shut up,' Tony barked, but the moment of levity was what Adam had needed to get over his fright.

He set off again. 'What's Bianca do—'

His leading foot stepped on something slick and jerked forward. He staggered, arms flailing.

He was going over . . .

He twisted and deliberately fell against the steep roof. The impact was hard, tiles grinding under his weight. The laptop bag thumped heavily against the rooftop.

His foot slithered over the edge—

He clawed at the tiles. Fingernails got a grip. Gasping, he held himself in place. His wayward foot found solidity again.

'Adam!' Holly Jo cried in his ear. 'Are you okay? Adam!'

'I'm okay,' he croaked. He carefully levered himself back upright and probed the edge with his foot. 'Shit.'

'What happened?'

'Like I said, shit. Literally. I just slipped on a big patch of bird poop.'

Her brief laugh was somewhere between relief and disgust. 'Jesus, Adam.'

'Kyle, get the UAV in closer and warn him if there's any more,' said Tony, concern clear even behind his professional tone. 'Adam, are you sure you're okay?'

'Just a scare. The PERSONA gear took a knock, though.'

'How bad?'

'No way to tell until we try to use it. Okay, I'm moving again.'

Kyle gave him warning of a couple more potential hazards. Adam stepped over them, heading out on to the overhang above Zykov's penthouse. 'What's the situation inside?'

'Bianca's still in the bathroom,' Holly Jo told him. 'Zykov doesn't look happy – he's pacing about in the lounge. I think he's getting fed up of waiting.'

'What about his bodyguards?'

'I don't see them. They must be in the back rooms.'

Adam pictured the penthouse's layout, recalling the floor plan Levon had procured. 'Which bathroom is Bianca in?'

'The one off Zykov's bedroom.'

'Damn.' To reach the balcony, he would have to monkey-climb down the support beam – making him fully visible to anyone in the main bedroom, and at risk of being seen from the lounge as well. 'Okay, tell me when he moves. I'm going to the corner of the roof.'

More carefully than ever, he advanced along the edge of the precipice.

'Adam's almost in position,' Holly Jo told Bianca. 'He'll be – uh-oh.'

'What?'

'Zykov's coming!'

She heard the muffled thump of footsteps outside, followed by sharp raps on the bathroom door. 'Bianca! What are you doing in there?'

'I'm fine, I'm nearly done,' she called out, fidgeting in near-panic before forcing herself to calm down. She flushed the lavatory. 'Just a second . . .'

It took exactly two seconds before he knocked again. 'Are you coming?'

She took several rapid breaths, trying to recover some facade of composure. 'Yes, yes.' Steeling herself, she opened the door.

Zykov was right outside. While he was a long way short of filling the doorway vertically, with his broad shoulders he blocked it widthways. He had a full champagne glass in each hand. 'I was getting worried,' he said.

'It was just . . . you know, foreign food. It takes a little time to adapt.'

He offered her a glass. 'You will be fine with this, I think!'

'Thank you.' She took it. He showed no inclination towards letting her through. 'So, ah . . .'

He smiled, exposing pointed teeth. 'What did you think of my bedroom? Nice, hey?'

'I didn't get a proper look, I'm afraid,' she said. 'I was in rather a rush to get in here.'

'So, you prefer the bathroom?' The smile widened, and he stepped into the room. There was still not enough space for her to get past him.

'I, ah, wouldn't say I prefer it,' she said, desperation behind her own, very tight, smile. He kept advancing. She tried to camouflage her retreat by turning as if to take in her surroundings. 'But it's a very nice— Oh!'

Completely unintentionally, she stumbled on her high heels. It was only a small trip, but it was enough to spill some of her champagne. She looked down at the puddle. 'Oh no, I'm sorry.'

'No matter.' Zykov backed her into a corner. He put his own glass down on the counter, then slipped his arms around her waist. 'So. Here we are. It is time that we—'

Sudden movement behind him – and Adam delivered a single hard chop to the base of his neck.

Zykov staggered, face contorted in pain, then his knees

buckled. The American grabbed him under his arms before he fell. 'Help me get him on the bed,' he said, voice low.

Bianca was too startled to move. 'What – what happened? What did you just do to him?'

'Knife hand strike. Come on, we don't have long.' He dragged the woozy Russian towards the door.

'But – I thought that sort of thing only worked in movies!'

'You'd be surprised. Hurry up. If he calls for help—'

'Okay, okay!' She gingerly took hold of Zykov's feet and they hauled him into the bedroom. Bianca saw the medical case and a bulky bag on the bed. The exit to the balcony was open.

'Shut the lounge door,' said Adam as he dumped Zykov on the mattress. 'Then work out the Hyperthymexine dose.'

Bianca quickly closed the door, then returned to the bed. 'How long will you be able to keep him from shouting for his bodyguards?'

Adam produced a silenced gun and pressed the muzzle against the Russian's forehead. 'Long enough.' He thumbed back the hammer with a loud metallic *click*. Even in his groggy state, Zykov recognised the sound and stiffened in fear.

'Oh God, oh God . . .' Flustered, Bianca tried to remember what Albion had taught her. Calculating the dose itself was straightforward enough; the associated theatrics was the hard part. She opened the case. The sight of a penlight torch reminded her of part of the show, but she struggled to recall anything more. 'Okay. Eyes. Check his eyes.' She took the torch and performed a quick arm's-length examination. 'Yes. Two. They look fine.'

Zykov screwed up his face in response to the bright light. 'What you doing? What is this?'

'Shut up,' Adam said firmly. 'Make a sound and I'll kill you.'

The Russian finally focused on his face. 'You! But—'

'I said shut up.' Adam pushed the gun down harder. Zykov fell silent, narrowed eyes burning with anger.

Bianca found a measuring tape in the case and stretched it out beside the prisoner. 'Okay, sixty-five inches, that's, ah . . .'

'Five-five,' Adam prompted.

'Five-five, right. Although . . .' She tugged at one of his shoes, revealing not only a stacked heel but a wedge inside. 'Jesus, his heels are nearly as high as mine! Okay, more like five-three. So, ah, the dose would be, let me think . . .'

He gave her an odd look. 'Aren't you going to weigh him?'

'Did you bring any scales?' she snapped.

'No.'

'Well, then! You just picked him up; how heavy would you say he is?'

'I'd guess about . . . a hundred and eighty pounds?'

'That means nothing to me – I work in kilograms!'

'Eighty-one kilos,' said Holly Jo through her earwig after a moment.

'Thank you!' Bianca backed away, trying to do the sums in her head and quickly finding that they were beyond the limits of her mental arithmetic. 'I need a pen and paper, or a calc—' Adam used his free hand to take out his phone and toss it to her. 'Okay, thanks.' She found the calculator app and started tapping in numbers.

Zykov was as confused as he was angry. 'Who are you? This is about more than just taking my money, isn't it?'

'Very perceptive, little comrade,' said Adam.

Zykov scowled. 'I will kill you for this. And her.'

'You won't even know it happened. Bianca?'

'Got it,' she said with relief. She loaded the jet injector with Hyperthymexine and set the dial to what she hoped was the right dose. 'Okay, I'm ready.'

Zykov started to struggle; Adam jammed his free hand down hard on his throat. The Russian rasped, choking. 'Shit!' Bianca gasped, afraid that he would alert his guards. She pushed the injector against his neck.

'No, wait!' said Adam, but it was too late. A brief *phut* of gas. Zykov's breathless rattle became a strained gurgle of pain as his entire body convulsed. 'Wrong order, you've done it in the wrong order!' He released the Russian and scrambled across the bed to the laptop bag.

'Sorry, I'm sorry!' Bianca squeaked, close to panic. 'I thought he was going to shout for help!'

'It's okay. Help me with this.' Dropping the gun, he unzipped the bag to reveal the PERSONA equipment. One corner of the recorder was cracked where it had hit the rooftop. 'Tony!'

His superior's voice came through the earwig. 'Yes?'

'The recorder's damaged,' he said, already opening the main unit's screen and starting it up. 'Do you want to risk—'

'No, just make a direct transfer,' Tony ordered. He didn't need to ask what had happened; the audio feed from their earwigs and the hovering drone's cameras had told the full story. 'Get as much as you can before the drug wears off.'

'I'm sorry,' Bianca said again as she prepared the skullcaps. 'I was—'

'It's okay, it doesn't matter,' he assured her. 'Just set everything up as quickly as you can.'

She gave one of the caps to Adam, who donned it and started to adjust the positions of the electrode clusters. 'I don't know what the margin of error is on this thing,' he said, as much to himself as anyone, 'so it's a good job I'm a gambler right now.'

Bianca pulled the second skullcap over Zykov's head. She had seen the effects of being injected with Hyperthymexine on video, finding it merely unsettling, but in person – and on an unwilling subject – it was extremely disturbing. 'How long have we got?'

'No idea. Roger was the expert. Does this look right?' Adam pulled the chin strap tight, then turned his head so she could see it from all angles.

'As far as I can tell.'

'Okay.' He took out the jet injector. 'I'll wipe Vanwall's persona. You connect everything up, and the second you're ready, start the transfer.' He lay back on the bed and put the injector's nozzle to his neck.

'Adam, I . . .' Bianca started to say, but he had already pulled the trigger. His body tensed . . . then the ever-etched smirk of Peter Vanwall slowly dissolved from his face.

She turned back to Zykov. The Russian was straining as if his muscles were trying to burst through his skin, eyes flicking rapidly from side to side. The drug was firing his synapses, forcing him to recall all his memories – but how many had already gone?

The thought galvanised her. She secured the skullcap, giving the electrodes one last quick check. If they were wrongly positioned, it was too late to do anything about it. She took the cable and plugged it into the PERSONA, then did the same with the lead from Adam's cap. 'Okay, here we go,' she said breathlessly as she tapped the keyboard.

ACTIVE: PERSONA TRANSFER IN PROGRESS.

The screen lit up, numbers scrolling up one window. The stylised graphic flared with pulsating colours as the electrodes read Zykov's brain activity and sent that data into Adam's mind. How much had her mistake lost? And how would only having a partial persona affect Adam? She had no idea; it was not a possibility Albion or Kiddrick had ever envisaged.

Adam's fingers were twitching, eyes moving as quickly as Zykov's. *Something* was being transferred, at least. Enough to get the information they needed? All she could do was wait and hope.

A minute passed. The data on the screen told her that everything seemed normal – so far. But for how much longer?

'Bianca,' Holly Jo said, giving her a start. 'One of the bodyguards just came into the lounge.' More urgency in her voice. 'He's heading for the bedroom!'

Bianca whipped round in helpless horror as someone knocked on the door.

20

The Face on the Bathroom Floor

A man said something in Russian. A question, Bianca could tell from his intonation. But she had no answer. And with Zykov trapped in the whirlwind of his own memories, there was no way she could force him to reply.

Another knock. If he didn't get an answer soon—

She didn't know what prompted her to do it, perhaps the half-forgotten memory of a scene from some movie or book, but she *giggled*, bouncing up and down on the end of the bed. The mattress creaked. Simultaneously blushing at the incongruous silliness of her actions and gripped with utter terror, she waited . . .

The door didn't open.

'He's going,' said Holly Jo, voice filled with relief.

'Bianca, stay still,' Tony added. Seconds passed. Bianca heard the faint clunk of a door. 'Okay, he's gone.'

She let out an explosive exhalation. 'Oh Jesus! Shit.' Her hands were shaking – no, her whole body. 'God, that was close.'

'Are you all right?' asked Tony.

'Yeah, yeah. I'm just . . . scared,' she admitted.

'You've done an amazing job, Bianca. Really. All you need to do now is wrap it up and we can get you out of there. How's the transfer going?'

She checked the PERSONA. The visual representations of the process were now quiescent. 'I think it's done,' she said, pecking at the keyboard with a quivering finger. 'It says the latency estimates are . . . God, I don't know. Not what they should be, is all I can tell you.'

'Check on Adam.'

She moved to him. His eyes were closed. 'Adam?' she said quietly. 'Can you hear me?'

'Yes.' He frowned, as if experiencing a mild headache.

'Ask him his name,' said Tony.

She did so. Adam opened his eyes, giving her a pained look. 'Adam Gray.'

'It didn't work,' she said, crestfallen. Everything had been for nothing . . .

'No, wait,' Adam said, raising a hand. 'It's there, it's just . . . fuzzy. Hold on. My name is . . . Ruslan. Ruslan Pavelovich Zykov.' His voice changed as he repeated the name, taking on some of the Russian's heavy accent.

'Your date of birth?' Bianca asked hopefully.

'January 1966. The . . . the tenth.'

'That's right,' said Holly Jo through Bianca's earwig.

Bianca decided to skip through the standard questions. 'What's your most guilty secret?'

Adam's reluctance to answer told her that at least some of Zykov's persona had been transferred to him. 'When I was a boy, I . . . I stole from our church. I broke in and took all the icons, and sold them to a trader for two hundred American dollars. The whole village was horrified, but they never found out it was me who took them.'

Bianca leaned back, surprised. Zykov was an arms dealer, a violent killer – and *that* was the event in his life of which he was most ashamed? 'Okay, I think it worked,' she announced to those listening. 'So now can we get out of here?'

Adam unstrapped his skullcap. 'We need to wipe Zykov's memory first.'

'And figure out a way to explain why he's missing ten minutes of his life,' Holly Jo added.

Bianca looked into the bathroom. 'I've got an idea. You move him in there – I'll pack up the gear.' She removed the cap from Zykov's head.

Adam took hold of the blank-eyed Russian and dragged him from the bed. 'Always the same. The man has to lift heavy stuff while the woman does nothing.'

'I hope that was Zykov saying that and not you,' Bianca chided, unplugging the cables and powering down the PERSONA.

Adam towed Zykov to the bathroom and manoeuvred him through the doorway. By the time he had pulled him inside, Bianca had packed everything up – except for the injector of Mnemexal. 'Okay,' she said, joining him. 'See where I spilled the champagne?' She indicated the splash. 'I'll yell for help, and when the bodyguards turn up I'll say he slipped on it and hit his head.'

'Good thinking. Help me turn him over.' They rolled Zykov on to his front. Adam regarded him for a moment – then took hold of him by the hair and slammed him face first against the tiles.

Bianca gasped in shock. 'What are you doing?'

'Making it convincing.' He lifted Zykov's head to reveal a bloodied mark on his forehead. The Russian moaned softly. 'He'll believe that headache. Now, give him the injection.'

She had at least remembered what Albion had told her about the dosages and effects of this particular drug. 'This should be enough to wipe everything as far back as coming into the bathroom.'

'If he loses more, it doesn't matter. As long as he doesn't remember seeing me.'

Bianca administered the drug. She passed the injector to Adam. 'Probably not a good idea to leave this lying around.'

'I'll put it in the case.' He went back into the bedroom.

'How are you going to get out?'

'I'll hide on the balcony. As soon as they're both in here dealing with you and Zykov, I'll go into the lounge through the other door and just walk out.'

'Easy as that, eh?'

'Hopefully.' He picked up both pieces of baggage and went to the balcony door. 'Okay. Get out as soon as you can.'

She gave him a pained smile. 'Oh, I will!'

He grinned back, the almost lustful way he bared his teeth unsettlingly redolent of Zykov, then went out on to the balcony. Bianca turned her attention back to the unconscious man, watching him intently for signs of recovery.

Adam crouched with his back against the glass at the corner of the bedroom. 'The lounge is clear, Adam,' Holly Jo told him. 'You could get to the front door now.'

'I don't want to risk it,' he replied. 'Not until I know where Bragin and Konev are.'

'Who? Oh, the bodyguards.'

'If we'd upgraded the UAV with a microwave radar like I suggested,' added Kyle, 'we could see right through the walls and know exactly where they are. Be useful, huh?'

'I'll bear it in mind at the next procurement meeting,' said Tony drily. 'Adam, are you sure you want to wait?'

'If they see me, I'll have to kill them. Not good for our cover.'

He already had the gun in his hand, ready for the worst-case scenario.

'Point taken. Just be careful, then.'

Adam listened for sounds of activity through the glass. When Bianca raised the alarm, the bodyguards would run to the bathroom to help their boss – leaving the way clear for him to head for the exit.

In theory. He squeezed the gun's grip more tightly . . .

Bianca's heels clattered on the tiled floor. He tensed, ready to move. A shrill cry from the bathroom, then: 'Oh my God! Hey, help! Help me!'

'They're coming,' warned Holly Jo. 'One guy – no, they're both coming. Hold on.'

Bianca was still putting on a performance. 'It's Ruslan, in the bathroom! We were in there, and – he slipped and hit his head! He's hurt, you've got to help him!'

He heard the bedroom door open, hurried footsteps. 'They're both going into the bathroom,' Holly Jo continued. 'Wait, wait . . . okay, their backs are to you. *Go!*'

Adam rose to his feet and strode along the balcony. He opened the glass door and slipped through into the lounge, silently closing it behind him. Without looking back, he headed for the exit. He emerged in the lobby. The concierge gave him a strange look, not recognising him . . .

'*Privet, kak pozhivaeteg?*' Adam said cheerily. The concierge blinked, uncomprehending. 'The boss's date, she is leaving.' He held up his baggage. 'I take these downstairs for her, yeah?'

The man nodded. 'Would you like me to order a taxi?'

'No, no, is fine.' He went to the elevators, pushing the call button. One of the sets of doors opened. He entered. 'Okay, I'm in the elevator,' he announced as it started to descend. 'Where's Bianca?'

★ ★ ★

She was helping the two bodyguards carry their boss to his bed. 'Ruslan, are you okay?'

Zykov put a hand to his head, wincing. 'What happened?'

'You slipped on the champagne,' she said. 'You hit the floor really hard – I was worried, I think you were knocked out. You should go to hospital.'

'No, no, I . . .' He sat on the bed and looked at his hand, seeing a small amount of blood. 'Oh. I don't . . . I went into the bathroom, I gave you a drink, and . . .' He closed his eyes, then his forehead wrinkled in confusion. 'I don't remember.'

'You should definitely see a doctor,' she insisted. 'I'll get the concierge to call someone.'

One of the bodyguards moved as if to block her, but Zykov waved him back. 'Yes, do that. I do not feel good.'

'Okay.' She paused at the bedroom door. 'I'm sorry the evening had to end this way. It's certainly been a very interesting night.'

He managed a faint smile. 'Maybe I see you again sometime, yes?'

'Maybe you will. Anything is possible.' Suppressing the urge to break into a run, she left the suite. 'Mr Zykov asks if you could call a doctor,' she told the concierge. 'He fell and banged his head.'

'I will see to it right away,' he replied, picking up a phone. 'And madam?'

She paused at the lifts, worried. 'Yes?'

'Mr Zykov's man has taken your bags downstairs.'

'Thank you very much.' The lift arrived. The doors closed, and she slumped against its wall. 'Oh God!'

'Bianca?' Adam's voice this time; Holly Jo had connected them. 'Are you on the way down?'

'Yes, I am. Finally! God, I need a drink.'

'We'll have something waiting for you on the plane,' said Tony. 'We're on our way to pick you up at the casino entrance. See you in a minute.'

Adam was waiting for her when the doors opened. He smiled at her. 'Ready?'

'Absolutely, yes. Let's get out of here.' They headed side by side through the glittering lobby.

'You know something?' He was still smiling.

'What?' she asked.

'For an amateur, you make a pretty good spy.'

She laughed. 'High praise indeed, coming from the man who's James Bond, Jason Bourne and Jack Bauer all rolled into one.'

'Just doing my job.' A man approached them: Lau. Without a word, Adam reached into his jacket and smoothly passed him the two casino plaques as he went by.

'Wait, that . . .' Bianca spluttered as Lau headed for the cashiers' cage. 'That was two million dollars!'

'It's US government money,' said Tony, amused. 'Sorry, but we don't get to keep it.'

They reached the main doors, emerging into the night. 'There,' said Adam. The van had pulled up amongst the taxis. They slipped through the crowd and climbed inside.

Tony, Holly Jo and Kyle were waiting for them in the back, the latter holding the UAV in his lap. 'So,' said Tony, 'I wouldn't say things went smoothly, but we got what we were after.' A cloud crossed his face. 'Didn't we?'

'We did,' said Adam. 'I know what Operation Lamplighter is.'

21

Lamplighter

The beach was a grim slate-grey, not sand, but gravel and shards of flint. The murky sea beyond was equally uninviting. It was the perfect setting for the objects at the centre of the photograph: rusted cage-like steel frames containing squat cylinders painted a sickly institutional green, metal vanes protruding from them. Corrosion-scabbed warning signs were attached to the cages. Most were unreadable to the majority of the observers, written in the Cyrillic alphabet, but one symbol was instantly recognisable. A trefoil, black on yellow.

The international radiation warning.

'This is Operation Lamplighter,' said Morgan, addressing the Persona Project team members gathered in the Bullpen. 'This is what Muqaddim al-Rais is willing to spend seven million dollars to obtain.'

'It's a Russian radioisotope thermoelectric generator,' Tony explained. 'Or Soviet, technically, since they date back to the Cold War. RTGs are basically nuclear batteries. NASA uses them in its deep-space probes and the Mars rover. The Soviets used them here on Earth. To power lighthouses.'

He clicked a remote, and the image on the video wall changed to a map of Russia. Along the long coastline of the vast country were marked hundreds of dots, each containing a miniature version of the radiation trefoil. 'They built them on the Arctic shipping lanes when they were free of ice,' Tony continued. 'But because large parts of the country are so remote and inaccessible, operating conventional manned lighthouses would have been a logistical nightmare. So they came up with an alternative. Build *unmanned* lighthouses, plug in an RTG, and then just leave them. In theory, they should have run without trouble for decades.'

'Except, as we all know, theory and practice are two different things when it comes to our former communist friends,' said Morgan. 'After the Soviet Union collapsed, there wasn't the money, or even the inclination, to maintain them as they started to deteriorate. And then there was the human factor.' He nodded to Tony.

Tony switched to a new image. This was another photograph: a makeshift camp in a snowy wilderness, the line of the leaden sea on the horizon. The flattened perspective suggested that the picture had been taken from a distance with a telephoto lens. At the centre was the core of an RTG, wrenched out of its protective cage and with several radiator vanes damaged or missing. Part of the case had been broken open, the crowbar and chisels used still lying beside it.

Also beside it were four bodies.

The Arctic cold had preserved them to an extent – enough to show how their faces had been burned and blistered, the skin a savage, molten red. From their agonised expressions and contorted positions, the men's deaths had been far from painless.

'August 2004,' said Tony. 'This is an island in the White Sea, north-west Russia. These men decided to break into one of the lighthouses and strip it of everything valuable. They got more than they bargained for. Either they didn't know what the warning symbol meant, or they didn't care. But when they busted open the core, they got a lethal dose of radiation, enough to kill them in minutes.'

'And this is not the only instance,' Morgan added. 'There have been more than forty reported cases of raiding or vandalism of RTG-powered lighthouses in the past ten years – in one case, a stolen core was found at a bus stop in a town in Leningrad Oblast. Then there are the accidents. At least nine RTGs have been dropped from helicopters during transport or were aboard ships that sank, and have never been recovered.'

'And these are just the ones the Russians have admitted to. Our intelligence sources have found out that as many as six RTGs have . . . disappeared.' Tony brought up another map, the same as the first – except that half a dozen of the dots, scattered along the Russian coast, were now circled in red. 'Teams went to check on the lighthouses, and found that their RTGs were *gone*. No trace, no dead looters, no signs of excessive radiation in the vicinity.'

'They're out there, somewhere,' said Morgan ominously. 'But our operation in Macau has given us a lead on one of them. Ruslan Zykov is acting as an intermediary between al-Rais and a Russian army officer, Colonel Kirill Makariy Sevnik.'

A new picture came up, a computer-generated facial composite of a middle-aged man, every deep line in his thin, tired face seemingly etched with a chisel. 'We don't have a photo of Sevnik, but Adam used Zykov's persona to produce this,' said Tony, with a brief sidelong glance at Adam on the group's periphery. 'It seems he's had enough of serving in Siberia and wants to take early retirement somewhere tropical. The RTG is his retirement plan. Zykov will take a big cut, of course, but the deal will still give Sevnik five million dollars – and al-Rais a new terror weapon. He won't be able to use it to build a bomb, but at our *minimum* estimate, the RTG contains enough radioactive strontium-90 to lethally poison two million people if it were released in a major city.'

A shiver of concern ran through the assembled group. 'Adam learned from Zykov that the deal has been agreed,' he went on. 'Zykov hasn't met al-Rais in person yet, but will be doing so soon to make the exchange. NSA's now monitoring all Zykov's phone and Internet use to find out when and where it's going to happen – a job we made a lot easier for them by giving them all his passwords, by the way.' The comment eased the tension slightly. 'Once we know that . . . we can catch al-Rais.'

'Fuckin' A!' said Kyle under his breath, though still loudly enough to draw a disapproving glare from Morgan.

'Will we be involved in the mission to capture him?' asked Holly Jo.

'That hasn't been decided yet,' Morgan replied. 'But considering the value of the information we got from Zykov, even if there were some, ah, hitches' – Bianca, standing near Tony, looked uncomfortably at her feet – 'I'd say we will be involved, yes. I want everybody to prep for an operation on that assumption. Once Zykov makes his move, we might not have a lot of time to react. So, get to it. Oh, and one more thing,' he added as the meeting began to disperse. 'Good work on the last mission.'

'Yes, good work, all of you,' added Kiddrick, stepping forward. 'What the Persona Project has done is bring us one step closer to smashing al-Qaeda. Excellent work, everybody.'

'Boo-yah!' Kyle pumped a triumphant fist, the sympathy shared more subtly by others in the room. Everyone started to head back to their posts. Kiddrick was about to leave when Morgan took him aside, his expression stern.

Tony joined Bianca. 'Martin *really* doesn't like it when people take credit for something they had no part in,' he said. 'Kiddrick will have a metaphorical boot-print on his butt for a week.'

'Shame it's not a real one,' she said.

'Yeah. So, how did you like being a field agent?'

'To be honest?' she said. 'Not much.' She took a moment to reconsider. 'All right, parts of it were *almost* enjoyable. The parts where I could pretend I was a glamorous international super-spy.'

'You weren't pretending,' he pointed out.

That caught her off guard. 'Wow. I suppose I wasn't, was I?'

'No. And you know something else?'

'What?'

He grinned. 'You did okay.'

'Well, except for the part where I completely cocked things up by injecting Zykov too soon.'

He pretended to wince. 'Yeah, that had us worried! But everything worked out okay. We got the information we needed from Zykov, and he doesn't even know we have it. He'll lead us right to al-Rais.'

'So what now?'

'Like Martin said, we wait for Zykov to make a move – and the President to decide whether we stay involved. I think we probably will be – in fact, I hope we are. I want to see this through.'

'Well,' said Bianca, 'can I stay in the van rather than needing Adam to rescue me?' She glanced in Adam's direction, expecting to see him retreating into the Cube, but instead found him still standing there, watching her thoughtfully. Wondering what was on his mind, she looked back at Tony. 'It seems a lot less stressful.'

'I'll see what I can do.' He checked his watch. 'So, do you have any plans for this evening?'

'Nothing beyond lying around in my hotel room . . .' Tired from what she had been through in Macau and the long flight back to the States, it took her a moment to pick up on his subtext. 'Why, do you have a suggestion?' she asked, with a hint of mischief.

Tony, on the other hand, got her meaning immediately. 'Well, it occurred to me that you haven't had a proper chance to experience Washington yet. Maybe you'd like someone to show you around?'

'That might be nice,' she said, flattered by his attention. It was certainly preferable to Zykov's. 'Although I really am exhausted after the last couple of days, so—'

'Bianca?' Adam appeared beside her as though he had teleported there, taking her by surprise. 'I wondered if you'd like to go for a drink with me this evening.'

She didn't quite know how to react. Tony was equally startled by the proposition. 'Er . . . what, after work?' she finally managed.

'Yes. I'd like to talk to you. Not about the mission,' he clarified, seeing that both Morgan and Kiddrick had now taken an interest. 'About . . . other things. Something that came up the other night, when you had that problem with your car.'

She was intrigued, but before she could answer, Kiddrick bustled over. 'No, no, that's absolutely out of the question,' he said, interposing himself physically between Adam and Bianca. 'I can't allow that. This is a United States government intelligence operation, not speed dating.'

While Adam's expression was normally inscrutable, it was now perfectly readable: disdain. 'Is that an order?'

'Yes, yes it is,' Kiddrick replied huffily.

'Well, *Nate*,' said Adam, surprising everyone again with the unveiled sarcasm in his tone. 'First: as the project's scientific *adviser*, you don't have the authority to give me orders, or anyone else for that matter. Second: what I do in my free time is my business, not yours.'

Kiddrick now resembled a beached fish, eyes wide and mouth uselessly gawping. 'Martin!' he finally protested. 'You tell him!'

Morgan was clearly still annoyed with the scientist. 'Tell him what? He's not a soldier; he's not confined to barracks when he's off duty.'

'But you know that—' He clammed up.

Bianca couldn't resist. 'Know what, Nate?'

Her use of the diminutive annoyed him even more. 'Martin!'

Morgan gave Kiddrick a stern look over the top of his glasses. 'I know what you're saying, but I don't see how that applies here. Or are you suggesting Adam can't be trusted to have one drink without bellowing national secrets down the length of K Street?'

'No, but – alcohol could cause complications,' he blustered. 'We don't know.'

'It never caused me any trouble,' said Tony. His expression told Bianca that while he was somewhat annoyed by Adam's unexpected usurpation of his social offer, he wasn't going to block it. 'And so long as it doesn't affect security, I don't see any problems.'

'Security!' exclaimed Kiddrick, seizing a lifeline. 'That *is* an issue. As an intelligence operative, Adam is strictly prohibited from unauthorised meetings with foreign nationals. And she' – he pointed at Bianca – 'is a foreign national.'

Bianca was already angry at his high-handed attitude, and the stab of his finger only increased her ire. 'Excuse me, *Nate*, but I have full security clearance granted to me by the Director of National Intelligence himself.' She held up her ID. 'I think that authorises me to talk to Adam whenever I like, inside or outside the office.'

All eyes turned to Morgan. 'I'd say that was correct, yes.'

Kiddrick went red with fury as he realised he had been

outmanoeuvred. 'This – this isn't over!' he spluttered, stalking away. 'I'll take it higher if I have to.'

Morgan started after Kiddrick. 'Nathaniel – my office. We need to talk in private.' He paused to look back at the little group. 'I'd prefer it if you *didn't* go bellowing national secrets down K Street.'

'I don't think that'll happen,' said Tony. Morgan nodded and followed the fuming scientist. 'Will it?'

'It won't,' Adam told him.

'Good. Of course, none of this actually matters unless Bianca actually wants to go.' He regarded her questioningly.

In the heat of the discussion she hadn't had a chance to think about that, but now she knew there was only one possible answer. 'Adam? Yes, I would love to go for a drink with you this evening.'

'Good. Thank you,' Adam replied. He didn't quite smile, but he still appeared pleased.

'Well, you kids have fun,' Tony said, before adding with faint warning: 'Don't do anything crazy, okay?'

'I'm too tired for that,' Bianca assured him.

Adam, on the other hand, said nothing.

22

Where Nobody
Knows Your Name

The bar to which Adam took Bianca was called the Rose &
Crown, an ersatz British pub incongruously located on the
ground floor of a glass and steel office block. 'I thought this might
make you feel at home,' he said.

The interior was more a caricature than a reproduction of the
real thing, but she decided to keep any mockery to herself. There
were more interesting things to discuss. 'Have you been in here
before?'

'I don't know,' he replied. On her questioning look, he went
on: 'It seems kind of familiar, but . . .' He shook his head. 'Which
is why I wanted to talk to you, outside of STS.'

They ordered drinks, then found a table. Bianca sat facing
him. 'What did you want to talk about?'

'The other night, when you were asking about my past, and I
wouldn't tell you?'

'Yes?'

'I realised afterwards that . . .' He searched for the right words. 'It
wasn't so much that I wouldn't tell you. It was more that I *couldn't*.'

'Why not?'

'That's the worst part – I don't even know. But once I started thinking about it . . .' He looked down at his drink for a moment, then back at her. 'Ask me something about my past. Anything.'

'Okay,' she said. 'Ah . . . do you have any brothers or sisters?'

'I can't disc—' he began, suddenly cutting the words off. 'You see? I didn't mean to say that, it just came out before I'd even had a chance to think about it. Like a programmed response.'

He was trying to cover it, but she could tell he was distressed by the realisation. 'But *do* you have any brothers or sisters?' she asked gently.

'I'm . . . not sure,' he managed to say.

'What about anything else?' The standard PERSONA questions came to her mind. 'Do you know your mother's maiden name?'

A look of pained puzzlement. 'I . . . no. I don't know.'

'Your best friend when you were a kid?'

'I don't know! I never thought about it until you brought it up; it didn't even occur to me to try. But now that I have . . .' He rubbed his temple with his fingertips. 'I can't remember anything about my past. At all.'

Bianca was shocked. 'Nothing?'

'Nothing specific. I know general things like . . . like I was in the military – I know how to field-strip weapons, unarmed combat techniques, things like that. I even know some obscene marching songs.' They both smiled a little at the brief injection of frivolity. 'So I've been trained, and I remember the results. But I don't remember *where* I was trained, or who trained me.'

'And it's the same for everything else about your past?'

'Yeah. I went to school, but I don't know where. I must have had a dog, because the other morning I saw a kid having trouble getting one to behave and I knew what he should do to train it, but I don't remember the breed, or even its name. And I obviously must have had parents, but . . .' A deep sadness filled his eyes. 'I don't remember them.'

She couldn't help but be affected, and reached across the table to put her hand on his. 'I'm sorry.'

'No need to be. It's not your fault.'

'No, but . . .' Even in her sympathy, part of her mind was still being analytical, scientific. 'This kind of very specific declarative memory loss is extremely rare, whatever Hollywood might think. Considering that it's also non-ongoing, because you aren't having trouble storing new memories . . .' She broke off, thinking.

'What is it?' Adam asked.

She leaned closer, lowering her voice. 'Isn't it obvious? Part of what you do involves giving people drugs to suppress their short-term memories. I think somebody's done the same to you.'

'But my short-term memory's fine. And I've never been given Mnemexal.'

'That you remember.'

Bianca hadn't intended the comment to be dramatic, but Adam reacted as if an electric charge had run through him. He straightened sharply, eyes wide. 'You think someone did this to me deliberately? It's not some PERSONA side effect?'

'Well – I don't know,' she said, flustered by his sudden intensity. 'I mean, Tony doesn't have the same symptoms as you.'

'You make it sound like an illness.' He considered her wording more carefully. 'You said symptoms, plural. There's something else besides the amnesia?'

She blushed, knowing she was about to broach an awkward subject. 'Um . . . okay, I don't want you to take this the wrong way and be offended . . .'

He withdrew his hand. 'After saying that, you'll have to risk it, won't you?'

'Yeah, I suppose I will.' She tried to think of the best way to phrase it, but all the alternatives seemed equally bad. 'Okay. When you aren't using someone else's persona, your behaviour tends to be . . . unusual.'

'In what way?' he asked, eyes narrowing.

She felt more embarrassed than ever. 'Oh God. How can I put this? You often seem, ah . . . blank.'

He certainly wasn't blank now. 'What the hell's *that* supposed to mean?'

'Look, I'm sorry, okay? But you asked, and I'm just telling you what I see. When you're at STS, you almost never show any kind of . . .' She trailed off.

Adam was not going to let her off the hook. 'Any kind of what?'

'Emotion?' she managed.

'That's not what you were about to say. Tell me. I want to know.' A beseeching look. 'I *need* to know.'

Bianca cringed in advance. 'I was going to say that you don't show any . . .' She forced out the word. 'Personality.'

That produced the expressionless mask she was used to – except this time, it clearly *was* being used to conceal some very strong feelings. 'You think I don't have any personality.'

'I'm saying that you don't often *show* it. That's not the same thing.'

'Maybe I'm just a naturally reserved kind of person.'

'Are you? You tell me.'

'I can't discuss . . .' The mask broke. 'God damn it! Why can't I remember?' His hands clenched into anguished fists. 'Why can't I even *think* about remembering?'

She took hold of his hands again. 'I'm sorry. Adam, it's okay. Look, if something was done to you to affect your memory, Roger'll know about it. He must do – he developed the drugs. I'll talk to him tomorrow and find out what he knows.'

'What if he won't tell you anything?'

'Then I'll poke his bullet hole until he does.'

It took him a moment to realise she was joking. 'You know, you Brits do that whole deadpan thing really well.'

'We *are* a nation of experts at hiding our true feelings.'

He smiled slightly. 'So that's how you made your assessment of me? It takes one to know one?'

'Something like that.' She returned the smile, which seemed to please him, before becoming a little wistful. 'Although . . . there's another reason.'

'What?'

She leaned back in her seat. 'I, ah . . . I lost two of my grandparents to Alzheimer's. It was awful, watching their minds – their *selves* – being eaten away. But one of the worst things was not knowing how much of them was still trapped inside. Up to a certain point in the illness, occasionally a flash of the real person would come through. And when it did . . . God, I would try to hold on to it *so* hard. But it always slipped away.' A morose sigh. 'I was always watching for those flashes, though. I still do. And . . .'

'You think you've seen them in me?'

'Yes. Maybe. I don't know.' She shrugged helplessly. 'Your case is different. It's not a disease, it's something that's been *done* to you.'

'But you still want to hold on to those flashes?'

'Well, I am a doctor . . .' Bianca stopped, seeing that something behind her had caught his attention. She looked round. Two men had entered the bar. She recognised them: Spence and Fallon, members of Baxter's tactical team in Macau. They scanned the room like human radars, locking on to Adam. 'I don't think they're here for a drink,' she said as they marched over.

'Nor do I.' Adam looked up as they reached the table. 'Yes?'

'We need you to come with us back to STS, Mr Gray,' said Fallon.

'Is there an emergency?'

'I can't say. We're just following orders.'

'Orders from whom?' Bianca demanded.

No reply. 'Well?' said Adam. 'Whose orders?' Still no answer. 'It was Kiddrick, wasn't it?'

The two men were losing patience. 'Mr Gray,' said Spence, 'come with us, please.' The final word was an insincere afterthought.

'Just a minute,' said Bianca. 'I think he deserves an answer.'

Fallon was unimpressed. 'This doesn't concern you, Miss Childs.'

She bristled, standing and rounding the table. 'First of all, it's Ms Childs, not Miss. And second of all, it's *Doctor* Childs to you. He asked you a question – are you going to answer it?'

'We've got our orders,' Fallon said, patience fraying. He raised a hand as if to shove Bianca aside. 'Mr Gray—'

Adam's hand snapped up and grabbed his wrist.

Fallon's reaction was almost instantaneous, the trained, automatic response of a soldier. He tried to pull his arm free, at the same time thrusting his other hand at Adam's elbow to break it—

Adam was quicker. He sprang up, dodging Fallon's blow. Faster than Bianca could even follow, he twisted the other man's arm up behind his back. Fallon gasped, but the sound barely had time to pass his lips before Adam scythed his legs out from under him with a spinning kick.

Fallon crashed against Spence, both men tumbling to the floor. The bar's other occupants looked round in shock. Bianca was in much the same state. She gawped at Adam – and found that he had a beaming, delighted smile on his face.

It widened. He grabbed her hand. 'Run!'

Before she could protest, he pulled her with him, heading for an exit at the bar's rear. Fallon and Spence struggled back to their feet, unhurt except for their pride.

That was enough to inflame them. Faces twisted in anger, they pursued.

'Adam!' Bianca cried, but his grip was unbreakable. He reached the door and barged it open. She had no choice but to run to keep up. They charged down a hallway. A glowing red sign marked a fire exit at the end. Timing his footfalls perfectly, Adam kicked the locking bar and sent it flying open. They barrelled through without stopping, emerging in an alley.

She expected him to head for the street, but instead he went the other way. 'It's a dead end!' she protested, seeing only dumpsters in a ragged line against a brick wall.

'Climb over,' he said. Before she could reply, he had effortlessly swept her up and deposited her atop one of the bins. She gasped in surprise. Down the alley, Spence and Fallon burst through the door and charged after their quarry.

Bianca thought Adam was going to fight them, but instead he leapt up beside her. 'Go on, climb up!'

Half scared, half exhilarated, she scrambled over the wall. The drop into another building's loading dock was about twelve feet. She hit the ground hard and fell to an undignified landing on her backside.

Adam climbed over after her – but didn't jump down. Instead he hung from the edge of the wall by both hands, feet up high to hold him in a frog-like crouch.

The mystery of what he was doing was revealed to Bianca a few seconds later. Metallic thunks came from the other side of the wall as Fallon and Spence climbed on to the dumpster. The latter's face appeared over the brickwork – then Adam popped up right in front of him. '*Boo!*'

Spence let out a startled yelp, losing his hold and falling back with an echoing crash. Twin explosions of swearing told Bianca that he had knocked Fallon down with him. Adam dropped to the ground beside her. His expression as he pulled her back upright was nothing short of mischievous glee. 'Come on!'

They ran to the street. Adam almost seemed to be dancing as he crossed the road, dodging and weaving through the cars. Bianca followed with rather more apprehension. They reached the other side and ran down the next block.

'Stop, stop!' Bianca gasped as they rounded a corner. While she tried to exercise as often as she could at home, the sheer unexpectedness of the chase had caught her unprepared.

Adam slowed to let her catch up. He was almost buzzing with energy. 'Damn!' he said, laughing. 'That was fun.'

'That's your idea of fun?' she complained. 'Being chased by – okay, I don't want to call them "goons", because you work with them, but . . . by goons?'

'They wouldn't have hurt you.'

'I don't know, they seemed pretty angry.'

'I wouldn't have let them.' There was a matter-of-factness to the statement that made her very glad he was on her side.

'Won't that cause you a lot of trouble at STS, though?'

He shook his head. 'Those two overstepped the mark. Anyway, don't worry about it. Are you okay?'

She recovered her breath. 'More or less. Oh!' She twisted to check her trousers, and found a dirty mark across her buttocks. 'Bloody hell. I landed in some mud.'

'Sorry. I'll take you somewhere you can get cleaned up.'

She was about to suggest her hotel, when impulsive curiosity took over. 'Your place?'

Adam appeared briefly surprised, but then nodded. There was

not a trace of lascivious intent, though. 'Sure. We can carry on our conversation.'

'About?'

Another smile, but one tinged with disquiet. 'About why that was literally the most fun I can ever remember having.'

23

The Impossible Dream

They took a cab to Adam's apartment. He received three phone calls en route, all of which he ignored. Once there, he watched Bianca's reaction as she looked around the living room.

'What do you think?' he asked. It was not the tone of someone awaiting praise for their taste, more that of a patient expecting the worst.

'Hmm,' she said.

'That bad?'

'It's very . . . minimalist.' She felt as if she had entered some sort of avant-garde art installation. The room was almost completely devoid of colour: white walls and ceiling, black furniture, the carpet a nondescript grey. Even the Apple laptop on a desk was monochrome aluminium.

There was something else unusual, but it took her a few seconds to work out what. When the answer came, it was startling in its obviousness. 'You don't have a television?'

Adam shook his head. 'I don't have a radio, either.'

'Why not?'

'I don't know. It just never occurred to me to buy one.'

'It reminds me of the Cube, back at STS.'

'Yeah, I know. And that's something else that hadn't occurred to me before – at least, not until you started making me think about it.'

She peered into the kitchen. It was as plain as the lounge; no mess, no clutter, everything neatly stored. 'Did you choose this place?'

'No. After I joined the Persona Project, they arranged it for me. All the furniture was already here.'

'And you didn't bring any of your own stuff with you?'

'I didn't have any stuff, now I think about it. Just clothes.'

'*Nothing* else? No books or CDs, anything like that?'

Another shake of his head. 'Now, I'm fairly sure that's not normal.'

'Not unless you're secretly a Trappist monk. And I can't picture you in a robe.'

'Maybe on a mission . . .' His phone rang again. He checked the screen. 'Tony.'

'You're still not going to answer?'

'Not yet. I want to see how panicked they get about all this.'

'Is that wise?'

'Probably not.' He cocked his head towards her. 'Well, there's something we've found out about my personality. Apparently I'm reckless.'

'I'm not sure I'd go that far,' she assured him. 'Maybe you like to test the boundaries, though.'

The ringing stopped. 'I'll get something so you can clean yourself off. Please, have a seat.'

She sat in a black leather armchair as he went into the kitchen. 'This apartment, then – have you ever done anything here except eat and sleep?'

'No. And you're actually my first social visitor.'

'In how long?'

'In, ah . . . seven months. That's when I moved in here.'

'Really? Wow. And you haven't felt lonely?'

'Like I said, it didn't occur to me.' He came back into the lounge, bearing a cloth. 'Here.'

'Thanks. Damn, I shouldn't have sat down first, should I?' She stood and rubbed the dirt off her trousers, then turned to wipe away the marks she had left on the chair.

'Leave it,' said Adam. She looked at him, questioning. 'Maybe this place could use some disorder.'

'I still have to sit somewhere,' she pointed out.

He gestured at the couch. 'Over here.'

'Okay.' She took a place on it. He sat beside her. 'I suppose the question that has to be asked is: what *do* you remember about your past? If you think back, what's the first thing that you can specifically recall?'

'I'm not sure.' He stared at the wall, but not in the blank way Bianca had seen in the Cube. He was making a genuine effort to probe his memory. 'I remember the first time I went into the Bullpen at STS, for sure.'

'Who else was there?'

'Roger, Kiddrick, Martin, Tony . . . some of the support staff too. Holly Jo, Levon, Kyle, a few more. There weren't many other people there, though. The project was suspended after Tony took medical leave – they were only just gearing back up to operational status.'

'When was this?'

'About seven months ago. After I'd recovered from the surgery to put in the PERSONA implants. Then I had five months of testing and training to make sure everything was okay, and after that we started warm-up missions. Low-level intelligence-gathering, to bring the team up to speed.'

'So what do you remember before that? Do you know how you actually joined the project?'

Another long moment of deep thought. 'No,' he finally said.

'Not at all? Roger told me that you volunteered for it.'

'I volunteered?'

'You didn't even know *that*?'

'Looks that way.' A resigned shrug. 'But I remember . . . I'm not sure what, actually. Bits and pieces. They must have been after the operation, because I was in a hospital. Kiddrick was there, and Roger. Tony, Harper . . . I think John Baxter, maybe?'

'But coming into the Bullpen is the first thing you definitely remember?'

'Yeah. Before that . . .' He shook his head.

'I don't get it,' said Bianca. 'It seems as if they deliberately affected your memory as some sort of conditioning for the PERSONA process. But they didn't do that to Tony. Unless they thought it would stop . . .' She paused, remembering that Tony had asked her to keep the details of his breakdown to herself, and not knowing how much Adam knew. 'Maybe they thought it would make the process work better.'

He frowned deeply. 'But why would I volunteer to have literally everything I knew about my past erased? Your memories make you who you are, so if you take them away, what's left?' He noticed her reflective expression. 'What?'

'It's funny – I said pretty much exactly that about the reason I went into Alzheimer's research.'

'So you're saying I've gotten artificial Alzheimer's?' He let out a sardonic huff. 'Maybe you were right – maybe I *don't* have a personality, because it got wiped.'

'That's not true,' she told him firmly. 'What I've seen of you in the past hour proves that. The real Adam Gray is definitely in there.'

'It still doesn't explain why I'd agree to go through with it. Unless . . .'

Whatever thought had occurred to him was clearly not one he liked. 'Unless what?' she asked.

'Unless there was something I didn't *want* to remember. But that would mean there was something that . . . that I couldn't face up to. And that would make me a coward.'

She put a hand on his arm. 'No. No, it wouldn't,' she insisted. 'Besides, you don't even know what might have happened.'

'I guess not. Although . . .'

'Do you remember something else?'

'I don't know. It's . . .' He seemed troubled, even worried. 'Okay. I have this recurring dream. Only I don't know how much of it actually *is* a dream.'

'You think it might be a memory?'

'I don't know. Some of it can't be real, though.'

'Why?'

He took a deep breath, working up the resolve to reveal some great secret. 'All right. I haven't told anyone this before.'

'It'll be just between us,' she said.

'Thanks.' Another long breath. 'Okay. It's always the same – I'm in a street somewhere, but I don't know where. Something bad's happened – there are people running and screaming all around me. Then I see a body on the ground.'

'Who is it?'

He looked at her, distress in his eyes. 'It's me.'

'You?'

'Yeah. I'm . . . I'm lying dead in the street. That's got to be a dream. Hasn't it?' His tone was almost pleading.

'It must be,' she said, trying to reassure him. 'I mean, you look very much alive to me.'

'Yes, I'd figured that much out,' he said, briefly sarcastic. 'But the rest of it feels . . . well, like a memory. And it's always the same, every time I have the dream.'

'How often do you have it?'

A grim look. 'Every night.'

'Do you remember any details about the street?'

'Not really. I don't think it's in America, but there's a lot of smoke in the air, so I can't really see. It might be somewhere—' He broke off, suddenly irritated. 'I'd wondered how long it'd be before they did that.'

'Did what?'

He pointed at his right ear. 'STS are trying to call me through my earwig. The transceiver's off, but there's a beeper they can use to alert me in emergencies – and somebody's holding down the button. I guess I'll have to answer just to shut it up.' He tapped at a spot behind his ear. 'Yes, what?' Several seconds passed as he listened to the message being broadcast directly into his skull. 'Yeah, okay, Holly Jo,' he said with annoyed resignation. Another tap switched the earwig back off.

'What is it?' Bianca asked.

'Tony's on his way over. It seems that business with Fallon and Spence put a fox in the henhouse. Mad panic, everyone wants to know what's going on.'

'I can imagine it might worry them. I'm sorry if I've got you into trouble.'

He managed a half-smile. 'I'm not. It's been an interesting evening.'

'It certainly has!'

The smile widened. 'We should do this again sometime. Assuming they don't put me under house arrest.'

The doorbell rang. Bianca looked round in surprise. 'When you said Tony was on the way, you weren't kidding.'

Adam stood. 'I'll get it.'

It was indeed Tony, looking rather more harassed than when they had last seen him. 'So much for not doing anything crazy, then,' he said as he entered. 'Want to tell me what happened?'

'Spence and Fallon overstepped the mark,' Adam replied, becoming businesslike. 'They were aggressive and threatening, and when Fallon was about to manhandle Bianca, I stopped him. He overreacted, so I shut him down. With minimum force.'

'You probably won't be surprised if I tell you that's not how their version of events goes.'

'It's what happened, though,' said Bianca, getting up. 'We were just chatting when they marched in like the Gestapo and said they had orders to take Adam back to STS.'

'They did have orders, though,' Tony said.

She gave him a cold look. 'From you?'

'No. From Admiral Harper.'

Adam's eyes widened. 'Harper?'

'That's right,' said Tony. 'Kiddrick complained to him directly – and Harper gave the order to bring you back. Then, after you both ran off . . .' He sighed. 'You know how two minutes doesn't sound a long time? Believe me, when you spend it being yelled at by the Director of National Intelligence, it's a goddamned eternity.'

Bianca shuffled her feet guiltily. 'Oh. Sorry . . .'

'It's okay, it's not your fault. I just didn't think Kiddrick would do an end run around Martin – or that Harper would back him up.'

'Why *did* he back him up?' asked Adam.

'Beats the hell out of me. But the upshot is that everyone at STS is going to get an email tomorrow reminding them of the rules on after-hours fraternisation – which,' he added to Bianca, 'are normally overlooked by supervisors because they're ridiculously restrictive. I don't agree that it's necessary, but it's not my call.'

Adam turned to Bianca. 'Sorry I dragged you into this.'

'No need to apologise. Like you said, it's been an interesting evening.'

'Unfortunately, you'll have to call it a night,' said Tony. 'Adam, Martin wants to see both of us tomorrow at eight sharp. Bianca, I'll take you back to your hotel.'

'You don't have to act as a chaperone, Tony,' she said. 'We were just talking.'

'No, it's okay,' Adam told her. 'I'll see you tomorrow.'

'Are you sure?'

He nodded. 'I'll be fine. Don't worry.'

After what he had told her, though, she knew it would be hard not to.

'I can't believe this,' Bianca snapped at Tony as he drove her through Washington. 'Since when has going for a drink with a colleague been a matter of national security?'

'Hey, I agree with you,' he replied. 'I don't know why Harper made such a big deal of it. But he did, and he's in charge, so . . .'

'It's still idiotic. Paranoid, even. But I suppose I should expect that by now.' She pursed her lips. 'Speaking of paranoid, how did those two know we were at that bar? And how did you know we were at his apartment?'

'Adam's comm system has a tracker built into it. So long as he's not too deep underground or in a shielded building, STS always knows where he is.' He caught her appalled look. 'Yeah, paranoid is only the beginning when you work in US intelligence.'

'Jesus.' Another, more worrying thought. 'You don't listen in through his earwig when he's off-duty, do you?'

'Why, have you been trying to persuade him to sell secrets to the Chinese?'

'I'm being serious, Tony. He might be a government agent, but he still has rights. You know, privacy and all that. I'm not even American and I know that's supposed to be one of the Amendments.'

'The fourth. Although when it comes to national security, rights get a bit fuzzy. Hey, I didn't say I approve,' he added, seeing her darkening expression. 'That's just the way it is. Trust me, it isn't any better in England. Or any other country.'

'That doesn't make it right.'

'Maybe not. But just to give you some reassurance that we're not all cogs in an Orwellian surveillance machine; no, we don't listen in on Adam. When he turns the earwig off, it's off.'

'Except for the tracker. And the beeper.'

'Hah! Don't get me started on the beeper. I just hope they toned it down for Adam. The damn thing was like an airhorn going off in my ear.'

'You had one too?'

'Yeah. I've got the same implanted gear as Adam. They deactivated the earwig – and the beeper, thank God – but it's all still in there. It would have needed surgery to take out, and since it wasn't causing any trouble we decided, hey, just leave it. You never know, I might need it again some day.'

'After what you said PERSONA did to you, I really hope you don't,' she said. That thought took her back to what Adam had told her. 'Tony?'

'Yeah?'

'What happened to Adam when he joined the project?'

'What do you mean?' There was already reticence in his voice.

'Why did they wipe his memory? They didn't do that to you.'

'I don't really know.'

'You don't know, or you can't tell me?'

He gave her an apologetic look. 'Some from column A, some from column B. What I do know is as much as you've obviously figured out for yourself – they did something to him that they didn't to me. What they did, or why they did it, I honestly don't know.'

'Who's "they"?' she asked, already suspecting she knew the answer.

'Kiddrick. And Roger Albion.'

She had been right. 'Roger . . .'

'Yeah. If you want to find out anything more, you'll have to talk to him.'

'Oh, I will,' she said, setting her jaw.

24

No History

Albion shifted uncomfortably under Bianca's stony stare. 'I don't suppose playing the helpless invalid card would get me any sympathy?'

'Not really,' she said.

'I thought not. Still, it was worth a try.'

A lengthy silence. 'Well?' Bianca prompted.

'Well what?'

'Are you going to tell me what happened to Adam before he joined the Persona Project, and why you and Kiddrick wiped his memory and brainwashed him into not thinking about it?'

'Oh, *that*.'

Another long pause. 'Roger,' Bianca finally said, exasperated, 'I told Adam yesterday that if you didn't tell me what I wanted to know, I was going to poke your bullet hole until you started talking. I was joking then, but now I'm starting to consider it.'

'Look, what can I say?' Albion protested. 'That whole part of the project is classified as need-to-know, and you don't need to know.'

'I disagree. I'm standing in for you—'

'Temporarily.'

'So what? You might think that I'm only here to keep your seat warm, but there are real people involved, real lives at stake. Whatever it was you and Kiddrick did to Adam, it's seriously affected his mental state. You must realise that.'

'Of course I realise that,' he snapped. 'I'm not blind – and I'm not devoid of empathy, either. But those were the orders we were given, so we carried them out.'

'So you were *ordered* to erase his memory?'

'It's hardly something we'd do for shits and giggles.'

The mere fact that he had sworn in front of her told Bianca that he was becoming stressed by her questions. She felt a stab of sympathy for the old man, trapped in his hospital bed, but knew she had to get closer to the truth. 'Who ordered it? Harper?'

He regarded her with suspicion. 'You seem to know so much already, I don't know why you're bothering to ask me. Yes, Harper.'

'You told me that Adam came from some special forces unit. But what was he like? As a person, I mean.'

Albion was reluctant to reply. 'He was . . .' he finally said, 'how best to put it? *Damaged.*'

'In what way?'

'Angry, disturbed. Very guilty.'

'Guilty?' The word came as a shock. 'About what?'

'I don't know. And I was specifically told not to ask. My diagnosis would be some kind of recent emotional trauma. But as for the cause, I have no idea.'

'So what you did to him was to erase this trauma?'

'Partly, yes. Although the main reason was to test the theory that the problems Tony had – I assume you know the basics?' She nodded. 'That Tony's problems were caused because the imprinted personas were clashing, for want of a better word, with his own memories. I created a modified version of Mnemexal to block specific protein kinases during the act of recall, effectively suppressing Adam's memories. Do that, and the imprinting process should work without the same risk of side effects.'

'But you weren't just suppressing the memories,' she said, appalled. 'You were wiping them! Do you even know if it's possible to recover them?'

'Adam didn't *want* to recover them,' said Albion. 'He volunteered for this, remember? Whatever happened to him, whatever it was he experienced, he wanted all memory of it *gone*.'

'And you went ahead and did it? Rather than try to help him deal with his problems, you just *deleted* them? Jesus, Roger! How can you possibly think that's in any way ethical?'

'Don't you preach to me about ethics, Miss Childs!' he fired back, his heart monitor warbling in early warning. 'The world I'm working in – that we're *both* now working in – puts ethics way down the ladder. This is about national security. It's about *results*. Whether something is ethical or not is a very low consideration.'

Bianca shook her head. 'What the hell happened to you? You never used to be like this.'

'It's called going through the looking glass. Only you find that what's on the other side is actually the real world. And it's not pleasant.'

She stared at him, disgust giving way to another emotion – a deep disappointment in her former mentor. 'I don't want to end up like that, Roger,' she eventually said. 'And I think I should get out before I do.'

For a moment he looked angry . . . then his expression sank into a resigned sadness. 'No, you're right,' he said. 'I'm sorry I got you involved. This is a very cynical little universe I've found myself in, and I'm afraid it's infected me. No reason you should catch anything too.'

'It's a bit late for that.'

A melancholy smile. 'There's still time to find a cure. Yes, you should go back to England. After all, you've got a very rewarding future waiting there.'

Grim pragmatism stepped on her idealistic outburst. 'It won't be if I don't stay here until you're back on your feet.'

'What do you mean?' he asked, puzzled.

She told him about Harper's blackmail. 'That son of a bitch!' he erupted when she finished, setting the heart monitor trilling again. 'I can't believe he'd . . . no, actually I can,' he decided. 'He's one of the most unpleasant men I've ever had the misfortune to meet.'

'No arguments there,' said Bianca wholeheartedly.

'That's a new level of pointless malevolence, though. Especially when you'd already agreed to help.'

'His justification was something like "when you've got no choice, you have to give the other person even less".'

'Yes, that sounds like him,' he said, with a short, sarcastic laugh. 'Oh, Bianca, I'm sorry. I shouldn't have dragged you into this.'

'No, you shouldn't,' she replied, but lightly. 'Although there's another reason to stay other than just being forced to by a loathsome old man.'

'Oh?'

'Yeah. Adam.'

'You want to help him?' She nodded, and Albion smiled. 'You know, there's still hope for the world yet. As long as there are people like you in it, rather than everyone being like Harper.'

'Thanks. Although sometimes I feel extremely outnumbered.'

'One good deed can outweigh fifty bad ones. So how do you want to help him?'

'I'm not sure. But I'm sure the real Adam Gray is still in there somewhere, underneath this . . . this *robot* they want to turn him into. If I can help him find those memories . . .'

Albion appeared unsure. 'Be careful, Bianca. I wasn't kidding when I told you that Adam *wanted* to have his memory wiped. Getting them back might not be the best thing for him.'

'But he lost *all* his memories,' she countered. 'That can't possibly be what he thought he was signing up for. He doesn't even remember his parents, for God's sake. Was erasing everything a deliberate part of the process?'

'I don't know. I devised the drug, but I wasn't involved with the actual procedure.'

'Who was? Oh, let me guess,' she said, before he could answer. 'Kiddrick.'

'Afraid so.'

She huffed. 'That man is an absolute arse.'

Albion laughed. 'Oh, you noticed?' He became more serious. 'That said, he might be an arse' – he rolled his tongue around the British pronunciation – 'but he's not stupid. And he has connections. *And* he's petty and vindictive. So, again, be careful.'

'I'll watch out for him. Anyway, I have to get over to STS.'

'So where do we stand?' Albion asked. 'Are we still okay?'

'We're still okay,' she replied.

Bianca was expecting a joke, but instead he said, 'I'm glad. Thank you.'

She gave him a smile. 'See you soon.'

From the frosty reception she received in the Bullpen, the staff of the Persona Project had obviously received the email Tony had mentioned the previous night, and figured out that she was part of the reason for it. 'So,' said Kyle loudly as she walked past his workstation, 'anyone want to go bowling tonight? Oh, wait, we can't. That'd breach protocol.'

Tony looked up from a discussion with Levon. 'All right, knock it off. Bianca, hi. Glad you're here.'

'Hi. Where's Adam?'

'In the Cube.'

She started for the door, but Tony called her back. 'Martin needs to see you.'

'Right now?'

'Yes.'

'Let me see if I can guess why,' she said with a sigh as she reversed course.

Morgan was in his office – along with Kiddrick, who had positioned himself next to his desk like some sort of twitchy hench-man. 'Good morning, Dr Childs,' said Morgan. 'Please, take a seat.'

She did so. Kiddrick remained standing. 'You're not going to sit down?' she asked him. 'Run out of Preparation H?'

The scientist bridled, but Morgan pre-emptively raised a hand to silence him. 'Dr Childs, that's enough. Now, we need to discuss last night's . . . incident.'

'You mean when two goons aggressively interrupted a perfectly innocent conversation?'

'That's hardly what happened,' Kiddrick sniffed.

'Oh, were you there? Funny, I didn't see you.' She turned back to Morgan. 'Look, what happened was—'

'Adam already gave me his account,' he interrupted. 'And Spence and Fallon gave theirs. I think the best way to deal with this is to say that both sides overreacted and escalated the situation unnecessarily, but since nobody was hurt beyond the odd bruise, the matter is now considered closed.'

She was taken aback, not expecting it to be concluded so quickly. 'Okay . . .'

'That's far from the end of it, though,' said Kiddrick, glaring down at her. 'We're going to—'

'Dr Kiddrick,' Morgan interrupted. Kiddrick reluctantly fell silent. 'However, as a result of this incident, all members of the Persona Project have been given a reminder to adhere to the USIC black agency rules and regulations on social interactions, to the letter. Normally, this is an area where I personally would allow some leeway in the interests of team morale, but a directive has been issued by the Director of National Intelligence, and it will be followed. By *all* team members. Do I make myself clear?'

'Perfectly,' she said, not hiding her disapproval.

'Since you didn't go through the standard STS orientation and training, you've been sent a copy of the relevant regulations. I'd recommend that you read them. To avoid any future problems.'

'I see. Is that all?'

Kiddrick was unable to stay quiet any longer. 'No, it's *not* all,' he said, stepping forward. 'As of now, you are *not* to talk to or communicate with Adam except for *strictly* work-related reasons.' His head jerked forward with each emphasis, reminding her of a strutting chicken.

'Well, excuse me,' Bianca shot back, 'but I think that Adam's mental well-being *is* work-related.'

'That's not your concern!'

'It should be *everyone's* concern! Without Adam, you don't even have a project.'

The tendons on Kiddrick's scrawny neck stood out as his anger rose. 'You're only here to work out drug doses for the PERSONA subjects. That's all! Adam's well-being is my responsibility, not yours. If he has any problems, I can handle them.'

'Like the great job you did for Tony?'

She knew the moment she said it that she had gone too far. Kiddrick looked to be on the verge of exploding with fury, but Morgan swiftly rose to his feet and slammed both palms flat on the desk. 'All right, enough!' he barked. 'Both of you. Dr Childs, for now, keep any interactions with Adam to nothing more than what you need to do your job. Understood?'

Face tight, she stood, refusing to allow herself to be physically intimidated by Kiddrick. 'I understand what you've said, yes. But I don't understand the reasoning behind it.'

'You don't need to know,' Kiddrick growled. 'And just because you're temporarily standing in for Roger, that doesn't give you—'

Someone knocked on the door. Before Morgan had a chance to respond, it opened and Tony leaned through. 'Sorry to interrupt,' he said urgently, 'but we've got something.'

25

Crossing the Line

'You know,' said Bianca, yawning, 'I think I've spent more time on planes in the past week than the entire ten years before that.'

'Too bad you don't get frequent flyer miles on US government jets,' Tony replied as he sat beside her. He gave her a bottle of water. 'Here.'

'Thanks.' She cracked open the cap and gratefully glugged down several mouthfuls. The dry air in the cabin of the Bombardier Global 6000, a large long-range business jet in an anonymous white and blue livery, had left her dehydrated and groggy during the long flight across the continental United States and Canada, and now over the frozen wilds of Alaska. 'How's everything going?'

'We're on schedule – we'll be landing in Provideniya in about an hour. Don't forget to turn your watch forward – we'll have crossed the International Date Line.'

'The Russians bought the cover story?'

'So far. To them, we're a team of climatologists. We're supposedly waiting for another group to arrive later in the day, which will explain why we don't get out of the plane after we land. We've got full authorisation from Moscow to be there.'

'And how did we get that at such short notice?'

'Better that you don't know. But if they check the plane, all they'll find – at least, unless they start unbolting panels – is exactly what they'd expect: winter gear, tents, skis. We've even got some weather balloons.'

'Cool. I can use the helium to sound like a duck.' They both smiled. 'So what about Zykov? And al-Rais?'

Tony's face became harder. 'Zykov's due to land two hours after we do. Al-Rais . . . we don't know yet. But we *do* know from the communications intercepts that he'll meet Zykov in person before they buy the RTG from Colonel Sevnik. We've got satellite surveillance on the airport to watch for his plane.'

Bianca looked up the cabin to where the rest of the team were sitting. She couldn't help but feel that she had been somewhat ostracised by the mission specialists, and among Baxter's squad of seven men were Fallon and Spence, so she had deliberately chosen an isolated seat to stay out of everyone's way. As for the team's key member . . . 'So, when am I going to be allowed to talk to Adam?'

That came out with more of an edge than she'd intended, but Tony took it in his stride. 'Nobody's stopping you now. I'm certainly not going to.'

'Really? I thought there was some sort of executive order forbidding it.'

'We're on a mission, so communication between team members is vital. That's my take, anyway. Besides, I'm not Kiddrick.'

'Well, no. You're a lot nicer to look at, for a start.'

'Careful!' he said, holding up his hands in mock warning. 'That might be considered *fraternising*! But it's nice of you to say so.'

'Well, you know.' She grinned sheepishly. 'I can talk to him, then?'

'Sure. Although it'd probably be wise to keep it work-related for now. And not just because of Kiddrick – we are about to go into a mission, after all. We don't need any distractions.'

'I'll keep things official. Ish.' Bianca headed up the cabin.

She passed Baxter and his men, ignoring Spence's glower. Holly Jo at least gave her a nod, though Kyle still appeared to be snubbing her. Adam was in the front row of seats. 'Okay if I sit here?' she asked.

He looked up at her. 'Sure.'

She sat beside him. 'So. Apparently there are certain topics we should avoid.'

'Yeah. Kiddrick's list started at A and went right through to Z.'

'He didn't include numbers? That gives us some wiggle room.'

He smiled slightly. 'Did you read the file on the persona I'll be using?'

'Yes. Dr Eugene Browning of the International Atomic Energy Agency.' The plan was for Adam to use Browning's persona to make a professional assessment of the RTG's condition, when located. If it were safe to transport, it would be loaded aboard the jet – along with al-Rais, if he was captured – and taken to the US; if not, it would be left in situ and the Russian authorities alerted so they could send one of their own nuclear recovery teams to secure it. 'Hopefully he knows his stuff.'

'If he doesn't, I might wind up glowing in the dark.'

Despite his joke, the thought gave Bianca a chill. She had on occasion worked with radioactive substances as a chemist, and always treated them with the utmost caution, finding the idea that something could kill a person without even touching them deeply unsettling. That anyone could even consider deliberately exposing others to something so toxic was more disturbing still.

'Dr Browning is about as far from a secret agent as I can imagine,' she said, changing the subject. 'What's it like when the persona you're using is so different from you?'

'It can be . . . tricky,' he admitted. 'There have been times when I've done something that's *so* far from how the person would actually behave that it's almost like a voice screaming in my head for me to stop.'

'Like when you answer the test question about the person's most guilty secret?'

'Yeah. Only much stronger. Macau was an extreme example, actually – Peter Vanwall had a serious fear of heights.'

'Has anything like that ever happened to you before?'

'Not to that degree, no. Kiddrick thinks it might have been caused by stress. I was already under pressure to get to you before Zykov did anything, and then suddenly coming up on that huge drop was a shock – which triggered Vanwall's vertigo. That started a kind of feedback loop; his fear stressed me out more, which allowed it to get even stronger, and so on. So when I was out on that roof . . . it was real hard not to be scared. But I managed it.'

'How?'

He looked at her as if the answer were obvious. 'Because I had no choice.'

'Has there ever been a time when . . . when that voice in your head got too loud? When it stopped you from doing something? Or made you do something else?'

'No. Not yet, and I hope it never does. But then,' he went on, looking over his shoulder at the seats behind, 'there are always other voices yammering at me to get on with the mission, so it shouldn't be a problem.'

Holly Jo looked up from her laptop. 'I *heeeeard* that,' she said, singsong.

'What're you doing there, anyway?' Kyle asked her.

'I sent Levon my solution to his puzzle,' she told him. 'I figured out how to get the diamond out of the vault. Just waiting for him to reply.'

'Hey! Watch out, that might be *fraternisation*!'

Tony came back up the cabin. 'I see that's going to be our running joke for the next few days. What did you come up with, Holly Jo?'

She gave him a smug smile. 'It's obvious, really. It takes an hour to break into the vault, but the guards check it every half-hour, yes? So you need to come at it from a different angle – literally. Get on to the roof, start cutting through it, time it so you stop cutting just before the guards start their rounds, then start again right after they finish.' Kyle began to chuckle. 'What?'

'I think he's planned for that,' he said.

'Why?'

''Cause my idea was to go into the vault through the *floor*. Didn't work. It's a big-ass vault, so it needs heavy-duty supports – six feet of concrete, reinforced with steel bars. Can't break through it inside the twenty-four-hour limit without making enough noise to warn the guards. So I'm kinda sure he'll have thought of putting a camera on the roof.'

'We'll see.'

'Yeah, we will.'

'Does Levon just make up reasons why a plan wouldn't work?' asked Bianca. 'That sounds like something he pulled out of the air.'

'No, no – the dude's tough, but fair,' said Kyle. 'He tells us the basics of each scenario, but keeps a file on the server with a list of everything he *doesn't* tell us. So if a plan doesn't work, he pulls out the bit that explains why. And 'cause it's time-stamped, we know he didn't just make it up.'

'But isn't he some sort of super-hacker? How do you know he hasn't changed the time stamp?'

Kyle and Holly Jo stared at each other for a moment. 'He wouldn't,' she gasped. 'Would he?'

'He'd better not have,' Kyle replied, flustered.

Tony laughed. 'Guys, you can trust Levon. He likes to outwit you fair and square.' Holly Jo's laptop chimed. He glanced at the screen. 'Besides, I guess we're about to find out. Although judging from the message title . . .'

Holly Jo pouted as she read it out. '"Not even close." Huh!' She opened the email and rapidly scanned through it. 'Cameras on each corner of the roof, and a vibration sensor on the ceiling directly above the vault. Damn. Although I'm definitely going to ask him if he's hacked the time stamp . . .'

The pilot's voice came over the cabin speaker. 'Tony, Mr Morgan is calling on the video link.'

Tony pushed an intercom button to reply. 'Okay, thanks.' He went to the forward bulkhead and switched on the flat-screen. 'Martin, we're here. What is it?'

'Just an update on your operation status,' Morgan replied. 'You have full approval to go ahead with a clandestine operation on Russian soil.'

That produced questioning looks throughout the cabin. 'I thought we already had it,' said Tony, mystified. 'Seeing as we're only an hour away from landing.'

Morgan rubbed the back of his head, seeming worn out from whatever meeting he had just endured. 'State had a fit when they found out what we were doing. They didn't want to antagonise the Chinese, and they want to antagonise the Russians even less. Even though the Admiral authorised the mission, it still got kicked upstairs to the White House. We managed to talk Alan Sternberg around – just barely, and the Admiral's still steaming about it – and once he was on board that pretty much meant the President would approve it. Same conditions as the Macau operation, though: the US will deny any knowledge if the Russians catch you.'

Tony regarded the screen grimly. 'Understood.'

'We've just been disavowed again,' Kyle muttered.

'There's one piece of good news,' said Morgan. 'If you secure the RTG and it's safe to transport, you'll have a fighter escort all the way home. F-22s from Elmendorf will pick you up as soon as you leave Russian airspace.'

'But before that, we're on our own?'

'I'm afraid so. Good luck.'

'Thanks.' Tony disconnected, facing the others with a conflicted expression. 'Well, you heard him. We'd better not screw this up.'

'Good thing we brought all that survival gear,' said Kyle. 'We might need it if we want to stay out of a Siberian gulag.'

'We won't need it,' said Baxter firmly. 'As soon as the bad guys bring the RTG into the airport, my team will move in, take them out and capture al-Rais. We'll be airborne before the Russians put down their vodka. We'll be out of Russian airspace in five minutes – and in *American* airspace in ten. St Lawrence Island is less than sixty miles from the Russian coast, and it's US territory. With F-22s backing us up, we'll be home free.'

'So long as nothing goes wrong,' Tony reminded him.

A short, sardonic laugh from Bianca. 'And what are the odds on that?'

26

The Edge of the World

Provideniya Bay airport, Russia

The little coastal town of Provideniya was one of the most remote settlements in Russia, located at the country's easternmost edge on the Bering Strait separating Asia and North America. Despite this isolation, close to two thousand hardy souls lived in the former military port. The town had gained an unlikely new economic lifeline following the fall of the Soviet Union, its relative proximity to the US – and the fact that it was home to one of the very few airports in the vast Chukotka region – turning it into a gateway for Siberian tourism.

The Persona team were not there for pleasure, however. In fact, the view outside suggested that any form of fun would be hard to come by. The worst of the Russian winter had passed, the icy waters now more or less navigable, but snow shrouded the bleak, treeless landscape. Heavy grey clouds warned that more was likely to fall. The even heavier coats of the shivering Russian customs officers who boarded the aircraft, making only a cursory check of its occupants and cargo after taking a 'gift' of several hundred dollars, made it clear that conditions were bitterly cold.

Kyle watched the departing officials through a porthole as they hurried back to the grim concrete block of the terminal. 'Man, I'm glad I don't have to get off the plane.'

'You'll have to go outside to launch the UAV,' Tony reminded him, to the younger man's dismay.

Bianca was still shocked by the openness with which the Russians had demanded – and received – a bribe. 'I can't believe they just shook you down like that.'

'Standard practice over here,' he replied. 'It must be annoying if you're a tourist, but it makes things a hell of a lot easier if you're a spy!' He addressed the others. 'Okay, let's set up the op centre.'

The cabin became a whirl of activity as equipment was removed from hidden compartments. Tony, Holly Jo and Kyle assembled their workstations. Baxter and his men meanwhile extracted more deadly hardware: weapons, an assortment of guns from pistols through angular G36 assault rifles painted in mottled grey Arctic camouflage to a hulking Barrett XM500 sniper rifle that looked to Bianca like a refugee from a science fiction movie.

She had equipment of her own, retrieving the medical case while Adam brought out the PERSONA gear. 'So, what happens now?' she asked.

'First we find out where Zykov is,' Tony told her as he brought his laptop online and checked the latest intelligence updates. 'Okay,' he announced, 'he's still in flight. ETA, ninety minutes.'

'What about al-Rais?' said Baxter.

Holly Jo also had her system up and running. 'Nobody's landed here except us. There aren't any other planes at the airport either, so it doesn't look as if he's got anything standing by to take the RTG out.'

'Perhaps he's not coming,' suggested Bianca.

Tony shook his head. 'The most recent intercepts said Zykov was going to meet him when he arrived.'

'Maybe al-Rais isn't coming in by air,' said Adam quietly as he looked through a window. The airport was on the eastern side of a fjord; across the mile of wind-whipped water was Provideniya itself, apartment blocks painted in shades of blue and yellow and pink standing out against the barren hillside beyond. But his attention was on the waterfront. Several ships were moored at the run-down docks. Most had been laid up there for the winter, blanketed in snow and ice, but a couple stood out as having been in recent use. 'This is a port, after all.'

'It's a hell of a long way to come by sea,' Baxter said, dubious.

'He wouldn't have to come all the way from Pakistan on a ship. We know that he's managed to travel by air before, despite all the security checks. If he got to Malaysia or the Philippines, a ship could reach here in two weeks.'

'Still a long time.'

'The man once spent six months in a cave. A couple of weeks on a ship wouldn't be much of a hardship for him. Especially not if he thinks he can get his hands on a terror weapon at the end of it.'

Tony joined him, looking out at the town. 'If he's planning to move the RTG by sea, that makes things a lot easier for us. With our satellites tracking it, the navy can intercept it anywhere.'

'I doubt he'd do that, though,' said Adam. 'If he's come in by sea, it's because he wanted to keep it quiet – but as soon as he gets the RTG, he'll want to get out of here with it as quickly as possible.'

Tony gave him an admiring look, like a teacher proud of a student's work. 'Good thinking. Okay, Holly Jo – new task.'

'Shipping?' she said.

'Yeah. See what we can get on ships coming into the port over the past few days. Kyle, get the UAV in the air and check the docks.'

'Oh man,' Kyle complained. 'You mean I have to go out in the cold?'

'It builds character,' Holly Jo told him. 'Which you need.'

Kyle made a face, then carried the UAV to the front of the cabin. The drone had been partially disassembled for transport. Bianca watched with interest as he attached the shrouded rotors to the main fuselage; this was her first good look at the machine. The entire underside of the body, except for a blister housing the camera lenses, was a smooth carapace inset with a hexagonal pattern. 'So how does it work?' she asked. 'I mean, it's not huge, but it's not invisible either. Won't people see it in the daytime?'

'Nope,' said Kyle smugly. 'It might not be invisible, but it's the next best thing. See these?' He tapped one of the hexagons. 'TCCs.'

'And those are . . . ?'

'Tri-polymer chromatic cells! Light-emitting plastic. There's a little camera aboard that looks up at the sky, and these change colour to match it. So if the sky's blue, the drone turns blue as well. It's like the Predator's cloaking device, brah! It's awesome.'

'He's actually not exaggerating, for once,' said Holly Jo. 'It's really cool.'

Kyle beamed with enthusiasm. 'Show her, show her.'

Holly Jo leaned over to his workstation and tapped the keyboard. After a moment, the UAV's shrouded belly turned from a neutral grey to a much lighter beige – matching, Bianca realised, the colour of the bulkhead behind Kyle. 'That *is* quite neat,' she said.

'Check this out.' He moved one hand over the little aircraft's dorsal surface. A second later, the hexagonal cells changed colour again – to a tanned pink. 'Give it a few years, you'll be able to put these on your car. Bored with red? Push a button and it turns blue, or green, or anything you want. I can't wait.'

'You'll have to, unless you want to pay a million dollars per square foot,' said Tony. 'Okay, switch it off. Save the batteries.' Holly Jo entered another command and the UAV flicked back to a dull grey.

'You know what else it needs, though?' said Kyle. 'A gun! Seriously, Tony, suggest it. Next time we see someone chasing Adam, pa-pa-pow, *boom*! Death from above!'

'You do know that flying a helicopter in *Grand Theft Auto* isn't a tactical simulation, right?' scoffed Holly Jo.

He gave her another sarcastic look, then continued to assemble the UAV. 'Okay,' said Tony when he was done, 'send it out.'

'Don't I get a coat?' Kyle moaned as Adam opened the hatch on the side of the aircraft facing away from the terminal building. A biting wind blew into the cabin. 'Whoa, whoa, *whoa*!' Kyle yelped as he ducked out on to the steps. He held up the little quadrotor, thumbing a switch. The translucent propellers blurred almost to nothing as the machine's underbelly changed colour to match the iron clouds overhead.

Kyle hesitantly eased his hold, leaving the UAV hovering in mid-air. Satisfied, he rushed back into the cabin. 'Okay, okay, close it!' he gasped as he scurried back to his workstation. 'God *damn*, it's cold out there! No wonder Russians drink so much vodka – they need it to stay warm.' As Adam shut the hatch, he took the controls. 'Okay, let's go have a look at some boats . . .'

The UAV tipped forward and glided away from the plane, gaining height. The camouflage really did work, Bianca saw; while it wasn't a perfect match for the surroundings, it was effective enough to confuse the eye. At cruising height, the drone would be almost impossible to spot from the ground.

'Okay, Adam, Bianca,' Tony said, 'I think you should imprint the persona now.'

'So soon?' said Adam. 'Zykov isn't even here yet.'

'I know, but I want everyone to be ready the moment he touches down. We don't know where the RTG is being kept – for all we know, it's right here at the airport. We can't afford to lose any time.'

'Okay,' said Bianca, opening the cases. 'Let's meet Dr Eugene Browning.'

'What is your name?'

'Eugene Browning. Middle name, Marcus.'

'Your date of birth.'

'That would be November fifth, 1955.'

'Your place of birth.'

'Riverside, California.'

'Your mother's name.'

'My mother's name was Florence.'

'Her birthday?'

'July tenth. I think. I was only seven years old when she died. Viral pneumonia. Very sad.'

'And your most guilty secret?'

Adam's eyes flicked evasively before he answered. 'That would be taking a ten-thousand-dollar bribe to overlook some safety infringements at a nuclear plant, when I was an inspector for the Nuclear Regulatory Commission. Nothing major!' he quickly qualified. There was a hoarseness to his voice, further increasing the oddness of his staccato speech pattern. 'They were fixed within a week. The plant owner just didn't want to risk a shut-down. And it was back in 1985!'

'I think the statute of limitations applies in this case,' said Tony. Bianca continued with the rest of the standard test questions. All the answers were as expected. 'Are you okay?'

'Yes. Fine.' Adam stood, looking around the cabin as if he hadn't seen it before. 'Very plush. It beats flying commercial.'

Tony and Bianca exchanged glances. Browning was more eccentric than any persona Adam had previously used. 'So long as he knows his stuff . . .' Tony muttered.

'Oh, I do, young man, I do,' said Adam. 'I've worked with these generators before. I'll be able to assess this one for you. We just have to find it.'

'I've got something,' Holly Jo announced. 'I tracked down the ships in the harbour through the Lloyd's Register. The *Anadyr Star* is Russian, and it doesn't seem to have been to any non-Russian port in the past five years; it's just a local transport. The *Woden*, though . . . Panamanian registry, departed Lingayen in the Philippines thirteen days ago. It got here last night.'

'So it *could* have brought al-Rais,' mused Tony. 'Kyle, give us a closer look at the *Woden*.'

The drone's cameras had provided the names of the two ships lacking a deep coating of ice. Kyle brought the miniature aircraft about to focus on the larger of the pair, an elderly thousand-ton freighter. The UAV was a few hundred feet above the bay, giving the observers an oblique view of the ship. Lights were visible in its portholes, but there was no activity on the decks. 'Whoever's aboard, they're not coming out,' he said. 'When it's this nut-freezingly cold, I can't blame 'em.'

'Someone might come out soon,' Tony replied, checking his laptop. 'We just got an update on Zykov's plane. Looks like he made good time; he'll be landing in ten minutes. We'd better be ready for him. Kyle, get the drone back over here so we can see what he does.'

'On it,' Kyle responded.

Baxter and his men finished preparing their weapons. Bianca

sat with Adam, unable to shake off a growing nervousness. Before long, Holly Jo provided an update. 'He's on final approach. Coming in from the south.'

Everyone moved to the right side of the cabin to watch. Lights shone above the sea as the incoming plane made its final descent. It hesitantly lined up with the narrow strip of snow-cleared runway, then dropped down to a bumpy landing. Before long, it had taxied around to the terminal building, stopping directly in front of it some three hundred metres from the Bombardier.

'There's Zykov,' said Kyle as he brought the UAV in closer. The squat Russian was the first out of the business jet, pulling a heavy coat tightly around himself. Two other men emerged behind him. Bianca recognised one as a bodyguard from Macau.

The pilot closed the hatch behind them. 'I guess al-Rais didn't fly in with them,' said Baxter, sounding disappointed.

Two Russian officials came out to meet the trio. After a brief exchange, all five men headed into the building. 'Tony,' said the Bombardier's pilot over the intercom, 'port side. We've got company.'

The rush to the other side of the cabin was enough to make the plane rock slightly. Everyone peered out of the windows. The Global 6000 was parked on a broad expanse of concrete north of the terminal, at the edge of which was a chain-link fence separating the airport from the snowy landscape beyond.

Something was making its way towards them along a track running around the bay's shore. 'What the hell's that?' said Kyle.

Baxter eyed the approaching vehicle. 'It's a Vityaz.'

'A what?'

'A Vityaz. DT-10 all-terrain vehicle. The Russians love 'em. Mud, snow, swamp, water – you name it, those things can drive through it.'

Bianca watched the Vityaz as it trundled towards the airport boundary. It was a low, wide slab of snow-caked metal painted a dingy military green, riding on broad caterpillar tracks. As it turned to follow the fence, she saw that it had two separately articulated halves, an equally boxy trailer on its own set of tracks connected to the forward section by a clutch of hefty hydraulic rams. From the way it was effortlessly carving through the snow, it appeared Baxter was right about its off-road capabilities, even if speed had not been high on its designer's list of priorities.

'Is al-Rais in it?' Tony wondered aloud. 'Kyle, get the drone over there. I want to see who's inside.'

It took another couple of minutes for the Vityaz to reach the terminal. By that time, the UAV had taken up station to observe it. 'Damn it, we can't see anything from this angle,' muttered Baxter, looking over Kyle's shoulder. 'Bring it lower.'

'If I do that, someone might see it,' Kyle shot back. 'I know what I'm doing, brah.'

'I'm not your *braaahhh*,' Baxter said, growling the word.

'Keep it at the same height,' Tony ordered. 'But pull back so we can see into the cabin.'

Kyle complied, zooming in on the Vityaz's row of four front windows. Reflections made it difficult to see inside, but movement within revealed a shadowy form at the controls. 'I don't see anyone else.'

'Could be someone in the rear cargo bed,' Baxter suggested. 'Or the trailer.'

But the only person who got out when the Vityaz stopped was the driver, an overweight, bearded man wearing a large fur hat. He waddled to the terminal entrance and went inside. After a couple of minutes he emerged, now accompanied by Zykov and his two bodyguards. Zykov asked a question; the driver responded by pointing in the direction of the little town across the fjord.

'Al-Rais is in the town,' Adam said suddenly. 'That's where they're meeting. We need to get over there.'

'We can track him with the UAV,' Tony pointed out.

'No, no. Something's not right.' The agent's concerns sounded incongruous in Browning's staccato speech patterns. 'You said yourself that al-Rais won't take the RTG away by sea. Too vulnerable. And Zykov won't be flying it out on his own jet. Far too risky. But there aren't any other planes here. So how's he getting it out?' He stabbed a finger at the Vityaz on Kyle's screen. 'Mr Baxter just said that thing can go anywhere.' Another jab, this time through the portholes at the cars parked by the terminal. 'The road into town's obviously passable. You don't need something like that just to be a taxicab. They're going somewhere else. Somewhere with no roads.'

'They'll have to come back to the airport, though,' said Holly Jo. 'I mean, this is literally the only way out of here.'

'No! No it isn't, young lady, no it isn't. Sevnik's an army colonel, he has command of helicopters.' Zykov and his men clambered aboard the Vityaz. 'We've got to follow them. Tony, how much more bribe money do we have? Roubles and dollars.'

The question surprised Tony. 'I'm not sure. A few thousand of each?'

'I'll need it all.'

'Why?'

'We need a car. I'm going to follow them into town.'

'The UAV can do that.'

'Tony, trust me. I need to stay close. We can't afford to lose them.'

'If anyone's going after them, it should be my guys,' said Baxter.

'I'm sure a team of armed commandos skiing through town

will pass completely without comment,' Adam retorted, to the Alabaman's annoyance.

'Okay. Adam, you go,' Tony decided. 'But don't get *too* close – Zykov knows you. And take a gun.'

Adam nodded. 'Bianca, come on.'

'*What?*' she yelped. 'I'm not going out there!'

'We might need the PERSONA. If we have a chance to record al-Rais's memories, we have to take it.'

'It's too risky,' said Tony, shaking his head.

'He's setting off,' Kyle warned. The Vityaz lurched into motion, bending like a metal caterpillar at its central joint and making a tight turn back along the track.

'Tony,' said Adam, more forcefully. 'We're running out of time. I won't take any unnecessary risks. Especially not with Bianca there. Zykov knows her too.'

'Okay, go,' Tony said, with reluctance. 'Both of you.'

'Don't I get any say in this?' Bianca protested.

'Sorry. But Adam'll take care of you, trust me.'

Adam was already moving down to the cabin to collect his gear. 'Come on,' he called over his shoulder to Bianca. 'And wrap up warm.'

27

The Face of Terror

'So you bribed some poor Russian to borrow his car?' asked Bianca.

'I gave him enough to buy a whole *new* car,' Adam replied as he carefully guided the ageing Lada around the edge of the bay. Even with chains on the tyres and following the Vityaz's tracks, the snow-covered road was still tricky to navigate. 'And then I had to pay off the others who were jealous that I didn't choose *their* cars.'

'Did you tell them why you needed it?'

'No. That's the whole point of a bribe. I pay, they don't ask.'

She was already irritable about leaving the comfort and security of the plane, and being patronised did nothing to help her mood. 'So, two new things I know about Dr Eugene Browning – he speaks Russian, and he's a sarcastic git.'

Adam laughed. 'Yes, sorry. Sometimes a persona comes through without my meaning it to.'

She regarded him quizzically. 'You're not in total control?'

'Oh, nothing like that, no. It's more a subconscious influence. Like picking up a local accent after moving to a new town.'

'Or saying "I" instead of "he", like you did when you were

talking about that bribe Browning took in 1985?'

'Just living the part. Less chance of messing up my pronouns in front of the bad guys.' He looked across at her. 'Are you warm?'

Despite wearing a thick hooded coat and padded overtrousers, she was hunched tightly in the seat, the medical gear and a case containing a Geiger counter in her lap and gloved hands wedged firmly under her folded arms. 'Do I *look* warm?'

'I'd turn up the heater, but as you can see . . .' The dial was already as far into the red as it would go.

'Adam,' said Holly Jo through his earwig, 'Zykov just reached the town. Looks like he's going to the docks.'

He looked across the fjord. 'It'll probably take us about ten more minutes to get there. Keep me informed.'

'Will do.'

Bianca gave him a questioning look. There had been no time to fit her with an earwig. 'Zykov's heading for the port,' he told her.

'Like you thought.'

'Yes. Al-Rais is almost certainly aboard the *Woden*. Two questions: one, where are he and Zykov going to meet Sevnik? And two, how many terrorists has he brought with him?'

'You don't think al-Rais has come alone?'

'Unlikely.'

'Well, that's . . . cheery.' She slumped back in her seat.

The car continued around the inlet. After ten minutes of slithering through the snow, it passed a sign: Провидения. *Provideniya*. Beyond was the town itself, strings of buildings stretched out parallel to the shore. Under the grey sky it looked thoroughly uninviting, even the brightly coloured houses providing little cheer.

'We've reached the town,' Adam told those in the jet. He looked along the waterfront. Dark cranes rose above the docks.

The *Woden* was visible, lights shining in its wheelhouse. 'Heading for the port.'

'Okay,' said Holly Jo. 'Zykov and his men just went aboard the ship.'

'No sign of al-Rais?'

'Not yet.'

'Right. Keep watching. We'll be there soon.' The road into the town had been partially cleared of snow, making progress easier.

Even in such bitter conditions there were still people out and about, moving briskly in heavy fur-trimmed coats and hats. A few regarded Adam and Bianca with curiosity – or suspicion – as they passed, recognising the car but not its occupants. 'Nice place,' said Bianca as she took in the run-down state of the buildings. Several of the apartment blocks were derelict, windows boarded up or broken.

'Now who's being sarcastic, young lady?' Adam retorted. 'The town's lost more than half its population in the past twenty years. That's why some of the buildings are abandoned.'

'I'm surprised not all of them are. Who just told me that, by the way? You, or Browning?'

'Me. I researched the town on the flight. But the "young lady" part was Browning.'

'Tell him that if he calls me that again he'll get a slap. And so will you.'

Adam grinned, then slowed as the car approached a junction. 'Okay, that looks like it leads down to the docks.' He turned on to the new road, rounding a large warehouse-like structure.

Bianca pointed ahead. 'There's the . . . the thing. Whatever Baxter called it.'

'The Vityaz. It means "knight".' The DT-10 was parked near some rusting shipping containers. The *Woden* was moored not far away. 'Kyle, any activity on the ship?'

'Not since Zykov and his two guys went aboard,' came the reply.

'Is the driver still in the ATV?'

'Yeah.'

'Okay.' Adam continued past the Vityaz.

'What are we doing?' Bianca asked.

'I want a closer look at the *Woden*.'

Alarm filled her voice. 'You're not going to go aboard, are you?'

'Don't worry. I'm not crazy.' He stopped the car behind a row of containers, out of sight of both the Vityaz and the ship. 'Wait in the car.'

He was about to switch off the engine when Bianca batted his hand away from the key. 'Leave it on!' she protested. 'There'll be no heat otherwise.'

'And I thought you'd be against pollution.'

'I'm against freezing to death even more!'

Amused, he acquiesced. 'I won't be long.'

He got out and quickly surveyed the docks. There was no sign of anybody, the cranes empty and unmoving and the other moored vessels dark. Pulling up his hood, he advanced to the last container in the line and peered round it.

The *Woden*'s black-painted hull and white superstructure were both scarred by orange streaks of rust. The freighter was at least fifty years old, a privately owned tramp that plied the Pacific on behalf of individual clients, taking their cargo between ports too small for bulk carriers.

And not just cargo. Such vessels sometimes carried passengers. The one he suspected was aboard would have paid very handsomely to travel while avoiding the usual customs checks.

He briefly considered going to look through one of the portholes, but it was entirely possible someone inside the ship was watching the docks. Instead he retreated back up the row of containers and slipped between them. A little labyrinth had formed where several of the metal boxes had been haphazardly dumped. He went through to the far side and glanced out at the Vityaz. A small flare of orange light revealed the driver in its cab, smoking a cigarette. The engine was still running; like Bianca, the Russian wanted to stay warm.

'Adam,' said Tony urgently. 'Movement on the ship.'

'Okay,' he whispered, looking back towards the waterfront. One of Zykov's bodyguards had emerged on to the aft deck. His coat was open, a hand inside. He wasn't impersonating Napoleon. He had a gun at the ready, surveying the shore for signs of danger. Adam retreated into the shadows.

The other bodyguard came through an open hatch, followed by Zykov. The arms dealer was talking over his shoulder to someone.

Another man appeared. Tall, rangy, with a long dark beard spilling over his coat's collar. Olive-brown skin, a thin, prominent nose.

Muqaddim al-Rais.

The world's most wanted terrorist. The man behind atrocities that had claimed hundreds, even thousands of lives across the globe, including that of the US Secretary of State.

And he was here, in a tiny town on the frozen fringes of Russia.

For a moment, Browning's persona vanished from Adam's mind. His only thought was a sudden urge for *vengeance*. From this distance, even his pistol would be more than accurate enough to score a killing shot. His vision seemed to tunnel, locking on to the terrorist leader's head. One bullet would do it . . .

His focus widened as more men followed al-Rais on to the deck. The majority looked to be Pakistani or Afghan. None appeared acclimatised to the cold. The mountains of the Hindu

Kush were far from hospitable in winter, but sub-arctic Siberia – Provideniya was only barely south of the Arctic Circle – was something else entirely.

The men kept coming. Five, six, seven in all, each carrying a bag containing something suspiciously similar in length to a Kalashnikov rifle. Two of them also bore suitcases; the seven million dollars? The last man out gave Adam an odd feeling of recognition. It took him a moment to realise why. His name was Qasid, one of al-Rais's lieutenants; Adam had pulled his face from Syed's memories during the debriefing on the flight from Pakistan. Holly Jo had also found his picture in the USIC database.

But a brief meeting and a single photograph didn't seem enough to have produced the feeling of familiarity. Was there something more? He wasn't sure.

He wasn't sure why he had felt such a surge of anger towards al-Rais, either. He was an enemy of the United States, yes, but this had been almost *personal*. Why? He hadn't encountered al-Rais before.

Or . . . had he?

There was no time to consider that. 'Tony,' he whispered. 'I have eyes on al-Rais. Repeat, Muqaddim al-Rais is here.'

'We see him,' came the reply. 'Stand by.'

The two bodyguards came down the gangplank on to the dock. Adam pulled back deeper into cover. Zykov followed his men, then the terrorists filed on to the shore, al-Rais shielded by their bodies at the centre of the group. They all marched towards the Vityaz. The two bodyguards, al-Rais and one of his men entered the cab; the other six clambered into the back compartment of the DT-10's front unit. Presumably the trailer would be used to carry the RTG.

Zykov, however, didn't get in. Instead he reached into his coat and took out a telephone. Its oversized antenna revealed it to be a satellite unit rather than a cellular.

The Russian started to tap in a number. 'Holly Jo,' Adam said, 'Zykov's making a call on a satphone.'

'I'll try to snag it,' she replied.

Zykov put the phone to his ear. After a few moments he frowned and peered at the unit's screen, then moved several paces away from the Vityaz and held the phone up to the sky. He turned in place, finally looking satisfied when he was facing south. Satellite phones depended on line-of-sight to their orbiting relays, and were also susceptible to local interference; the Vityaz, a big metal box housing a powerful engine, would not help reception.

He put the phone back to his head, waiting several seconds before getting a connection and starting to talk. Adam – or rather Browning – could make out most of what he heard, his current persona having acquired a fair knowledge of Russian during his years as an international atomic energy inspector. Zykov was talking to Colonel Sevnik: his seller.

A tension – no, an excitement, the thrill of the hunt – rose in Adam as he realised what Zykov was doing. 'They're arranging the meet,' he told the team. 'This is it – they're going to collect the RTG.'

He was about to ask Holly Jo if she had tapped into the call when Zykov suddenly waved to the driver, who leaned out of the cab. 'Put these in!' Zykov called out in Russian. 'Sixty-four! Twenty-five! Thirty-three, north! One-seven-three! Four! Thirty-seven, west!' The driver typed each number in turn into a unit on his dashboard.

A GPS. He was entering the coordinates for the rendezvous with Sevnik.

Adam hurriedly relayed the figures. 'Where is that?'

'It's about four and a half miles due east of your current

position, up in the hills,' Tony replied. 'That's as the crow flies – it's a lot further going round the inlet.'

Adam glanced around the container. The desolate snow-covered hills rose steeply and uninvitingly on the fjord's far side. He guessed the summits to be well over a thousand feet high. 'What's there?'

'Nothing, as far as I can tell. Looks like a glaciated valley.'

Zykov concluded his call, then returned to the Vityaz and climbed into the cab. The driver revved the engine, a plume of dirty exhaust smoke spouting skywards. Wherever they were going, Adam knew he had to follow. But the borrowed Lada would not get far off the road, while the articulated Vityaz could negotiate almost any terrain. So how . . .

Only one way. He hurried back to the car, pulling Bianca's door open. She looked up at him in surprise. 'Come on. Bring the PERSONA – quick!'

She had not seen the terrorists leave the ship. 'What's happened?'

'Come on, now! They're moving out.'

Still bewildered, she scrambled from the car. 'Who's moving? Zykov?'

'Yes – and al-Rais.'

'He's here?'

'Yes, but not for long. Hurry up!' They retrieved the PERSONA's cases, taking one each, then ran along the row of containers. Adam cautiously checked the road. The Vityaz was performing its caterpillar trick again, bending at the middle to drastically tighten its turning circle. Snow and gravel spitting up from its tracks, it ground back the way it had come.

Adam waited for the driver's mirrors to be blocked by the trailer, then broke into a run after it. 'Move, quick!'

Bianca followed, confused. 'What are we doing?'

'We've got to get aboard!' Adam quickly caught up with the crawler. The trailer's rear entrance was a wide bottom-hinged tailgate with only a canvas flap above it to shield the interior from the elements. He pulled the canvas away and swung the case inside, then clambered in after it. 'Come on!'

Bianca was some way behind, weighed down with the second case, the medical kit and the Geiger counter. 'Wait, wait!'

'I can't, I'm not driving!' He held out his arms. 'Give me the case, then take my hand!'

She strained to lift the weighty case up high enough for him to get hold of it. He swept it into the trailer, then reached back to grab her hand. 'All right, jump in!'

He pulled her up as she leapt at the tailgate, hooking her free arm over it. For a moment she wobbled, then Adam tugged harder and she rolled into the trailer. 'Ow! Bloody hell!' she cried.

'Are you okay?'

She clutched her arms protectively across her chest, grimacing in pain. 'No, that really bloody *hurt* when you dragged me over that thing!'

'Sorry. But I needed you to come with me.'

'Why?'

'That's a very good question,' Tony said in Adam's ear. 'What the hell are you doing? The UAV can follow Zykov – it's tracking you right now.'

'Sevnik isn't just going to hand the RTG over then and there,' Adam replied. 'It's a rendezvous, but I doubt it's the end of the journey. If Sevnik was bringing the RTG in by helicopter or in another ATV, he could have delivered it straight to the airport. No, it's stashed somewhere – somewhere protected from the weather, and where some random hunter won't trip over it.'

'Okay, we'll see where this takes us,' said Tony, though doubt was clear in his voice. 'Not that we've got much choice, now that you've jumped in the back of Zykov's truck!'

'It'll take us to the RTG. I'm sure of it.' Adam pulled the canvas flap back down, then surveyed the trailer's interior. It was as bare as the landscape beyond the town, plain metal benches running the length of each side and a small mound of dirty tarpaulins and sheets piled at the far end. He gestured to one of the benches. 'You might as well sit down,' he said to Bianca. 'This could be a long ride.'

28

Out in the Cold

Adam had been right. The drive out of Provideniya and up into the hills took some time. While the Vityaz was extremely capable off-road, it was not fast.

Nor was it comfortable. 'I feel seasick,' Bianca moaned after a particularly rough series of lurches almost pitched her from the bench. It was taking the pair's full effort to stop the cases from skittering about like pinballs.

Adam pulled back the canvas to look outside. 'At least this is as high as we're going.' The Vityaz had reached the end of a particularly steep climb and was now on more or less level ground as it rumbled across a hilltop. Provideniya was still visible on the far side of the inlet, though the weather was deteriorating, a light snowfall rendering the view hazy.

'Yeah, but I'm getting the horrible feeling we might never go back down.'

'We'll be okay.'

'Really? *Really?* We've jumped into the back of a snowmobile-tank thing full of terrorists on their way to buy a nuclear weapon, and it's not as if we've got anywhere to hide in here. If they find us, they'll kill us!'

'Then we'll have to make sure they don't find us.' Adam nudged the tarps with one foot. 'The only person who knows what's in here is the driver, and he doesn't seem to want to get out of his nice warm cab. We can lie under the benches and cover ourselves with these. It's pretty dark; we should be okay.'

'And if they put the RTG in here, and it has radiation pouring out of an enormous crack in one side?'

'Then we'll have to hide on the *other* side.'

It took a moment for her to realise that he was joking. 'That's not very funny.'

'But "not very" still means "a little", doesn't it?'

A tiny, reluctant smile appeared on her lips. 'A *very* little.'

'That's still enough. Browning's good at reassuring people. He has to be, considering his line of work. He always had to convince his kids that he wasn't going to come back home radioactive.'

'Browning has kids?' He nodded. 'Is that . . . does that feel weird to you? Knowing all the everyday little details of somebody's life when it's so completely different from yours?'

'It does now that you've brought it up. Thank you!'

She smiled again. 'Sorry. But once you mentioned his kids, what happened in your mind? How does it work for you? Do you just know the details about them, like their names and their birthdays, or do you . . . *feel* how he does about them?'

'I feel it,' he replied, after a moment – one filled with a rush of memories that weren't his. A summer afternoon in the garden, whooping as he jumped into the paddling pool with his son and daughter and the sluice of displaced water sent a plastic duck whirling across the lawn, Janey and Bobby squealing and giggling at the sight . . .

Not *his* daughter, or *his* son. Browning's. It took a conscious mental effort to stop the flow of images and sounds and smells—

'Adam?'

'Yeah,' he said, snapping back. 'It's strange. When I've got someone's persona in my head, some memories bring back emotions. Sometimes really strong ones. But once the persona's gone, it's different. I still have the memories I accessed, but . . . they're just facts. I was at a place, I was with a particular person, I did this or that – but I don't remember how it felt.'

'But you do remember that the persona *did* feel something?'

He nodded. 'I remember that Zykov was mad as hell when I took all his money. But the actual anger itself . . . no, it's gone.' That thought suddenly took him back to the dock. When he'd seen al-Rais emerge from the ship, a feeling almost of *rage* had struck him, nearly overpowering. It couldn't have come from one of the personas he had used in the past. But he had never encountered the terrorist leader himself.

As far as he knew.

'Holly Jo?' he said. 'I'm going off-comms. Bleep me if anything happens.' He pushed the little bump behind his ear, cutting her off before she could reply. A faint click told him that the radio channel was closed.

'What is it?' asked Bianca.

'Something happened on the dock, when I saw al-Rais. Just for a moment, I got *mad*. Really mad. I was ready to pull out my gun and put a bullet in his head before I got myself back under control. The thing is, I have no idea why.'

'He *is* the world's most wanted terrorist,' she pointed out.

'No, it's more than that. It felt . . . *personal.*'

She leaned closer, concerned. 'You think you might have met him before you joined the Persona Project? Before your memory was . . .'

'Wiped? I don't know.' He was silent for several seconds, brooding. 'Maybe I had him in my sights once before, and for some reason I didn't take the shot. If I had done . . . it could have saved lives.' Another pause. 'Is that why I volunteered to have my memory erased? Because I felt guilty about missing the chance to take out al-Rais?'

'I don't know,' Bianca said softly. 'But . . .'

'What?'

'If seeing him provoked a response like that, then maybe your memories *haven't* been erased. Not fully, anyway. They might still be there, just buried. There could be a way to get them back.'

'How?'

'I don't have the slightest idea. I'm just the hired help.'

He realised that this time, she was the one not being entirely serious. 'I suppose I was asking for that.'

'Just a little. But I don't even know what they did to you in the first place, so I'm not the one to ask. You'd have to talk to Kiddrick, I suppose.'

'Somehow I don't think he'll tell me anything.'

'You could always beat it out of him.'

'Now I'm not even sure if you're joking.'

'Maybe I'm not!' She grinned. 'But I suppose—'

Adam suddenly waved her to silence, hearing something over the Vityaz's engine. A moment later, a bleep sounded in his ear. He reactivated the transceiver. 'What is it? Sounds like we've got company.'

'You have,' Tony replied. 'The UAV just saw a helicopter. A Hind, it looks like.'

'It must be Sevnik. What's it doing?'

'It flew in for a closer look at your ride, then turned east towards the valley. Landing at the rendezvous point?'

'That'd be my guess too. Tell Kyle to keep a watch on it.'

'Will do. What's your situation? Why did you go off-comms?'

'Just something I wanted to ask Bianca, that's all. How far are we from the rendezvous coordinates?'

'About a mile,' said Holly Jo. 'You're approaching a steep hill down to the valley, so you might want to hold on to something.'

'Thanks for the warning. Okay, I'll leave the link open. Out.'

Bianca's nervousness had returned in full force. 'What's happening?'

'A helicopter just flew past. Probably Sevnik's. Looks like Zykov is about to introduce his buyer and seller for the first time.'

'Okay, so . . . what do we do when we get there?'

'To quote you, I don't have the slightest idea.'

'I'm not reassured,' she said sulkily.

The trailer jolted violently, one of the cases bashing against the side wall, then tipped sharply downhill. 'Hold on to me!' said Adam as he braced himself, stretching one leg across the cabin to pin the escaped case in place. Bianca clung to him, trying to keep the other from sliding away.

The descent lasted for several uncomfortable minutes before finally levelling out. Adam pulled the case across the trailer with his heel, then went to the back of the cabin. 'What are you doing?' Bianca demanded.

'Reconnaissance.' He peeled the flap aside, then leaned out and cautiously raised his head above the roof to look ahead.

The wind that hit his face was simultaneously hot and cold, exhaust fumes mixed with the biting gusts rolling across the landscape. He grimaced and narrowed his eyes. The flat-floored valley ran roughly north to south, hills rising steeply on each side. There was not so much as a tree in sight, or even shrubs, just the occasional boulder poking out above the snow.

The helicopter had landed, the Vityaz plodding towards it. It was a Hind, as Tony had said: an ugly and deadly Mil Mi-24P gunship, its stubby wings laden with rocket pods and a cannon mounted on its nose. Unlike its American counterparts, it also doubled as a troop carrier, a compartment in its fuselage able to carry up to eight people.

Some of them had debarked. Even from this distance, he could tell they were soldiers, his sharp eyes picking out their AKs. Sevnik was obviously as untrusting of al-Rais as vice versa.

He withdrew. 'The chopper's landed,' he told Bianca. 'Get under the bench – I'll cover you up.'

The prospect didn't please her. 'What about the cases? And what about you?'

'I'll put them under the sheets. Go on.'

Bianca reluctantly crawled under the bench. Adam took one of the grubby tarpaulins and draped it over her. In the half-light inside the trailer, it was unlikely anyone would give it a second look. He pushed the cases to the forward bulkhead and pulled the sheets over them, then held the remaining tarp over his shoulders like a cape and squeezed beneath the other bench. A quick check that his feet were fully covered, then he concealed his head and waited.

The Vityaz's bumpy journey finally stopped. The engine noise dropped to an idle grumble. Over it, Adam heard the clunk of doors opening, and voices. 'Holly Jo, I can't see outside,' he whispered. 'What's happening?'

'They're getting out of the ATV,' she replied. Her words were slightly distorted, interference crackling in the background. Even with the quadrotor relaying the signal, they were now far enough away from the op centre aboard the plane for it to be degraded. 'Some more people are getting out of the chopper.'

'That must be Sevnik,' Tony added. 'That's a colonel's uniform.'

Straining to listen, Adam could just about make out parts of the conversation outside. Zykov greeted the other Russian cheerfully, though Sevnik's response was more restrained. The arms dealer then introduced al-Rais to his seller. Neither was impressed by the other, their mutual disdain clear, but matters moved straight on to business.

'Two of al-Rais's men have brought out suitcases,' Holly Jo reported. 'Al-Rais is opening them . . . they're full of money.'

'They're full of a *shitload* of money,' Kyle cut in excitedly. 'So that's what seven million big ones looks like, huh?'

'Sevnik is checking it,' Holly Jo went on. 'He seems happy. They're closing the cases – wait, now they're coming back towards you.'

The Russian voices drew closer. 'So where is the RTG?' asked Zykov.

'In a mine, not far from here,' said another man: Sevnik.

'Near the lagoon?'

'How did you know about that?' The officer's voice suddenly filled with wariness – and threat.

Zykov remained relaxed. 'An educated guess. I checked a map – considering how the RTG is going to be transported, it seemed logical.'

'I see.' Sevnik was not pleased to have been out-thought, but continued: 'Very well. I will give you the position so you can land your plane.'

'Zykov's making a call,' said Holly Jo.

'Can you intercept it?' Adam asked.

'Already on it – I got his number last time, and NSA has a backdoor into the satellite network.'

Once Zykov had got a connection, Sevnik gave him a set of coordinates, which the arms dealer relayed to his contact. 'Did you get that?' Adam asked as the call ended.

'We got it,' Holly Jo replied. 'The coordinates are about five miles south-east of your position. There's a long lake – they're on the western shore.'

'The RTG is there. Tony, they're not taking it to the airport – they're going to fly it out directly!'

'A seaplane?' Tony asked.

'It has to be. Baxter and his team need to get out there, right now. It's our only chance of stopping them.'

'Those coordinates are over eight miles from us! We'll never make it in time.'

'You've got to. I'll do whatever I can to slow them down – hold on.' Zykov, Sevnik and now al-Rais were talking again.

'You want to come with us?' Zykov asked, surprised. 'Your helicopter is a lot more comfortable than this thing – and faster!'

'I'm staying close to the money,' Sevnik replied. 'A couple of my men will come with me. The others will fly to the mine.'

'You do not trust me?' al-Rais growled.

'I don't trust *anyone*. I am committing an act of treason by selling you the generator – if the government finds out, I will be shot! I want to be a long, long way from Russia before anyone realises what has happened.' He shouted orders. 'Now, let's go.'

'Some of your men will have to ride in the trailer,' Zykov told al-Rais. 'There isn't enough room for everyone up front.'

Alarm filled Adam. He lifted the tarpaulin from his face – to see Bianca peeking out from under her own cover, unable to follow the Russian conversation outside and wanting to know what was going on. 'Hide, hide!' he hissed at her. She hurriedly pulled the tarp back down.

Adam did the same. Movement outside, muttered words – then the trailer shook as the tailgate was dropped. Men clambered in. The bench above Adam creaked as a man sat heavily on it, followed by another.

He raised the edge of the tarp just enough to see the floor. Four pairs of boots were planted on it, two on each side of the cabin. He glanced towards the front of the trailer. The cases containing the PERSONA gear were partly visible under the sheets, the clean metal contrasting sharply with the dirty surroundings. If the terrorists noticed that they looked out of place and investigated . . .

One of the men closed the tailgate. Outside, the helicopter started up. The Vityaz's engine snarled, the ATV lurching back into motion. All Adam could do was hold himself in place and endure the journey to their final destination – and hope Bianca could do the same.

'The crawler's moving,' Kyle said. His main monitor showed the Vityaz turning south-east across the valley, the Hind lifting off in a whirling cloud of rotor-blown snow behind it.

'God, I hope they're okay,' said Holly Jo anxiously. 'How many bad guys got into the back?'

'Four.'

'I would *so* not want to be in there. Bianca's braver than I thought.'

'Or stupider.' Kyle looked up as Tony hurried past him – wearing a heavy coat and carrying a handgun, to which he was attaching a silencer. 'Brah, uh . . . what're you doing?'

'That's a good question,' said Baxter. His team had assembled at the front of the cabin, Fallon peering through binoculars at the terminal. 'We can handle this, Tony.'

'You're outnumbered at least two to one,' Tony countered as he shoved the pistol inside his coat and donned a radio headset. 'You need all the help you can get.'

'That's not—'

'This isn't open for discussion, John,' he said firmly. 'If al-Rais gets the RTG on to a seaplane, it could end up anywhere. We're only sixty miles from US soil. No matter what, we've got to stop that plane from taking off.' He picked up a G36 rifle and loaded it. 'Are we being watched?'

'Doesn't look like it,' replied Fallon.

'Good.' Tony looked back at Kyle. 'Get the UAV to the coordinates at the lake – I want to know what we're dealing with. Okay, everyone grab your skis. We've got eight miles to cover, and we need to do it fast!'

29

Enemy Mine

The second leg of the Vityaz's journey was as uncomfortable as the first; all the more so for the two stowaways. The vehicle made another steep ascent out of the valley. It took considerable effort for Adam to hold himself in his hiding place.

Making matters worse, one of the cases slid out from under the sheets as the Vityaz climbed. Several heart-stopping moments passed – would any of the terrorists be curious enough to look inside? – before a man irritably kicked it away, but it ended up jammed against Adam's legs. Each time it moved, it tugged at the tarpaulin. If it slithered loose again, it would expose his feet . . .

Fortunately, the ATV eventually reached more level ground, before dropping sharply back down on the hill's far side. Another long trudge across the snowy landscape, and finally the torment ended as the Vityaz rattled to a halt. The tailgate clanged down, and the four men jumped out.

Adam waited until he was sure they had moved away before raising the tarp. 'Bianca?' he whispered. 'Are you okay?'

She hesitantly looked out from her own cover like a small animal emerging from its nest. 'I haven't been killed, so . . . yes. What's happening?'

'Baxter and his team are on their way. Holly Jo?'

'Yes?' came the reply through his earwig. There was even more interference than before.

'Where's John?'

'They're about five miles out.'

'That didn't sound like a good answer,' said Bianca, seeing his grim expression.

'It wasn't. At that rate, it'll take them well over an hour to get here.'

'They're on skis, so they'll make better time once they reach the downhill slopes,' Holly Jo assured him. 'They can follow a valley down to the lake and approach your position from the south.'

It was better than nothing. 'Is the UAV here?'

'Yeah,' said Kyle, 'but the signal's pretty weak 'cause of the distance and the hills.'

'Do the best you can. What do you see?'

'You're about a quarter-mile from some buildings by the lake, but they're wrecks. The chopper's landed not far from you.'

'What are the bad guys doing?'

'They're walking to the helicopter. They didn't leave anyone guarding the ATV, but the driver's still inside.'

'Okay.' Adam crawled out from under the bench, standing and stretching with relief before moving to the open tailgate. Bianca got up behind him. He gestured for her to stay put, then looked out.

Beyond were the first trees he had seen since arriving in Russia, a stand of stunted, snow-heavy conifers. The Vityaz had stopped on relatively level ground between the long lagoon and the steep hill to the west. The waters around the shore were still frozen, but not far out the ice had thawed and broken up enough to be navigable.

As if his thought had acted as a trigger, he heard the distant drone of an engine.

But it was no boat.

He leaned out of the trailer, searching for the source. More trees along the shore blocked his view. 'Kyle, there's a plane coming in from the south. Can you see it?'

'Hold on, I'll have to turn the drone around . . .'

While he waited, Adam surveyed his surroundings. The Hind had landed a hundred yards away. Zykov, al-Rais and Sevnik were leading their respective followers towards it. Two of the terrorists carried the cases of money. Past the helicopter, something stood out even under the snow – a line running from a cutting through the trees across the flat ground and up the side of the hill. A railroad track? It led to a tumbledown structure about two hundred feet higher, rusted machinery around it.

The mine entrance.

Probably dug to extract tin or tungsten, according to Adam's research on the area, it now contained a far more deadly element. Somewhere inside was a container full of radioactive strontium.

And the world's most wanted terrorist was about to take delivery of it.

The thought of al-Rais again caused a brief surge of hate to rise inside him. But why?

He forced the question – and emotion – aside as Kyle's distorted voice sounded in his earwig. 'Adam, I've got a seaplane on camera. It's a Beriev Be-200 amphibious jet – pretty cool, actually.'

'It's a jet?' That made matters worse; if al-Rais got away with the RTG, he would have the advantage of both speed and range over the image of the lumbering boat-like turboprop Adam had associated with the word 'seaplane'. Even with the US's array of satellites attempting to track it, over the empty wilds of eastern

Russia or the vast nothingness of the Pacific it could easily be lost.

'Yeah. Looks like the pilot's overflying the lake to check the ice. He's probably going to come back from the north to land.'

That meant only minutes before the Beriev splashed down. Adam looked at the helicopter. The group had now reached it. Sevnik and al-Rais apparently still did not trust each other, an animated debate taking place before agreement was reached over who should keep hold of the money. The cases were placed on the ground by the Hind, wary Russian soldiers facing two of the terrorists over them. The others continued towards the mine.

'What's happening?' Bianca asked.

'They're going to get the RTG. There's a seaplane on the way in – we've got to stop it from being loaded.'

'How?'

'When I figure it out, I'll tell you.' He reached into his coat and took out his gun. 'Okay, bring the cases. We need to get into those trees.'

Bianca collected the gear. 'Will we be safe?'

'Safer than in here if they put the RTG aboard.'

Her eyes widened. 'Yes, yes, we should absolutely get out of here,' she said, quickly convinced.

Adam jumped from the trailer, then helped Bianca down. He peered round the side of the Vityaz. The vehicle would shield them from the men by the helicopter. The driver was more of a concern, but Adam caught sight of him in the wing mirror, watching his former passengers as they headed up the hill. 'Okay, come on,' he said, leading the way to the woods.

They quickly reached cover. 'Wait here,' he told her.

'Where are you going?'

'To check the lake. Keep out of sight.'

Adam slung the Geiger counter's case from his shoulder, then picked his way through the trees. The woods were far from dense; he soon had a clear view of the lake. A snow-covered jetty extended about a hundred feet out into the icy waters.

An echoing sound from behind. He looked round to see the Beriev, its lights standing out clearly against the rising hills to the north. The seaplane, red and blue stripes running along its white fuselage, descended towards the lake. It dropped to just feet above the dark surface, jet wash from its high-mounted twin engines kicking up a great plume of spray behind it, then almost hesitantly lowered its keel into the water. More spray exploded outwards, the jet bouncing before falling again. This time it stayed down, the shrill of the engines echoing across the valley as the pilot engaged reverse thrust to slow it.

Adam turned away from the sight and set off again. Before long he arrived at the cutting and cautiously crouched behind some snow-covered logs at its edge.

At the shore end of the jetty were several buildings, all in disrepair, with broken windows and missing planks. The workings were long abandoned. A line of battered, corroded mine carts, some of them overturned, was not far to his right; he had been right about the railroad track. Further away was another little train. He looked up the hill at the mine entrance. The purpose of the machinery there was now clear. It had been a simple gravity-assisted system, full carts being sent down the slope under their own weight, using a cable and pulley to bring the other, empty train back up to be loaded.

He also saw Sevnik leading the way into the mine. Once al-Rais confirmed that the RTG was genuine and the money was exchanged, the terrorist leader would load his prize into the seaplane and leave. 'Holly Jo, how far away is Baxter?'

'They're still about four miles from you. I've told Tony the situation – they're trying to get there as quick as they can.'

That surprised him. 'Tony's with them?'

'Yes, he wanted to even up the numbers. There are a lot more of them than us.'

'I'd noticed. Look, al-Rais is going to take possession of the RTG. I'm going to delay things for as long as I can.'

'How?'

The mine carts gave him an idea. 'Just tell Kyle to keep watch.' The noise of the Beriev's engines grew louder as it pushed through the drifting ice towards the pier. Keeping low, Adam headed for the nearest row of carts.

A steel cable, scabbed with rust, was attached to the leading wagon's frame. When the mine was operational, the line would have led all the way up to the entrance, then looped around the pulley to link up to the other train.

He gave the cable an experimental tug. Coils of it popped up from under the snow like a startled snake. It had been broken or cut. Another wary glance uphill. A couple of men were at the mine entrance, but the others had all gone inside.

Still crouched, he followed the line of the cable, staying close to the trees. The skeletal remains of a tractor lay beside the tracks, surrounded by discarded scrap. 'Heavy metal . . .' he muttered.

'Say again?' said Holly Jo.

'Nothing. Am I still clear?'

'Yeah,' said Kyle. 'The plane's coming up to the jetty.'

He had to act fast. Gripping the cable with his gloved hands, he pulled more of it free of the snow and headed along the edge of the cutting to the tractor. He brought the rusted line around the front of the machine, then crouched by its rotted tyre and looked up the hill.

The two men, one Russian soldier and one of al-Rais's followers, were still at the mine entrance. The Beriev was holding their attention as it moved towards the dock. He needed to get to the other side of the cutting, but if he crossed the open, snow-covered ground they would spot him immediately . . .

Both men turned, looking down the darkened shaft. The others were coming back out. Adam seized his chance. Running the cable through his hands, he bolted across the tracks.

The steel line twanged, resisting him. He yanked at it. More coils burst from the snow. He headed for a mound of mouldering logs. Twenty feet to go, the cable heavier with each step. Ten feet, five. The Russian soldier turned back round—

Adam dived behind the logs, the Geiger counter's case digging hard into his side. Had he been seen? Heart thudding, he flattened himself against the wood. 'Kyle! The men at the mine – what are they doing?'

No alarm in the younger man's voice. 'Looks like they're coming out. I can see Zykov, al-Rais . . . Sevnik's waving to the guys by the helicopter.'

He was safe – for now. But he still had to set up his plan. He reeled the cable in to pull it semi-taut across the cutting at ground level. One log had the large stump of a severed branch jutting from it. He formed the metal line into a loop and hooked it around the wooden stub, then wedged the cable under the log itself.

The whine of the Beriev's engines died down – and at the same moment, he heard the growl of the Vityaz setting off. As he'd hoped, al-Rais was going to use the all-terrain vehicle to carry the RTG to the jetty. He took out a pair of compact binoculars and looked up at the mine.

The deal had obviously been agreed. Sevnik was considerably happier than before. Even the terrorist leader seemed in a better mood. Whatever he had seen inside the mine had been to his liking.

Zykov clapped Sevnik on the shoulder, his expression

suggesting that he could almost taste the champagne. Al-Rais shouted something into the shaft.

His men were bringing out the RTG.

'How far out are Tony and John?' Adam asked.

'Still more than three miles away,' Holly Jo told him apologetically.

'They're not gonna get there in time, are they?' said Kyle.

'They might if I can stall things here.' Adam picked up the cable again and gave it an experimental shake. Sinuous steel ripples ran across the cutting.

The Vityaz's engine note changed. He looked up the hill to see it crawling laboriously but relentlessly towards the mine's entrance. It would reach it in a couple of minutes. He raised the binoculars again.

Before long, al-Rais's men came into view, along with the Russian soldiers. They were clustered together, carrying something extremely heavy.

The nuclear generator.

Browning's thoughts resurfaced, almost excited about what he was about to see. *What have they got? Is it a Senostav, or one of the older units? Is it damaged?*

The RTG was now out in the open, but he still couldn't see it properly past its bearers. *Put the thing down, damn it!* 'They've got the RTG,' he reported grimly. A look back towards the lagoon. The Beriev was at the end of the jetty, a man using a rope to secure the seaplane to the dock. A hatch was open, ready to accept cargo.

The Vityaz snarled, the articulated crawler bending as its driver made a tight turn just below the minehead to position the trailer for loading. Those who had stayed at the helicopter climbed out with the money. The cases were placed on the ground.

The shuffling men brought the RTG to the vehicle. Adam was

concerned that he wouldn't get a proper look at the device before it was placed aboard, but then al-Rais gave an order. With obvious relief, the men set down the generator and stepped back.

Adam focused the binoculars. Browning's knowledge instantly told him what he was looking at. An IEU-2M, the core's green-painted radiator fins visible within its outer frame. Weight: six hundred kilograms, of which just five was the strontium – the rest was mostly shielding. Planned service life: fifteen years. This particular unit was well beyond that. But its fuel was still deadly. Strontium-90 had a half-life of close to thirty years, so even though its radioactive emissions were far down on what they had been when the RTG was built, it remained active enough to be lethal.

Nobody at the mine appeared concerned about taking a terminal dose, though. As far as Adam could tell, the core was intact and undamaged. He put down the binoculars and switched on the Geiger counter. Even at this distance, an exposed nuclear core would set it crackling furiously, but the reading was only slightly above normal background levels. He wouldn't want to spend any appreciable time in close proximity to the unit, but for short periods it was safe.

At least . . . until it was deliberately opened.

He couldn't allow that to happen.

Adam returned the counter to its case, then retrieved the binoculars. An order from Sevnik, and the men heaved the RTG off the ground and brought it step by careful step to the Vityaz's tailgate. The entire vehicle lurched on its suspension as it was placed aboard.

Another couple of minutes passed while the generator was secured for its short journey, then people climbed aboard the crawler. Zykov, al-Rais and Sevnik got into the cab, two of the terrorist group picking up the money cases and joining their leader. A sort of musical chairs began amongst the others, nobody wanting to ride in the trailer with the RTG, but some unlucky soldiers drew the short straw.

The Vityaz revved up and started down the slope. It followed the tracks, heading straight for the cutting. Adam crouched lower behind the logs. He would only get one chance: his timing had to be perfect.

The engine noise grew steadily louder. He didn't dare lift his head to check the Vityaz's position in case he was seen. Instead he inched forward to look past the logs at the dilapidated tractor across the cutting. The cable he had run around it was partially visible in the snow, a dotted rust-orange line.

His own footsteps ran alongside it.

Nothing he could do about that. He was committed to his plan. If it failed, he would be left with only two choices: either watch impotently from hiding as al-Rais flew the RTG and its deadly contents to parts unknown . . . or make a desperate suicide attack in the hope of at least killing the terrorist leader before he could escape.

Neither appealed. It *had* to succeed.

His hands tightened around the cable. The Vityaz drew closer, the growl of its engine making the logs tremble. Only seconds away. Wait, wait . . .

It drove past, the fat tracks kicking up clods of snow. The cable bucked in his grip as the ATV rolled over it. Not yet—

Now!

The instant the first of the two articulated units was past, Adam whipped up the cable and snapped it forwards to hook it over the caterpillar tracks.

It caught on one of the deep rubber blocks and was yanked along the top of the tread. The line was snatched from Adam's open hands. If he had kept hold of it for a fraction of a second longer, it would have sliced off his fingers. The log he had looped the cable around leapt from the pile and spun across the cutting, smashing against the Vityaz's side in a shower of rotten flinders.

The ATV jerked sharply off course. The cable had jammed the track – and also become entangled in the clutch of hydraulic rams linking the forward unit to the trailer. The two sections of the vehicle convulsed, the trailer slewing sideways and crashing to the limit of its articulation. Metal shrieked. The Vityaz slithered to an emergency stop, the back end of the trailer about thirty feet from Adam.

He pressed himself against the piled logs. 'Tell me what's happening,' he hissed. His cover was already slight enough that he couldn't risk looking out from it.

'They don't know what the hell just happened,' Holly Jo told him. He heard shouted Russian. 'Sevnik's yelling at the driver, the driver's yelling at him, all the other guys are piling out – lots of guns.'

'Maybe they'll shoot each other and save us the trouble,' Kyle added.

Adam doubted he would be that fortunate. Instead he lay still, listening to the commotion. Zykov implored everyone to calm down, with mixed success. 'We hit a mine!' someone cried.

'It wasn't a mine – it was a *log!*' the arms dealer yelled back. 'Look! We ran over a log, that's all.'

'No, it's not all,' said another voice – the driver, Adam realised. 'The tracks are jammed, there's something – what the hell? Shit! Look at this.'

'They've found the cable,' Holly Jo reported. 'The driver's trying to pull it out – nope, not happening.'

'Is it stuck?' Sevnik asked.

'It's caught in the hydraulics!' A few strained grunts of exertion. 'Balls! It's jammed in there.'

'You didn't see it?' al-Rais said with suspicion.

'It was under the snow! I don't have X-ray eyes.'

'Can you get it out?' asked Zykov.

'I'll have to cut it. I've got the tools, but it'll take time.'

'How long?' demanded al-Rais.

'I don't know. Twenty minutes, half an hour? I need to check that the driveshaft isn't damaged too.'

'That is too long,' said the terrorist leader. 'We'll carry the generator to the plane.'

Although he couldn't see him, Adam somehow knew that the driver was shrugging. 'Up to you. But I'll have to cut it free anyway.'

'Get it out,' al-Rais ordered. Muffled footsteps followed as the men headed to the trailer.

Frustrating minutes passed, Adam still unable to risk moving. The running commentary from Holly Jo and Kyle told him that the RTG was being taken from the Vityaz, then slowly carried down to the waterfront. Tony and his team were still over two miles distant. 'It's all downhill from here,' Holly Jo added hopefully. 'Oh, wait, that didn't come out quite like I wanted . . .'

'I know what you meant,' said Adam. 'Is anyone close to me?'

'Just the driver. Everyone else is almost at the jetty.'

'Which way is the driver looking?'

'He's got his back to you,' Kyle said.

Adam raised his head. The driver was kneeling at the Vityaz's central coupling, using a small saw to cut the cable. Beyond the stalled all-terrain vehicle, he saw the scrum of men bearing the RTG, Zykov's bodyguards having joined in to lighten the load. He was unsurprised that the leaders of the three groups were not volunteering their own services. 'Okay, I'm going to get closer to the plane.' He cautiously backed up to the tree line. The conifers' drooping branches, laden with snow, provided good cover. He looked east, seeing the buildings through the trees. Still watching the driver, he headed towards them.

'Adam!' Kyle, urgent. He ducked behind a trunk and froze. 'I just saw movement on the infrared camera, other side of the tracks. I think it's Bianca.'

'I told her to stay still,' he muttered, peering across the cutting. The Vityaz obstructed his view.

'I guess she got cold.'

'I don't see her. Where is she?'

'Two o'clock from the ATV, looking north. About thirty yards from the edge of the trees. I think she's following your tracks.'

He couldn't see her. 'Damn it! We should have given her a headset.'

'Hindsight's always twenty-twenty, brah. Oh, wait – she's stopped. She's about twenty yards from the cutting. Hold on, I'll zoom in . . . yeah, she's hunkered down. Doesn't look like she's planning to get any closer.'

That was a relief, but she was far from out of danger. There was no way he could tell her to retreat without exposing his own presence to the conspirators. 'Okay. Warn me if she moves.'

He set off again. Through the trees he saw the RTG's porters gingerly bringing it along the jetty. While the wooden structure had been built to carry heavy loads of minerals to waiting boats, many harsh winters had passed since it was last maintained, and nobody appeared fully convinced that it would take the weight of the generator – to say nothing of the men themselves.

Before long he reached the largest building. He quickly made his way to the rear. A door hung off its hinges. He drew his gun and stepped inside.

The former headquarters of the mining operation had been ravaged by weather and looters. Anything of value had been stripped from its interior, only trash remaining. He moved carefully through the derelict structure to a front window.

It gave him an excellent view of the jetty. He got his first proper look at the Beriev. It was a big aircraft, its high wings over a hundred feet in span and the fuselage very nearly as long. The hatch in its flank was still open, a bored young man sitting in it smoking a cigarette. Lights in the cockpit revealed the pilot watching the ponderous advance of his cargo.

Adam looked back to the shore. Sevnik, Zykov and al-Rais were less than fifty feet from him.

His hand tightened on the gun's grip. One shot, and Muqaddim al-Rais would be dead . . .

But the threat his organisation posed would not. Somebody else would take over. Unless al-Rais was captured alive, and the PERSONA used to extract all his secrets. *Patience.*

'And so, we are done,' Sevnik proclaimed loudly. 'I suppose you want your share now, Ruslan Pavelovich.'

Zykov gave him a sarcastic smile. 'It would be nice to have it before you leave for your tropical paradise, yes.'

Sevnik did not appreciate the joke, but nevertheless he crouched and opened one of the cases. He took out and unfolded a nylon holdall, then started tossing bundles of banknotes into it. Zykov counted them off. 'Two million,' he said before long. He zipped up the bag and lifted it. Two million dollars in tightly packed hundreds required surprisingly little effort to carry. 'Good doing business with you, Kirill Makarovich.' Sevnik grunted in response, closing the case and standing to watch the men on the jetty.

'Tony's just over a mile out,' Holly Jo told Adam through a crackle of static. 'Coming from the south-west. They'll be there in about eight minutes.'

'Okay.' But did he *have* eight minutes? Despite their concern about the state of the jetty, the men had still managed to get the

RTG to the plane. The man with the cigarette flicked it into the water and disappeared inside the cabin. The porters eased their heavy burden through the hatch. The Be-200 listed, the float beneath the end of its starboard wing dipping lower into the icy water.

The terrorists climbed into the aircraft to secure the RTG. The Russian soldiers and Zykov's bodyguards, meanwhile, decided that their part in the heavy lifting was done. They returned to the shore. 'All right!' said Sevnik. 'Let's go!' Hefting the cases, he set off back through the cutting. The soldiers followed, one taking out a walkie-talkie and issuing a curt instruction. A few seconds later, Adam heard a muffled whine through the trees. The Hind had started its engines.

That was good: with the Russian troops and their gunship gone, Tony's team would no longer be so drastically outnumbered. But if they didn't arrive soon, their numerical advantage would be worthless. Al-Rais and his men would have left with their prize, leaving only Zykov, his bodyguards and the Vityaz's driver.

He looked up the cutting at the stalled Vityaz as Sevnik's group, moving at a rapid trot, passed it. The driver finally freed the cable from the hydraulics. He watched the soldiers go, then turned to toss the metal line into the snow—

Something made him freeze.

Adam knew immediately what the driver had seen. *His footprints.*

None of the Vityaz's passengers had crossed the cutting. The driver peered into the woods, puzzled, then plodded to investigate the mysterious tracks.

It wouldn't take him long to work out that someone else had been there. Adam checked the plane. The RTG was being lashed into place. 'How far away is Tony?'

'A few minutes.'

'Do they know the situation here?'

'Yes. They're moving as fast as they can.'

'Adam,' cut in Kyle urgently. One of al-Rais's men, Qasid, was coming back along the jetty, but that was not what he was warning about. 'The driver – he's following your tracks into the woods.'

Adam looked back along the cutting. 'I don't see him. Is he behind the buildings?'

'No – he's following them back the way you came. He's heading straight for Bianca!'

30

Firefight

A mixture of cold and fear had driven Bianca deeper into the trees. The longer she spent crouching amongst the firs, hands and feet slowly numbing, the more exposed she felt. With no idea what was happening outside the little woods, her imagination came up with its own frightening possibilities. Were soldiers patrolling the area? Were al-Rais's terrorists combing the forest for intruders?

A loud bang followed by a commotion from the stalled Vityaz had been the final straw. Something had happened – but what? Was Adam in trouble? Even knowing that it directly contradicted Adam's instructions, she followed his trail. Just being able to see what was going on, she felt, would calm her nerves. At the very least, she would know if she *had* a genuine reason to be scared.

It had not taken her long to lug the PERSONA gear to a position with a partial view of the jetty and the ruined mine buildings. The Vityaz was stationary and silent off to her right. Most of the men were clumped together, slowly shuffling through the snow towards the lakeside. She realised they were carrying something.

The RTG. Al-Rais had got what he came for. And now he was about to take it away.

She assumed Adam had somehow sabotaged the Vityaz. But there was no sign of him – and since the men were carrying the generator rather than scouring the woods, he had obviously remained undiscovered. That realisation eased her tension, slightly. If nobody was looking for Adam, they weren't looking for her either. She hunched behind a tree, keeping watch.

The men carrying the RTG reached the jetty, then the plane. Some talking – she recognised Zykov's voice – and then the soldiers headed back the way they had come. The helicopter started up. Sevnik and his men were leaving.

What about the terrorists? And where was Adam? All she could do was wait, the cold gnawing at her again. The noise of the helicopter grew louder. She turned her head towards the sound, but couldn't see the aircraft through the snow-heavy trees.

She looked back—

The stab of cold through her heart had nothing to do with the temperature. It was pure fear.

Someone was moving through the woods.

It wasn't Adam. Too broad, coat the wrong colour. The Vityaz's driver? He was looking down at the ground.

Following Adam's tracks.

The tracks that would lead right back to her.

Bianca choked the breath in her throat, afraid she would be heard. She had to run! But if she did, the driver would see the sudden movement. All she could was crouch behind the tree trunk and make herself as small as possible, terror rising within her as he drew closer . . .

★ ★ ★

'How far is he from her?' Adam demanded. He glimpsed the driver through the trees, but still didn't know where Bianca was in relation to him.

'About a hundred feet, maybe?' Kyle replied, unsure.

Adam stared into the gloom beneath the branches, but saw no trace of her. At least that was something; she was hiding. Maybe the driver would give up and return to the Vityaz . . .

'Is it secure, Qasid?' al-Rais asked his comrade as he reached the shore.

'Almost,' came the reply. 'You are finished here?'

'Yes.' Al-Rais glanced round as the gunship took flight, the pounding thrum of its rotors fading as it wheeled about and headed west over the hills. But a new noise rose to replace it – the Beriev's engines starting up.

'If you need any more weapons,' Zykov said to al-Rais, 'you know how to reach me. But for now, we go our separate ways, eh?' He looked up the cutting to see how work on the Vityaz was progressing. 'Hey, Ogurtsov! Where are you?'

'Over here,' came a reply from the trees.

'What are you doing there? Is the Vityaz fixed?'

Al-Rais had no interest in Zykov's transportation issues. He spoke briefly to Qasid, then the pair started down the jetty. Adam tensed, bringing up his gun. Time was rapidly running out.

'There's something weird,' the driver called. 'I found some footprints.'

On the dock, al-Rais stopped abruptly. 'What footprints?'

Adam took aim—

Bianca had no idea what the driver was saying, but he was getting closer. She hunched up more tightly, shivering. Maybe he wouldn't see her, maybe Zykov would call him back, maybe . . .

She heard a muffled metallic clack.

A gun!

Ogurtsov drew a revolver and cocked it as he advanced on Bianca's hiding place. 'There's someone here!'

Al-Rais whirled, yelling to the men in the plane. 'It's an ambush! Get your guns, get out of the—'

Adam fired.

Not at the terrorist leader, but at the driver. The Russian crumpled to the ground less than ten feet from Bianca, blood spraying over his coat from a head wound.

Adam brought his gun back towards al-Rais, but his target was already moving, drawing a weapon of his own as he and his companion raced back to the shore. They dived behind a snow-covered pile of rusted machinery. The American's second shot clanked off the corroded metal a fraction of a second later.

'Find them, kill them!' al-Rais screamed. His men started to scramble from the Beriev, AKs at the ready.

Zykov and his bodyguards had also hurried into cover behind a mound of rubble. 'They're in the buildings!' he shouted.

Al-Rais glared at him. 'You set us up!' he snarled, raising his gun. Qasid rolled on to his front and aimed his Kalashnikov at the Russians.

Zykov's eyes widened. 'No, I swear—'

Al-Rais fired, four bloody holes bursting open in the arms dealer's head and chest. Qasid opened up with his AK on full auto, spraying the bodyguards with lead. Their bullet-riddled corpses flopped to the ground beside Zykov.

The last of the terrorists jumped from the plane, following his comrades down the jetty—

Shots tore into them, sending three men spinning into the icy water amid spouting trails of gore. A fourth was hit in the arm.

He staggered, screaming – only to take another shot to the throat and collapse dead on the dock. The last two men managed to hurl themselves behind the ice-encrusted scrap on the shore.

Adam had been as surprised as the terrorists by the onslaught – but he knew where it had come from.

Tony, Baxter and his men had joined the battle.

He could tell from the sound of the gunfire that they were still some distance away, using their rifles' scopes to engage from extreme range. 'Holly Jo! Where are they?'

'They're coming along the shore to the south,' she replied. 'About five hundred metres from you.'

It only took him a moment to visualise the relative positions of all the combatants – and to realise that if the terrorists moved a short distance further from the lake, the American team's sight lines would be blocked by the buildings.

Al-Rais had come to the same conclusion. 'Cover me!' he shouted. Adam briefly saw him gesturing towards a single-storey building on the cutting's north side, but wasn't able to line up a clear shot. 'Get into there!'

The whine of the Beriev's engines rose sharply. The young co-pilot reached from the open hatch to unfasten the mooring rope as the seaplane shifted, ice churning and bobbing around its belly—

A hole suddenly exploded in the windscreen, the pilot's head snapping back out of Adam's sight as a gunshot echoed along the shore. Not the dry mechanical rattle of the G36s, but the enormous boom of Rossovich's XM500 sniper rifle. Five hundred metres was nothing for the Barrett; the weapon was designed to hit targets well over a mile away. The co-pilot shrieked and ducked back inside. The Beriev jerked to a stop, held by the line.

Al-Rais made a break for the building. Adam took aim – but

forced himself not to fire. The mission objective was to *capture* al-Rais, not kill him. Instead he found a new target as the other three terrorists sprinted after their leader. This time, he didn't hesitate to pull the trigger. One of the running men fell from a bullet wound to his upper back.

He tracked the next man – but al-Rais had already kicked open the broken door, his remaining followers piling in after him. Unlike the other ruined structures, this had stone walls rather than wood, giving the terrorists much more cover.

But they hadn't gone there purely for protection. For Zykov to have contacted him, al-Rais must have had a satellite phone of his own. If he warned his organisation, anything Adam learned from the terrorist's persona would be rendered worthless.

It would take Tony and his team a couple of minutes to reach him. More than enough time for al-Rais to make a call . . .

Adam ran back through the building and out of the rear door, rounding the side of the derelict structure. He paused at the corner, glancing across the tracks at the stone building. Movement behind a broken window, one of the terrorists pointing an AK towards the shore.

He ran—

The Kalashnikov swung towards him, but Adam raised his own gun and fired five rapid shots as he raced across the cutting. The bullets smacked off the stonework. The AK briefly jerked away from the impacts – then returned, unleashing a burst of automatic fire. Rounds sliced through the air just behind him. He fired once more, then dived headlong behind a couple of overturned mine carts.

Snow sprayed in his face as he landed. He wiped his eyes, then ejected his SIG's magazine. It still had three bullets remaining, but he wanted to reload while he was still in cover.

The new mag clacked home. He popped his head out from the

side of the wagon, seeing broken planks piled against the stone building's windowless side wall, then ducked back as the gunfire resumed. Screaming ricochets bounced off the thick metal, but an AK couldn't rock 'n' roll on full auto for long . . .

The gun fell silent. Now it was the terrorist's turn to reload, the thirty rounds in the curved magazine gone.

Adam burst out from behind the carts. He heard a warning shout, but kept running for the stacked planks. They were slippery with ice and rot, but he had enough momentum to charge up them and vault on to the roof.

There was a large hole where decay and the weight of a winter's snow had made a combined attack. He jumped down through it, landing with a thump inside a back room.

Al-Rais was just six feet from him, whirling in surprise at the noise. He had a satphone in one hand, gun in the other.

The pistol came up—

Adam charged, slamming his shoulder into the Saudi's stomach and driving him back against a wall. He lashed out with his gun hand, metal striking metal and sending the terrorist's weapon clattering across the room, then whipped it back up to smash against his opponent's skull. Al-Rais slumped to the floor.

Movement to one side—

Adam spun and fired three shots into the chest of one of the terrorists as he rushed into the room. The dead man tumbled to the ground.

Where was the third? He had—

Something hit him hard from behind.

Adam stumbled, landing painfully beside al-Rais. Another blow struck his arm. The SIG was jarred from his hand. He cried out, twisting to look up at his attacker. It was Qasid, fumbling to reload his AK after using it as an impromptu club.

The magazine slotted into the receiver with a solid *clack*. Qasid yanked back the charging handle, then pointed the gun at the downed American—

Shock filled his face. 'You! But—'

Adam took full advantage of the moment of confusion to sweep a foot up at Qasid's leg. The steel-reinforced toe of his boot cracked against the other man's kneecap. The Pakistani shrieked, his leg buckling and pitching him to the floor. The AK barked as he landed, bullets tearing into the ruined ceiling. Before he could recover, Adam scrambled to him and drove a savage punch into his face. Qasid went limp.

The American pulled the Kalashnikov from Qasid's hand and used it as a support to get back to his feet. He checked on the two terrorists. Qasid's face was twisted in pain, blood oozing from his nose. Al-Rais moaned, head lolling. The satphone lay nearby. A number had been entered . . . but not sent, the last digit missing.

Adam kicked the terrorist's gun away, then recovered his own pistol. 'Adam!' said Holly Jo in his ear. 'What's happened?'

'We have al-Rais,' he announced. 'I repeat, we have captured Muqaddim al-Rais.'

31

Dominate the Mind

Bianca didn't dare move. Curled into a tight ball, she flinched with every gunshot and scream. Who was shooting at whom? Had Adam been hit, or even killed? Was she stranded in the Russian wasteland with a group of angry terrorists?

Even after the shooting stopped, she heard activity around the buildings. Petrified, she stayed hunched in the snow. Was she about to be saved – or shot?

'Bianca!' Adam's voice. 'Bianca, where are you?'

Relief rose in her heart – almost immediately stamped back down by paranoia. Was it a trick? Had he been captured, forced to draw her out of hiding? She peeked fearfully round the trunk. There were men with guns near the jetty, but she couldn't make out their faces. *Oh God, he'd been caught . . .*

'Bianca!'

Another voice. Tony's. The feeling of relief returned with full force, overcoming her coldness and fear. 'Here!' she cried, jumping up. 'I'm over here!'

Figures hurried through the woods: Adam and Tony. 'Are you okay?' the latter called as he approached.

'I'm fine,' she replied gratefully. 'Is everyone all right?'

'We're all okay,' said Adam. 'We've captured al-Rais.'

Tony regarded the cases. 'Is the PERSONA gear okay?'

'As far as I know,' she replied.

'Good. We're going to need it.'

'Soon as we make the recording, we should just kill this asshole,' muttered Baxter. Al-Rais had been secured with flex-cuffs, as had Qasid and the Beriev's terrified co-pilot, the three survivors held at gunpoint inside the stone building. 'These two as well.' He pointed his G36 at Qasid, who recoiled.

'No!' Adam said firmly, interposing himself. 'He knows something. I want to find out what.'

'That's not the mission. We got al-Rais, that's all that matters. Everyone else . . . well, I know *my* orders. Eliminate the terrorists and anyone helping them.'

'What?' exclaimed Bianca, who was taking the repaired recorder from its case. 'But they're prisoners – that's murder!'

'It's war. And the only prisoner we were supposed to take was al-Rais. Everyone else should have been shot, if we'd all been following orders.'

'Nobody gave me that order,' Adam replied.

Baxter's only response was a look of contempt. Tony stood beside Adam. 'Well, we've got prisoners now, so we'll treat them by the book, okay? Besides, we can use this guy,' he indicated the co-pilot, 'to fly the plane back to the airport.'

'Seriously?' said Baxter in disbelief.

'The RTG weighs over half a ton. You want to carry it all the way back? Adam, what was your assessment of it? Browning's, I mean.'

After finding Bianca, Adam had boarded the Be-200 with the Geiger counter to examine its cargo. 'It's not in the best condition,' he said, his borrowed persona's clipped speech patterns unconsciously returning. 'But there was no sign of radiation leakage. The casing is intact.'

'Good.' Tony reactivated his headset. 'Holly Jo? Put us through to Martin.'

Morgan's distorted voice came on the line. 'What's the situation?' he asked.

'We've secured al-Rais and the RTG,' said Tony. 'It seems to be intact and safe – as safe as these things get, anyway.'

'Good. Will you be able to bring it back to the States?'

'Yeah. They'd already loaded it into their seaplane.'

'In that case, transfer it to our jet and bring it back home. Better we have it than it's left lying around in the Russian countryside until they can be bothered to collect it. What about al-Rais?'

'Dr Childs is prepping the PERSONA right now.' Bianca glanced up at the mention of her name. 'We're going to make the transfer as soon as she's ready.'

'And a recording.' It was a reminder rather than a question.

'Yes, the recorder's ready.' Tony's gaze moved to Qasid and the co-pilot. 'There's, ah . . . something else. We have two additional prisoners.'

Morgan was not pleased. 'What?'

'A pilot, and one of al-Rais's men. Adam captured him.'

'I see. Adam?'

'Yes?' said Adam.

'Care to explain?'

'I think Qasid's got valuable information. Once we've got what we need from al-Rais, we should interrogate him too.'

'What kind of information?'

Adam hesitated before answering. 'He recognised me. But I've never met him before. At least . . . I don't remember doing.'

That brought surprised reactions from Tony, Bianca and

Baxter. Although Morgan was out of sight half a world away, the silence from the other end of the line suggested that he shared the feeling. 'Okay,' he finally said. 'Bring him back as well. But al-Rais takes priority. We need to get as much as we can from him as soon as possible, before al-Qaeda realise he's missing.'

'We'll start the debriefing as soon as we leave,' said Tony.

'Good. Oh, and . . . one more thing.' Morgan sounded uncomfortable. 'Considering al-Rais's importance as an intelligence source, approval has been given to imprint Adam with his persona as many times as necessary to extract information from him.'

'Wait a minute,' said Tony, as startled as Adam at the news. 'What about the rule on multiple imprints? It's too risky.'

Bianca looked up again. 'What is?'

'They want to imprint al-Rais on to me more than once,' said Adam.

'But – I thought that was too dangerous?'

'So did I. John? Headset.' He clicked his fingers and held out a hand. Baxter was affronted, but at a nod from Tony took off his headset and gave it to Adam, who passed it on to Bianca. 'Martin, Bianca's on the line.'

'Correct me if I'm wrong,' she said, adjusting the microphone, 'but wasn't the rule about only imprinting Adam once with a particular persona put in place because of the risk of his suffering the same side effects as Tony?'

'That's correct,' said Morgan, not appreciating her confrontational tone, 'but in this case, the value of the information we can get from al-Rais has been deemed to outweigh other considerations. We've captured al-Qaeda's leader – we can cripple the entire organisation.'

'And the price is Adam's health?'

'Dr Kiddrick is sure it'll be possible to do it within the bounds of safety.'

'I don't suppose anyone asked Dr *Albion's* opinion, did they?'

Morgan's patience had already run out. 'Dr Childs, this is not a discussion. The decision has been made. We will use every possible means to attack al-Qaeda. Your job is to make that happen – while monitoring Adam's condition, of course. If it looks as if there are going to be problems, we'll decide whether or not to continue. But for now, we need to know what al-Rais knows. So make the transfer, please.'

'Martin,' said Tony, 'I want to state on the record that I don't approve of this decision.'

'Noted, and understood. But you have your orders. Out.'

'For Christ's sake,' Bianca snapped, pulling off the headset and returning it to Baxter. 'Tony, you're not going to go through with this, are you?'

'Right now, we don't have much choice. Besides,' he added, 'at this stage all we're doing is a standard transfer. I'll take this up again with Martin once we're back at STS, but until then he's right: we need that information. Are you both ready?'

'Yes,' said Adam. Bianca reluctantly nodded.

'Okay.' Tony indicated Qasid and the co-pilot. 'John, take those two into the other room. No point in them seeing more than they need to.'

'I still say the only thing they need to see is a bullet,' Baxter told him.

'Just move them, okay?'

Scowling, Baxter and a couple of his team hauled the two prisoners through a doorway into another part of the derelict building. Tony turned back to Bianca. 'All right. Let's do this.'

Al-Rais was guarded by two of Baxter's men, Cope and Trenton, their guns trained on him. He had maintained a defiant silence, glaring at his captors. The sight of the PERSONA equipment as Bianca set it up prompted a reaction, however. 'You will never make me talk,' he rasped. 'It does not matter for how long you torture me. I will not tell you anything.'

'We don't need you to tell us anything,' Tony countered. 'Bianca, wire him up.'

She took out the skullcap and unwound the cable. 'Aren't you going to examine him first?' Adam reminded her.

'Hmm? Oh, oh yes! That would help, wouldn't it?' The stress – she hesitated to call it excitement – had completely thrown her. She quickly went through the motions of Albion's spurious procedure. Al-Rais snarled at her, making her flinch; one of Baxter's men kicked him hard in the side. 'Hey, hey!' she protested.

'This piece of shit deserves a lot worse than that,' Cope replied sourly.

'Maybe so, but I can't examine him if your boot's in the way, can I?' She completed her checks, the two guards pulling him upright so she could measure him, then used the scales in one of the cases to weigh him. Al-Rais resisted, getting a punch in the stomach for his troubles. 'Okay, thank you.'

The terrorist leader was dropped back to the floor. Bianca calculated the drug dosage in a notebook, then began to fit the skullcap over his head. Even with Trenton and Cope pinning him, he struggled, trying to strike the back of his skull against the floor to break the electrodes. Tony took hold of his coat collar to pull him up. 'This bloody thing,' Bianca complained, repositioning the cap. 'Why couldn't Kiddrick have just designed it as a hat?'

'I'll put that on the requirements list if he builds a Mark Two,' said Tony with a wry smile.

She secured the Velcro strap, then took the Neutharsine from the case and turned to Adam, who was sitting facing al-Rais. 'Are you ready?' He nodded. 'Okay. Hold still . . .' While the drug did its work, wiping the memories and personality of Eugene

Browning from Adam's mind, she put the other skullcap in place on him. Seeing all expression drain from his face at such close range was even more unsettling than before.

Baxter came back in to watch as the final preparations for the transfer were made, taking distinct pleasure in pinning al-Rais down with a foot on his chest as Bianca gave the terrorist his injection. That done, she activated the PERSONA. The transfer and recording process started. Minutes passed as the machine processed the vast amount of data flowing through it.

Finally it stopped. Bianca checked the readings, then powered it down. Unfastening the skullcap, she asked Adam: 'Can you hear me?'

Adam's eyes slowly opened. For a moment they were unfocused – then they locked on to her with a malevolent, hawk-like sharpness. 'Yes, I hear you,' he said quietly. His accent was now several time zones removed from that of a West Coast scientist. His gaze flicked past her to al-Rais. His startled reaction reminded Bianca of someone who had glanced in a mirror to discover something unexpected stuck to his face. 'Wait, I am—' He looked back at her, anger briefly burning in his eyes before he brought himself back under control. 'Bianca?'

'Are you all right?' she asked, concerned. She had never seen him so intense following a transfer.

'Yes, but . . . it's different, somehow. Al-Rais's persona, it's . . . *stronger* than anything before.'

Tony crouched beside him. 'Like it's fighting with you?'

'Yes.'

'You can beat it. Take it from me, I know.' He put a reassuring hand on Adam's shoulder. 'I had the same thing with Najjar. These guys aren't mooks – they're leaders, they're strong-willed, they have to be. But you're stronger. Trust me.'

'I'm stronger,' Adam repeated. 'I can beat him.' He clapped

one hand over Tony's, then looked back at Bianca. 'I don't think we need a cheat sheet to know that the transfer was successful.'

'I guess not,' she said. 'Are you *sure* you're all right?'

'I'll be fine.' He stood, Bianca and Tony helping him up. 'I'll just . . . need a minute.'

'We'll get al-Rais on to the plane,' said Tony.

'What about the Mnemexal?' Bianca asked.

'It doesn't matter if he remembers what we did now that we've got him.' He faced the two men holding the dazed terrorist. 'You two, with me.'

'You're *seriously* going to commandeer that Ruskie boatplane out there?' said Baxter incredulously. 'Why don't we just use the snowcat?'

'I want to get out of here as quick as we can. Rossovich speaks Russian – get him to make that pilot fly us back to Provideniya airport. Bring him to the plane when you're done.'

'What about the other prisoner?'

'We're taking him too,' Adam said firmly. Baxter looked to Tony, who nodded. With a disgruntled shrug, the ex-Marine went into the other room. Cope and Trenton picked up al-Rais and dragged him out of the building after Tony.

Bianca watched them go, then looked back at Adam. His fingertips were pressed to his temples, eyes closed. 'Are you okay? Does it hurt?'

He opened his eyes. 'No, it's not like a headache. But it's . . .' A deep breath. 'Not pleasant.'

'None of this is,' she said, starting to pack away the equipment. She pulled the memory module out of the recorder and regarded it ruefully. 'After what happened to Tony with Najjar, now they want to do the same to you with al-Rais. It's mad.'

Adam glanced towards the doorway through which Baxter had

gone, checking that nobody was listening. 'Holly Jo, I'm going off-comms,' he said, pressing his finger behind his ear to deactivate the link before lowering his voice. 'To be honest, I'm worried. This isn't just finding out someone's guilty secret about an affair. Al-Rais controls a terrorist group that's killed thousands of people. It'll take a lot more than a single interrogation session to break him – and the same will be true of his persona. I can tell. He'll be fighting me all the way.'

'When you say "fighting",' Bianca asked hesitantly, remembering the fleeting moment of hatred in his eyes immediately after the transfer, 'do you mean that literally? Is his persona . . . is it trying to take control of you?'

'No, but there's . . . *resistance*.' Seeing her questioning expression, he expanded: 'Remember what I said on the plane about Vanwall's fear of heights? When I was using his persona to play cards, I could call up his memories as easily as my own – I wasn't doing anything against his interests, or his instincts. But when his fear of heights kicked in, it took effort to overcome. It's the same thing here, like a kind of mental wrestling. I can overpower him, but . . . it takes work.'

'But you'll be okay?'

'I'll be fine – for now. If they imprint al-Rais's persona on me again, I don't know.' He shook his head. 'I really don't know.'

'I'll do everything I can to stop them from doing it,' she assured him. 'However much *that'll* be worth.'

'It's worth a lot to me,' he said. 'Thank you.'

She smiled at the unexpected compliment. 'No problem.' He returned it, faintly. 'So, this other guy you took prisoner—'

'Qasid.'

'Bless you. You said he recognised you?'

'Yes. But I don't know why.'

'Well, you've got al-Rais's memories now. Maybe *he* knows.'

Adam nodded thoughtfully. 'He probably does. So ask me.'

'What?'

'It's easier for me to remember things spontaneously by being asked direct questions than by making random associations. Ask me something about Qasid.'

'I'm not really a master interrogator, but . . . okay. What does Qasid do in al-Qaeda?'

'He's one of my most . . . reliable men,' Adam said, hesitating mid-sentence. 'One of *al-Rais's* men, I mean. Qasid's one of *his* best people. He has contacts in Pakistani intelligence, in the government—' He suddenly stopped, shocked.

'What is it?'

'There's a mole. Qasid was given information by a high-ranking mole! It's how they knew the Secretary of State's route in Islamabad, how they were able to set up an ambush. Qasid got it from someone working in intelligence.'

'Who?'

He frowned in concentration. 'Al-Rais doesn't know. Qasid kept all his sources secret so they couldn't be exposed if someone else in the organisation got captured. But he knows it was someone with access to highly classified information.'

'That should narrow things down, though, shouldn't it?'

'Definitely. The Secretary's entire *visit* was top secret, never mind the route she was taking to the meeting. They've *got* to let me take an imprint from Qasid. He knows who the mole is!' He reactivated the earwig. 'Holly Jo, put me through to—'

Two sharp cracks came from somewhere outside. Adam's head snapped round at the noise. 'Kyle! That was gunfire – what's happening?'

'I dunno,' said Kyle, confused. 'I landed the UAV to save power – the camera's off.'

Adam drew his SIG and ran to the door. Baxter had also heard the noise, hurrying up behind him with his rifle raised. 'What was it?'

'I don't know. Bianca, stay back,' Adam warned as he surveyed the scene. No movement . . .

'Tony!' he shouted. Tony was sprawled on the ground near the jetty, blood on his face. Nearby was Trenton, red lines oozing over his coat from a ragged wound in his back. No sign of Cope – but then he saw the other man's legs at the water's edge, his upper body half-submerged amongst the broken ice where he had fallen.

Al-Rais was gone.

32

Ambush

'Adam!' said Holly Jo. 'Zykov's satphone – someone's using it!'

'Tap it,' Adam ordered. He heard a shrill whine nearby as the UAV took off. 'John, cover me!'

He hurried across the tracks to the fallen men. Tony was alive, but barely conscious, a deep cut on his temple. Both Cope and Trenton were dead, shot. Trenton's G36 was missing. Adam looked round. Al-Rais had gone to Zykov's body to get his phone. The nearest cover from there was in the woods to the north.

He signalled for Baxter to watch in that direction. 'Tony! What happened?' The only reply was a groan.

'I've got al-Rais,' Holly Jo reported. 'He's talking to Sevnik – oh, crap.'

'What?'

'He's turning round. Adam, the gunship's coming back!'

'Kyle, find the Hind,' said Adam. 'I need to know the second you see it. John! Help me with Tony!'

As the rest of Baxter's men took up positions to watch the woods, their leader ran to Adam. 'What the hell happened here?'

'Get him up.' They picked up Tony, who moaned. 'We need

to get everyone on the plane, now. The Hind's on its way back.'

The older man regarded his fallen comrades with anguish. 'We can't leave them behind!'

'The living have priority. Get everyone aboard. Did you talk to the pilot?'

'He'll do what we tell him,' Baxter assured him coldly. They started for the jetty, carrying Tony between them. 'Everybody, get to the plane! Rossovich, bring the pilot! Spence, you've got the other guy!'

'Stay with me, Dr Childs,' said Perez as Bianca emerged fearfully from the building, carrying the cases. Rossovich, the XM500 slung from a shoulder, followed them out, one hand clenched on the co-pilot's collar as the other shoved his pistol into the young man's back. Behind him, Spence pushed Qasid at gunpoint. 'Okay, let's move.'

Everyone headed for the pier, eyes sweeping the trees. 'Kyle, do you see the gunship?' Adam asked as he reached the jetty.

'Not yet.' They might have enough time to get airborne, then . . .

Morgan cut in through the earwig. 'Adam, where's al-Rais?'

'In the woods somewhere.'

'You've got to recapture him!'

'There isn't time.' He checked the trees to the north again. Still no sign of the terrorist leader. 'We've got the imprint, we can—'

A crackle of gunfire – from the *south*.

Rossovich was hit by several bullets and tumbled to the snowy ground. The co-pilot took another round to his abdomen. He fell, screaming. Everyone else on the shore scrambled for cover, Perez practically throwing Bianca behind a pile of scrap before diving alongside her.

Adam and Baxter, Tony still hanging limply between them,

were completely exposed on the jetty. They turned to find the threat, knowing that a second burst would finish them . . .

It didn't come. 'Go!' said Baxter. They ran back along the pier and jumped down into the meagre cover it provided at the shoreline, ice crunching and snapping underfoot as they landed. Freezing water splashed over Adam's feet. He ignored it, concentrating on locating their enemy.

He should have known. Al-Rais was always willing to take calculated risks. Instead of going straight for the nearer trees, he had stayed in the open for the extra seconds needed to cross the tracks and find cover on the cutting's southern side. Part of him felt a gloating pride at having outsmarted the infidels—

He crushed the feeling. 'Where is he?' he called.

'I think he's in the big building,' someone shouted back.

Adam cautiously peered at what had not long earlier been his own hiding place. Several windows, and the terrorist could be behind any of them – or none. *Never stay still*, said the unwelcome resident in his mind. *A fly that lands gets swatted.*

Seconds passed. Still no further gunfire – but a wail from the wounded Russian told Adam that al-Rais had fired all the shots he needed. Without the pilot, the American team had no way to escape. Some of them, Adam included, had received basic flight training – but none knew how to pilot a jet-powered seaplane.

The Hind was no more than five minutes away. They wouldn't stand a chance against it . . .

Another scream – and he knew what he had to do.

'Bianca!' Adam yelled. 'Set up the PERSONA!'

'What?' she shrieked back, on the verge of panic. 'What for?'

'The pilot! If we transfer his persona, I can fly us out of here!'

'No!' gasped Tony, stirring weakly. 'It'll wipe al-Rais's persona. We can't afford to lose it.'

'We've got the recording. And keeping it in my head won't be any use if we're all dead. John, you've got to get the pilot to Bianca. It's our only chance.'

Baxter was uncertain, but set his jaw. 'We'll get him. Listen up!' he shouted to the others, issuing orders.

'Adam,' said Morgan through the earwig, 'Tony's right. If we lose al-Rais—'

'We've already lost him,' Adam said, curt. 'Tony, what happened?'

'I don't know,' Tony said, eyes screwed up in pain. 'I was walking just ahead of him, and – he must have gotten free somehow, grabbed Trenton's gun and hit me. I don't remember anything after that.'

'How the hell did he get free?' growled Baxter. 'His hands were cuffed behind his back!'

'He had a knife,' Adam remembered. 'But – no, your team found it when you searched him. He knew how to break flex-cuffs, though. Najjar taught him. That doesn't matter now, though. John, are you set?'

'Yeah.' Baxter brought up his rifle. 'Okay, guys, ready – and *go!*'

He aimed the gun at the large building, ready to fire at the slightest sign of movement. Along the cutting, other squad members did the same, covering Perez as he ran into the open to drag the pilot back to cover. The Russian screamed again, his cry echoing off the ruined buildings.

Adam raised his own pistol. Where was al-Rais? What was he planning? Would he attack Perez and the pilot while they were vulnerable in the open? *No*, the terrorist's persona told him. *Even if I hit them, the moment I fire the Americans will shoot back. All I have to do is stop them from reaching the plane, and wait until Sevnik arrives . . .*

He was covering the jetty, then. From where? A clear vantage point, but with cover. The wooden walls would give no protection against rifle bullets. Adam looked along the icy shore to the south.

There was a small hut behind the former mine offices. Near it was a pile of snow-covered debris; broken wood, garbage—

Something moved behind it.

Adam fired three shots. The shape ducked, then reappeared, running for the hut. Adam fired again, but al-Rais had already thrown himself behind the little structure.

'Watch Tony,' Adam told Baxter as he ran to Bianca. Perez pulled the pilot behind the scrap pile. 'He's behind that building!' he warned the troops, pointing.

'Adam, I've just spotted the Hind,' Kyle said.

'How long before it gets here?'

'A few minutes, but it's coming at full steam. You've got to get out of there.'

'That's the plan. Bianca, are you ready?'

She regarded the writhing pilot, appalled. 'We can't make a transfer from him! He's been shot!'

'Yeah, and *we'll* be shot in about three minutes if you don't. The gunship's coming back!'

She hesitated, then began to put the skullcap on the Russian's head. He cried out, babbling. 'Hold him down,' she told Perez.

Adam took the jet injector from the case, then sat with his back against the scrap pile. 'This is still set for the right dose, yes?'

'It should be,' Bianca replied. He brought the device to his neck. 'No, wait! I'll do it.'

'No time.' He gasped at the sharp pain, then lay back and waited for the drug to take effect.

He felt al-Rais's persona clawing at his mind, desperate to hold on as the Neutharsine washed through it. But even the terrorist leader's willpower was not enough to resist the chain reaction of chemical processes. The other voice in his head seemed to scream before dissolving to nothingness . . .

'Adam!' He opened his eyes to see Bianca leaning over him

anxiously, and realised that his own skullcap was now in place. 'Did it work? Is al-Rais's persona gone?'

'I . . . I think so.' He tried to think of the Saudi's parents, his lovers. No memories came to him. 'Are you ready?'

She had the other injector primed with a dose of Hyperthymexine. 'Yes, but . . . he's injured, I don't know what'll happen. It might kill him!'

'It's our only chance. Do it!'

Reluctantly, she injected the co-pilot. He let out a gurgling shriek, flecks of spittle around his mouth tinged with blood. Bianca grimaced, then activated the PERSONA.

At the jetty, Tony struggled to sit up. 'John,' he groaned. 'Give me a hand.'

Baxter pulled him into a crouch. 'Are you okay?'

'I'm gonna need a truckload of Advil, but I'll live.' He reached into his coat and took out his silenced SIG. 'Where's al-Rais?'

'Somewhere behind that building.'

'Adam?'

'With Childs. They're using the machine on the pilot.'

'Damn it. I told him – never mind.' His headset had been dislodged; he fumbled it back into place. 'Holly Jo, Kyle, what's the situation?'

'Chopper's coming in fast,' Kyle warned.

'Okay, whatever happens here, you need to be ready to get into the air. Tell the pilot to start the engines and stand by. If you lose contact with us, then he takes off *immediately* and heads back to US airspace at maximum speed. Understand?'

'But we can't leave you behind,' protested Holly Jo.

'If that Hind does what it was designed to do, there won't be anything of us *left* behind. That's an order, okay? Tell him to power up, now.'

'What do we tell the Russians?'

'Anything you have to. Just get the plane ready for takeoff. Out.' He exchanged a grim look with Baxter, then they turned their eyes and weapons back to the search for al-Rais.

Despite the cold, Bianca was sweating. She watched the columns of scrolling figures with a growing sense of hopelessness. 'Come on, faster,' she muttered, willing the numbers to speed up – but knowing that they wouldn't.

She couldn't bring herself to look at the pilot, shuddering in the snow. Instead she checked Adam. His eyes were flickering as he took in the Russian's memories. Another look at the screen. What had been normal was now excruciatingly slow. 'Come *on!*'

Perez scuttled from the scrap pile to duck behind an overturned mine cart some forty feet away. Rifle raised, he surveyed the woods opposite before glancing up at the mine. 'Dr Childs – you'd better move back into the trees.'

'I can't leave them,' she protested, indicating the two men beside her.

'You need to get out of sight.' A distant drumming became audible, the rapid tattoo echoing off the surrounding hills. 'We're about to have company!'

With a despairing look at Adam, Bianca unwillingly backed up to the trees. The sound grew louder—

The gunship rose over the summit like a bird of prey and swooped down towards the lake.

Fire flashed from the Hind's nose with a fearsome chainsaw rasp as its twin-barrelled autocannon spewed out fifty rounds every second. A line of eruptions ripped along the ground. They raced towards the Vityaz – which shook under the metallic hammer-blows before disintegrating in a blinding fireball, a black mushroom cloud swelling skywards.

But the line didn't stop there. It raced snake-like through the cutting, hunting for prey – then finding it, and striking.

The cart was no protection against the gunship's explosive 30mm rounds. They ripped through it, shattering the corroded steel – and hitting the man behind it. Perez didn't even have time to scream as he was torn apart by shells and shrapnel.

And the deadly serpent raced on, seeing more victims ahead – the pilot and Adam, lying helpless on the ground—

The line of fire suddenly swerved. Shells hit the pile of rusted scrap rather than the men behind it as the Hind banked. The gunship blasted overhead, rotor wash kicking up a freezing whirlwind of snow in its wake. It crossed the shoreline and headed out over the lagoon, beginning a long, sweeping turn for a second attack.

The downdraught had dislodged lumps of snow from the trees, leaving Bianca covered. Coughing, she shook off the icy deposits and looked out with trepidation into the cutting. To her relief, Adam was unharmed – but the sight of what was left of Perez almost made her vomit. Acidic bile burning in her throat, she stumbled out into the open and crouched beside the agent, wiping snow off the PERSONA.

The activity on the screen was dying down. Heart pounding, Bianca pulled off a glove and stabbed at the keyboard. CALCULATING LATENCY ESTIMATES. The figures finally appeared. They were only just within the limits she had been taught were acceptable – but she didn't care. 'Adam, wake up!'

She tugged at the skullcap. Adam stirred – and sprang upright with an anguished scream. Bianca fell backwards in fright. He clutched at his side, wailing in Russian – then stopped, panting.

'What is it? What's wrong?' Bianca gasped.

'His strongest memory – it's being shot!' He looked down at

himself, almost surprised to find that he was unhurt. 'I thought I'd been shot too.'

'You nearly were! The helicopter – it killed Perez!' Keeping her eyes averted, she pointed towards the mine carts.

'Jesus,' said Adam as he saw the dead man. He looked for the Hind. It was still making its turn; the heavily armoured flying tank did not possess dragonfly manoeuvrability. 'Get the gear packed up. We've got to get to the plane.'

'Can you fly it?'

Despite the tension of the situation, the emotion that crossed his face was embarrassment. 'Ah . . . kind of.'

'What do you mean, "kind of"?'

'I mean, this guy was still learning! He's only made two takeoffs from water, and both times he had an instructor helping.'

'Well, that's just fantastic!' Bianca started to remove the co-pilot's electrode cap, only to pull back in horror. The Russian was still and silent, unmoving eyes staring at the leaden sky. 'Oh, God!'

Adam knew what she was thinking. 'You didn't kill him,' he assured her, indicating the spreading red stain in the snow at the pilot's side. 'Al-Rais shot him, not you.'

'But – but if we'd done something for him, he might—'

'Bianca, if we don't get out of here, we'll be dead too. Come on!' He yanked the skullcap off the dead man and tossed it into the case, then slammed the PERSONA's screen shut and shoved the machine into its foam bed. 'I'll take this – you carry the recorder.' He looked round at the lagoon – and froze.

The Hind was coming back.

33

Cut Off

Sevnik was in the gunner's seat, finger on the cannon's trigger as he surveyed the scene below on the hooded gunsight screen. It had been many years since he had flown in actual combat, attacking rebels in the Second Chechen War, but he had not forgotten how to fight.

'Come right three degrees,' he told the pilot in the seat behind him. Unlike earlier models of the Mi-24, which had a rotating turret, the 30mm autocannons on this machine's nose were fixed and required the entire aircraft to be lined up on its target. The chopper banked gently. 'Hold.' He switched the gunsight's mode to infrared, the cold landscape becoming a dark grey with hot white spots revealing the Americans al-Rais had warned him about.

Two of the spots were at the shore end of the jetty. The line showing where the cannon shells would impact ran right over them. 'Move in.'

Small flashes of light on the IR display. The Americans were shooting at him! An act of pure desperation: even if they scored a hit, the gunship's armour was impervious to anything smaller than a .50-calibre round.

His finger tightened on the trigger, ready to fire . . .

Something flicked through his peripheral vision – not on the screen, but outside the cockpit canopy. The pilot reacted in surprise. 'What—'

The helicopter shuddered as something hit the engine intakes above the cockpit and exploded.

'What the hell?' shouted Baxter as fire and smoke burst from the Hind's upper fuselage. Debris dropped into the water. The gunship banked sharply, turning away from the pier and crossing the shoreline to drop behind the trees to the south. 'We didn't hit it that hard!'

Tony knew what had happened. 'Kyle! Was that you?'

No answer. Kyle had used the UAV's self-destruct to make a kamikaze attack on the helicopter – but with the drone destroyed, they had also lost its communications relay. Their headsets, and Adam's earwig, only had limited range and power. Transmissions to the op centre aboard the plane were now blocked by the hills.

'Sounds like it's landing,' said Baxter. The rumbling slap of the Hind's rotors changed in pitch as it moved into a hover. 'We're gonna be outnumbered any minute!'

'Adam!' shouted Tony as two scurrying figures approached. 'Can you fly the plane?'

Adam jumped down into the cover of the jetty, Bianca following. 'Touch and go,' he said.

'What does *that* mean?' Baxter demanded.

'It means we'll either go, or we'll touch something – very hard.'

'Make it the first one,' said Tony. He glanced at the Beriev. 'How long will it take to get that thing moving?'

'I can do an emergency start-up quickly enough – it's getting it into the air that'll be tricky.'

'Get aboard,' Tony ordered. He called out to the others. 'Everyone give Adam cover!'

'Bring Qasid,' Adam told him.

'It's too risky,' Baxter objected. 'If we waste time moving a prisoner while under fire, it'll get someone killed!'

Tony was silent for a moment, then nodded to Adam. 'We take him with us,' he announced. Baxter was about to protest, but he cut him off. 'No arguments – get him on that plane.'

Adam gave Tony a nod of thanks, then rose. The Hind had landed somewhere on the other side of the woods. The Russian soldiers would be here in a few minutes – but al-Rais was already somewhere much closer. Even without the terrorist leader's persona, Adam knew he would try to stop the Americans from leaving with the RTG.

No sign of him, though. 'Okay, I'm ready.'

'Good luck,' said Tony.

Adam jumped up on to the jetty – and ran.

Despite some of the covering snow and ice being cleared by the men carrying the RTG, the surface was still slippery. The tip of the Beriev's starboard wing reached halfway back along the hundred-foot pier. He passed it, skirting a dead terrorist. If al-Rais were going to take a shot, it would be now—

A sharp crack of gunfire – but he had already ducked. The bullet snapped over him and punched a hole in the Beriev's fuselage.

More shots, these from a G36 as a teammate opened fire on the terrorist leader's position. Boots skidding over the old planks, Adam threw himself through the open hatch into the Be-200's cabin. He rolled into cover – and hit something hard and heavy.

The RTG. The nuclear battery squatted inside its protective frame, secured to the deck by thick straps. The core's green paint was cracked and flaking, exposing the metal of the casing.

The shooting stopped. He glanced through the hatch. Tony

and the others still had guns at the ready. They hadn't hit al-Rais. Beyond the trees, he heard the throb of the Hind's engines at idle. The pilot probably had no idea what had hit his aircraft, and was unwilling to risk the Americans having more of them.

But Adam knew that as soon as the Beriev started up, Sevnik would not allow the gunship to remain grounded.

He hurried into the cockpit. A moment of terrified shock as he saw the dead pilot still slumped in his seat, the Barrett round having blown half his head away. But he suppressed the young co-pilot's horror at the sight of his dead instructor and friend and dropped into the empty second seat. The Beriev was a modern aircraft with a relatively high degree of computerisation; he engaged the auxiliary power unit to activate the main systems, then began the procedure for an emergency start-up.

Holly Jo ran back into the Global 6000's cabin from the cockpit. 'Better strap in!' she warned Kyle as she sat and buckled her own seat belt tightly.

'I can't believe we're doing this,' Kyle said as he followed suit. The lights flickered, then the airframe trembled as the engines rose in power. There was a whine as the thrust reversers opened. The plane began to move – backwards, trundling towards Provideniya's main runway.

Holly Jo put her headset back on. 'Oh, they are *not* happy about this,' she said as she heard the control tower's demands to know what was going on.

'They want us to stop and power down,' said the pilot. 'What do we do?'

'We've got our orders – take off and get to US airspace,' she replied, looking through a porthole. A couple of Russian officials were running across the snow-covered concrete after the retreating jet. 'Uh-oh.'

The plane swung sharply through ninety degrees to face down the runway. Kyle peered through the window. 'What're they gonna do, try to shoot out the— Oh shit. Oh shit! They've got guns – they *are* going to shoot out the tyres!' He reactivated his own headset. 'Dude, get us out of here!'

'Miss Voss, can you keep your people's chatter down, please?' the pilot replied testily. The thrust reversers retracted, the jet lurching to a stop.

'What?' snapped Kyle. 'No, wait – I'm not *her* people! She doesn't give me orders!'

'You are *such* a gynophobe, Kyle,' Holly Jo said, clutching her armrests as the engines shrieked to full power.

'No, I'm not, whatever that is – oh Jesus!' The Russians were taking aim. 'Go, go go *go!*'

The pilot released the wheelbrakes. Holly Jo and Kyle were shoved back in their seats as the jet surged forward. One of the Russians gawped at the Global 6000 as it raced past.

The younger of the pair opened fire—

He was aiming at the wheels rather than the fuselage. His bullets hit nothing but concrete and snow. The plane left the officers behind in moments and took to the sky, climbing steeply and banking to head south-east.

Holly Jo was still monitoring the radio traffic. 'They're warning the Russian air force about us,' she said, alarmed.

Now that they were airborne, Kyle had relaxed. 'Pfft. What're they gonna do?' he asked dismissively. 'They can't even afford to keep up a proper interceptor screen. Besides, we'll have an F-22 escort as soon as we're out of Russian airspace. Nothing'll be able to touch us.'

'Maybe,' said Holly Jo, less convinced. 'But we've got to *get* out of Russian airspace first . . .'

★ ★ ★

A rising shrill announced to those on the shore that Adam had started the Beriev's engines. Baxter waved to his men. 'Let's go, let's go! Bring the prisoner!'

Spence hauled Qasid upright and pushed him along the cutting. The two other soldiers quickly caught up.

Tony kept a close watch on the buildings. Al-Rais had fired from behind the largest one, its wooden wall now ravaged by G36 bullets – but he was certain the Saudi had escaped unharmed.

Al-Rais was no longer the only threat, however. Sevnik's soldiers were somewhere in the woods – and getting closer. 'Okay, John,' said Tony, 'get Bianca to the plane. I'll cover you.'

'You should take her,' Baxter said.

'There isn't time to argue. Go!'

Baxter frowned, but helped Bianca up. 'Can you carry both those cases?' he asked.

'They're heavy, but – yeah, I can,' she said, realising that he was effectively offering to take one himself, which would leave him holding his rifle one-handed.

'Good.' He turned to cover the cutting's southern side. 'Okay, head for the plane as quick as you can. Go!'

She swung the cases on to the jetty, then clambered up. Baxter hopped on to the structure with considerably more grace. Arms straining, she scurried along the pier. The Alabaman moved at a backwards trot behind her.

'Movement in the woods!' yelled one of the men on the shore. 'South-west!'

Tony looked past the derelict buildings, seeing shadowy figures ducking between the snow-laden evergreens about a hundred yards distant. Three, maybe four men – which meant the rest of Sevnik's squad would be moving in from a different direction. 'Suppressing fire!' he ordered. 'Get to the plane!'

Spence drove Qasid towards the pier as the other two men

opened up, firing three-round bursts into the trees. The shots weren't intended to kill, simply to force the approaching Russians to drop and find protection – preventing them from shooting back. Bark splintered, white powder exploding from the drooping branches. The soldiers scrambled for cover.

Tony checked on Bianca and Baxter. They were halfway along the jetty, Baxter still watching the shore. 'Tony!' the ex-Marine shouted, gesturing with his rifle.

More figures in the trees, these emerging from behind the buildings to make a pincer movement along the lagoon's edge. Baxter fired a burst in their direction. The Russians hurriedly pulled back.

'Come on, move!' yelled Tony as Spence and Qasid passed him. The remaining two men backed towards the pier as they unleashed bursts of fire into the woods.

'Reloading!' said Levin, ejecting a spent magazine. He crouched behind a pile of mine debris and fumbled for a replacement. Fallon reached the jetty.

'Levin, hurry up!' Tony yelled as he climbed on to the wooden structure to start his own retreat. Another look back. Bianca boarded the plane, Baxter pausing to untie the mooring rope. 'We are *leaving*!'

Levin finally loaded the new mag. He popped up to fire across the cutting, then raced for the jetty.

One of the Russians in the woods shot back, his Kalashnikov on full auto. Some of the rounds were tracers, lines of green fire streaking like laser beams across the tracks.

Homing in—

A shot ripped through Levin's left shoulder with a spray of blood.

'Man down!' Tony cried, seeing him fall. 'Cover me!'

He opened up with his SIG at the shooter, who ducked into

cover. The men on the jetty also fired, Baxter and Spence aiming at the soldiers behind the buildings while Fallon put down more suppressing fire on Tony's target. Tony ran to the fallen man. 'Can you move?'

Levin had dropped his gun, his free hand clamped over the bloody wound. 'I – I think so.'

Tony hauled him to his feet. 'Get going – I'll give you cover. Run!' He picked up the G36 and backed up, firing into the trees.

Baxter pulled the last loop of the mooring line free. 'Get that asshole aboard!' he shouted to Spence, who forcefully shoved Qasid through the hatch before turning to continue shooting. 'Tony, come on!'

Tony fired one last burst – then his rifle clicked empty. He dropped it and ran, quickly catching up with Levin and pulling him with him.

Baxter retreated into the plane, the others following suit. Despite their suppressing fire, retaliatory gunshots rattled from the shore. Bullets clunked against the Beriev's hull. Bianca shrieked, flattening herself on the deck and shielding her head. 'Get moving, go!' shouted Tony, waving furiously for the plane to set off.

In the cockpit, Adam saw him and pushed the throttles. The engines rose in power. The float on the seaplane's starboard wing would have hit the pier if he had simply gone forward, forcing him to engage reverse thrust and back the thirty-ton jet away from it.

Still hauling Levin with him, Tony reached the open hatch just as it slipped from the end of the jetty. Hands dragged them inside.

'They're aboard!' Baxter yelled to Adam, before leaning back out of the door to resume firing. 'Get us out of here!'

Adam pushed the port engine's throttle further forward. The

extra power on that side drove the aircraft into a slewing turn, its tail swinging towards the shore. Ice crackled under the hull. He looked through the side window. Was the float clear?

A hailstorm rattle of bullets told him that it would have to be. He closed the thrust reversers and pushed both throttles forward. The Beriev's nose tipped upwards like a surging speedboat before the water's drag on the aft fuselage slammed it back down in an explosion of spray. Shouts came from the cabin as people were thrown off their feet.

Fear gripped him, the co-pilot's inexperience fuelling the emotion. *I've only done this twice before – and Stepan is dead!* He worked the controls, extending the wing flaps for maximum lift. With the RTG aboard, the Beriev was heavily laden, its hull low in the water and both wing floats carving deeply into the lagoon's surface. The nose thumped through the choppy waves as the plane moved out into open water. *What do I do? Elevators – use the elevators, set the right pitch angle . . .*

Adam made the adjustments, the seaplane's nose slowly tipping back up. Another wave impact, but this time the Be-200 skipped over it rather than ploughing through. He increased power and looked ahead.

Hills filled his vision. The plane's turn had left it pointing diagonally across the long lagoon. He needed to head due south to have enough room to take off. *I've never turned at this speed! We might capsize!*

Despite the persona's warning, he pushed his foot down on the rudder pedal. The Beriev changed course, centrifugal force rolling it heavily on to its left side. *Slower, slow down!*

But he couldn't. Off to his right he saw movement above the woods. The Hind had taken off again.

Sevnik was trying to stop their escape.

34

Outflanked

A dam pushed the rudder pedal down harder. The Beriev tipped further, the pilot's corpse flopping grotesquely over the armrest. The hillside swung away. Grey sky almost touched grey water in the distance ahead, separated only by a thin bar of land across the lagoon's mouth.

He eased pressure on the rudder, lining up the plane with the open sky. The Hind pulled ahead, sweeping out across the water. He realised what Sevnik was doing. The Russian didn't want to risk losing the RTG – maybe he even had some sliver of conscience that drew the line at poisoning the Motherland with five kilograms of strontium-90 – and rather than destroy the seaplane, he was trying to stop it from taking off.

The easiest way to do that would also be the simplest: block its path.

Adam opened the throttles, changing the elevator pitch to bring the nose back up. The Beriev bounced over the waves as it gained speed. It needed at least a kilometre of open water and to reach 120 knots to take off. The Hind could easily match its pace and move to obstruct it. A collision would be catastrophic for both aircraft, and Sevnik was surely banking that

351

the American team was not on a suicide mission.

Tony entered the cockpit and braced himself against the dead pilot's seat. 'Can we make it?'

'Yes – if we can get past the Hind!' The gunship was now directly ahead, slowing to a hover and turning to face the oncoming seaplane.

'Is he playing *chicken*?' Tony said in disbelief.

'If we hit him, we'll lose the tail and probably the engines too. All he has to do is force me to cut power and splash down again, and I won't have enough room left to get back up to takeoff speed.'

'What are you going to do?'

Adam indicated the body. '*He's* the one who'd know what to do. I'm just trying to stop this thing from nose-diving into the lake!'

He checked the airspeed indicator. Fifty knots and rising. The Beriev crested a wave with a loud *whump*, spray speckling the windshield. *More pitch on the elevators!* He adjusted the trim. The young Russian was at least a qualified pilot in conventional aircraft, even if his seaplane experience was far too slim for comfort. It was only then that Adam realised he didn't even know the man's name. *Gennady*, the persona told him, almost indignant. *Always the middle brother, always overlooked* . . .

Orange flashes from the Hind's cannon. Waterspouts kicked up in the Beriev's path. Sevnik was giving him a shot across the bows, trying to scare him into aborting the takeoff.

Eighty knots. The Be-200 skipped over each wave, producing a momentary roller-coaster sensation in his stomach before the keel sliced back into the water. Ninety knots. 'Everybody hold on!' he shouted over his shoulder.

More flames – this time from one of the gunship's rocket pods. Two great white geysers erupted just ahead of the seaplane,

the Beriev ploughing through the spray. Adam's view through
the windshield was obliterated, water gushing into the cockpit
through the bullet hole. It took him – rather, Gennady – a
moment to remember where the wiper controls were. He found
the switch, the blades squealing across the rectangular panes.

The Hind was dead ahead, an ugly bug-eyed creature hanging
above the lake.

He applied more rudder as the Beriev bounced up again, the
seaplane curving to port. The gunship tilted to follow. The way
was still blocked. One hundred knots.

Another burst of cannon fire—

This time, the Be-200 hit the line of waterspouts. There was a
piercing bang somewhere below the cockpit's right side. Adam
felt the jolt of impact through the joystick. His eyes snapped to
the display screens. The computers weren't reporting any damage
– but that did not mean the wound was harmless.

One-ten. He jammed the throttles to the detent and
pulled back on the stick. The Beriev was still short of takeoff
speed, but if it didn't get airborne now it would never clear the
gunship.

Another wave – and the seaplane's nose pitched upwards.
A hundred and fifteen knots. The hull cleared the surface
completely . . .

It wasn't enough.

He felt the roller-coaster sensation again as the plane reached
the top of its arc. The Hind hovered gloatingly ahead, weapons
pods curled down like mantis claws. If he didn't cut power
immediately, he would crash into it—

The flash of lunatic inspiration was not Gennady's, but Adam's
own. He didn't pull back the throttles. Instead he shoved the
joystick forward, throwing the plane into a power dive. The
Beriev pitched down sharply, water rushing up to meet it . . .

The seaplane hit the lake hard, another eruption of spray blinding its pilot – as he yanked the joystick back and slammed the elevators to their maximum pitch.

The Be-200 skipped off the surface like a thrown stone and climbed again—

Passing right under the gunship.

The tip of the seaplane's tail scraped the Hind's belly with a metallic shriek, but the damage it inflicted was nothing compared to the impact of the Beriev's jet exhaust. With both engines at full power, it was blasting out over thirty thousand pounds of thrust – swatting the helicopter out of the sky.

The gunship was hurled into a corkscrewing spin, rolling as it fell. Its rotors slashed into the water – and the engines' torque flung the fuselage around in the opposite direction, slamming it down like a hammer. The Hind disintegrated, wreckage tumbling in all directions before being swallowed by the icy void.

But the Beriev was not out of danger. The forced touchdown had slowed it, the airspeed indicator dropping. The bar of land across the lagoon's mouth was coming up fast – and the seaplane was falling towards it.

Adam grappled with the controls, desperately trying to find extra lift. If he pulled the stick back to climb without increasing speed, it would result in a stall, smashing the Be-200 on the frozen ground. But the indicator needle was rising too slowly. The plane reached one hundred knots again, but it was not enough to stay airborne.

Despite every instinct of Gennady's screaming for him to stop, he pushed the stick forward again. The altimeter spun down faster – but the plane picked up speed. One-ten, one-fifteen, but the Beriev was only fifty feet above sea level.

Rocks and snow filled his vision . . .

One hundred and twenty knots.

Adam felt the plane's wings flex, as if it were coming alive. He pulled the stick back. The icy land dropped away—

A fearsome grinding noise echoed through the fuselage as the Beriev's keel grazed the bar, kicking up a spray of snow and gravel – then the seaplane angled upwards, gaining height.

'*Slava bogu!*' cried Adam, whooping. 'We made it!'

'Jesus!' gasped Tony, still clinging to the other seat. He looked back shakily into the main cabin. 'Is everyone okay?'

Baxter and his men gave more or less positive responses, the team leader closing the hatch before checking Levin's wound. Bianca flipped strands of spray-soaked hair off her face. 'Oh yes, fine,' she said with withering sarcasm. 'So what's the in-flight movie? *Alive*?'

Adam ignored her, turning the plane south-east. He found a pair of headphones on a hook and donned them, then switched on the radio and listened to the rapid chatter from Provideniya's control tower. 'This isn't good,' he said.

'What is it?' Tony asked.

'Our plane got away from Provideniya – but the controllers have requested Russian military support to bring them back.'

The blond man was unimpressed. 'The nearest airbase is, what, two hundred miles from here? There's no way they'll catch up before we reach US airspace.'

'They don't *have* to,' Adam said urgently. 'They already had two fighters in the air on a long-range exercise – they're moving to intercept!'

The Global 6000 had levelled out at ten thousand feet, on course for St Lawrence Island. Kyle hoped for a sight of American soil in the distance, but clouds obstructed his view. 'God *damn*, that was close,' he said, leaning back in his seat. 'I'd better get danger pay for this.'

Holly Jo glowered at him. 'Jesus Christ, Kyle!'

He looked affronted. 'What?'

'Is that all you can think about, yourself? Some of our people just *died*! We lost at least three members of the tac team – and we don't know what happened to everyone else after you blew up the UAV.'

'Hey, I was trying to *save* them by doing that.'

'That's not the point! You're sitting there whining about how dangerous things were for you, when—'

The entire plane lurched violently, loose items flying across the cabin. Only Kyle and Holly Jo's seat belts kept them from following suit. A thunderous roar shook the aircraft, followed a moment later by another vicious jolt and a second rumbling scream that rapidly dopplered away into the distance.

Holly Jo grabbed her armrests in panic. 'What the hell was that?'

Kyle looked back through the window. 'Holy shit!'

Two sleek jet fighters powered away from the American plane, having just crossed its path at near-supersonic speeds so that it would slam into their turbulent wakes – the aerial equivalent of throwing a stinger strip in front of a speeding car. They circled behind the business jet, giving Kyle a better view as they passed. He identified them instantly: Sukhoi Su-35E 'Super Flankers', painted in angular grey dazzle camouflage. The pride of the Russian Air Force, and among the most deadly aircraft on the planet. Each Flanker had four missiles mounted beneath its wings.

He doubted that the weapons were harmless training dummies.

Holly Jo used her headset to talk to the cockpit. 'What's happening?'

Tension was clear in the pilot's voice. 'They're ordering us to turn about and head back to Provideniya.'

'They can't do that!' Kyle protested. 'We're in international airspace.'

'We just violated *Russian* airspace with an unauthorised takeoff. They're kinda pissed about it!'

'But what about our F-22s?'

'Gee, I don't see them,' the pilot replied scathingly. 'Do you?'

Holly Jo listened in on another transmission, from one of the Sukhois. 'Oh my God,' she said, going pale. 'They just said that if we don't turn round, they'll open fire.'

'We don't have a choice,' said the pilot. 'I'm taking us back.'

Kyle pressed his face against the porthole. One of the pursuing Flankers swung into sight as the Global 6000 banked, the military aircraft effortlessly matching the Bombardier's movements. 'Crap. Crap, oh *crap*!' he cried, close to panic. 'What happens if they arrest us? I mean, we're technically spies.'

'There's no "technically" about it,' said Holly Jo. 'We *are* spies! We've got to destroy the hard drives, wipe anything containing classified data—'

She was interrupted by an astonished shout from Kyle. 'Holy *shit*! Look at this, look!'

She rushed to the other side of the cabin to see what was happening – and reacted with the same amazement.

Another plane had joined the chase.

The pilot of the leading Sukhoi adjusted his course to follow the larger jet as it turned. Even though it had followed his instructions and was heading back to land, he still kept the gunsight on his head-up display locked on to it. Where east met west over the Bering Strait, the Americans were always up to something sneaky. This time, they had been caught red-handed—

He flinched at a shocked yelp in his helmet's earphones – his wingman. 'Drop, drop!' the other pilot cried. 'Break off!'

Nothing on the radar or threat warning indicator. He looked back . . . as a shadow fell over his cockpit.

The second Flanker had made a hurried rolling descent – away from the looming underbelly of the large transport aircraft now plunging down at him like a giant's fist.

'He's diving, he's gone!' said Tony, leaning over the pilot's body to see what was happening outside. He had pressed a gloved hand against the bullet hole in the windshield to block the shrieking wind. The two Sukhois disappeared into the clouds below. 'You did it! You scared them off.'

'Not for long,' Adam said grimly as he levelled out. He selected a new radio frequency. 'Two-zero-one, do you read me? This is Adam, on an open channel. Do you read?'

'We read you,' came the reply – the pilot of the Global 6000, its tail number ending in 201. 'What's your situation?'

'The situation,' said Kyle, cutting in with enormous relief, 'is that he's just saved our asses!'

'I only bought us a little extra time,' Adam corrected. 'Two-zero-one, turn back to the south-east, maximum speed. You've got to reach US airspace.'

'Those fighters will catch up again long before then,' the pilot pointed out.

'Just get as far as you can. We'll do the same. Out.' He banked the Beriev away from the business jet. As he turned, he saw two faces gawping at him through the cabin portholes: Holly Jo and Kyle. He gave them a brief wave, then looked back at the controls.

'They're following us,' Tony reported as the Bombardier changed course.

'They're not the only ones.' Although he couldn't see them, Adam knew the Russian fighters were still out there.

And now they were mad.

The lead Su-35 pilot powered his plane back up through the clouds. He was shaking; both with shock at the near-miss, and with anger. Attacked – by a *seaplane*! It was almost insulting that somebody in a tub of a Beriev had tried to intimidate him. What made it worse was that they had succeeded.

Now he would show the Beriev's pilot the true meaning of intimidation.

He activated his fighter's fire-control systems. The Flanker's Irbis radar was capable of detecting targets as far as four hundred kilometres away, but the two he was now hunting were only at one hundredth of that distance. 'Bandits at eleven o'clock high, bearing one-one-zero degrees,' he told his companion. 'Let's get them.'

Both Sukhois banked hard, afterburners flaring as they surged in pursuit.

Adam watched the Bombardier overtaking his plane. Even with its two powerful engines, the aerodynamic compromises needed to make the Be-200 amphibious limited its maximum speed to just over five hundred knots. The Global 6000 had almost a ninety-knot advantage.

Not that it mattered: both aircraft were in a losing race. The Flankers could achieve well over Mach 2, getting on for three times faster.

He switched one of the displays to a computerised map. The plane was now about halfway between the Russian coast and the north-western tip of St Lawrence Island. US airspace officially began twelve nautical miles from the land's edge, matching the limits of its territorial waters.

At the seaplane's top speed, it would still take more than two minutes to reach it.

And he didn't have two minutes. 'Attention seaplane, attention unidentified seaplane,' said a voice in his headphones. The Russian pilot was speaking in thickly accented English, but his barely restrained fury was clear. 'You have committed an aggressive act against military aircraft of the Russian Federation. You will turn to three-two-five degrees and land at Provideniya airport, where you will be placed under arrest. I have missile lock on your plane. If you do not obey, I will shoot you down. You have twenty seconds to comply.'

'Not good?' said Tony, seeing Adam's expression.

'Not good. They're going to fire if we don't turn back.'

The Global 6000's pilot had already made his decision, the other jet peeling away. One of the Flankers followed it. 'I guess that settles it,' Tony said mournfully. 'See you in the gulag . . .'

'You now have ten seconds,' said the Russian. The Beriev was dead centre in his HUD, a trilling warble in his headphones assuring him that he had a solid missile lock on his target. 'Nine. Eight . . .'

A new sound, an insistent, piercing shrill. Threat warning indicators flashed red. Someone had locked weapons on to *him*! But who—

'Russian fighters, Russian fighters,' said a new voice. American. 'We have missile lock on both your aircraft.'

The display revealed that the radar beam pinning him was coming from astern. The pilot twisted in his seat to spot its source. He glimpsed an ominous grey shadow against the sky, closing in from behind.

An F-22 Raptor, the most advanced fighter aircraft in the world.

'You will disengage immediately and allow the two civilian aircraft to proceed on their way,' the Raptor pilot continued. 'If you do not, we will use all necessary force to protect them.'

'What do we do?' asked the Russian's wingman, frantic.

The pilot choked back his rage. He had always wanted to know how a dogfight between a Flanker and a Raptor would play out, not believing for one minute the American claims of the latter's superiority and certain that he was more than a match for any US pilot . . . but from such a weakened position, any challenge would be suicide.

'Withdraw,' he snarled. 'Break off and withdraw.'

Tony was pressed against the window again, watching the Flanker curve away. An F-22 followed it, a hound corralling its prey. 'They're bugging out!'

'Attention two-zero-one and companion aircraft,' said one of the American pilots through Adam's headphones. 'This is Raptor One. You are now free and clear to reach US airspace. Once we're sure these guys have gone, we'll escort you to Elmendorf.' A pause, then, pointedly: 'Whatever you were doing, I hope it was worth it. There's gonna be diplomatic hell to pay once you're on the ground.'

'Thanks for your assistance, Raptor One,' Adam replied. He looked back into the cabin, seeing the RTG still secured to the deck, Bianca near it with the PERSONA cases – and Qasid, bound and under guard. 'We got what we came for.'

35

Double Jeopardy

Washington, DC

The atmosphere in the meeting room was caustic, to say the least.

Gordon Harper sat at one end of the table, glaring at the STS personnel around it with utter contempt. 'So. I bust my ass and call in a lot of political favours to give you the chance to follow up on what you found out in Macau. And in return, I get' – he jumped to his feet, banging both hands down on the table as his voice rose to a roar – '*a colossal cluster-fuck!*' Holly Jo flinched.

'With respect, Admiral,' said Morgan hesitantly, 'the operation wasn't a complete failure.'

'You want to call it a *success*?'

'We stopped al-Qaeda from getting the RTG,' said Tony, more firmly. 'And we have a recording of al-Rais's persona. The information we get from that—'

'Will be utterly useless!' Harper bellowed. 'Because you let him get away! The Russians haven't caught him, so he's still out there somewhere – and now he knows we're on to him, so whatever plans al-Qaeda had in the works, they'll change.'

'It'll still be valuable,' Tony insisted. 'Al-Rais knows names, contacts. With that information we can attack al-Qaeda from the top down, go after the captains rather than the foot-soldiers.'

Harper couldn't deny that he had a point, so switched to another angle of attack. 'And speaking of the Russians, do you have any idea of the size of the swirling shitstorm you've started at State?'

'Awesome alliteration,' said Bianca quietly.

Not quietly enough. Harper's searing gaze turned upon her. 'I don't think you appreciate how serious this is, Dr Childs.' He was somehow *more* threatening now that his voice had returned to a normal volume. 'Not only are three members of the Persona Project dead and two more injured,' he nodded towards Tony, who had a dressing over his head wound, 'as a result of the failure of this operation, but it's caused a major diplomatic incident. The Russians have raised their military alert status in response to what they call an aggressive invasion of their sovereign territory, so we've been forced to do the same. The United States is now at DEFCON 3 – and the last time it was that high was on September eleventh, 2001. *Now* do you see how serious this is?'

She nodded, abashed. 'Yes.'

'Good. Now, the State Department has brought out its chopping block, and it wants to see heads on it. Specifically, all of yours. Convince me not to hand them over.'

Adam spoke up. 'We still have the other prisoner, sir – Qasid. I learned from al-Rais's persona that he knows the identity of a mole who gave away the Secretary of State's route in the Islamabad bombing.'

That produced surprise around the table. Harper flicked through some papers. 'Qasid? According to everything we have on him, he's just some low-level thug.'

'Al-Rais didn't think so. He considered him one of his most reliable people.'

The Admiral didn't appear convinced, but before he could say anything the telephone in front of Morgan rang. He picked it up. 'Morgan . . . Okay, thank you.' He ended the call and turned to Harper. 'Mr Sternberg is ready at the White House.'

Harper looked less impressed than ever. 'Put him through.'

Morgan used a remote to activate the big screen. The National Security Adviser appeared on it. The camera shooting him was positioned below his eyeline, increasing the impression that he was looming over everyone seated around the conference table. 'Good afternoon, Gordon, Martin,' he said, apparently not considering anyone else worthy of a greeting. 'I won't mince words – the President is furious about this situation.'

Harper went straight on the attack. 'A situation that you recommended to him.'

'At your insistence,' Sternberg countered smoothly. 'But at this stage, I'm not here to apportion blame. I just want to know what you're doing about it. Have we got any actionable intelligence?'

'Not immediately actionable,' Morgan replied. 'Agent Gray was imprinted with Muqaddim al-Rais's persona, but circumstances forced the team to erase it before he could be debriefed. However, we still have a recorded copy of that persona. Our plan is to re-imprint it and get as much information as we can.'

'I thought using the same persona twice was unsafe?'

'Given the circumstances, it's the only logical option,' said Kiddrick. 'We think the risk is minimal.'

'*You* think the risk is minimal,' Bianca said pointedly.

'All right, Dr Childs, that's enough,' said Morgan. 'We need that information.'

'See to it,' said Sternberg. 'Hopefully we can salvage something out of this mess.'

'We did get the RTG, sir,' Tony reminded him.

'There is that, I suppose. NEST has secured it at Elmendorf. The question now is what we actually *do* with the thing. I doubt the Russians will ask for it back, considering how much it'll cost them to make it safe. Anyway, do you have anything else to say at this stage?'

'You've been told everything I have, Alan,' said Harper. 'As soon as STS gets anything more, you'll be copied in on it.'

'Good. The President wants to be kept fully informed – after all, he has to smooth things over with our Russian friends. In the meantime, get as much as you can from al-Rais's persona.' He leaned forward, face filling the screen like a gargoyle before he disconnected.

'Well,' rumbled Harper, 'looks like you all get a stay of execution – for the moment. Get to it, then. Re-imprint al-Rais's persona and get everything you can out of him.'

'I still think that's potentially dangerous,' Bianca objected.

'You've made it very clear what you think, and right now I don't care. A second imprint isn't going to kill him.'

'But what about a third? Or a fourth, or fifth?'

'Just get it done,' snapped Harper. He gathered his papers and stood up to leave.

'What about Qasid?' asked Adam.

'What about him?'

'He knows the identity of a mole in Pakistani intelligence, sir. We need to find out who that is.'

'Al-Rais is top priority. You heard the man.' He jerked a sarcastic thumb at the screen. 'Let's gut the big fish before we bother with the small fry.' He turned to Morgan. 'Where is this guy Qasid?'

'In holding,' Morgan replied.

'Get a team over here to do a prelim and process him, then

render him to Gitmo on the first available flight. Cuba's the best place to interrogate these people, not DC. Whatever he knows, we'll find out there.'

Adam started to protest. 'Sir, I don't think—'

'We need to get as much as we can from al-Rais's persona while the intel is still actionable, Agent Gray! If we waste time and resources on nobodies like Qasid, al-Rais's people will find new rocks to hide under, and the men who died in Russia will have done so for nothing. Get your priorities straight. Is that understood?'

'Yes, sir,' Adam replied emotionlessly.

'Good.' Harper headed for the door. 'Keep me posted,' he said without looking back.

Uncomfortable looks passed around the table after the door closed. 'Well, that was . . . pleasant,' said Levon. 'And I wasn't even *in* Russia!'

'What's happening about recovering the bodies of our guys?' Baxter demanded.

Morgan shook his head dolefully. 'That's all in State's hands at the moment.'

'We can't just leave them there to rot.'

'I know, I know. I've already pushed for an answer. But until we get one, let's get on with the job in hand. Dr Kiddrick, Tony, Adam, Dr Childs – use the recording of al-Rais's persona and start a debriefing. And yes,' he added, raising a hand to block any objections, 'I know some of you have problems with that. They've been noted.'

'Are they also going to be ignored?' said Bianca.

'Dr Kiddrick thinks it's safe, and he's the senior adviser, so we'll proceed on that basis. Now, are there any further questions?'

'I had one about hazard pay?' said Kyle. All eyes turned to him, none approvingly. 'But . . . I can put it in an email, I guess.'

'I look forward to reading it,' said Morgan scathingly. 'Okay. Let's get back to work.'

Everyone filed out. In the corridor, Adam was about to follow Tony and Bianca to the lab when Holly Jo stopped him. 'Adam?'

'Yes?'

'There's, er . . . something I want to say.' She glanced down the corridor to check that Morgan was out of earshot.

'Yeah, me too,' added Kyle.

'What is it?' Adam asked. Bianca and Tony halted, watching with curiosity.

'I know the mission didn't go all that well,' said Holly Jo. 'But you . . . well, you saved us. When you flew in and scared off those Russian planes—'

'That was absolutely *awesome*, brah!' Kyle exclaimed. 'Seriously, an unarmed seaplane taking on two Flankers? You are . . .' He was briefly lost for words, settling for raising his right hand in a fist and making a bumping motion with it towards Adam's chest. 'The man!'

'What he said. Only less *Jersey Shore*,' Holly Jo added, peeved at being interrupted. 'But that really was amazing. And you kept us from a diet of prison borscht and cabbage, so thanks!'

'Anything you need, brah,' said Kyle. 'Any time.'

'Thanks,' said Adam. 'But I was just doing my job.'

'Speaking of jobs . . .' said the amused Tony.

'Yes, I guess we'd better get back to the Bullpen,' Holly Jo said. 'But I just wanted to say—'

'*We* just wanted to say,' Kyle cut in.

'All right, God! *We* just wanted to tell you how we felt. Thank you.' The pair headed down the corridor. 'You are *such* a child,' she snapped at Kyle.

'What? What'd I do?' he replied, bemused.

'Looks like you've got a fan club,' Bianca told Adam with a smile.

'It's better than the opposite, I suppose.' He watched Holly Jo and Kyle go, then turned back towards the lab. 'Okay. Let's get this over with.'

'Bianca.' The word drifted in through a languid fog. 'Bianca?'

Bianca jerked awake as something touched her arm. She looked round in startled confusion before awareness fully coalesced, finding herself on a couch in one of STS's soundproofed debriefing rooms. Tony stood over her, a cardboard cup in each hand. 'Oh! Tony, hi. What . . . how long was I asleep?'

'I'm not sure – I dozed off for a while myself,' he admitted with a smile. 'Here.'

He passed her a cup of coffee. Bianca looked at her watch. It was approaching six in the morning. 'Where's Adam?'

'In the Cube. Asleep.'

'I'm not surprised after all that.' She waved a hand at the battery of recording equipment. The interrogation had gone on for over fourteen hours before its participants finally succumbed to exhaustion.

'You sat through most of it with him. You didn't have to – I said you could have gone back to your hotel as soon as the transfer was complete. Hell, Kiddrick left the second he'd packed up the PERSONA gear.'

'I wanted to make sure Adam was okay.' She sipped the coffee.

'Not good?' Tony asked, seeing her grimace.

'It's vending machine coffee – is it ever?' They both grinned. 'Thanks, though. I needed it, whatever it tastes like. God, I can't believe I actually fell asleep while you were questioning Adam.'

'You *were* very tired,' he pointed out. 'You've been through a lot in the past couple of days, so I can't blame you for taking a nap. I just hope that when they play back the tapes, they can filter out your snoring.'

'I *don't* snore,' she protested, before realising that he was teasing.

Another grin. 'You do drool, though.'

'I do not!' she cried, putting a hand to the side of her mouth – and finding it damp. 'Oh. Apparently I do. Ugh.'

He chuckled, then sipped his coffee. 'It's kind of cute, so don't worry about it. Anyway, I wanted to say thank you.'

'For what?'

'For everything you've done. However the mission turned out, the fact remains that we *did* stop al-Qaeda from getting hold of nuclear materials. And we still got a lot of actionable intel from al-Rais's persona.'

'You didn't get the man himself, though.'

'We will. Next time.'

'If there is a next time. The way Harper was carrying on, it sounded like he wanted everyone at STS court-martialled, or whatever it is you do.'

'We'll see. But you . . . you've got absolutely nothing to be ashamed of. You should be proud, in fact. We asked you to do things that were way beyond what you expected – what *we* expected – and you came through amazingly.'

She blushed, even as she basked in the compliment. 'Thanks. Although I really would have preferred not to be shot at.' Her mood dampened as she remembered that others in the team had also been fired upon – and not all had escaped unharmed. 'God. We could all have been killed. We nearly were.'

Tony crouched in front of her, putting a hand on her arm. 'Hey. The main thing is that it's over. And you . . . you did great.'

'Thank you,' she said quietly.

They were both silent for a long moment, looking into each other's eyes. Tony was the first to break the spell. 'So. You should get some proper sleep.'

'I think that's a good idea,' she said, stifling a yawn.

'You want a ride to your hotel? I'm probably going to head home myself soon.'

'Thanks, but there's something I need to do before I go.'

'Check on Adam?'

'Good guess.'

'It wasn't a guess.' He stood. 'And this isn't a guess either – you want to ask me about the side effects of having a persona imprinted more than once.'

'You're good at this. You should be a spy or something.'

Tony laughed. 'I wanted to design skyscrapers when I was a kid, but things didn't work out that way.' He sat on the couch beside her. 'The second time I took on Najjar's persona, it felt . . . smoother, maybe, like it was quicker for me to adjust to it. But it was also . . .'

His expression became troubled. 'What is it?' Bianca asked.

'It's hard to describe. It felt like . . . like a *tumour*. Something that shouldn't be there, growing inside me. It was a relief every time the persona was wiped, but . . . it made coming in for the next interrogation worse because I knew this *thing* would be back. I started getting sick to my stomach every time I went to the lab.'

'Did you tell anyone?'

He shook his head. 'No, because I'm a macho idiot.' The self-deprecating admission made her smile. 'And I wanted to bring al-Qaeda down using that son of a bitch Najjar's own knowledge. Which we did – we took out a whole bunch of his top men. Unfortunately, not all of them. Al-Rais survived. And now we're back in exactly the same situation.'

'Not quite the same. This time it's Adam doing it.'

'Yeah. And I hope he doesn't go through what I did, but . . . well. It's like that definition of insanity: doing exactly the same thing and expecting a different outcome.' He straightened. 'You should talk to him. Persuade him *not* to be a macho idiot.'

'That might be tough.' They both smiled. 'But yes, I'll try.' She stood. 'And Tony . . . thanks.'

'For what?'

'For telling me all that. I know it must have been hard.'

'Not as hard as actually doing it. If you can help Adam avoid it, you've certainly got my blessing.'

'I'll see what I can do.'

She left the debriefing room and headed through the corridors to the Bullpen. Only a few of the workstations were manned at this early hour, a skeleton night-shift crew standing in for the regular team members. She went to the Cube and hesitantly tapped on the door.

Adam replied immediately. 'Yes?'

'It's Bianca. Can I come in?'

'Sure.'

She entered. Adam had changed his clothes, an open wall panel revealing a small wardrobe. 'Morning,' she said.

'Hi. Are you okay?'

'That was going to be my opening question. Did you get any sleep?'

'Some.'

She detected an unsettled air to his answer. 'Did you have the same dream again?'

'I *always* have it. But there was something about it this time . . .'

'Was it different? Did you remember something?'

'Not remember, as such, but . . . I'm more certain than ever that it was something real – up until the part where I see myself dead, anyway. Qasid's got something to do with it. I don't know *how* I know, but . . . I know.' He shook his head. 'As for how much sleep I actually got, it was enough to erase al-Rais's persona.'

'That must be a relief.'

'It is. But you're still worried about the effects, right?'

'Yeah.' She sat facing him. 'I just talked to Tony about . . . about what he went through with Najjar's persona. I want to make sure you're okay.'

'Thank you. I'm fine, though.'

'You're not just being a macho idiot when you say that, are you?' He raised an eyebrow. 'Tony's words, not mine.'

'Tony called me a macho idiot?'

'No, that's what he called himself. For not telling anyone what he was going through.'

'Right.' He said nothing for a moment, lost in thought. 'It did feel different the second time.'

'How so?'

'It's hard to put into words. It felt . . . like getting into character for a play, I suppose. If you've rehearsed it, it's easier to do.'

'So I assume you've acted in a play before, if that's the first metaphor you thought of.'

'Huh. I hadn't thought of that. Maybe I was in the drama club at school.'

'Well, you are a spy. There's a lot of acting involved.'

A wry grin. 'It'd be good to have a complete script once in a while.'

'Preferably one with a happy ending. But did you feel any ill effects from taking on al-Rais's persona again? Anything . . . deep down?' She didn't want to use Tony's words to prompt him, hoping he would come up with his own description.

None was forthcoming, though. 'No. Unless you count disgust, now that I know some of the things he's done. John was right. We should have killed him when we had the chance. He deserves it. Only now . . .' He sighed. 'He's on the loose again. And he knows about the Persona Project.'

'He can't know all that much, surely?' said Bianca. 'Even

though we didn't give him any Mnemexal, all he'll remember is that we did something to him – but he won't know what. Maybe he just thought the PERSONA machine was a fancy lie detector or something.'

'He knows our faces.'

That thought cast a pall over the room. 'Hopefully someone'll catch him before he can find out who we are.'

'We need more than hope.' Adam leaned back, thinking. 'He's got assets he can use against us. But we've got one we can use against him.'

'His persona?'

'No. We got the most crucial information in the first interrogation – anything else is just going to be extra detail. But we've also got Qasid. He knows one of al-Qaeda's moles – someone high up in Pakistani intelligence. If we find out who . . . maybe we can turn them.'

'And get them to tell us where al-Rais is?' Adam nodded. 'Only problem is, Harper doesn't think Qasid's worth the effort. What if you can't get permission to make a transfer before he gets shipped out to Guantanamo Bay?'

'I already know I won't get it,' he said. 'They're only interested in al-Rais. But Qasid *knows* something. And not just about the mole – about *me*, too. He's seen me before.' Another thoughtful pause, then he stood. 'I'm going to find out where.'

'You're going to interrogate him?'

'No. I'm going to use the PERSONA on him.'

'What?' Bianca gasped. 'Wait a minute – if you don't have permission, won't that get you into a lot of trouble with Morgan? And with Harper?'

'I'll have permission – they just won't know about it. I can hack into the system and give myself authorisation.'

'That sounds like a really bad idea, Adam.'

'Oh, it gets worse,' he said, giving her a humourless smile. 'Because I can't do it without your help. So . . . will you help me?'

Visions of orange jumpsuits jumped unbidden to her mind. 'Are you insane? I don't want to end up in the cell next door to Qasid!'

'Nobody'll ever find out. And this is the best time to do it – there's hardly anyone on duty. The full day shift won't come in for another couple of hours. I'll only need a few minutes to get what I need from Qasid's persona.'

'What about the security cameras? And the guard on the cells?'

'If nobody knows anything happened, they won't have any reason to look at the security records. And the guard will check his computer, see we've got permission and not think anything more about it. Bianca, *please*!' he said, suddenly pleading. 'I've *got* to do this. Qasid knows something about my past. If he's taken away, I'll never find out what it is.'

'I want to help you, really I do,' she replied. 'But it's too dangerous!'

'You went undercover with a violent arms dealer. *That* was dangerous. So was hiding in the back of a snowcat full of terrorists. All you have to do here is get the PERSONA gear from the lab and oversee the transfer – it'll take ten minutes, tops.'

'But if we get caught . . .'

'We *won't* be,' he insisted. 'I know what I'm doing.' Seeing that she was still reluctant, he softened his voice. 'Bianca, I'm not going to let anything happen to you. You've done something for me that nobody else has – you made me start thinking about who I really am. And now, I've got a chance to find out . . . but I'll never know if you don't help me. I *need* to do this, Bianca. Please.'

Several seconds passed before she gave him a reply. 'Are you *absolutely* sure you can do it without anyone finding out?'

'Yes, I am. Do you trust me?'

Another pause, but shorter. 'Yes,' she said, before repeating the word with more certainty. 'Yes.'

'Will you help me?'

Seconds passed before she replied. She would be risking a lot: her career, the Luminica deal, even her freedom.

But Adam was right. She had started his search for answers about his past, and since he had saved her life – more than once – in Russia, she owed him the chance to find them.

'I . . . yes,' she said. 'But if anything happens . . .'

'I'll take all the blame,' he said firmly. 'But it won't come to that. Like I said, I'm not going to let anything happen to you.'

'I'd better not get mud on my bum again,' Bianca told him, her old spark resurfacing. 'Okay, so what do I have to do?'

'Go to the lab and bring the PERSONA gear.'

'Including the recorder?'

'No, I won't need it.'

'Good. The damn thing weighs a ton.'

He smiled. 'Then meet me outside briefing room C in five minutes.'

'Briefing room C, that's, ah . . .'

'Out of the back-left exit from the Bullpen, turn left, then right.'

'Gotcha.' She rose and went to the door – then hesitated, looking back. 'Adam . . .'

'Trust me,' he said. She nodded and left the room. Adam followed her out, going to one of the unoccupied workstations. A surreptitious check to make sure none of the night-shift staff were paying him any particular attention, then he started to enter commands.

36

You Know My Name

Bianca went to the lab, feeling as though everyone she passed was regarding her with deep suspicion. She almost expected her ID card to be rejected when she put it into the lock, but the light turned green as normal.

Heart pounding, she entered and opened the cabinet to collect the equipment. It was the first time she had done so without Kiddrick watching hawkishly over her shoulder, and she still couldn't escape the sense that there was someone right behind her.

But a glance round assured her that she was being paranoid. Relieved, she turned back to her task, collecting everything she needed. She picked up the cases and was about to nudge the cabinet closed with her knee when she paused, noticing something. One of the memory modules containing the recorded personas of the test subjects was labelled with a familiar name: CARPENTER, A. Tony was short for Anthony, obviously. She looked along the cases for a GRAY, A., but saw none.

No time to wonder about the omission. She shut the cabinet and hurried out, heading through the building to briefing room C.

Minutes passed as she waited outside it, feeling increasingly conspicuous and nervous. If anyone wandered by and wondered why she was hanging around with the PERSONA cases at her feet . . .

She heard someone approaching. Wishing that she had spent the time devising a semi-plausible excuse for being there, she turned – and to her relief saw Adam. 'What kept you?' she demanded in a half-whisper.

'I had to get something from the equipment room. You've got everything?' She gestured at the cases. 'Okay, good. Come on.'

He picked up the large case and started down the corridor. Bianca collected the medical equipment and followed him to a security door bearing the sign HOLDING. Adam inserted his ID card. The light on the lock turned green, and he opened it.

Beyond was a short, windowless corridor with three heavy doors leading off it. A uniformed security guard sat at a desk beside the entrance. Monitors showed the interiors of the cells; one was occupied. He hurriedly put down his newspaper, evidently not expecting visitors this early in the day. 'Mr Gray, sir. Morning. Uh . . . what can I help you with?'

'We need to talk to Qasid,' Adam told him, matter-of-factly. 'Mr Carpenter's authorised it.'

'Okay, sir, let me just check . . .' He tapped at the computer on the desk. 'Ah, yeah, here we go. He's in number one.' He indicated the nearest of the three doors, then pushed a button on a control panel. A loud *clack* came from the door as the lock was released. 'He's all yours. Just wave at the camera when you want to come out.'

'Thank you.' Adam opened the cell and entered, Bianca behind him. The door swung shut.

Qasid lay on the bed. A metal toilet bowl and a tiny washbasin set into the wall were the only other furnishings. The terrorist had been asleep, the noise of the lock rousing him. He looked blearily at the new arrivals – then sat bolt upright, scrambling back as he recognised Adam. 'Gray!' he snarled. 'You bastard, you traitor! You set us up!'

Adam put down the case. 'Do you know me?'

'Of course I know you! What sort of stupid question is that?'

'Where did you meet me? Before Russia, I mean. Where do you know me from?'

Confusion joined anger on Qasid's face. 'Why are you asking me things you already know?'

'Answer the question.'

'I won't tell you anything!'

'Yes, you will.'

'Are you going to torture me?' he sneered. 'And you Americans call *us* animals!'

'I'm not going to torture you,' said Adam, taking something from a pocket. 'But that doesn't mean I won't *hurt* you.' Before Qasid could react, he pushed the prongs of a stun gun hard against the terrorist's chest and pulled the trigger. There was an electric flash. Qasid instantly slumped into a twitching heap.

'Jesus!' gasped Bianca, nearly as shocked as the Pakistani. 'You didn't tell me you were going to do *that* to him!'

'Did you want to put the cap on him while he was still awake and resisting?'

'Well, when you put it that way, no. But—'

'We don't have a lot of time,' said Adam, stepping back.

Still shaken, Bianca booted up the PERSONA before taking out the first skullcap and pulling it over the stunned man's head. 'What about the camera?' she asked, glancing at the lens staring glassily down from above the door. 'The guard'll be watching us.'

'We won't be doing anything he hasn't seen before.' Adam started to put on his own skullcap.

'You know, I don't find that very reassuring.' She secured Qasid's cap and connected its cable to the PERSONA. 'Okay, now I need to work out the drug dose . . .'

'Don't go through the full routine,' said Adam. 'We don't have time.'

'What do you mean?' she asked hesitantly.

'I mean, the whole charade Roger asked you to do so he can stay on the project.'

She looked up at the camera again. 'I, uh . . . I've got no idea what you're talking about.'

'It doesn't have audio. Your secret's safe with me. I *said* you can trust me.'

Bianca glared at him. 'How long have you known?'

'Well, you just confirmed it.' On her horrified realisation that she had dropped herself and Albion in it, he went on: 'But I suspected in Macau. You did things in the wrong order, missed out steps – but it still worked, so it got me wondering. After Russia, I was sure.' He handed her his skullcap's cable. 'Is this on right?'

'Do you even need me to check any more?' she replied, both relieved by his discretion and irked at the amusement he was taking from her embarrassment.

'I'd rather be safe.' He dropped lower so she could examine the electrodes.

'Looks fine,' she said, plugging in the cable. 'But if it gives you an electric shock, don't expect any sympathy.'

'I trust *you* not to let that happen. The drug?'

'Yes, yes. How much would you say he weighs?'

Without the need for pretence, the correct dose did not take long to calculate. Bianca took out the jet injector. 'Are you sure you want to do this?'

'I've never been more sure of anything. At least,' he added, 'that I can remember.'

'You're starting to develop quite a smart-arsed sense of humour, did you know that?'

'Maybe I'm picking it up from you. Okay, give me the shot.'

She put the nozzle against his neck. 'Let's hope it's worth—'

Clack!

They both whirled at the sound of the lock. The door opened – and Tony entered the cell. His expression was the coldest Bianca had ever seen it. 'Morning, guys,' he said, the casual greeting not reflected by his tone. 'How's it going?'

Bianca was frozen with fear, but Adam simply asked: 'How did you know?'

'Because the system logs everything, and sends out "Hey, did you really authorise this?" warnings if an order's issued under somebody's login from a terminal they don't normally use. If you were going to hack it, you should have waited for Levon to come in. I should probably ask how you got my login in the first place, but that can wait. Right now, what I want to know is: what the hell are you doing?'

'What I have to,' Adam replied. He looked down at the semi-conscious Qasid. 'He knows something about my past. I need to know what.'

'Harper said to leave him to the interrogators at Guantanamo.'

'Do you agree with him?'

'It doesn't matter whether I do or not. If the Director of National Intelligence gives an order, it gets followed. End of discussion.'

'But I've got to *know*, Tony!' Adam cried with sudden desperation. 'Qasid's met me before – but I don't know where, or why. This is the only way I can find out.'

'Look, I completely understand why you want to do it,' said Tony, with more sympathy, 'but this isn't the way to go about it.'

'It's the only choice I had! He'll be in Cuba by the end of the day.'

'Where he'll be interrogated. They'll find out what he knows.'

'And how long will that take? A week? A month? A year? Tony, I can find out everything he knows in five minutes! And not just about me – he knows who leaked the Secretary of State's route in Islamabad. Qasid gave it to al-Rais – and a mole gave it to Qasid. I can get the name of that mole *right now*.'

Tony seemed conflicted. 'If there's a mole, I can't deny that we need to know who he is sooner rather than later. But this isn't the way to go about it.'

'There isn't any other way,' Adam insisted. 'And I'm willing to take the consequences for it.'

'But it's not just about you.' Tony looked at Bianca. 'If you drag her into this too . . .'

'He didn't drag me,' said Bianca firmly. 'I *want* to help him.'

He sighed and shook his head. 'I wish you hadn't said that. I don't think you realise how serious this is.'

'No, I do realise,' she replied. 'And I'm still willing to help him, because – because he's had part of his *self* taken from him. To me, that's one of the most horrible things that can happen to somebody. I've spent my whole career trying to save people from that. This might be the only way to help Adam remember who he really is. Please, Tony. If anyone can really understand what's happened to him, it's you.'

A long silence. 'If you do this,' Tony finally said, 'or rather, if I *let* you do this, we could all end up in jail.'

'If you weren't going to let us,' Adam pointed out, 'you would have arrested us by now.'

'I still might. But are you absolutely certain Qasid knows the identity of the mole in Pakistan?'

Adam nodded. 'Al-Rais was.'

Another pause. 'Okay,' Tony said, 'if there's actual, actionable intelligence you can get from this, that's the angle I'll use to justify it.'

'You're letting us do it?' Bianca asked.

'As head of field ops, I've got the authority to make snap decisions critical to a mission's outcome.'

'But the mission's over,' said Adam.

'Yeah, I know. I'll have a hell of a job spinning it! But if it changes the outcome from "near disaster" to "partial success", maybe we'll get away with it. It's results that count.'

'And what if we don't find the mole?' said Bianca.

'Well, then we're all screwed! But if you don't get any useful intel, I'll do what I can to make it look like none of this ever took place. If Martin or anyone higher up hears so much as a whisper, though, there's no way I'll be able to cover it up.'

'I won't tell anyone if you don't,' said Adam, with a faint smile.

Tony looked at his watch. 'Okay. You've got ten minutes, and then you're out of here, no matter what. Just don't forget to give him the Mnemexal after you're done, okay?' He stabbed a finger at Qasid, who was starting to recover. 'I'll get back on the system and confirm that I authorised you to come in here so it doesn't get kicked up a level for a security check.' He looked up at the camera, signalling to the guard. The lock clacked. 'Ten minutes, no more.'

'That's all we'll need,' said Adam. 'Thanks.' Tony nodded, then opened the door. 'One thing – what changed your mind?'

Tony looked back at him. '"Knowledge of the self is the mother of all knowledge," said Khalil Gibran. And in this business, we need all the knowledge we can get.'

Bianca was impressed that he could quote the Lebanese poet. 'That's very philosophical. Especially for this early in the morning.'

'I'm full of surprises. Now do what you need to do.' He left, closing the door behind him.

'We'd better get on with it, then,' said Adam.

'I just hope we're not making a horrible mistake,' Bianca replied.

'Me too. Do it.'

Bianca injected both men, then activated the transfer process, watching the PERSONA's screen carefully for any signs that the unplanned procedure had gone wrong. There were none. Minutes passed before the flood of electrical impulses began to slow. She made the last checks. The computer told her that everything was normal. She gave Qasid a dose of Mnemexal, then knelt beside her companion. His eyes were shut. 'Adam? Did it work? What's your name?'

'My name is . . . Mohammed Nithar Qasid,' said Adam, a Pakistani lilt to his accent.

'When were you born?'

'The twelfth of Ramadan, 1407.'

'*What?*' she gasped.

He opened his eyes and smiled crookedly. 'Islamic calendar. May tenth, 1987.'

'God, for a minute there I thought you'd taken on his past life or something.' She unfastened his skullcap. 'Come on, we've got to pack all this up.'

Adam didn't move, an odd expression on his face. 'What is it?' she asked.

His look slowly became one of dawning horror. 'I know how Qasid recognised me. He *had* met me before. In Islamabad, ten months ago.'

Bianca realised the significance of the date. 'That was when the Secretary of State was killed, wasn't it?' He nodded. 'What were you doing there? Were you trying to find the mole?'

He scrambled to his feet, reeling away from her. 'No, no – you don't understand!' he cried, his voice anguished. '*I* gave the Secretary's route to al-Qaeda! I *am* the mole!'

37

Inside Man

Adam paced back and forth across the Cube, struggling to keep his head above the rising whirlpool of emotion threatening to swallow him. Horror, panic, shame . . . and guilt.

And those were only *his* feelings. Qasid's were also trying to pull him under, the terrorist filled with gloating pride at having turned an American agent to the cause. He was caught in a downward spiral, the other man's triumph worsening his own stress and self-loathing.

The more he tried to deny it, searching Qasid's memories for some hint of deception, the more he knew it was true.

Qasid had met him three times. The first had been a sounding-out mission for the al-Qaeda operative, simply to check if the supposed sympathiser could be trusted. The meeting had been in a small café – with five armed men lurking nearby. At any sign of Pakistani or American security forces, the man calling himself Adam Gray would have been the first to die.

But there had been none. He seemed genuine.

Adam relived Qasid's memories, the vision of his own face disorienting, surreal. Nightmarish. The two men had been brought together by a mutual contact, an al-Qaeda supporter within the Ministry of Foreign Affairs. He listened to himself explain to Qasid why he was there. His grandfather on his father's side was Waziri, from Pakistan's mountainous western regions bordering Afghanistan. This family connection was what had brought him to Pakistan, as an intelligence officer – and it had also fuelled his disgust at his own country's actions, as American drones bombed the tribal lands with impunity. The CIA claimed publicly that only terrorists were being killed by the missiles, but he knew, having seen the raw intelligence reports before they were sanitised, that innocent civilians were being murdered.

Now, blood demanded blood.

Qasid believed him enough not to have him killed, but was still not fully convinced. The American had to provide proof of his sympathies.

So he did.

The next time the two men met, this time in a filthy slum house in Sector G-7 of Islamabad, Adam handed over a DVD containing footage of a Reaper drone strike two days previously. The Pakistani government had condemned the attack on a village in South Waziristan, in which the Americans claimed that four al-Qaeda fighters were killed – but the recording not only made it clear that numerous civilians in nearby houses had died in the blast, but also that Pakistani military intelligence officers were working directly with the CIA to guide the attack, picking out targets. The footage was quickly released to Al Jazeera and other news networks. Pakistan and the United States immediately declared the audio portion to be fake, but it still roused popular anger for several days.

Qasid was pleased – as were his superiors. They wanted more.

And on the third and final meeting, Adam Gray provided it.

The memory was as clear as if it had just happened. This time, the two men met in the open, spending barely twenty seconds together. Qasid brought a bag containing fifty thousand US dollars; his contact, a memory stick. 'The details of the Secretary of State's visit,' Adam heard himself say as he handed over the little flash drive. 'The route, the timing, decoys, security assignments – everything. Make good use of it.'

'We will,' Qasid replied, giving him the bag in return. 'Allah be praised.'

The American nodded, then walked away.

The drive contained a full itinerary of the politician's impending assignation – so comprehensive, in fact, that Qasid at first thought it too good to be true. Was Gray a double agent, trying to draw the al-Qaeda cell into a trap? But the more he checked, the more certain he became that the information was genuine.

Muqaddim al-Rais himself made the final decision.

Go.

The bomb was prepared, over a hundred kilograms of high explosive jacketed by ball bearings and ragged fragments of scrap metal in the trunk of a nondescript Toyota parked near the location of the meeting. Because the Secretary of State's visit to discuss the security of Pakistan's nuclear weapons was secret, the roads were not blocked off or cleared of other traffic. This allowed a confederate in a truck to get ahead of the three-vehicle convoy, controlling its speed as it approached the kill zone.

Qasid was half a kilometre away, watching through binoculars from a high rooftop. Adam felt his nervous anticipation, reliving the terrorist's growing excitement as he took phone calls from spotters along the route.

'This is Azim, they've just passed me . . .'

'Salim here – they just turned right at the junction, like you said they would.'

'It's Imran, they're coming up to me now . . .'

The truck deliberately dropped to a crawl, backing the convoy up behind it on the busy street. According to Gray's information, Sandra Easton would be in the middle car, SUVs driven by undercover agents ahead and behind.

He shifted his gaze back and forth between the Toyota and the approaching vehicles, the movement shorter each time. Less than a hundred metres to go.

Fifty. 'Get ready, get ready . . .' he whispered into his phone's headset. The operation could not be trusted to radio control. There was a man in the car holding a switch directly wired to the detonators. The first SUV passed the waiting Toyota. 'Here she comes . . . *now*!'

He held his breath. Time seemed to freeze, for a moment nothing happening—

Then the Toyota and the car beside it vanished in a cloud of dust.

It took over a second for the sound of the explosion to reach Qasid. When it did, it was shockingly loud, a single sharp basso crack that shook the building beneath him. Other noises followed: shattering glass, splintering concrete, the thunderous echoes of the detonation.

Adam felt Qasid's surge of exultation overpower his own horror at the sight. The memories kept coming, even though he no longer wanted them. The terrorist looked back through the binoculars. Nothing was visible except swirling dust and smoke.

Then shapes began to resolve.

Mangled wreckage. Shredded bodies. Rubble and debris surrounding a crater at the roadside, flames gouting from a severed gas main. More sounds reached him – distant screams of panic and pain. Those people on the street who had not been cut down by the blast started to flee.

There was nothing left of the Toyota, and the trailing SUV was barely recognisable as a vehicle. The leading 4x4, which had been moving away from the bomb, lay on its side, ripped open, its occupants spilled out like sardines from a can. The Secretary of State's car had been reduced to burning fragments.

As had everyone inside.

We did it!

'No,' gasped Adam, reeling. He couldn't stop the flood of images from Qasid's mind.

He had been responsible. He had given the information to al-Qaeda. He had betrayed his country.

The more he tried to deny it, the stronger the memories became, taunting him. It *was* him. The face, the voice of the man Qasid had met – they were his.

He was a traitor.

'No!' It was a cry of pure anguish.

Panic rose in him. Conflicting thoughts warred in his mind – a desperate urge to escape, to run from the punishment that awaited if the truth was discovered versus the need to confess to what he had done. He *had* to turn himself in. He was a security risk, an al-Qaeda sympathiser.

A traitor.

He looked around frantically. The exit—

I have to run.

His thought, or Qasid's? He didn't know. *This is my only chance, I have to get out of here before they catch me . . .*

The door opened. He jumped in alarm. It was Bianca, having returned the PERSONA equipment to the lab. She held something in one hand. The Englishwoman immediately picked up on his fear. 'Are you okay?'

She's the only other person who knows the truth.

Qasid. It *had* to be. It couldn't be his own mind regarding as a threat the woman who had done nothing but try to help him. It *couldn't*!

'Yeah, yeah, I'm – I'm fine,' he gasped.

'No you're not,' she replied, anxious. She gestured towards the couch. 'Look, sit down.'

'No, I'm okay.' He opened the panel concealing the wardrobe. There was a mirror on its back. He looked into it, not even sure who he was going to see staring back. His face, or Qasid's?

It was his own, but wide-eyed, brow beaded with sweat. 'Really, you don't look good,' said Bianca.

He whirled. 'Of course I don't look good! I've just found out that I'm – I'm a traitor!'

'I don't believe it,' she insisted. 'I can't! There's got to be some other explanation.'

'There isn't,' he said, pacing again. 'I remember – *Qasid* remembers. We met in Islamabad, three times. I gave him a flash drive with all the security details for Sandra Easton's visit. And they were genuine.'

Why am I telling her this? She already knows too much! I'll have to elimin—

He tried to crush the thought. But it wouldn't die, writhing and squirming under his mental boot heel. Growing stronger. Fear roiled through his body. What if he couldn't resist?

'But that doesn't make sense,' she protested. He saw that the object she was holding was a jet injector. 'If you were really a traitor, why would you join the Persona Project? The entire thing is about finding out people's deepest secrets!'

'To get rid of the guilt. That's why I wanted my memory erased. It's the only explanation.'

'No, I don't accept that.' Bianca moved closer. 'It doesn't fit with your personality.'

'I don't *have* a personality!' he said with a desperate near-laugh. 'You said so yourself!'

'I was wrong. I know you better than that now.'

Adam pulled away. 'You don't know me at all. How can you? *I* don't know me. But now I know what I've done. I've got to—'

He broke off abruptly. He had been about to say that he had to turn himself in, but another voice in his mind drowned out the words. *I've got to get out of here, before they catch me . . .*

'What is it?' she asked.

Adam said nothing, staring at her. *She's the only person who knows the truth. The only person who can tell the Americans what I did.*

The only person who can stop me.

He stepped towards her. Panic faded, replaced by a cold resolution. *I have to get out of here. She's the only witness.*

She has to be eliminated.

Images of the other people Qasid had killed flashed through his thoughts. Shot, stabbed, burned, strangled . . . *Killing is easy. All you need is the will.*

'Adam?' He saw the uncertainty in Bianca's eyes change to concern. *It's the only way. Do it.*

Another step. She backed away, confused – and starting to feel fear. He had seen it before, many times; the realisation that death was approaching . . . and there was nothing they could do to stop it.

Do it. Kill her! I have to get away.

'Bianca, I—' Again, the words froze before they could reach the air.

Kill her! Qasid's voice grew ever louder, drowning out his own thoughts. The more he struggled against it, the more insistent and deafening it became. *I have to escape! Kill her! Kill her!*

'Adam!' Bianca gasped as he grabbed her arm. She tried to twist away, but his grip was too strong. He pushed her against the wall. 'Adam, no! What are you—'

Kill her!

His other hand took hold, tightened . . .

Around the injector.

He tore it from her, jammed it against his neck – and pulled the trigger.

No! I have to escape, I need to . . .

Qasid's voice faded. Adam reeled back, collapsing on the couch as the Neutharsine took hold. His heart raced, every breath as loud as a hurricane. Mind churning, he slumped, struggling to regain control.

'Adam!' Bianca's voice seemed to come from a great distance. But when he forced his eyes open, she was right beside him. 'Oh my God, are you okay? Can you hear me?'

He slowed his breathing. 'I'm . . . I'm okay,' he croaked.

She helped him sit up. 'What happened?'

'Qasid. It was Qasid, his persona. It – it almost took over.'

'But I thought that was impossible!'

'Apparently not.' He took a deep breath. 'Are you all right? Did I hurt you?'

She glanced at her arm. 'No, I'm okay. You scared me, though.'

'I scared myself,' he admitted. 'What did you see?'

'I'm not sure. It was like – like there was someone else behind your face, is the only way I can describe it. Your eyes went so . . .' She shuddered. 'Cold.'

The injector was still in his hand. He let it drop on to the couch. 'It's a good thing you brought this. I don't know what I would have . . .' He trailed off, partly so as not to disturb her any further.

And partly to stop himself from thinking about what he had almost done.

Would he have done it? Would he actually have killed her? He didn't know. That was in some ways the most frightening thing of all.

She knelt before him, holding his hand. 'Jesus. You're shaking. Do you need anything?'

'No, I'm okay. But thank you.'

'So what happened? How could Qasid's persona take over?'

'Maybe because I was panicking? It was like the feedback loop with Vanwall's vertigo, but worse, much worse. I was losing it – and that gave him an opening.'

'What did . . . *he* want?'

'To escape – to get out of here before he was caught. Before *I* was caught.' He gave her a look of anguish. 'Bianca, I've got to turn myself in. I betrayed my country.'

'No, I still can't believe it. It doesn't fit.' She leaned back on her haunches, still holding his hand. 'The Persona Project is so secret, even other parts of STS don't know about it. So how could *you* have known? Nobody here had ever met you before you joined.'

'If I had access to the Secretary's security details, I would have had access to other classified information.'

'So, what, you planned all along to give the information to al-Qaeda, and then join Persona to wipe your guilt?'

'Something like that. It has to be.'

'But if you knew you were going to feel that guilty, why would you do it in the first place? Was Qasid blackmailing you?'

'No. I approached them.'

'Okay, so . . . what did Qasid make of you? Did he think you were conflicted about handing over the files?'

Adam thought for a moment. Qasid's memories of the encounters remained in his own mind, but now stripped of feelings. 'No. I seemed nervous, I guess, the first time I met him, but the other two times I was . . .' He paused, the image incongruous. 'Businesslike.'

'That doesn't sound like you were racked with guilt, then.'

'But it's the only explanation.'

'No, it isn't. Maybe you were doing your job – as a spy.'

'But I gave Qasid the damn details!' he cried, pulling his hand from hers. 'I took fifty thousand dollars of blood money in exchange for the information. And they used it! They planned an attack on the Secretary of State – and it succeeded! They killed her, and over a hundred other people. Qasid watched it happen—' He stopped, realising with shock that there was something familiar about the scene.

Not from television, or a photograph. He had *been* there, seen the buildings and people and smoke around him …

'The dream,' he said, as the answer came to him. 'The dream I always have – that's where it was. The bombing in Islamabad. I was there, I was *right there* after it happened!'

Bianca was confused. 'But the dream always ends with you seeing yourself lying in the street. How is that possible?'

'I don't know. But I was there, I'm certain of it. It doesn't change anything, though. I'm still guilty of treason.'

'*No,*' said Bianca, more insistently. 'There's got to be another answer.' She looked thoughtful. 'Maybe it's a cover-up. The mission went horribly wrong, so someone wanted to erase the memory of the only person who knew what really happened. They might have—'

A knock on the door. 'It's Tony.'

'Don't say anything,' Bianca told Adam quietly, before raising her voice. 'Come in.'

Tony entered. He half smiled at the sight of Bianca kneeling before Adam. 'Remember those fraternisation rules, guys,' he said. The smile disappeared as he took in their tense expressions. 'What is it?'

'Adam had a bad reaction,' said Bianca, before Adam could reply. She stood. 'Something went wrong with the transfer. I had to give him a shot of Neutharsine to clear Qasid's persona.' She picked up the injector.

'Are you okay?' Tony asked, concerned. 'What kind of reaction did you have?'

Again, Bianca spoke first. 'It was almost like . . . like a panic attack, I suppose. After what you told me about what happened to you, I was worried, so I gave him the injection. He's back to normal now, thank God.'

'That's a relief. Did you get anything from Qasid's persona? Did he really know you?'

'I'm not sure,' Adam said quietly. 'Everything was . . . confused.'

'What went wrong with the transfer? Is Qasid okay? It'll be kinda hard to cover all this up if our prisoner dies because of it.'

'He's fine,' said Bianca. 'I don't know what went wrong, though. Maybe I miscalculated the drug dose.'

'You're damn lucky things didn't turn out worse, then,' Tony said sternly. 'I've been into the system and made sure everything looks to be in order, but like I said, it won't stand up to higher-level scrutiny. This needs to end right here.'

'I think that's a very good idea.'

'What about you, Adam?'

Adam said nothing for a moment, then nodded. 'Yeah.'

'Good. Let's hope this doesn't come back to bite us all in the ass.' Tony checked his watch, suppressing a yawn. 'Okay. It's been a hell of a long day. Once I've wrapped everything up, I'm going to go home and get a few hours' sleep, and I'd advise you both to do the same before it starts all over.'

'You're going to imprint Adam with al-Rais's persona again?' Bianca asked. 'After what just happened to him?'

'Well, unless you want to go explain to Martin and Harper that your unauthorised transfer went bad, we don't have much choice. All right, I'll see you later.' He turned to leave.

'Tony?' said Bianca, stopping him. 'Can I ask you something?'

'What?'

'When I got the PERSONA gear from the lab, I saw a disk with your name on it. Did you have your persona recorded?'

'Yeah, not long after I joined the project.'

'Before you had the surgical implants?'

'Yes. They wanted it as a backup, for comparison if there were any after-effects from the procedure, but they never used it. Why did you want to know?'

She shrugged. 'Just curious. I wondered why you had a disk and Adam didn't.'

'No idea. I guess Roger and Kiddrick felt confident enough second time around not to need one.'

'I guess. Okay, see you later.'

'What was that about?' Adam asked after Tony left.

'I was just thinking . . . what if there *is* a disk with your persona on it, from before you had your memory wiped? If we imprinted you with that, then you'd know for sure what happened in Pakistan.'

'Maybe, but there isn't a disk like that.'

'Well, it's not something they're going to leave lying around the office, is it? Especially now that you've started trying to find out more about your past.'

'So where would they keep it?'

Bianca glanced towards the Bullpen. 'I think there's a way we can find out.'

38

Safe Keeping

When Levon arrived at his workstation, he was surprised to find two people waiting.

'Wow, you guys look terrible,' he told Adam and Bianca as he sat. 'You been here all night?'

'Afraid so,' said Bianca. 'But then, we had a lot to cover with interrogating al-Rais.'

'Yeah, I guess you're not going to get everything out of the world's most wanted terrorist in time for Letterman. Still, pulling an overnighter's hard work. Darleen hates it when I do 'em.'

'Darleen?'

'My wife.' He saw Bianca's look of surprise, and raised an eyebrow over his thick glasses. 'Oh, what? Just 'cause I'm a big fat nerd, I can't find true love? I got my moves.'

'No, that's not what I was thinking at all!' she lied. 'It's just that you never mentioned her before.'

'You never asked. You want to see her picture? I got a whole bunch on my phone.'

'No, that's okay, thanks. But there was something we wanted to ask you.'

'Yeah? What is it?'

Adam leaned closer to him, dropping his voice. 'Tony said that you know how to bypass the system's security.'

Levon shrank into his chair, eyes darting furtively. 'I don't know why he'd tell you that. What is this, some sort of loyalty check?'

'Yes, I'm actually Harper's mole,' said Bianca sarcastically.

Adam remained serious. 'This is off the record, Levon. In fact, it's off the books. Can you do it?'

The bald man was still reluctant to answer. 'Why would you want to know?'

'Because I need you to find something for me – without Tony or Martin or anyone else knowing about it.'

'Seriously?' Levon glanced at the nearby workstations to make sure nobody was eavesdropping. 'What kind of thing?'

'I need to know if I had my persona recorded when I first joined the project. And if I did, then I also need to know what happened to the disk containing it.'

He was startled by the request. 'For real? You're actually asking me to hack into the system?'

'Yes. And nobody else can know about it. It has to stay completely under the radar.'

'Hell *yes*, it has to remain under the radar!' Levon insisted. 'You know what would happen to me if I got caught accessing data above my security classification?'

'The same thing that would happen to us,' said Bianca.

'Not quite! Irreplaceable intelligence asset; pretty white lady; black guy. Who do you think'll come out worst of those three?'

'But you won't get caught, will you?' Adam said. 'You never have been before.'

'Again, I don't know where you got the idea that I've been doing any . . .' he couldn't hold back a hint of pride, *'awesome* hacks.'

'So you can do it?'

'Hypothetically speaking,' said Levon, straightening, 'there ain't a system built I can't get into. Speaking *purely* hypothetically, of course.'

'Of course,' Bianca echoed with a smile.

'How long will it take?' asked Adam.

'Well, with the security that STS runs, if I were trying to get in from the outside it could take days, even weeks. But since I'm sitting right here . . .' He gestured at his monitors and grinned.

'You'll help us?' said Bianca.

'Yeah, I'll help you. Hell, after what you did in Russia, everyone in America should be doing favours for you. You got hold of all al-Qaeda's secrets! Even if you didn't manage to bag al-Rais himself, we've still got enough to kick their asses. Plus, Holly Jo and Kyle wouldn't shut up about how awesome you were when you scared off those fighter planes. Almost wish I'd been in the field to see that. I figure saving their lives is worth something. Well, Holly Jo's, anyway. Kyle? Eh.' He waggled one hand in a *so-so* gesture, then smiled to assure them he was joking. 'So, you want it right now?'

'Can you do it?' Adam said.

Levon snorted. '"*Can I do it?*" the man says. Weren't you listening?' He turned to his computer and started typing, fingers flicking over the keyboard. 'Give me a minute here.'

More of the project's day-shift members had arrived in the Bullpen. Adam saw Kyle approaching, on the way to his own workstation, and was concerned that he would be curious – but then he veered off to start a sports-themed conversation with someone else.

'Okay, here we go,' said Levon, pointing at a particular file. 'This might be what you're after. It's the index of all the recordings of people's personas.' He opened it and quickly scrolled through.

'All these here, they were done early on, when Tony was in training. Once he went active, there were only a few done at the lab, like if they needed an expert in something specific. Then, after the project was suspended, there's obviously a gap – until it started up again with you, Adam.'

Adam regarded the screen intently. His name leapt out at him from the list. The date beside it was ten months earlier – less than two weeks after the car bombing in Islamabad. 'Is there any more information?'

'One sec, man . . .' Another rapid burst of typing. 'Yeah, here.'

Bianca examined the new text. 'They *did* record your persona. So what happened to the disk?'

Adam had already read on. 'It doesn't say – but I know who can tell me.'

Twenty minutes later, Kiddrick arrived at his office – and like Levon, found someone waiting for him. In this case, it was Adam alone. 'Good morning, Dr Kiddrick.'

'Morning, Adam,' said Kiddrick, mildly surprised. 'Something I can do for you?'

'I need to ask you something. In private.'

'Of course.' Kiddrick opened the door. 'Come in.'

Adam followed him inside. Kiddrick's framed qualifications were mounted prominently on the wall behind his desk, positioned to be the first thing a visitor saw on entering. The other walls were home to photographs, also in frames: Kiddrick shaking hands with prominent figures from the scientific and political worlds, the latter including Harper and even the Vice-President.

The scientist took his place at the desk and airily waved for Adam to sit before him. 'So, how's the interrogation of al-Rais proceeding?'

'It's going well,' Adam replied. 'We've got a lot from him. But that's not why I'm here.'

'Oh?'

'I wanted to ask something about the PERSONA procedure itself. Specifically, about when I joined the project.'

Kiddrick's demeanour changed, a subtle wariness creeping over him. 'Yes?'

'I noticed in the lab that there's a recording of Tony's persona. Is there a disk containing mine too?'

Kiddrick's gaze momentarily flicked up to one wall. Adam followed it to a large photograph of the scientist shaking hands with a distinguished-looking older man. 'Why do you want to know?'

The brief dart of his eyes had been unconscious, defensive. Was there a wall safe behind the picture? 'Is there a disk? Is that where you keep it?'

'There is no disk,' said Kiddrick in a dismissive tone. 'Why would there be?'

'You recorded Tony's persona.'

'That was just a precautionary measure. It was the first time we'd tried the full procedure on a person, so we wanted a point of reference. We didn't need to do the same with you.'

Adam regarded him in cold silence. He knew Kiddrick was lying; Levon's hack proved that. But how to challenge him without giving away his source?

He stood and crossed the room to the photograph. The younger Kiddrick, hairline slightly lower on his domed forehead, beamed smugly back at him. 'What are you doing?' the present-day version demanded.

Adam ignored him, pulling one side of the frame. The picture swung away from the wall, revealing a concealed safe. 'What's in this?'

Kiddrick jumped to his feet, eyes bulging with outrage. 'Classified documents! What the hell do you think you're doing?'

'I'm finding out the truth. I think you *did* make a recording of my persona. Is the disk in here?'

'That woman put you up to this, didn't she?' Kiddrick said, scowling. 'Distracting you from the project, poisoning your mind. We should never have gotten her involved.'

'This is nothing to do with Bianca. But it's *everything* to do with me. Answer the question. Have you got the disk?'

'This conversation is over,' snapped Kiddrick. He stalked around his desk to Adam, slamming the picture back to cover the safe. 'I suggest that you drop this, right now. Otherwise . . .'

Adam met his gaze without blinking. 'Otherwise what, Nate?'

The use of the diminutive made Kiddrick twitch with anger. 'Otherwise,' he began, his voice almost cracking before he cleared his throat and repeated himself in a lower register. 'Otherwise, I'll report you for security violations.'

'What security violations would those be, *Nate?*'

'Asking about a disk that's above your security clearance, for one!'

'A disk that you said doesn't exist? Are unicorns above my security clearance too?'

'You *are* spending too much time with that woman,' said the scientist, his face tightening. 'Now look! I don't know what's brought all this on, but I'd advise you to forget about it.'

'I've forgotten too much already,' Adam replied. 'I'm trying to get some of it back.'

Outright worry flashed across Kiddrick's features before anger covered it. 'I'll remind you of something you've forgotten, for free: you *asked* us to erase your memory. In fact, you *begged* us to! We gave you something a lot of people would give their eye teeth to have – a clean slate, with all of that pain in your past wiped away. We did it before . . . and we can do it again. So drop it!'

He glared at Adam, who stared back at him without emotion. Kiddrick was the first to look away, ire dissolving to discomfort under the other man's level gaze, but it was Adam who broke the silence. 'Okay,' he said simply. He turned and left the office.

Breathing heavily, Kiddrick watched him go. Even after the door had closed he remained still for several seconds, trying to compose himself – then he hurried to his desk and picked up the phone, stabbing in a number. He waited impatiently for the call to be transferred from Tony's office line to his cell phone. 'Tony!' he barked, on getting an answer. 'Have you been talking to Adam?'

Even through his tiredness, Tony's sarcasm was clear. 'Well, yeah. It's a lot easier than using semaphore.'

'What is this, comedian day? I meant, why did you tell him we recorded your persona when you joined the project?'

'Because he asked? Look, what is this? I'm on my way home, but I can come back in if there's a problem.'

'No, no, there's no problem.' Kiddrick hung up without a further word, regarding the phone grimly as he pondered his next action before entering another number. 'I need to talk to Admiral Harper.'

Adam entered the Cube. 'What did he say?' Bianca asked.

'Nothing helpful. And nothing I liked, either.'

'Did he say anything about the disk?'

'Only that there wasn't one. But I know he's lying. I'm sure he's got it in his office safe.'

'Maybe we should use the PERSONA on him to get the combination.'

'There's an easier way.' The coolly matter-of-fact way he said it made Bianca give him a curious, slightly unsettled look. 'I think you were right, though.'

'About what?'

'About there being some sort of cover-up. Kiddrick didn't say anything outright, but he implied that he knew what had happened to me before I joined the project. So if I really am a traitor, then he's involved in concealing it . . .'

'And if you're not, then there's a lot more to whatever's going on,' Bianca finished excitedly. 'I know which I believe.'

'I know which I *prefer*. One way or another, though . . . I've got to find out the truth.'

'How are you going to do that?'

He thought for a moment – then made what he knew was a fateful decision. 'The only person who knows what really happened is me – the *original* me, before I had my memory wiped. I've got to get that disk. Are you still willing to help me?'

She nodded. 'Yes, of course.'

'Whatever I have to do?'

Another nod, though somewhat hesitant. 'Yeah . . . although I'd be happier if I knew exactly what you had in mind.'

He gave her a lopsided grin. 'Really, you wouldn't. But we're going to need the PERSONA gear again. Can you get it from the lab?'

'The whole lot?'

'Yes. Do you know where the emergency stairwell is?'

'The one past the break room?'

'That's right. Take the gear there and wait for me – I'll meet you in about ten minutes. Oh, and . . . put your foot in the door to keep it open.'

She cocked her head, puzzled. 'Why?'

'Just a precaution.' He collected a jacket from the wardrobe and donned it.

'And what do I say if somebody wants to know why I'm standing there with my foot stuck in the fire door?'

'Tell them you thought you smelled smoke. Okay, I'll see you there.' He went to the door, then looked back. 'Thank you.'

'Glad to help.' Her smile faded. 'I hope . . .'

He left the room, making his way out of the Bullpen and heading for the armoury. His ID card opened the security doors; as lead agent, he had full access to STS's inventory.

He made use of it, first collecting a few items from the equipment storage area and putting them into a holdall before opening another locked door to enter the weapons room. A couple more objects went into the bag, then he collected a SIG-Sauer P228 and a magazine. He loaded the weapon and pulled back the slide to chamber the first round. He very much hoped that he wouldn't need to use the gun, but he had a horrible suspicion that once he committed to his goal, matters would escalate very quickly . . .

The door opened behind him.

He didn't look round, somehow knowing who it was. 'Tony.'

'Adam. Not planning something else crazy, are you?'

'That depends on your definition.' He slipped the gun into his jacket and turned to face the new arrival. While Tony appeared tired from the long night, his eyes were anything but, watching him intently. 'I thought you'd gone home.'

'I was on the way. Kiddrick called me. From the way he was ranting, it sounded like I needed to get back here.' His gaze flicked to the angular bulge beneath Adam's lapel. 'I guess I was right.'

'I'm not planning to hurt anyone.'

'Glad to hear it.'

'But I need to know the truth,' insisted Adam. 'I need to know who I am. This is the only way I can do that.'

'Are you sure of that?'

'Kiddrick threatened me with erasing my memory again if I didn't drop this. He's part of it – he's actively trying to stop me from finding out what really happened to me in Islamabad.'

'So you *did* get something from Qasid.' Tony didn't sound surprised – but there was clear disappointment at not having been trusted enough to be told.

'Yeah. And I didn't like any of it. Qasid *had* met me before – right before the Secretary of State was killed. I was connected to it, somehow. I've seen Qasid's side of what happened – now I need to see mine.' His voice became imploring. 'Tony, please. I *have* to know what really happened. Someone's trying to keep the truth about the bombing hidden.'

Tony looked concerned. 'Who?'

'I don't know. It might even . . .' He hesitated. 'It might even be *me*.' At the other man's shock, he continued: 'That's why I have to do this. Kiddrick has a recording of my persona from when I joined the project. The truth's on that disk. But he's never going to give it to me voluntarily.'

'So you're going to threaten to shoot him if he doesn't give it to you? What if he calls your bluff?'

'He won't. This *is* Kiddrick we're talking about.'

'Point taken,' said Tony with a wry smile. 'But have you thought about what happens after he gives you the disk? And I don't mean about finding the truth. I mean, what happens to *you*, personally.'

Adam squared his shoulders. 'I'll take whatever's due to me – whether for this, or for anything I did before. That's a promise, Tony. But I've got to know, one way or another. I'm not asking you to help me openly – but I need to know if you're going to try to stop me.'

Tony looked back down at Adam's chest. 'I'd feel a lot better if I knew you weren't going to pull a gun on anyone at STS. Even Kiddrick.'

Adam was still for a moment, then took out the gun. His

thumb moved to the magazine release, about to press the button . . . then he lifted it, extending his arm to the other man. 'Here.'

'How do you know I won't take you in?'

'Because I trust you to do the right thing.'

Tony hesitated, then took the gun. The muzzle pointed at Adam . . .

Then it disappeared into Tony's jacket. 'Okay,' he said, voice somewhere between encouragement and resignation. 'Do what you have to. Just remember what you promised.'

'I will,' Adam replied. He picked up the bag. 'Thanks.'

'I hope that what you find out is worth it,' Tony said.

Adam didn't reply.

39

Catch the Wave

Adam checked his watch as he exited the armoury and headed quickly through the building. Talking to Tony had cost him time. Bianca would be at the stairwell by now – and the longer she waited there, the more chance there was of her attracting unwanted attention.

His destination was just ahead. He took a breath to prepare himself – then burst into Kiddrick's office.

Kiddrick jumped in shock at the unexpected intrusion. 'What – what the hell do you think you're doing? You can't just—'

Adam dropped the bag as he marched around the desk. He grabbed the scientist and yanked him to his feet, slamming him against the wall. The framed diplomas rattled, one dropping from its hook and falling to the floor with a crack of glass. 'Open the safe,' he growled.

'Are you mad?' Kiddrick spluttered. 'I'm not going to—'

Adam hurled him bodily over the desk. The computer and phones crashed down around him, scattered papers whirling like snowflakes. Before Kiddrick could recover, Adam rounded the desk and dragged him across the office.

'Open it!' he barked, swinging the framed photograph aside

with such force that one of the hinges broke. He pushed Kiddrick's face hard against the cold steel door.

The older man tried to break free, but Adam was too strong. 'Help!' Kiddrick shrieked. 'Somebody help me!'

Adam was unfazed. 'It's a secure office,' he reminded him. 'Soundproofed.' He shoved Kiddrick across the safe door until the combination dial was pressed hard into his cheek. 'If it's not open in ten seconds, I'm gonna smash your teeth out on that dial.'

'You're out of your fucking mind!' Kiddrick croaked. 'You won't get away with this!'

'And you won't be eating solid food. Open the safe!' He forced Kiddrick's head harder against the metal with each word. 'Five! Four! Three!'

'Wait, wait!' screeched the scientist. One hand clawed desperately at the dial. 'I'll open it!'

'If you set off an alarm—'

'I won't, I won't!' He fumbled with the dial, squinting to read the figures etched into its surface. 'Seventeen left, fifty right, and, uh . . .' A gasp of fear as Adam pressed harder. 'Thirty-eight left! That's it, that's the combination!'

Adam pushed him away, sending him stumbling to the carpet, and opened the safe. If an alarm had been tripped, it was a silent one. He looked inside. Folders bearing the TOP SECRET: SCI classification, a small stack of optical disks and flash drives . . .

And at the back, a plastic box like an extra-thick DVD case. He pulled it out. The label on the spine read GRAY, A. He opened it. One of the blocky memory modules was inside.

He snapped the case shut and picked up the bag, dropping the disk inside. Kiddrick recoiled as Adam walked towards him and reached down, but it was only to pick up the fallen phone. He yanked out the cable and threw the handset against the wall. It broke apart, plastic pieces scattering. 'Don't move,' he ordered as he went to the door, knowing that he would not be obeyed.

He left the room, moving briskly down the corridor. He had ten seconds, fifteen at most, before Kiddrick summoned the courage to get up and scream for help. There was a security door ahead. He inserted his ID. The wait for the green light felt interminable. He snatched the door open and hurried through, moving at a trot now. Any moment . . .

'Help!'

He looked back, seeing through the door's reinforced glass that Kiddrick had left his office. 'Security, get security!' the scientist yelled. 'Help me!'

Adam broke into a run. 'Clear the way!' he barked. The people in the corridor hurriedly moved aside to let the agent through.

He rounded a corner, Kiddrick's yells fading behind him. Another security door. 'Coming through, move!' he shouted. More STS personnel cleared his path. He reached the barrier and jammed his card into the slot. Waiting, waiting—

Green light.

He barged through the door – barely a second before an alarm sounded, a strident two-tone klaxon signifying a security breach. All the security doors were now locked, every exit from the building sealed, and STS's squad of security protective officers placed on full alert to hunt him down.

It wouldn't take them long to find him. And if Bianca hadn't held the stairwell door open, their job would be even easier . . .

Another corner, and he entered the short passage leading to the emergency stairs. Bianca was there, with the PERSONA cases – and one foot in the doorway. 'Open it!' he shouted.

'What's going on?' she asked, confused and scared.

'We're in trouble! Go!'

She picked up the cases and entered the stairwell. 'What did you do?'

'I persuaded Kiddrick to open his safe,' he said as he followed. She was about to start down the stairs. 'No, go up! They'll be coming from below.'

Bianca reversed direction. 'Who will?'

'Security.'

'I take it your persuasion wasn't the gentle kind!'

'Like they say, flattery gets you nowhere. Here.' He took one of the cases from her as they reached the next landing. 'Keep going, all the way to the top.'

'Where are we going?'

'The roof.'

'Ah . . . why?'

'It's the only exit that won't have armed men guarding it.'

'But – it's the roof! How are we supposed to get down?'

Adam didn't answer. They reached the top landing. A utilitarian door marked with a DANGER: NO ADMITTANCE WITHOUT AUTHORISATION sign awaited them. He pointed to the corner of the landing. 'Wait over there.'

'What are you doing?'

He took a hemispherical object the size of an orange from the bag. 'It's locked. I'm going to open it.' He peeled a plastic sheet from the item's flat side.

'What's that?'

'A bomb.'

Bianca spluttered in disbelief. 'A – a *what*?'

'A bomb.' He slapped the half-sphere against the door beside the card lock. It stuck fast. There was a small switch set into the curved casing; he flicked it. A red LED started to flash. 'Cover your ears.'

He ran to her and shielded her with his body. The light flickered faster, then turned solid as a shrill bleep sounded. Adam pressed his hands to his head—

A piercing *bang* shook the stairwell as the shaped charge detonated. Adam looked round. A ragged hole the size of a fist had been blown through the door. 'Okay, come on,' he told Bianca as he picked up the case again and hurried back to the exit. He pulled at the door handle. It rattled, but didn't open. For a moment, he thought they were trapped – then something inside the frame gave as he tugged again.

He waved Bianca through. The echoes of the explosion had faded – but he could now hear another sound.

Charging footsteps. A security team was clattering up the stairs after them.

'Adam!' Morgan's voice boomed from the building's PA system. 'Whatever it is you're doing, I want you and Dr Childs to stop and turn yourself in, right now!'

Adam had no intention of doing so. He went through the door after Bianca. The rumble of machinery surrounded him as he entered the maintenance level. 'Follow the yellow line,' he told her, pointing at a painted marking on the concrete floor. 'It goes to the roof access.'

She saw that he had stopped, and paused to wait for him. 'What're you doing?'

'I need to slow them down. Go on, keep moving!' He took out another charge and placed it facing the doorway at the base of a large metal tank.

Morgan spoke again, his tone more sombre – and threatening. 'Adam, this is your last warning. If you don't surrender immediately, I'll have no choice but to declare you a category one security threat.'

'What does that mean?' Bianca asked.

He flicked the switch and raced after her. 'It means they're authorised to use deadly force.'

Her reply was almost a shriek. *'What?'*

'Just get to the roof. Quick!'

'Agent Gray! Dr Childs!' someone shouted from the landing. 'Put your hands in the air and show yourselves! This is your only warning!' Red laser lines lanced through the machine level – then suddenly converged on one spot, drawn by an electronic trill. 'Oh *shit*! Back, get ba—'

The bomb exploded.

Adam had placed it on a seam running up one of the tanks containing the building's emergency water supply. The steel split along the welded join – and the pressure of the thousands of gallons of water behind it ripped the metal wall open.

A deluge burst out, sweeping through the doorway on to the landing. The security team, already reeling from the detonation, were knocked off their feet by the frothing flood. They crashed against the railings, a couple of luckless tail-enders tumbling back down the stairs.

That was not the only damage. A waterfall cascaded over the edge of the landing down into the building, another wave sweeping through the maintenance level and dashing against banks of humming machinery.

Sharp bangs rippled through the space as equipment short-circuited in showers of sparks. The lights went out. A moment later, yellow emergency bulbs came to life, casting a sickly glow over the churning water.

The wave raced after Adam and Bianca, but too late to catch them as they reached the stairs to the roof and pounded up them. He opened the door. 'Come on.'

Bianca followed him outside, squinting at the bright light of day. Her eyes focused on the flat expanse of the roof – and the drop beyond each edge. 'You haven't got a helicopter, have you?'

Adam took something else from the bag. 'Just an umbrella.'

The Bullpen was in chaos.

The video wall had been switched to show views from the STS building's internal CCTV cameras, tracking the fugitives as they made their way to the uppermost floor. The coverage was not total, so none of the observers had seen Adam planting the charge on the water tank . . . but it was impossible for them to miss its effects.

'God *damn!*' Morgan exclaimed as he saw the water sweep away his men – then all the screens went black. The overhead lights flickered and died, plunging the room into darkness for several seconds.

'My system's down!' Levon cried as illumination returned.

'Mine too,' added Holly Jo in dismay. The computers were linked to a backup battery system that was supposed to keep them running long enough to allow the emergency power supplies to kick in, but something had clearly gone very wrong.

Kyle was the first to realise the cause. 'The *hell*? I'm gettin' rained on!'

Everyone looked up. Water was dripping from several points on the ceiling. One of the lights buzzed furiously before going out with a crack and a small puff of smoke. Kiddrick, standing beside Morgan, flinched. 'That maniac's destroying the entire *building!*'

Desktop monitors started to flick back to life as machines rebooted. 'Martin!' shouted Tony in alarm as he checked one of his screens, then entered frantic commands. 'The security system's gone into failsafe mode!' He looked at one of the doors. The green light was flashing, telling him that the lock had been deactivated. In dire emergencies, the failsafe was intended to allow people to evacuate the building without fear of being trapped behind a security barrier. 'I can't reset it, everything's— *Shit*! Qasid!' He ran for an exit. 'Martin, get security to the cells!'

Morgan had already picked up a phone from a nearby desk, stabbing at one of the keys. There was no response. 'Phones are down,' he reported. 'Levon, we're deaf and blind! How long before all the systems are back up?'

Levon gestured helplessly at his screens. 'I'm still rebooting! Couple of minutes, at least.'

'Damn it!' Morgan slammed the receiver back down and took out his cell phone, swiping through the contacts list to find a particular number. 'This is Martin Morgan. I need to speak to Admiral Harper – it's an emergency.' He waited impatiently for the call to be transferred. Finally, he got a reply. 'Admiral! It's Morgan – we have a major situation at STS.'

'What's going on?' Harper demanded.

'Agent Gray has gone rogue. We don't know the full situation, but he assaulted Dr Kiddrick and stole a PERSONA module.'

'Which module? Who's on the disk?'

'*He* is, sir. It's a recording that was made when he first joined the project.'

There was a long silence from the other end of the line. When Harper spoke again, he sounded both angry and strained. 'If what Adam Gray knows – what he *used* to know – gets into the wrong hands, there will be major implications for national security. That disk has to be recovered, Morgan. At any cost. Do I make myself clear?'

'You do, sir,' said Morgan, frowning. 'If I may ask . . . when you say "the wrong hands", do they include Agent Gray's?'

Another pause. 'That is correct. Where's Gray now?'

'We're not sure. He's knocked out our systems.'

'*What?*'

'He blew a water tank and shorted out a lot of the building's electrics. We're trying to bring everything back online now. We think he's on the roof, but—'

'Whatever it takes, Morgan, you have to recover that disk. Put Baxter and his team on it. They're authorised to use any means necessary to take Gray down.'

Morgan was shocked. 'Take him *down*, sir? Are you saying—'

He broke off, whipping round at a muffled sound from somewhere outside the room. Kyle jumped. 'Was that a *gun*?'

'Everyone stay calm,' Morgan ordered, as more distant retorts reached him. 'Stay at your posts – we need those cameras! Get our systems online!' He brought the phone back up. 'Sir, there have been shots fired. I'll report back as soon as I know the situation.' He ran from the Bullpen, following Tony's path through the building.

He passed frightened workers rushing the other way. 'Did you see what happened?' he asked one woman.

She shook her head, desperate to get away. 'No, sir. But I saw Mr Carpenter run past my office – and then we heard the shots.' She pointed down the corridor.

'Get to safety,' Morgan ordered, running the way she had indicated. Towards the cells. It struck him that he could be heading straight into danger, unarmed, but he shook off his concerns. He was in charge; he *had* to know what had happened.

A security door ahead, the green light flashing. He hurried through. Beyond was the holding area. The door was open – and he caught the sharp scent of gun smoke in the air. 'Tony!' he called, going to the entrance. 'Tony, are you okay?'

Silence, then—

'Martin? Yeah, I'm all right.' Tony sounded anything but.

Morgan looked cautiously through the doorway. Tony was leaning over the guard's desk, supporting himself with both hands and breathing heavily. The guard himself, a man named Rivers, was sprawled on the floor outside Qasid's cell – which was open, and empty. A pool of blood slowly swelled around him. He was unmoving, eyes and mouth frozen open.

Qasid was slumped against the wall by the door. Ragged splatters of blood were splashed across the paint, smeared downwards where the terrorist had fallen. A SIG lay near him, several shell casings glinting on the floor. 'What happened?' Morgan asked.

Tony shook his head. 'I wish I knew. Maybe Rivers didn't realise that the failsafe system had unlocked the cell and went to check the door after the lights went out, I don't know. But Qasid must have caught him by surprise and got his gun.' He looked down grimly at the dead guard. 'Jesus.'

'What about you?'

'I came in just as Qasid was going *out* – we ran right into each other. We started fighting for the gun. He nearly got me with it, but I managed to take it off him.'

'So I see.' Morgan checked the Pakistani's corpse. Three holes had been ripped through his chest and abdomen, blackened and burned by the muzzle flare from point-blank shots. 'My God. Are you sure you're okay?'

'Just shaken up, that's all. What's the situation with Adam?'

'Right now, you know as much as I do. But Harper wants him taken down.' Tony reacted with shock. 'Come on, we've got to get back to the Bullpen.' They left the cells at a run.

40

Leap of Faith

Bianca peered nervously over the edge of the roof. Traffic cruised along the street, a long way below. She looked back at Adam. 'You must be joking!' she said as he pushed a button to snap open the very flimsy-looking umbrella.

'Trust me, it'll work,' he replied. 'I've used one before. I jumped off a four-storey building.'

'Well, that's great,' she protested. 'But this has got more than four floors. And there are two of us, *and* we're carrying a lot of heavy cases! There's no way that'll get us down to the ground in one piece.'

'We're not going to the ground. You see that tree?' He pointed at one of the lindens lining the sidewalk, this one somewhat younger and shorter than its neighbours. Even so, it was still a good thirty feet high.

'What about it?'

'That's what we're aiming for. It'll break our fall.'

'It'll probably break a lot more than that!'

Adam put down the open umbrella, taking the medical case from Bianca and squeezing it into his bag. 'We can't drop straight to the sidewalk,' he said, as he slung the holdall over one shoulder.

'The Mary Poppins won't slow us down enough from this height.'

'The what? Oh, never mind, I get it. But you can't seriously—'

'The guys with guns will be here any time now.' Holding the umbrella in one hand, he hefted the heavier of the two PERSONA cases in the other. 'And they've been told they can shoot us. You want to wait for them?' Her expression made her opinion clear. 'Then grab the other case and hang on to me as tight as you can.' He hunched down a little, gesturing for her to move in front of him.

Bianca put both arms over his shoulders, gripping the case's handle as hard as she could. The forced intimacy of being nose-to-nose with Adam was the least uncomfortable thing about her situation. 'Are you ready?' he said.

She licked her suddenly dry lips, trying to cover her rising fear. 'It's a bit late to back out now, isn't it?'

A crash of metal. The access door had been kicked open. Uniformed men, their clothing darkened by water, burst out on to the roof. 'Over there!' one shouted, seeing the fugitives. His gun came up. 'Freeze!'

Adam looked into Bianca's eyes, giving her unspoken reassurance – then he swept her with him over the edge.

Gravity caught them. Bianca screamed as they plunged. The umbrella's carbon-fibre spokes creaked alarmingly, the tough nylon straining as wind resistance tried to rip it free.

The floors of the STS building flashed past. Even with the umbrella's air-braking effect, it wasn't slowing them enough . . .

'Close your eyes!' Adam shouted.

An order, not fatalism—

Bianca did as she was told – as they hit the top of the tree with a huge crackle of snapping twigs. Leaves burst around them like confetti, broken wood clawing at their clothes and skin.

ANDY MCDERMOTT

They kept falling, the topmost branches too slender to resist their weight. The fabric and spokes were ripped from the umbrella's shaft. Bianca felt a slashing pain in her thigh as a wooden shard tore through her trouser leg. She cried out – then the breath was knocked from her as she slammed down on a more solid bough.

She lost her grip on Adam. The case was jarred from her hands, bouncing through the foliage. She tumbled, hitting another branch side-on. It cleaved from the trunk with an earsplitting snap. More leaves lashed at her hair and face as she dropped—

A hard impact, this time on something cool and flat and solid. She was on the ground.

Head spinning, pain messages from different parts of her body competing for attention, she blearily opened her eyes . . .

And saw a car coming straight for her.

She screamed—

The sound was drowned out by the screech of tyres. The car juddered to a halt, the front wheel less than a foot from Bianca's head.

A thump nearby told her that Adam had landed. He pulled her up. The bag was still slung from his shoulder, and he had some-how kept hold of the case. Its twin lay on the sidewalk, leaves dropping around it like green snowflakes. 'Get the PERSONA!'

She limped to pick it up. Adam ran around the car, an ageing Hyundai Elantra station wagon, and yanked open the door. 'Out!' he roared, pulling the startled driver from her vehicle. 'Bianca, come on!'

Bianca collected the case and hobbled to the passenger door. 'Sorry,' she called to the driver as she climbed in. Adam had already tossed his case on to the back seat, putting the car in drive. The Hyundai peeled away with as much power as it could muster, leaving shocked onlookers in its wake.

'Take this,' said Adam, passing the bag to her.

With the case in her lap, she had to perch the extra baggage on top of it – making it all but impossible for her to fasten her seat belt. She struggled to brace her legs in the footwell as Adam took a corner at speed, the station wagon's roll making her slither sideways in her seat. 'Where are we going?'

'We need to get underground.'

'Why?'

'To block the tracker. If we stay in the open, they'll box us in.'

'But – if we go into an underground car park or whatever, they'll still know where we are. It won't take them long to find us.'

'That's why you'll have to work fast.'

'At what?'

He glanced at the bag. 'There's an emergency surgical kit in there. I need you to cut me open and disable the tracker.'

She gawped at him. 'You couldn't have told me all this *before* we jumped off the roof?'

'Would it have changed your mind about helping me?'

'It might! I'm a neurochemist, not a surgeon!'

'I'll tell you what to do.' He swerved the car on to the wrong side of the road to overtake some slow-moving traffic, then skidded through an intersection, eyes scanning the street ahead.

'Everything's back online,' Levon reported, checking a system diagnostic on one of his monitors. The video wall lit up again, showing the views from various STS security cameras.

The images were well behind the action, however. 'They did *what*?' Morgan barked, listening to a call on his cell phone.

'They jumped off the roof!' reported the leader of the security team. 'They used one of those trick umbrellas to land in a tree, then took some woman's car.'

'Did you get the licence plate?'

'We couldn't see it from up here. Some sort of station wagon, light blue, fairly old.' He paused as someone spoke to him. 'Thomson thinks it's a Hyundai. They went south down 20th, then turned east.'

'Hook us into the DC traffic cameras,' Morgan barked to Levon. 'We're looking for a light blue station wagon, heading east.' He turned to Baxter, who had just arrived and received a rapid briefing from Tony. 'John, get your team and go after him. The Admiral wants you to handle this personally. I'll link you in with DC police.'

'On it,' said Baxter. He took out his own phone as he hurried to an exit. 'Spence! Get the guys geared up and down to the parking garage – we're moving out!'

'You're sending our tac team after him?' asked Tony. Holly Jo also looked concerned.

'In case you've forgotten,' said Kiddrick, face tight with anger, 'he attacked me and stole classified information! Then he wrecked half the building while resisting arrest!'

Tony ignored him. 'You are going to try to *capture* them, right?' he said to Morgan. 'Not shoot them on sight? We need to find out *why* Adam's done this.'

'That's what I'm going to ask him, right now,' Morgan replied as he donned a headset. 'Holly Jo, patch me through to Adam.'

She entered commands. 'You're on, sir.'

'Adam! Whatever it is you're doing, I want you to—'

Holly Jo shook her head. 'Sorry, sir. He's turned off the earwig.'

'Damn it,' Morgan muttered. He went to her workstation. 'Use the alert bleeper, see if that gets his attention.' She pushed the button, but there was no response.

'Do we have the tracker?' Tony asked.

'Yes,' Holly Jo told him. Another flurry of commands. 'Putting it on the wall.'

A block of screens switched to a map of Washington. A green square appeared on the street grid, heading across the city. It was already several blocks from the STS building.

'I'm tied in with Metro,' Levon announced, pudgy fingers rattling across his keyboard. More markings appeared on the map. 'We've got live LoJack trackers of all the MPD patrol cars in the city.'

'The nearest one's four blocks from him,' said Kyle.

'Holly Jo, link in with the police and give them Adam's position,' Morgan ordered. 'But tell them just to corral them, not arrest them – I want our people to make the capture. Maybe we can find out what the hell's going on.'

Kiddrick stared at the green square as it turned north at an intersection. 'Where's he going? Is he trying to get out of the city?'

'No, he's trying to find cover,' said Tony. 'He knows we can track him – so he'll be looking for somewhere to block the signal so he can disable it.'

'How can he do that?' Kiddrick demanded. 'The tracker's implanted in his body!'

There was a brief silence as the answer came to everyone simultaneously. 'Ew, gross,' said Holly Jo, wrinkling her nose. 'I hope he's got some Band-Aids.'

Morgan crossed to Kyle's workstation. 'Have we got a drone available?'

'Yeah, one of the new ones,' the younger man told him.

'Get it in the air. When Adam goes to ground, I want us to have eyes on every possible exit from his location. We can't let him get away.'

While Morgan was talking, Tony went to Holly Jo and leaned over her shoulder. 'Do you trust Adam?' he whispered.

'Of course I do,' she answered, surprised. 'Tony . . . do you know what he's doing?'

'No – but I trust him too. Do what you can to help him. I'll try to get Levon and Kyle on board.' He moved away, leaving her staring after him in surprise before she returned her attention to the screens . . . with a surreptitious glance at Morgan to see if he was watching her.

He wasn't, instead finishing giving instructions to Kyle. The UAV pilot hopped from his seat and headed across the Bullpen – to be intercepted by Tony. 'Kyle, hold on.'

'What is it?' Kyle asked.

Now it was Tony's turn to check that Morgan wasn't eavesdropping. 'You trust Adam, don't you?' he said quietly.

'Course I do. The dude saved my life!' It took a moment for him to realise that the question had a subtext. 'Whoa, hold on, brah. You asking what I think you're asking?'

'There's more going on here than we think. Adam and Bianca are the only ones who know what that is. Try to help them if you can.' Another sidelong glance, and he saw that Morgan was glaring impatiently at them. 'Use the computer's auto-tracking to tag all the MPD vehicles,' he said, more loudly. 'Their trackers aren't as accurate as ours – we need to know the exact positions of everyone involved in the pursuit.'

'Huh? Oh, yeah – sure, brah,' Kyle said, finally getting it. He hurried from the room.

Tony went back to Morgan, just as the director's phone rang. 'Yes?'

'It's Baxter,' came the reply. 'We're just leaving STS. Where is he now?'

'I'll tie you in,' Morgan told him. 'Levon! Relay all our tracker data to the mobile units – and put their positions on the screen.'

Levon nodded, then turned back to his computer. A couple of seconds later, new symbols appeared on the map: three green triangles. They moved east, then quickly turned north, heading after Adam.

But another symbol was much closer. One of the DC police cars was now less than two blocks from the Hyundai's position, racing to intercept it.

'I can hear a siren,' Bianca warned.

'I'm surprised it took this long,' Adam said, grim-faced. He looked ahead. There was a red light at the approaching intersection. The street they were on was one-way, all four lanes filled with stationary vehicles. 'Hold on!'

He pressed one hand on the horn and swung the station wagon up on to the sidewalk. The well-worn shock absorbers compressed with a bang as they mounted the kerb, the steering wheel jerking in his hands.

He kept control and straightened out. The sidewalk was only narrow, a tree at its edge forcing him to smash through some small bushes beside a building to avoid it. Another yank on the wheel to dodge a fire hydrant, and the station wagon pounded back on to the road. Bianca shrieked.

'You should put your seat belt on,' he told her.

'I would if I could!' she protested, still trying to keep hold of the luggage on her lap.

He brought the Hyundai back on to the northbound street. There was another set of traffic lights not far ahead, but these had just turned green. Only two lanes were occupied. A twist of the wheel took the Elantra into an empty one. He accelerated.

The siren was getting closer. On the left—

They shot through the intersection at over sixty. The other traffic had just pulled away from the lights – only to stop abruptly as a police car, strobes pulsing, tore through the red in front of them and made a screeching, skidding turn to pursue the station wagon.

Bianca looked back in dismay. 'I don't think we'll outrun them in this thing!'

Adam pushed the accelerator down harder, but he knew she was right. He could hardly have chosen a less suitable getaway car. The Hyundai had been far from over-powered even when brand new, and the general poor condition of the elderly vehicle implied that maintenance and tuning had not been high on its owner's agenda. The engine was already straining to reach seventy.

Another intersection at the end of the block. The lights were green. Only one of the lanes was empty. He wove round a slower car to get into it, feeling the Elantra wallow on its suspension. A glance in the mirror. The MPD Crown Victoria grew larger even in the brief flick of his gaze.

This was going to be a very short chase.

He shot through the intersection – and realised in a split second that something was wrong. Even though the lights were green on the northbound street, the cars heading east and west were also moving . . .

Bianca gasped as an SUV pulled out of the side road on a collision course, halting abruptly as the speeding Hyundai cut in front of it. 'Oh my God!'

Adam looked in the mirror. More vehicles were crossing the junction behind him, stopping sharply in panicked confusion as their drivers realised that traffic was still coming the other way. The police car skidded under hard braking and slammed into the side of a van.

'What the hell happened?' Bianca cried.

He turned his eyes back to the road ahead. 'I think someone's giving us some help.'

41

Race and Chase

Bewilderment spread through the Bullpen. The symbol representing one of the MPD vehicles was right behind the green triangle on the map . . . then came to a sudden stop, Adam's Hyundai leaving it behind. 'What's going on?' demanded Morgan.

Holly Jo was monitoring police frequencies. 'The cops just crashed!'

'Have we got the traffic cameras yet?' said Tony as he put on a headset.

'Coming up,' said Levon, hurriedly closing the window on his monitor from which he had been overriding the traffic lights at the intersection. A view appeared on the video wall. Cars were scattered like a bored child's toys across the centre of the crossroads. The police cruiser tried to move, but one of its tyres was flat, battered bodywork cutting into the rubber. 'Damn! That's a mess.'

'Yeah,' said Tony, giving him a tiny nod of thanks.

Kyle ran back in and hurried to his workstation. 'Man, there's a lot of water upstairs!' he said as he brought the UAV on line. His screens lit up, displaying the roof of the STS building. The viewpoint rose sharply as the drone took off. He looked up at the traffic chaos. 'Did I miss something?'

'*Way* too easy,' said Holly Jo quietly. A couple of people smiled at the joke even through the tension.

Morgan was not one of them. 'Minds on the job, people!' he snapped. One screen now showed the view from the drone's camera; his gaze fixed on it. The vehicles on the streets below were little more than coloured specks. 'Kyle, why are you flying so high?'

'So I don't crash into anything,' Kyle replied, as if it were self-evident. 'Sir,' he quickly added as Morgan's glare turned on him like a laser.

'What?' said Kiddrick incredulously. 'The buildings in DC have a height limit – there's hardly anything more than seven storeys. You'd be looking down on the Washington Monument from that altitude!'

'I told him to go that high,' said Tony. 'So we can use the computers to tag and track all the vehicles involved in the chase. We need maximum situational awareness to avoid any more incidents like that.' He jerked a thumb towards the scene at the intersection – not adding that with the drone flying far higher than necessary, it would make the job of tracking Adam and Bianca much harder if they left their car.

Morgan appeared dubious, but accepted the explanation. 'Just find them,' he said, before turning back to the map. The three green triangles representing the positions of Baxter and his men were now racing diagonally through the city along Rhode Island Avenue. The tactical team's SUVs were fitted with strobe lights and sirens to help them carve through the Washington traffic.

They would not catch up with the Hyundai before the police did, however. Two more MPD cruisers were rapidly closing on the green square from different directions.

Holly Jo gave Tony a conspiratorial glance, then her hand moved to the button for the emergency bleeper.

Adam twitched as a tone sounded inside his ear – three shrill beeps, a second of silence, then a repeat. Bianca saw his irate reaction. 'What is it?'

'Someone's using the alert beeper, and they won't shut up.'

'Can you switch it off?'

'No. I'll just have to not let it distract me.' The pattern continued, more insistently.

A pattern . . .

The rising sound of a siren elbowed the thought aside. The police were getting closer – but he couldn't tell from which direction, the electronic wail echoing off the surrounding buildings.

The Hyundai was fast approaching an intersection. The siren didn't sound close enough to be coming from one of the side streets, so the police car was probably at least another block away. If he turned now, he had more chance of evading it.

Which way? Left or right?

He chose the former, braking as little as he dared to sweep the station wagon through the apex of the corner. Bianca gasped, trying to hold herself in her seat as the Hyundai listed. No sign of the cops ahead, or in the mirror. He swung across to the left side of the road to overtake a couple of cars.

The sound in his ear became more frantic. The pattern had changed, now four beeps. Short, long, short, short . . .

Morse code!

Adam had already committed to turning right at the next crossroads as the realisation struck him, the lanes ahead full of traffic – but even as he made the move he knew it was a mistake. Morse code was obsolete, but he had still been trained in it, and some recess of his mind told him that the signal represented the letter L.

L for *left*.

'Adam!' cried Bianca, but he had already seen the danger. There was a police car dead ahead, running silent with strobes but no siren. It turned sideways to block their path. Parked cars lined both sides of the street, not enough space for him to get past.

Instead of braking, he accelerated—

Bianca screamed – but Adam was not planning to ram the obstruction. Instead he yanked the handbrake lever, simultaneously flicking the steering wheel to full right lock. The Hyundai's tail end swung wide – and clipped the Crown Victoria's front wing.

The impact threw Bianca against him. Metal crunched, the station wagon's rear window bursting apart. But it was still driveable, smoke pouring from its front tyres as they scrabbled for grip. The Elantra's mangled rear bumper was ripped from its body as it lurched away.

The police car started to follow – but didn't get far.

Like a supermarket trolley with a bad castor, it suddenly veered off course and slammed into a stationary car. The Crown Victoria's right front wheel bounced free and wobbled away down the street, the stub of the broken axle protruding from its hub.

Bianca recovered from her shock and looked back. 'What – what happened? Why did they crash?'

'I took out their front wheel,' Adam told her.

'You mean you *deliberately* hit them when you skidded?' He nodded. 'Where did you learn how to do that?'

'I have no idea.' The bleeper sounded in his ear again. Dot-dash-dot-dot: L. He turned the car back down the road along which they had come. 'I'll tell you what I do know, though – Holly Jo's helping us.'

'How?'

'The beeper. She's sending Morse code, telling me which way to go.' Another message came through, this time three beeps. Dot-dash-dot: R. *Right.* He followed the instruction. Only normal traffic ahead.

'You think Tony asked her?'

'Yeah. And Levon, too – he must have hacked the lights at that intersection.'

'So we'll be able to get away from the cops?'

'Not until we deactivate the tracker – and we need more of a lead to do that. But I think our chances just went up.'

'From what baseline?'

'You know when we jumped off the roof?'

She gave him a pained look. 'How could I forget?'

'The odds weren't much better than if we'd jumped *without* the Mary Poppins.'

'Oh. Now I see why you didn't tell me any of this before we started.'

Another signal came through the bleeper, telling him to go left. Adam put the Hyundai through a tyre-torturing turn, listening for sirens. He heard one – but it was a few blocks away, fading with every moment.

Morgan glared up at the video wall. The map had turned into a bizarre version of Pac-Man, Washington's streets representing the maze and the symbols of the pursuing vehicles the ghosts moving through it.

The green square was the avatar of the person playing the game. And at the moment, he was winning.

'Damn it, he's got past them!' he growled, watching the square make another turn. The nearest MPD vehicle was now two blocks away from the fugitives, and heading in the wrong direction. 'Tell the cops he's heading north again! They're reacting too slowly.'

'They don't have a live tracker feed,' Tony reminded him.

'It's still not good enough.' He glanced down the map. Unlike the police, the three STS vehicles *did* have real-time tracking of Adam's position – and were closing on him remorselessly.

★ ★ ★

'Take the next left,' Baxter ordered from the passenger seat of the lead SUV. A map on his open laptop showed him exactly what those in the Bullpen were seeing. 'He's six blocks from us, going north. We should be able to intercept—'

He broke off as his phone rang. He had assigned a specific tone to this particular caller, and knew that no delay in answering would be tolerated. 'Baxter.'

'Situation?' Harper demanded.

'We're closing on him, sir,' he replied.

'You know that you're authorised to use deadly force?'

'Yes, sir.'

When Harper spoke again, his voice was unnaturally clipped and precise. 'Let me restate that, in the strongest possible terms. You are *authorised* to use *deadly force* to stop Gray. He cannot be allowed to learn what is on that disk. You know why. Confirm that you understand.'

Baxter responded without hesitation. 'Yes, sir. I confirm.'

'Good. Clear this up quickly, Baxter.' The line went silent.

Baxter lowered the phone and turned in his seat to address Fallon and Spence behind. 'I've just received new orders. Gray is now considered an imminent threat to the security of the United States. We do whatever's necessary to take him down.'

Neither man could quite suppress a brief expression of satisfaction. 'Understood, sir,' said Spence, readying his gun.

Morgan's frustration grew as he watched the chase play out on the screens. Every time the police started to close in, the Hyundai turned to evade them, widening the gap.

Kiddrick was even more agitated than the STS director. 'This is ridiculous! How does he keep avoiding them? It's like he's psychic!'

'It's just luck,' said Tony firmly. 'There's no way he can know where the Metro PD cars are.'

'What if he's got access to our system? Baxter and his team are using laptops to track what's going on – maybe he's got one too.'

'If he were logged in, we'd know,' said Morgan, shaking his head. But an idea had been planted. He frowned, turning his gaze back to the map. One of the police vehicles turned on to an east–west street . . . and just a few seconds later, the Hyundai changed direction as if in response, moving on to a new course to take it further away. 'Kyle, how long before the drone will be able to spot him?'

'Couple of minutes,' Kyle reported.

'That's too long,' complained Kiddrick.

'It's going as fast as it can, brah. It's not a jet.'

Morgan waved a hand impatiently to silence them. 'Tell the cops going west along R Street to make the next turn south.'

The instruction was passed on. After a short delay, the vehicle's icon altered course . . . and soon after that, the Hyundai turned away once again. 'He knows,' he muttered. 'He knows what route to take to avoid the other cars.'

Tony tried to hide his concern. 'Martin, that's not possible. Like you said, if he had access to our system, we'd know.'

'He wouldn't need direct access if someone was helping him.' Morgan slowly turned, his eyes locking on to one particular workstation. 'Miss Voss.'

Holly Jo looked up in alarm, hurriedly jerking her finger away from the beeper. 'Uh, sir?'

'Why are you using the emergency signal?'

'I'm, ah . . . trying to distract him?' she said, flustered. 'I thought that if he had a constant beeping in his ear that he couldn't shut off, it might drive him nuts enough to make a mistake.'

Morgan was unimpressed. 'You're relieved, Miss Voss. I want you to— Miss Voss!' he barked as Holly Jo tapped a frantic tattoo on the button. 'Security! Get her out of here!'

A pair of security protective officers had taken up station by one of the Bullpen's entrances when the building was placed on alert; they hurried across the room and pulled Holly Jo from her seat. She gave Tony a despairing look as she was hustled away.

'Take her to holding,' Morgan snapped. 'Someone take over her station. Maybe now we'll have a chance of catching them!'

Behind him, both Levon and Kyle swapped nervous glances with Tony.

'I think we just lost our guide,' Adam told Bianca. 'Holly Jo sent me an SOS.'

'So now what do we do?' she replied, worried.

'STS will be able to direct the cops right to us. We need to disable the tracker.'

'By "we", you mean me, yes?'

'Afraid so. Hold on.' He threw the battered Hyundai into a sharp left turn.

Bianca clung to the cases as she was thrown sideways. 'Where are we going?'

'I think there's a building with an underground parking garage a few blocks from here, near a subway station. It should be—'

He saw rapidly pulsing blue lights reflecting off the flank of a car ahead – a moment before a black Chevrolet Suburban SUV roared out of an intersecting street and powered towards the Elantra.

Baxter leaned out of the passenger-side window, aiming an MP5 sub-machine gun—

'*Down!*' Adam shouted. He hunched lower in his seat, reaching across to shove Bianca's head down as Baxter opened fire. Bullets clanked against the Hyundai's nose, shattering a headlight. More chewed into the hood before the stream of automatic fire punched holes through the windscreen. One round smacked into the headrest mere inches above Adam's skull.

His view was obscured by spiderweb cracks in the glass, but he could still see enough to make out the Suburban still charging towards him. He swerved sharply to avoid it, riding the car up hard on to the sidewalk.

Plastic recycling bins lined up outside a brownstone apartment building scattered like tenpins as the Hyundai ploughed into them. The SUV whipped past, tyres shrieking as its driver hurled it into a skidding U-turn.

Baxter's vehicle was not alone. Another two Suburbans charged around the corner, strobes flaring. One tried to block the Hyundai's path – but the hulking vehicle couldn't turn fast enough. The Elantra shot past and swung back on to the tarmac as the SUV spun out.

Baxter fired again, more bullets searing down the street—

They hit the Hyundai's tail as Adam flung the car around the corner, cutting off his line of fire. It would take the Suburbans several seconds to come about and rejoin the pursuit – but the government-issue SUVs were equipped with upgraded suspensions and more powerful engines than the standard civilian models. The station wagon stood no chance of outrunning them. And unlike the police, the STS pursuit team had direct access to his tracker, pinpointing his position.

No escape. And Baxter had fired not at the car, but its occupants. He had been given clear instructions.

Kill the fugitives.

42

Field Surgery

A section of the video wall had been switched to the live feed from the UAV's camera. The drone was still several blocks from its target, the view partially obscured by buildings – but enough of the street was visible to show flashes of fire coming from one of the Suburbans. 'Whoa!' exclaimed Kyle. 'Are Baxter's guys *shooting* at them?'

Tony rounded on Morgan. 'Martin, what's John doing?' he demanded. 'If he kills Adam and Bianca, we'll never find out what the hell all this is about!'

Morgan hesitated uncomfortably before replying. 'Orders from Harper. Use whatever force is necessary to take Adam down.'

'Take him down – or take him *out*?' Tony turned to Kiddrick. 'What's on that disk that's worth killing him for?'

'The contents of the disk are classified,' Kiddrick said stiffly.

'Even from Adam? How the hell can somebody's own memories be kept a secret from them?'

'We have our orders,' said Morgan, face grim. 'If Adam had surrendered immediately, it wouldn't be necessary.' He sounded as if he were trying to convince himself as much as anyone else.

Tony made a disgusted sound and looked back at the screens. All three Suburbans had rejoined the pursuit, panthers bearing down upon their smaller and weaker prey.

Bianca risked lifting her head enough to peer into the wing mirror. 'Oh God! They're catching up!'

'Stay down,' Adam warned her. But he couldn't follow his own advice, needing to see the street ahead through the damaged windshield.

And that was not the only part of the Elantra that had suffered injury. He heard a piercing hiss from the engine compartment – steam escaping from the bullet-punctured radiator. The Hyundai was dying.

But he couldn't stop. That would spell death for more than just the car.

Sirens ahead – several of them. Getting closer.

He looked in the mirror. The Suburbans were about two hundred yards behind, but quickly gaining. Without Holly Jo's guidance he no longer knew which way to turn to evade the approaching cops – although if they beat him to the next intersection it wouldn't make any difference.

He willed the car to go faster, but the stench of boiling coolant and oil told him that the hope was futile. The speedometer needle, which had been pinned at seventy, started to fall.

Wisps of steam blew back along the hood. The engine was overheating, strained beyond its limits.

Sixty-five. Sixty. The chase was almost over . . .

The Elantra shot through the intersection just ahead of three charging police vehicles off to the right.

Adam checked the mirror. The lead cruiser appeared—

But it didn't follow him. Instead it screeched to a stop, the two other cars following suit to form a ragged barricade across the junction. Cops jumped out, raising weapons – but not at the Hyundai.

They were aiming at Baxter's team.

'What the *fuck*?' yelled Baxter as the MPD vehicles blocked his path. Cops took up position behind them, aiming pistols and shotguns over the hoods and trunks. 'What are these assholes doing?'

'Stop your vehicles!' boomed an amplified voice. 'Stop or we open fire!'

The driver looked at Baxter in alarm. 'What do I do?'

There was not enough room to get past without ramming the cars aside – injuring or killing the cops behind them. 'Stop,' Baxter reluctantly ordered, the cold thrill of the pursuit replaced by anger. The driver braked hard, the Suburban halting ten yards short of the roadblock. The other two SUVs pulled up behind it. 'I'm gonna rip someone a new one for this . . .'

Morgan blinked in surprise as he watched the aerial view of unfolding events. The cops advanced on the stationary Suburbans, weapons drawn. 'What the— What are they doing? Why are they stopping Baxter's team? Get me the Metro commander, now!' he barked at Holly Jo's replacement. 'And keep track of Adam!'

Kyle zoomed out, catching the Hyundai just before it made a turn and was lost to view behind buildings. 'Get him back in sight!' Kiddrick demanded.

'Let me just switch to X-ray mode,' Kyle said sarcastically. 'Patience, brah. Another thirty seconds and the drone'll catch up.'

Morgan was connected to the police commander. 'What the hell's going on? Your guys just stopped my pursuit team!'

'The hell are *you* talkin' about?' was the truculent response. 'We're doin' what you told us to do!'

'What do you mean?'

'I got your APB right here! "Highest national security priority, stop and detain armed and dangerous suspects in three stolen black US government Suburbans." That's what you asked for, and that's what we're doin', right now!'

'That's not what we told you!' Morgan said, bewildered. On the screen, the cops were making the SUVs' occupants get out at gunpoint. 'Our suspects are in a Hyundai station wagon – you're arresting the agents who were chasing them!'

'Look, I'm just goin' by what you gave us,' the commander complained. 'First you told us it was the Hyundai, then you sent an update about the Suburbans.'

'We didn't send—' Morgan broke off, casting an accusing glare over the Bullpen's occupants. 'All right. I guess Holly Jo isn't the only person trying to help Adam. So who else has a good reason to feel loyal to him?' His gaze fell upon Kyle. 'Someone he saved from being shot down by a Russian jet, maybe?'

'I'm just flying the UAV!' the young man protested. 'I don't even have access to that kind of stuff.'

Kiddrick moved to Morgan's side, sour-faced. 'But I can think of someone who does.'

'So can I,' said Morgan. 'Levon? Did you change the APB?'

Levon looked up at him with a guilty expression. 'If I say yes, do I get some leniency?'

Exasperated, Morgan waved to another pair of guards. 'Put him in with Voss.' Levon held up his hands in surrender and stood as they approached.

'We're gonna need more security guys in here,' said Kyle as the two men took Levon away.

'We'd better not,' Morgan rumbled. He turned back to the screens. 'Where's Adam now?'

'I'm on him,' Kyle assured him. 'Okay, got a fix with the auto-tracking.' A blue outline was overlaid on one particular vehicle as it reached an intersection. 'He's going west – no, wait, he's turning again.'

The Hyundai pulled on to an access road running behind a large office building of dull red brick. It headed down a ramp beneath the structure. 'We've got him,' said Kiddrick. 'If he tries to hide, the police can just sweep the place floor by floor until they find him.'

'That's not why he's gone in there,' said Tony. As if in response, the green square began to jitter, before vanishing entirely. 'He's blocking the tracker!'

'Will this work?' asked Bianca as Adam brought the car into the underground garage.

'Hopefully. They'll know we're in here, but they won't be able to pinpoint exactly where,' he replied.

'Our car's fairly easy to spot, though.' With its mangled back end and bullet-pocked nose and windscreen, the Elantra was no longer anonymous.

'That's why we're not staying with it.'

'Oh, so we're going to steal some other poor sod's car?'

'I'll pick something that looks like the owner can afford theft insurance.' He drove along the garage until he spotted a space and slewed the steaming vehicle into it. 'Follow me.'

'Like I have much of a choice,' she said as she got out, fumbling with her baggage.

Adam pulled the other case from the back seat, then hurried along the row of cars until he reached the end wall. 'This'll have to do,' he said, crouching behind the last parked vehicle. 'Give me the bag.'

Bianca handed it to him, looking fearfully back towards the ramp. 'How long do you think we'll have before they get here?'

'Not long. You'll have to work fast.' He opened the holdall, extracting an emergency surgical kit he had taken from STS. 'Okay, here's what I need you to do,' he said, handing it to her and then untucking his clothing to expose his lower back. 'Just above the base of my spine there's a thing like a large coin under my skin. That's the kinetic power pack. You'll have to find it by feel.'

'So – so you actually want me to do this?' she said. 'You want me to cut you open?'

'It's the only way. Find the power pack.'

Bianca hesitantly touched him, fingertips moving down his backbone. She felt something under the skin, hard and unnatural, a circular object about four centimetres in diameter. 'Okay, got it. What now?'

'You're going to cut through the skin just above it. Use a sterile wipe to clean it.' She found one in the surgical kit and did so. 'Now take the scalpel and make a horizontal incision across the top.'

There was a scalpel inside a plastic tube. She took the instrument out. Even in the gloomy half-light of the parking garage, the razor edge of the stainless-steel blade still glinted. 'Oh God, I can't stop my hands from shaking,' she warned him.

'You'll be okay,' Adam replied. He knelt down, leaning forward. 'Find the pack again – use your left hand.'

She tried to control her breathing as she relocated the disc beneath his skin. 'Okay.'

'Now, put the tip of the scalpel just above it, about half an inch to the left of its top.'

Bianca brought the blade into position, but hesitated before the metal touched him, her hand trembling more than ever. 'Adam, I'm scared. If I do something wrong . . .'

'You won't. I know you can do it. I trust you, *Doctor* Childs.'

That didn't stop her from shaking, but at least it gave her the courage to press the scalpel's tip against his flesh. 'What about anaesthetic?'

'There isn't time.' He tensed, taking a deep breath. 'Make the incision.'

Another hesitation – then, wincing, she pressed the blade down.

Adam flinched at the pain, drawing in air sharply through his nostrils. Blood swelled from the cut, rising like a tar bubble before trickling down his back in a crimson stream.

Bianca gasped. It was not so much the sight itself that caused her alarm, rather that she was responsible for it. 'Oh God. The blood's coming out really fast!'

'You'll have to be fast too,' said Adam through gritted teeth. 'Make the cut – left to right, about an inch.'

She tried to slide the scalpel sideways, but the blade refused to move. 'I can't, it's stuck!'

'You have to – push harder. Like cutting a steak.'

'Is this a bad time to tell you I'm a vegetarian?' But she applied more pressure – and the scalpel shifted, slicing through the skin and the thin layer of fat beneath. A sudden gush of blood made her jerk in shock. 'It's bleeding, a lot!'

'Keep cutting,' Adam told her, voice strained. 'You're almost done.'

Wincing, Bianca edged the scalpel across until the incision was the size he had demanded. 'Okay, okay! Now what do I do?'

'Don't put down the scalpel, you'll still need it – but you're going to have to use your other hand to open the incision. There's a wire coming out of the top of the pack – the earwig's power line and antenna. Use the scalpel to cut it.'

'Oh God, oh my God . . .' Bianca whispered as she moved her quivering left hand to the gory opening. Blood oozed out as she touched it. She probed deeper, feeling the curved edge of the implant against her fingertips. 'I've found the power pack – but I can't feel the wire.' Desperation rose as she kept searching without result. Another bloody rivulet rushed down Adam's back. 'Oh God, I can't find it!'

'Stay calm,' Adam rasped, muscles and tendons drawn tight. 'It's there. Right at the top. Just keep feeling . . .'

Her right hand was shaking so much she almost dropped the scalpel. She clamped her hand tightly around its handle, then slid her fingertips deeper into the incision. Still nothing but the smooth plastic curve of the power pack and the awful warm softness under his skin – then suddenly she felt something else that did not belong. It was much thinner than she had expected, more like a hair drawn taut than an electrical wire. 'I've got it!'

'Okay,' said Adam. 'Now put the scalpel blade under it, and pull outwards.'

She did so. There was resistance, the edges of the cut rising upwards as the wire pulled against them – then with an almost musical *tink* it broke. Bianca gasped. 'It's gone!'

Adam's own relief was less vocal, but just as heartfelt. 'Okay,' he said, exhaling sharply. 'There's some gauze in the kit. Put a piece over the cut, then stick a bandage over it.'

'What about cleaning it?'

'No time. We need to get out of here.' As she covered the wound, he rummaged in the bag, producing something the size of a smartphone.

'What's that?' Bianca asked.

'Something that would have every auto manufacturer in the world suing STS if they ever found out about it.' He tapped at the buttons on the device's face. A line of tiny LEDs along the top of the gadget flickered – then the garage echoed with the chirps of dozens of remote locking systems, indicators flashing.

Bianca looked up from her nursing work in amazement. 'How did you do that?'

'It's an override – it's got the lock and alarm codes for just about every car on the market.' He pocketed the remote. 'Are you done?'

She finished pressing the bandage into place. 'Yes. Does it hurt?'

'Yeah, but there isn't time to worry about it. Get the gear, we need to find a car.' He stood, pulling his clothing back into place as he turned to survey the garage. 'Something fast, but not too showy . . .' He managed a smile. '*There* we go.'

Bianca collected the PERSONA, then turned to see what he was looking at. Not knowing anything about American auto-mobiles, all she could tell was that the vehicle in question was some sort of glossy black muscle car. 'Is that good?'

'Hell *yes*, it's good,' Adam replied. 'And I guess I just found out something else about myself.'

'What's that?'

'I'm a Ford man.' Suppressing a wince at the pain in his lower back, he picked up the other case and the bag and hurried down the row to the waiting Mustang.

Bianca followed. 'I used to have a Ford Ka. One-point-two litre. I'm guessing this is a bit more powerful.'

'Just a bit. Get in.' He opened the driver's door, dropping the case on to the back seat, then took out the override and climbed inside.

She saw his face twist with pain as he sat, putting pressure on the wound. 'Are you sure you're all right?'

'I'll live. Assuming we actually get out of this alive.' He flipped the remote around in his hand, thumbing open a panel in its base. 'Okay, let's see. Ford, Ford . . .' He turned a small knurled wheel, then pushed it. A sliver of metal sprang out of the remote with a click. He slid it into the ignition slot and turned it. The Mustang's five-litre V8 started up with a rumble that echoed through the garage. 'All right!'

'That's the happiest I've seen you since we ran out of that pub,' Bianca said, almost teasing.

'Apparently I like my wheels. You ready?' She nodded, and he pulled out of the space, turning back towards the ramp. He accelerated up it, the exhaust note booming in his wake.

'There!' said Morgan, pointing at the screens. A dark shape emerged from the bowels of the office building the drone was observing. 'Someone's leaving. Kyle, follow it.'

'We don't have his tracker,' said Kyle. 'It could just be some dude going home early.'

'He went in there to *disable* the tracker. We can't risk losing them.' He glanced at the map. Baxter and his men had been released, the three STS Suburbans now racing with the police vehicles towards Adam's last known location – but they were still two blocks distant.

'It could be a decoy,' Tony cautioned. 'They might be splitting up.'

Morgan shook his head. 'Adam somehow persuaded Dr Childs to help him do this, even though she must have known the consequences. They'll stick together.' He looked back at the view from the UAV's camera. 'Kyle, why isn't the auto-tracking on that car yet? And zoom in closer – we can't even tell the model from this height!'

'There's, uh, some sort of glitch in the system,' Kyle replied unconvincingly. 'I can't get a lock on it – uh-oh.' The image rocked as the drone slewed around. The black car swept off the edge of the screen. 'Must be turbulence or something! A jetstream, maybe.'

'Over Washington?' spluttered Kiddrick.

'Air's a weird thing, brah.' He waggled the controls, putting the UAV into a spin.

'I see we *do* need some more security guys in here,' growled Morgan. 'Hamilton, take over from him. Kyle—'

'I know, I know,' said Kyle, standing. 'I'm busted.'

'Just stand over there and wait for the SPOs. Hamilton! Where's that car?'

Kyle's replacement took over the controls, stabilising the drone. The office building came back into view – but there was no sign of the target vehicle. 'I can't see it, sir.'

'Search wider. We've *got* to find it.'

'I don't even know which way it was heading, sir. It could have gone in any direction from the nearest intersection.'

'We can't exactly tell Metro to put out an APB on "a black car",' said Tony. The camera panned across another block – revealing at least half a dozen vehicles that would fit the description.

Morgan simmered, glaring at the wall screens. 'Okay. Tell them to search that building, just in case they're still inside. It's a long shot, but we have to check. Then get MPD to set up roadblocks – ten-block radius.'

Tony looked at the capital's expansive grid on the map. 'That's a hell of a lot of streets. They'll never be able to close them all off.'

'We have to try, damn it!' He turned and glared at Kyle, who was being escorted away by a pair of guards. 'Wait, don't take him to holding. Take him to my office. And bring Voss and James, too. I want to know what the hell's going on here. Tony, come with me.' He started towards an exit, then stopped as he realised the Bullpen's staff were staring at him in confusion. 'Well? You've got your orders – get on with them! Find that car! Find Adam Gray!'

★ ★ ★

'Put your head down,' said Adam as he saw a police car approaching from the other direction. 'They're looking for two people, not one.'

Bianca squirmed lower in her seat, dropping below the window line. The MPD cruiser drew closer, the driver's eyes flicking towards the Mustang – then it passed. Adam checked the mirror. The cops disappeared into the distance. 'Okay, they're gone. They're not looking for this car.'

She cautiously lifted her head. 'What now?'

'Go somewhere quiet, then use the PERSONA to see what's on that disk.' He glanced at the bag in her lap. 'Find out what was in my mind.'

He looked ahead. An alley led between some run-down commercial buildings. He slowed and turned into it. 'The neighbourhood's a bit grotty,' said Bianca.

'We're not going to get carjacked by drug dealers in broad daylight.' He slowed the Mustang. 'This should do.'

It was a brick structure with a small loading dock set into its rear, real-estate signs proclaiming that the property was available to rent. The windows were boarded up. Adam turned the car into the space and stopped. They were completely hidden from the main street; anyone looking for them would have to come down the alley to find them.

If someone *did* do that, the Mustang would be blocked in by their vehicle. But it was a chance he had to take.

He twisted to get the cases from the back seat – and let out a grunt of pain. 'Stay still, I'll do that,' Bianca told him. 'Let me see.' He reluctantly shifted position. 'Oh, God. You're still bleeding – it's all over your back!' A blotchy dark patch had swollen outwards from the wound, soaking his clothing.

'It'll look worse than it is,' he said, trying to reassure her – and himself. 'It's just spread because I've been pressed against the seat.'

'Are you sure? How do you feel?'

'I'm feeling . . . that I wish I'd used anaesthetic. But I'm okay. Really.' He managed a small, strained smile. 'Get the PERSONA set up.'

It was awkward doing so in the confines of the coupé, but after a few minutes Bianca had connected both units of the PERSONA device and switched them on. Despite its rough treatment since leaving the STS building, the system appeared to be in working order. She took out the memory module. 'Are you sure you want to do this?'

Adam finished donning the skullcap. 'I don't know if I'm going to like what I find out. But I've *got* to find out.' He faced her. 'Is this on okay?'

She reached up to adjust the electrodes. 'There. You're good.' Her hand stayed against his skin for an extra moment as she regarded him with concern. 'What are you going to do if it really is something bad?'

'I don't know,' he said in a quiet voice. Then, more firmly: 'Give me the shot and start the transfer. Let's get this over with. However it turns out.'

'Okay.' She took the jet injector from the medical case. 'Are you ready?'

'Do it.'

'Good luck.' She positioned the nozzle against his neck and pulled the trigger, then watched the now unsettlingly familiar sight of all expression fading from his face. Thirty seconds passed. 'I'm going to start the transfer,' she whispered. Adam's only response was a slight nod.

She touched the controls. The PERSONA's screen came to life, beginning to feed the recorded memories back into their owner's mind.

43

Know Thyself

Morgan's mood had not improved by the time he reached his office.

'Right,' he said, glowering at the three young specialists lined up before his desk. 'I want answers, and I want them now. All three of you were working to help Adam get away. Why?'

Holly Jo, Levon and Kyle exchanged unhappy looks, none wanting to be the first to speak. 'Let me spell it out for you,' Morgan continued. 'You deliberately impeded an operation to capture a rogue agent who had stolen highly classified information – *and* assaulted a senior STS official in the process, in case you'd forgotten. That means you can be charged under the Espionage Act! We're talking a good thirty years in federal prison here – assuming you aren't all packed off to Guantanamo. So this is your last chance. Why did you help Adam?'

Tony spoke before any of them could answer. 'Because I told them to.'

It took Morgan a moment to fully process what he had heard. When he did, his tone was calmer, yet more dangerous than ever. 'Would you care to explain that?'

'I *ordered*,' Tony placed emphasis on the word, 'them to help

Adam evade capture. They were acting under my instructions as their superior, so the responsibility for everything they did is mine.'

'Very noble of you,' said Morgan. He looked at the trio. 'And would you all back up that statement?'

'Yeah, totally,' Kyle gabbled. 'I mean, it's *Tony* – he's our boss, we all trust him, and we do what he says, right?' He took in the disapproving expressions of his companions. 'What?'

'He's right,' said Tony, before Holly Jo or Levon could add anything. 'They were following my orders.'

'While disobeying mine,' Morgan replied. He regarded Tony in silence for several tense seconds. 'All right, if that's how you want to play it . . . You three,' he snapped, turning back to the specialists. 'You're all relieved of duty pending further investigation. Report to the security office and turn in your IDs, then get out of my agency. I'll deal with you later.'

They mumbled shamed affirmations, then left the room. 'You asshole,' Holly Jo hissed at Kyle.

'What?' he protested. 'That's what Tony wanted!'

Morgan waited for the door to close behind them. 'So, what *do* you want, Tony? Why have you decided to risk your career – your freedom – for Adam?'

'Because he deserves to know the truth about himself,' Tony answered.

'But you don't know what that truth is.'

'Do you?'

'No,' Morgan admitted. 'But the Admiral vouched for him as an ideal candidate to replace you – and whatever the reasons Adam had for wanting to forget his past, he *asked* to forget it.'

'But he's changed his mind. Now he wants to remember – or at least to find out *why* he wanted to forget. He wants to learn who he really is, and what we took away from him. I think he has a right to know.'

'You don't have the authority to give him that information,' Morgan said sternly. 'And nor do I, for that matter.'

'You're saying it's entirely Harper's call?'

'It is.'

'You can't tell me you agree with that.'

'Whether I do or not is irrelevant. And for God's sake, Tony, even if I sympathise with Adam's motives, he's gone about this in the wrong way. He assaulted Kiddrick, stole classified data, sabotaged a government facility and wreaked havoc in the capital! You know we can't tolerate that. And I can't tolerate insubordination.'

Tony took a deep breath, then nodded. 'I understand. What are you going to do?'

'I don't know yet. For now, you can wait in holding until I figure that out.' The phone on his desk rang. 'Yes?' He listened, expression hardening. 'Right.' He put it down and regarded Tony grimly. 'Speak of the devil. Harper is here.'

The Director of National Intelligence was in Morgan's office barely a minute later. 'I want to know what in the name of the good Christ is going on,' he snarled. 'How the hell did Gray get away?'

'I helped him,' Tony said.

Harper seemed about to explode. '*What?*'

'Tony just admitted to me that he was passing information to Adam that allowed him to evade capture,' explained Morgan – the truth, but not in its entirety. Tony gave him a brief look of gratitude on behalf of his three co-conspirators. 'I put him under arrest just before you arrived.'

Harper stared angrily at Tony. 'Then why is he still here and not in a cell?'

Morgan picked up the phone. 'Get security to my office,' he ordered.

The white-haired man marched up to Tony, almost nose to nose with him. 'What the *fuck* are you playing at, Carpenter?'

Tony didn't blink. 'Why is it so important that Adam doesn't remember his past, Admiral?'

Harper's fury rose at being challenged. 'That's not your goddamn concern!'

'My concern is the people under my command – and Adam is one of them.'

'And my concern is the security of the United States! By taking that disk, Gray is a direct threat to that security. If it gets into the wrong hands—'

'It's in *Adam's* hands,' Tony cut in, raising Harper's ire still further. 'They're his own memories! How can finding out about his past be a threat to national security?'

Before Harper could reply, there was a knock at the door. 'Come in,' Morgan barked. Two security officers entered. 'Take Mr Carpenter to holding and keep him there until further orders.'

'What did Adam know?' Tony demanded. 'What's on that disk, Admiral?'

'Get him out of my sight,' Harper growled.

'And what about Adam?' asked Tony as the two men ushered him to the door.

'We'll catch him,' replied Morgan.

'And if he's used the PERSONA to re-imprint his own memories?'

Harper said nothing – but the concern clearly visible even through his mask of anger was an answer in itself.

Bianca watched the rush of data on the PERSONA's screen subside. She checked that the diagnostic readings were in order, then turned to Adam. 'Are you okay?'

He opened his eyes. 'Yeah. I think.'

'I'll try to do a memory check. What's your full name?'

'Adam Peter Gray.'

'So you are really you, then.' She remembered something he had said a few days earlier. 'What was your dog called?'

'Grover,' Adam replied, a smile breaking. 'I *did* have a dog, I remember him! He was an Irish setter.'

'Where did you grow up?'

'Crescent City, Florida.'

'Your parents' names?'

'Steven and Lucia.' Brief gloom crossed his face. 'My dad passed away in 2004 – but my mom's still alive! She's still in Florida, she moved to Fort Lauderdale.' His downcast look was completely swept away by delight. 'My God, I can remember her! I can remember everything, my fam—'

He flinched as if he had taken a physical blow. His exhilaration instantly vanished, replaced by horror. 'What is it?' Bianca said, alarmed.

'I have a brother,' he mumbled. 'I – I *had* a brother, a twin. He looked just like me. The dream, it wasn't – oh God.' He fumbled at the door handle, trying to get out of the car. The cord attached to the skullcap pulled tight. He clawed at it, tearing it off. 'Oh God, no!'

He staggered from the Mustang, almost collapsing against the wall of the loading dock. Now genuinely scared, Bianca jumped out and ran to him. 'What is it? What's wrong?'

'The dream's not a dream,' he gasped. 'My brother, Michael – he worked for the State Department, he was one of Secretary Easton's staff. He was with her in Islamabad when – when al-Qaeda blew up her convoy. I was waiting to meet him, we were going to catch up . . .' He tried to stand, but reeled again, overpowered by the rush of memories pummelling his mind. 'I heard the explosion – I ran down the street to help, but I found him, I found him . . .' He slumped to his knees, retching.

'Oh God,' whispered Bianca, a hand covering her mouth in dismay as she realised the truth. Adam's recurring 'dream' had been reality, an image so shocking and traumatic that it had resisted the purge of his memory, searing itself into his subconscious.

But now it had been brought back into the open. And Adam was feeling the pain of that moment all over again.

She crouched beside him, a hand on his back. 'Adam, I'm here for you. What can I do to help?'

'Nothing, there's nothing you *can* do,' he replied, stricken. 'Oh, God! It's all my fault!'

'No it isn't,' she said, trying to reassure him. 'You couldn't have—'

'But I did!' He raised his head, tears streaming down his cheeks. 'I really *did* sell the information to Qasid. I gave al-Qaeda the Secretary's route – and I killed my own brother!'

44

A Life Lost

Bianca stared at Adam in disbelief. 'You mean . . . everything you found out from Qasid's persona was true?'

He struggled to regain control over his emotions as he answered. 'Some of it. I was – I was on a CIA-SOCOM joint op. It was meant to be a sting operation. The idea was that I'd pose as a disaffected embassy worker. My grandfather was Syrian, so I looked the part enough for it to be plausible that I'd have local sympathies. They wouldn't have bought it if I'd been blond-haired and blue-eyed like Tony.'

'So what happened?'

'I had to establish myself as a credible source, so I gave them classified information. It was all part of the plan,' he quickly clarified. 'It caused some diplomatic blowback, but it did its job.'

'It got Qasid to trust you.'

'Yes. So the next stage of the plan was to give him information about the Secretary of State's secret visit to Pakistan.'

Her eyes widened. 'You mean your bosses *deliberately* told al-Qaeda about it?'

'No! That's not what happened – not what was supposed to happen,' he replied, correcting himself. 'I was supposed to give them *mis*information. They wouldn't get the real itinerary. They'd get a fake route, one we'd be watching. There were only a couple of places along it where they'd be able to carry out an effective attack – and we'd cover them. When they showed themselves, we'd take them out all at once – captured or killed, either way would be a win.'

'But it didn't work out like that . . .'

'No. And I don't know why.' The anguish returned. 'I did everything I was supposed to. I followed my orders to the letter, gave Qasid the fake information – but somehow they saw through it. I wasn't good enough to convince them. So they found a way to attack the real convoy. And they murdered over a hundred people. They killed the Secretary, and . . . and . . .' His voice cracked. 'And Michael. They killed my brother. *I* killed him – I gave them what they needed to do it!'

He slumped again, head buried in his hands, shaking as he wept uncontrollably. Bianca tried to comfort him. 'I'm sorry, I'm sorry. Is there anything I can do?' She looked back at the car. The door was open, the medical case visible inside. 'I could give you another injection of Neutharsine. It'd wipe the memories, take the pain away—'

'No.' He shook his head. 'I don't want it to go away.'

'Why not?'

'I don't *deserve* it to. It's my fault, it's all my fault . . .' He curled into a tighter ball, shuddering.

'It's *not* your fault,' Bianca insisted. 'You were on a mission – you did exactly what you were ordered to do. There's no way you could have known what would happen. And,' she went on, more forcefully, 'I'm not going to let you torture yourself over it out of some sort of misplaced guilt. I'm getting the injector.' She stood.

Adam's hand snapped up and gripped her wrist. He raised his head. 'Don't,' he said. 'Please. It hurts, but . . . it's all I've got left of him. If you wipe it, some of the memories will still be there, but . . . none of the *feelings*.'

'Then don't just think about what happened in Pakistan,' she pleaded. 'Think about all the other times with him – with your parents. With your dog! Try to remember the good stuff, the times when you were happy.' His hand was still around her arm; she wrapped her other hand over it as she crouched again. 'Get all the other memories while you can – and all the feelings that go with them too. Tell me about them.'

Despair returned to his face. 'I want to, but . . . it's too hard. All I can see is Michael lying in the street. I can't – I can't get back past it.'

'Then go forward,' she said. 'What happened afterwards? How did you join the Persona Project?'

His shivering subsided as he focused on recalling the memories. 'I was taken back to the US embassy. I . . . I had to identify Michael's body. But I couldn't even phone my mom to tell her what had happened, because I was on a classified operation – officially I wasn't even in Pakistan.'

'I'm so sorry. It must have been terrible. I'm sorry.'

He wiped his eyes, and sighed. 'Thank you. After that . . . Harper came to see me.'

'What, at the embassy?'

'Yeah. And . . .' He frowned, puzzled. 'Baxter was with him.'

'What was he doing there?' Bianca asked, surprised.

'I don't know. I didn't speak to him, but he arrived with Harper – I'm certain it was him.'

'What did Harper say to you? That what happened wasn't your fault?'

A pause. 'No. The opposite.'

'What?'

'He blamed me for it. He said . . .' Adam's tendons tightened in a mixture of resurgent guilt, and anger. 'He said I must have done something wrong. I made Qasid and his cell suspicious, so they realised the information I gave them was a trap. He said everything was my fault.'

'That – that *bastard*!' Bianca cried. 'What did you do?'

'I believed him. He's the Director of National Intelligence – the only person above him in the chain of command is the President. If he says you've screwed up . . .'

'But *did* you screw up? Did you do anything wrong?'

'No – not that I can remember. But . . .' He fell silent, deep in thought. 'Qasid *wasn't* suspicious of me. He believed my cover story – and he believed that the information I gave him about the Secretary's visit was genuine. He and al-Rais used it to plan the attack.'

'So you gave them the real itinerary?'

'No, that's just it! I gave them exactly what I was supposed to. I was working with one of the embassy staff – a CIA agent. He gave me the files that I passed to Qasid.'

'Maybe he was the one who screwed up.'

'There's no way of knowing,' said Adam, shaking his head. 'He's dead. He died in the bombing.' Another frown. 'But he wasn't directly involved with the Secretary's visit – he shouldn't have been in the convoy . . .'

'Did you actually read these files?' asked Bianca.

'Yes – I had to, in case Qasid asked me any questions about them. But . . .' He searched his newly reacquired memories. 'I didn't know what the genuine itinerary was going to be – I didn't need to.'

'So if you'd given Qasid the real files rather than the fakes, you'd have had no way to know that, would you?'

'No,' he admitted. 'No, I wouldn't.'

'So it *wasn't* your fault, no matter what Harper told you. God, the more I learn about him, the more I hate him!'

'You're not alone,' said Adam. 'It was just him and me in an interrogation room. But he wasn't interrogating me – it was more like an inquisition. He just kept on and on, hammering it into me that I'd fucked up. And finally I . . .' His face filled with shame. 'I cracked, just broke down in tears in front of him. I couldn't take it any more. The guilt was too much.' His voice fell to a whisper. 'I wanted to die.'

He released his grip on Bianca's wrist, but she kept hold of his hand, squeezing it in sympathy. 'What did Harper do then?'

An almost sarcastic exhalation. 'He offered me a job.'

'*What?*'

'Not right away. First he ordered me back to Tampa – SOCOM headquarters – to be debriefed. In isolation; I wasn't allowed to talk to anybody except the intelligence officers doing the debriefing. I couldn't even call my mother. And the agents were nearly as bad as Harper, just saying over and over again that I'd screwed up the mission. I was practically on suicide watch by the time Harper saw me again.'

'And that's when he told you about the Persona Project?'

'Yeah. He said it was a way that I could . . . God, he actually used the word "atone", for my mistakes and go on serving my country – and have my pain and guilt taken away. And I was hurting so much that I took him up on it. I would have . . .' He cleared his throat, the very feelings that had been erased along with his past returning. 'I'd have done anything to make it stop.'

'So you let them wipe your memory,' Bianca said quietly.

He nodded, saying nothing for several seconds before finally whispering: 'Does that make me a coward?'

'No,' she told him. 'It makes you human.'

A bitter smile. 'Good to know there's *something* human about me. The cyborg secret agent without a past.'

'But you do have a past. Now, I mean. You know who you are again.'

'Only until I fall asleep.'

She gestured towards the PERSONA equipment. 'I can imprint you with it again tomorrow. Since it's your own personality rather than somebody else's, I don't think it'll be nearly as risky. Then we can get out of Washington.'

He shook his head. 'It might make a good TV show, but I don't think the two of us going on the run in a black Mustang'll work out in real life.'

'So what are we going to do?'

He wiped his eyes, then straightened. 'Harper was *determined* to wipe my memory. Even after I'd agreed to join the Persona Project, he kept up the pressure – he even once had me come see him at his house to make sure I wasn't going to back out. But he wasn't doing it to save me from any emotional pain – that's not how he works.'

'He's more the type who likes to *cause* it,' Bianca said.

'Right. So he had a reason for doing it. But what was it? He wanted me to forget what happened in Pakistan – my mission to give false information to al-Qaeda. So if I didn't remember it . . .'

She completed his thought. 'You couldn't tell anyone else. He's trying to cover it up!'

'Looks that way.'

'But why?'

Adam stood, filled with a new sense of purpose. 'There's one way to find out.'

The sun was setting over Washington as the luxurious Cadillac CTS crawled north-west out of central DC along the traffic-clogged Massachusetts Avenue. In its back seat, Harper shouted incredulously into his phone. 'You've *still* got nothing? How the hell is that possible! You've got the entire resources of the US government at your disposal, and you can't find one man?'

Morgan's voice at the other end of the line was tired, beaten down after a long and stressful day. 'With all due respect, Admiral, Adam Gray *is* a highly trained agent in his own right, even without the help of the PERSONA system. If he's gone to ground—'

'Morgan, I'm getting fed up of your excuses,' the older man snapped. 'Gray is your man – and your responsibility. And right now, he's an ongoing threat to national security. Find him!'

He disconnected, then immediately scrolled through his lengthy contacts list to make another call. 'Baxter,' came the reply.

'STS still has nothing, and nor do the cops. What about you?'

'No joy, sir. I've got men watching Gray's apartment and Childs' hotel, but they haven't shown. Nothing on their credit or ATM cards either. Sir,' he added, 'are you sure you don't want to block their cards? They'll need money sooner or later – if we cut them off, it might force them into the open.'

'No, leave them active,' said Harper. 'Gray won't just be hiding – he'll be planning something. If we track any financial transactions they make, it could give us a clue to what that is. We have to assume that Childs gave him back his memories, so now he knows everything up to when the recording was made. He'll be trying to put the pieces together.'

Baxter sounded uncomfortable. 'Could he expose us?'

'No – he doesn't know anything more than he did before, remember. The risk is if he causes the wrong people to start asking questions.'

'Morgan?'

'I can handle him, and anyone else in the intelligence community. It's people outside the chain of command who are the problem.'

'Like Sternberg?'

The mention of his rival's name provoked a scowl. 'Yeah. I've already had demands for updates on the situation from the White House. But even if Gray remembers everything, he still doesn't know anything that directly links us to what happened.'

'I'll make sure he never does, sir. Now that he doesn't have any more inside help, we'll find him. What's happening with Carpenter, by the way?'

'He's locked up at STS. Once Gray's been dealt with, I'll decide what to do with him. It might be that I'll need you to handle him.'

'Understood,' Baxter replied with malevolent meaning. 'I'll call you with any updates, sir.'

'Good.' Harper disconnected again, then sank back into the plush leather, thinking.

It took another fifteen minutes before the Cadillac finally pulled into the driveway of his house. The leafy neighbourhood was both expensive and exclusive; amongst its residents were a number of embassies, as well as the Washington homes of several major politicians. 'Will you be needing the car again tonight, sir?' the driver asked as he opened the rear door for his passenger.

Harper shook his head. 'Pick me up at the usual time tomorrow morning.'

'Yes, sir. I'll see you at six.' The driver waited until Harper had opened the front door of the house, then climbed back into the Cadillac and drove away.

Harper entered the hall, going to the alarm panel and checking that everything was as it should be. The Director of National Intelligence was not granted round-the-clock protection by the Secret Service, but he still required a high degree of security. The fact that he had once summoned Adam Gray to his home – meaning that Gray surely now remembered where he lived – had been weighing on his mind, but requesting a bodyguard would have raised questions about his past connections to the rogue agent.

However, the display told him that the house remained secure. Satisfied, he entered a disarm code. The system chirped in confirmation. He headed down the hall, going into the kitchen—

A savage kick slammed into his stomach, knocking him breathless to the floor.

Despite her loathing of Harper, Bianca couldn't help but wince at the violence of Adam's ambush. 'Don't move,' the agent ordered, drawing a gun – the DNI's own, taken from a cabinet in his study.

Harper clutched at his midsection. 'How – how did you get in here without tripping the alarms?' he rasped, struggling to draw breath.

'It turns out I was trained by the best,' Adam replied. 'Now, I want answers.'

'Go fuck yourself, Gray,' came the snarled reply. 'I'm not going to tell you anything.'

'I don't need you to.' Adam glanced across the kitchen to Bianca, who was setting up the PERSONA on the oak dining table.

Harper saw what she was doing. His eyes widened in alarm, and he tried to get up – only to have Adam's heel crunch down hard on his sternum, forcing him back to the floor. Even through the pain, however, the older man was still defiant. 'You just earned yourself a lifetime ticket to Gitmo,' he gasped. 'That's if you're not executed for treason!'

'Shut up,' Adam snapped. 'I'm going to find out the truth about what happened in Pakistan. That's what you're afraid of, isn't it? That's why you pressured me into joining the Persona Project – so I couldn't tell anyone what I knew.'

'You didn't know shit, Gray,' Harper replied. 'You didn't then, and you still don't. You've got your memory back, sure – but what does it tell you? Only that you fucked up, and got the Secretary killed – and your own brother!'

Adam stared at him for a moment – then bent down and delivered a fierce blow to his forehead with the butt of the gun, drawing blood. Harper let out an agonised cry.

'Jesus!' Bianca shrieked. 'Adam, what are you doing? You'll kill him!'

'If I wanted to kill him, he'd be dead,' he replied coldly. 'Wire us up.'

She took out the skullcaps – then hesitated. 'Adam, are you sure you want to do this? It'll wipe your own memories.'

'I don't want to, but I *need* to. It's the only way to find out what really happened. And we've still got the disk – you can re-imprint them.'

'In theory,' she reminded him.

Harper fought back through the pain, squinting up at his captor as Bianca placed the skullcap on Adam's head. 'You do this, and it's all over for you,' he said. 'The US government will never allow someone to run around with all the DNI's secrets in their head. They'll take you out – both of you.'

'Seems like that's what you were trying to do anyway,' Adam countered. 'Baxter wasn't shooting at my tyres. Did you order him to kill us?'

Harper ignored the question. 'You should think about what you're doing, Dr Childs,' he said instead. 'If you back out now, I'm prepared to be lenient.'

'I suppose you'll just drop the whole matter and I can go home, right?' she said sarcastically.

'Not exactly. But there'll still be a possibility of your seeing merry old England again before you die of old age in a federal prison. You get one chance. I'd recommend that you take it.'

'And I'd recommend that you take your offer and shove it up your arse,' Bianca replied, drawing a quick smile from Adam – and a glare of furious outrage from Harper. 'You've done nothing but bully and intimidate me ever since I arrived in the States. Well, not this time.'

'It's easy to act tough when your boyfriend's pointing a gun at someone, huh? You think you're Bonnie and Clyde? Well, remember how it ended for them. It'll go the same way for you.'

'He's not my boyfriend,' she told him. 'No offence,' she added to Adam as she secured the strap.

'None taken. Okay, *sir*,' he said to Harper as he lifted his foot from the other man's chest, 'get up and sit in that chair over there.'

Harper scowled. 'Like hell I will—'

Before he could even finish speaking, Adam's foot came down again, grinding brutally against Harper's ribcage. The white-haired man tried to scream, but all that came from his mouth was a choked gurgle. 'You know what I've been trained to do,' Adam said in a low, level voice. 'This is nothing. I can make you *beg* to feel this good again.'

'Adam, please,' said Bianca, fearful of how far he might go. 'Don't.'

He reluctantly eased the pressure. Harper drew in a deep, whooping breath. Adam bent down and pressed the gun against the gasping man's head before dragging him across the room and dumping him beside the table.

Bianca hurriedly fitted the second cap as Adam kept the gun pointed at Harper's face. 'Okay, it's ready,' she announced.

Adam took the Neutharsine injector from the medical case. 'Keep him covered,' he said, handing her the gun. 'If he moves, shoot him in the leg.'

'*What?*' she protested, regarding the weapon as if it were toxic. 'I can't do that – I've never used a gun in my life. I've never even held a real one before!'

'It's easy. Hold it with both hands, point, pull the trigger.'

'But I might kill him!'

'Aim for the outside of his thigh. It'll minimise the chances of hitting a major blood vessel. But if he's smart,' he continued, as much for Harper as for her, 'he'll keep very still. Like you said, you've never held a gun before. You might easily rupture the femoral artery – or blow his balls off.' Harper's face twitched at the prospect. 'Just point it at him and count to thirty.'

She was about to object further, but Adam put the injector to his neck and squeezed its trigger. He dropped on to a chair as the Neutharsine swept through his system.

This time, it wasn't just erasing a borrowed persona. It was erasing *him*. Bianca had coaxed memories out of him during the wait for Harper to return home, trying to ensure that at least some of what he had rediscovered would remain . . . but it wasn't enough. The sensation was almost physically painful this time, a lifetime being neurochemically torn away before he had even had the chance to experience it again.

And his *feelings* were being eradicated too. The resurgent pain of the grief and guilt that had almost destroyed him ten months earlier was fading . . . but so too were all the flashes of brightness to which his thoughts of Michael had led him. His brother, father, mother, other family members, friends, lovers – countless moments of happiness, love, pleasure, laughter, warmth, joy . . .

All leeching away, flattening to bland cardboard. Nothing left but second-hand descriptions of emotions, not the emotions themselves.

Michael was gone. He knew he had once had a twin brother, closer to him than anyone else, and that his loss had been shattering. But he could no longer remember *how* his brother's death – or his life – had made him feel. It was merely a fact.

Another emotion rose in him. *Anger.* Not for what he had lost, but that it had been taken from him. Stolen. He opened his eyes, seeing the cause of the anger. Harper.

'Thirty,' said Bianca, the gun still shaking in her hands. She glanced at Adam. 'Are you okay?'

'Yes,' he said, trying to control his feelings. He stood. 'Give me the gun, then inject him.' She passed the weapon back to him with great relief.

'Dr Childs!' said Harper. 'This is your last chance to save yourself. You've got your whole life in front of you – don't throw it away.'

'Adam had his whole life ahead of him too, until you threw away his past,' she responded, taking the other injector from the case. It was loaded with a vial of Hyperthymexine.

The Admiral eyed it with concern. 'Wait – aren't you going to do an examination? What about all the measurements you need to take? If you get the dose wrong, it could kill me!'

Bianca smiled sardonically. 'I've done a whole four transfers from unwilling subjects now; I think I can wing it. Six foot two, about ninety-five kilos, wouldn't you say, Adam?'

'Call it ninety-eight,' Adam said.

She looked Harper up and down, then adjusted the dial. 'Yeah, that's probably about right. Sitting at a desk all day adds a bit extra, no matter how hard you try.'

The DNI was caught between fury and fear as she crouched beside him. 'If you get it wrong and you kill me, it'll be on your hands. You'll be a murderer, Childs! I read your file – you went into medicine to *save* lives. Is that what you want? To be a killer?'

'Like you?' Adam said, voice cold.

'I've never killed anyone in my life!'

'Not yourself. But you gave the orders – to people like me. I want to find out what other orders you gave.' He nodded to Bianca. 'Do it.'

'No!' Harper roared, trying to scramble to his feet. Adam kicked him back down. Before he could recover, Bianca fired the injector into his neck. His yell was abruptly choked off as his entire body convulsed.

Adam quickly returned to the chair as Bianca tapped the keyboard.

ACTIVE: PERSONA TRANSFER IN PROGRESS.

With more nervousness than usual, she flicked her gaze between the flaring colours on the screen and the two men before her. Guessing the drug dose really was a gamble; there was leeway in Albion's overly theatrical calculations, but not so much that some degree of accuracy was unnecessary. She had estimated Harper's height and weight as best she could, but if the dose of Hyperthymexine was too low, it could affect Adam's ability to access the stolen memories.

If it was too high . . . Harper was right. It could kill him.

But the readings on the screen seemed in line with what she had seen with Zykov, al-Rais, the Russian pilot and Qasid. Reassured, slightly, she removed the vial from the injector and replaced it with one of Mnemexal. Adam did not want Harper to retain any memory of their visit – though it would be impossible for him to dismiss the cut on his head. She eyed the tiled kitchen floor. Maybe they could make it seem as if he had slipped and banged his head, as they'd done in Macau . . .

The screen's swirl and scroll slowed. The transfer was almost complete. She gave Harper a cursory check, then ran the final diagnostic before turning her full attention to Adam. 'Did it work?' she asked as he stirred.

He opened his eyes – and regarded her with the same cold,

reptilian intensity as the Admiral himself. A brief chill ran through her. 'Yes,' he said. 'It did.'

'I'll do a memory check anyway—'

'No!' He jumped from his seat. 'We've got to get out of here, right now!'

'Why? What's wrong?'

He pointed across the kitchen. Beside a door leading outside was an alarm panel, a smaller version of the one by the front entrance. 'There's a secondary system. If it's not deactivated within three minutes after the main alarm, it sends an alert to the Secret Service. They'll already be on their way!' He tore off the skullcap, then hurriedly rummaged through Harper's pockets to find his phone. 'Come on!'

'What about the PERSONA?' Bianca cried as he ran for the hall.

'Leave it! There's no time! Bianca, *move!*'

She looked helplessly at the equipment on the table, then turned to follow him – before impulsively stopping to fire the dose of Mnemexal into Harper's bloodstream. Then she tossed the injector on to the table and hurried after Adam.

They reached the front door and rushed outside. The drive was not yet filled with SUVs and sharpshooters, which was something, but Adam knew – Harper knew, from a false alarm when the DNI had once forgotten to deactivate the secondary system – that the Secret Service would only take a few minutes to arrive. He pictured the neighbourhood in his mind as the pair ran down the driveway. There were two roads out of the exclusive little enclave; the Secret Service would be coming from the south-west.

The obvious exit route was north-east, then. But the agents knew that too . . .

They ran through the gates to the Mustang. Adam listened for approaching vehicles. Nothing yet – but they would not be coming with sirens wailing. If there was an intruder in the Director's home, the agents' orders were to capture or kill, not scare away.

He used the override to start the engine. 'Wait, wait!' Bianca gasped as she scrambled into the passenger seat.

Adam revved up, slamming the car into gear and making a rapid getaway – then abruptly jerked the wheel, flinging the Mustang into a 180-degree handbrake turn. Bianca shrieked as she was thrown against the door. He straightened out and headed south-west.

To her surprise, rather than accelerating, he slowed to the legal speed limit. 'What're you doing?' Bianca asked.

'Making us seem less suspicious. Look relaxed.'

'Oh, nothing could be easier!'

Vehicles appeared ahead. A pair of black Lincoln Navigators, red and blue lights pulsing behind their radiator grilles. They rushed towards the Mustang – and whipped past, continuing to Harper's home.

Bianca turned to look out of the rear window. 'Do you think we fooled them?'

'Their first priority is Harper's safety,' said Adam. 'Or rather, his security. They need to make sure he hasn't been compromised.'

'I think they'll work that out pretty quickly once they see what we left on his kitchen table.' She gave him a doleful look. 'Adam, the disk – *your* disk. We left it behind! It's still in the recorder.'

'I know.'

'But it's the only way to get your own memories back.'

'Harper was more important.'

'Is that you saying that, or him?'

He gave her a sharp look. 'What do you mean?'

'It's evidence against Harper. If his persona *made* you leave it behind . . .'

469

'No,' he said firmly. 'I'm in control. If we'd taken another ten seconds to get out of there, the Secret Service would have seen us leave. I had to do it.'

'I hope it was worth it.'

'So do I. But once we're somewhere safe, we'll find out the truth.'

'Sir, are you all right? Admiral Harper!'

Harper struggled back to wakefulness, painfully opening his eyes to see two men in dark suits standing over him. He squinted, making out coiled wires running from behind their ears into their collars. Secret Service agents.

But why were they here?

'What happened?' he grunted. More pain rolled through him as they helped him to sit up. His head was throbbing like the mother of all hangovers, but he hadn't been drinking. He'd been . . .

What *had* he been doing? He remembered being in the car, talking on the phone, and then . . . he was here, lying on his kitchen floor. The orange glow of sunset was still visible outside, so not much time had passed.

He glanced at the panel by the door. A small red light was on, indicating that an alarm had been tripped. That explained the Secret Service's presence – he must have not switched off the secondary system. Had he slipped and hit his head?

'We don't know what happened, sir,' said one of the agents. 'We're doing a sweep of the house and grounds, but haven't found anyone else here. Although . . . we did find something unusual. We don't know what it is, though.'

'What thing?' He touched his forehead, wincing at a sharp pain.

'On the table, sir. Can you stand?'

'Yes, damn it, I can stand.' He shook off their helping hands and struggled upright . . .

And froze, staring at the table.

The PERSONA device told him everything he needed to know.

'You were wearing this when we found you,' said the second agent. He held up the skullcap. 'Sir, do you know what it is?'

'Yes, I do,' Harper growled, using anger to cover his fear.

Adam Gray had got what he came for.

45

The Traitor

The Mustang was parked outside an apartment building on a tree-lined street in Washington's north-western quarter. It attracted no attention from passers-by; indeed, there was an almost identical vehicle a few spaces away. If a search was under way for the black Ford, it had yet to reach this part of the capital.

Adam lowered his window and, after checking that nobody was watching, casually dropped Harper's phone down a drain. 'I hope you got everything you needed from it,' said Bianca.

'I did.' He had memorised a select few of the phone's hundreds of contact numbers. 'Now they won't be able to use it to track us.'

'Is that why you got me to chuck my phone?' He had made Bianca dispose of it earlier in the day. 'Great. Now I'll have to re-download all my apps.'

'I'm glad you've got your priorities straight, Dr Childs.' There was an acerbic disapproval in his voice that immediately reminded her of Harper. 'Sorry,' he added, more normally. 'I meant Bianca.'

'So, you've definitely got Harper's persona in your head. What does he know? What's he hiding?'

'A lot.' Flashes of the Director of National Intelligence's

memories had already come to Adam. Harper had forty years of dark military and political secrets stored in his mind. 'But I'm not going to tell you what.'

She gave him a hurt look. 'Why not?'

'Because they're highly classified, and even though I'm on the run, I'm still an American intelligence officer. I took an oath, and I intend to honour it.' He considered that. 'The spirit of it, at least. The letter, I've kinda broken.'

'Just slightly. So what *can* you tell me? Why did Harper push you so hard to join the Persona Project?'

'Because he knew Kiddrick and Roger could wipe my memory.'

'And why was that so important to him?'

'Because . . .' Adam fell silent as the answers came to him, one thought calling up a memory, which in turn opened up another, and another, a domino effect of conspiracy. He slumped back in the seat. 'My God.'

'What is it?'

'Harper . . .' Adam began, barely able to believe what he was discovering. 'Harper was behind it all.'

'All of what?'

Harper's persona resisted, desperate to keep the secret, but he pushed the words out. 'The bombing in Islamabad – the Secretary of State's assassination. He was behind it!'

Bianca's eyes widened in shock. 'You mean – he's working with al-Qaeda?'

'No, not at all,' Adam replied, shaking his head. 'They're a threat to American interests – he wants them all exterminated. But he's willing to *use* them to help achieve his own goals. Giving Qasid the Secretary's itinerary was supposed to be a set-up so we could take out a major al-Qaeda cell. But Harper was setting *me* up.'

'How?'

'He changed the fake itinerary for the *real* one. He *wanted* them to kill Sandra Easton.'

Bianca was confused. 'Why would he do that? What would he gain from it?'

'Two things. Firstly, she was a political opponent. The Pentagon and the State Department have always been rivals, and Easton had been doing a good job of pushing her agenda with the President. Harper detested her. And secondly, al-Qaeda killing such a high-profile target meant that the War on Terror would be reignited.'

'How could anyone possibly *want* that?'

'They would if it meant expanding their power base. Billions of dollars more for the US intelligence community and the Pentagon – more special-ops units, more drones, more satellites, more surveillance systems. As the Director of National Intelligence, Harper is effectively in charge of all of it. The Secretary's assassination showed that there's still a major threat against America – and he's been given the extra money and manpower to deal with it.'

'You mean . . . Harper did all that just to get more power for *himself?*' said Bianca, incredulous.

'It's not like that at all,' Adam snapped. 'It's about protecting America – by reminding everyone that there are forces out there who will stop at nothing to destroy our way of life! I did what needed to be done to make that threat clear—' He stopped abruptly, realising what he had said. '*Harper* did what had – what he *thought* had to be done.'

'He actually believes that paranoid crap?'

'It's not crap,' he said sharply. 'And that's not Harper talking, that's me. I've been in the heads of these people – like al-Rais. He doesn't just want to destroy America, he wants to tear down the whole of Western civilisation and replace it with an Islamic theocracy. His ultimate goal is basically the Taliban as a model for global government. Is that something you want?'

'Of course it's not,' she replied. 'But al-Qaeda wouldn't have been able to kill the Secretary if Harper hadn't given them the information in the first place. He was using you as an agent provocateur!'

He shook his head again, more sadly. 'And I didn't even know it.'

'If you didn't know, why did he still want to wipe your memory? You couldn't have been a threat to him.'

'Risk minimisation,' he said, following another rippling chain of memories. 'I'd read the documents I gave to Qasid. Harper thought there was a chance I might put two and two together and realise they were real, not fakes. He couldn't allow that.'

'Not to be morbid, but if he was willing to go that far to get what he wanted, why didn't he just have you killed?'

A cold shiver ran down Adam's spine. 'He considered it. That's why John Baxter was in Pakistan. If I realised the truth, he'd been ordered to kill me.'

'Baxter?' gasped Bianca. 'You mean – all the time he was working with you at STS, he was really keeping watch on you?'

'Yes. And he was still under the same orders, even after my memory was erased. If I remembered what had happened, he'd take me out. Quietly, though – he would have made it look like an accident.' Another memory made his eyebrows rise in dismay. 'That's what happened to the CIA officer I was working with in Pakistan! He *didn't* die in the bombing. He worked it out – but made the mistake of telling Harper directly. Baxter killed him.'

'It's a good thing you didn't work it out at the time, then.'

'I should have done. I had all the information, but . . . I wasn't thinking straight.'

'You can't blame yourself for that.'

'I suppose not.' He stared morosely through the windscreen. 'You know what's funny? In a twisted way, I mean. Harper actually thought that my *not* figuring it out made me the perfect candidate to replace Tony. One of Kiddrick's theories about why Tony had his breakdown was that he was too strong-willed, that he was subconsciously resisting the persona imprints. But I was a good soldier who followed orders and didn't ask questions . . . and I was broken. I *wanted* to forget who I was.'

An image from Harper's mind came to him, as disconcerting as the similar one from Qasid's memories: himself, as seen through the eyes of another. But the quiet confidence of the agent on a mission was gone. This Adam Gray was a shattered wreck, crippled by loss and guilt. The only thing keeping him from a complete breakdown was his sense of duty.

And Harper had taken advantage, filled with contempt for the younger man's emotional weakness even as he saw the potential to make use of it. *Persona . . . That puffed-up little prick Kiddrick claimed he could wipe a man's mind, and condition him not to think about it. Two birds with one stone – reactivate a promising project, and make sure that Gray never puts the pieces together. I could assign Baxter to keep an eye on him . . .*

So events had been set in motion. Harper had 'persuaded' Adam to join STS, and Kiddrick and Albion had erased his memories – without ever being told the complete story, just enough to convince them that his mental injuries had been sustained on a mission of the highest secrecy, and that he should never be allowed to remember it. For his own emotional protection.

The procedure had worked. More effectively than either doctor expected. As they had explained to Harper, the trauma they were trying to delete was intimately linked to countless other memories . . . and the process had wiped them all away. Albion was uneasy about it, but Kiddrick had been positively crowing. Their new agent was an empty vessel, perfectly primed to take on the other personas that would allow him to complete his missions.

And I was safe . . . except that idiot Kiddrick had made a recording of Gray's original persona without telling me!

'Adam?' He blinked as Bianca gently touched his arm, emerging from the Admiral's thoughts back into the real world.

'Yeah, I'm here, I'm fine. I was just . . . just seeing things from Harper's side.'

She bit her lip. 'He's not trying to take control, is he?'

He knew she was worried about what had happened in the Cube, when his despair had almost allowed Qasid's persona to overcome him. 'No. Absolutely not. I won't let him. That bastard *used* me. He took literally everything from me and tried to turn me into some kind of – clockwork soldier.' Bitterness and anger coloured his words. 'Wind me up and watch me go.'

'Well, nobody's telling you what to do now. Except yourself. So what *are* you going to do?'

His response was immediate. 'I'm going to bring that son of a bitch down. Tell people what he did – and make him pay for it.'

'How?'

'I don't know yet.' A cold smile. 'But he does.'

The answer was already in his mind. All he had to do to find it was think. *What is Gordon Harper's worst fear? How can he be exposed?*

Harper knew. And now, despite his persona's attempts to deny him, Adam did too.

He sat in silence for a long moment, absorbing the flood of information and images and feelings. A name and face jumped out: Alan Sternberg, the National Security Adviser. A rival – and a threat. The nightmare scenario for Harper was Sternberg discovering the truth about the events in Pakistan. There would be no bargaining, no deals, no quiet cover-ups. Sternberg would destroy him without hesitation if he ever had the opportunity.

Was there a way to give him that opportunity?

Yes.

Adam felt Harper rage in protest inside him, but he pushed the DNI's fury down and started the car. 'Where are we going?' Bianca asked.

He smiled. 'A hardware store.'

She was surprised. 'Why?'

The smile widened. 'To solve Levon's puzzle.'

'Sir,' said one of the Secret Service agents, listening to a message through his earpiece. 'A Mr Baxter just arrived. He says you asked to see him.'

'Let him in,' Harper ordered. He irritably waved away another agent still fussing about him. The cut on his forehead had been bandaged and he had been given some painkillers, but refused to take them, wanting to keep his mind sharp.

Gray knew everything he did. That meant Gray also knew how to expose him. Even though he had done what he did solely to protect America's interests, he knew that the snivelling left-wing parasites infesting Washington would not accept that as justification. If they learned about it, they would twist it in the media to bring him down in a howling witch-hunt of a kind not seen since the trial of Oliver North. He would be accused of treason; every past decision second-guessed, every black operation under his watch dragged into the light. A disaster for American intelligence – no, a disaster for *America*.

As a patriot, he would do whatever it took to stop that from happening.

At the back of his mind for the past ten months had been the concern that something might emerge that could destroy him. The risk was minimal – he had taken every possible precaution, from the deletion of incriminating files at the small end of the scale all the way up to Gray's mind-wipe and the elimination of his CIA contact in Islamabad. But there were some things that even the Director of National Intelligence could not simply erase from the record.

One of those was foremost in his thoughts right now – which meant, he was sure, that it was also foremost in Gray's. It would not be easy for the rogue agent to obtain. He had seen the facility for himself; security through obscurity was backed up by security through physical barriers – and beyond them, physical force. But if anyone could do it . . .

'Admiral!' A familiar voice caught his attention. He looked round, seeing Baxter hurrying into the kitchen. 'Are you okay?'

'Yes, yes,' Harper replied with irritation. He addressed the Secret Service agents. 'All right! The situation's under control. Go back to your duties.'

'Are you sure, sir?' the first agent asked. 'If there's been a security breach, we should—'

'You've got your orders, agent,' he snapped. 'Is my car here yet?' After summoning Baxter, he had called back his chauffeur.

'Yes, sir. It just got here.'

'Good. Take its driver to wherever he needs to be. Mr Baxter will handle everything from now on.'

The agents were clearly unhappy about surrendering authority, but had little choice except to follow his orders. They filed out.

Baxter regarded the PERSONA equipment with grim dismay. 'Did Gray use the machine on you?'

'I don't know – I don't remember,' Harper replied. 'Which means I have to assume that he *did*, and then wiped my memory.'

'Son of a bitch,' the former Marine muttered. He went to the table, staring at the gear upon it . . . then with a snarl threw the PERSONA device to the hard floor. The screen broke loose and skittered across the tiles. He was about to do the same to the recorder unit – then his eyes widened as he saw what was inside. 'Sir – Gray's disk! It's still in the recorder.' He pulled out the memory module and held it up.

'Why would he leave it behind?' Harper wondered, before the answer came to him. Of course – as soon as Gray had been imprinted with his memories, he knew that the secondary alarm hadn't been deactivated and had to make a hurried departure before the Secret Service arrived. So he had been forced to abandon something vital . . . 'Destroy it.' Baxter gave him a look of puzzlement. 'Smash it! Now!'

Baxter dropped the disk to the floor and stamped on it, grinding it under his heel. The plastic shell cracked and split, exposing densely packed microcircuitry. Another blow and it broke in half, silicon splinters scattering.

Harper regarded the destruction, satisfied. 'There are only two pieces of evidence against me, and that was one of them. As for the other one . . . come on. We need to get to Suitland.'

He marched for the door, Baxter hurrying to catch up. 'Why?'

'Because,' said Harper, grim-faced, 'there's a federal secure data storage facility there. It's the only place Gray can get proof about what happened in Pakistan.'

Shock crossed Baxter's craggy face. 'You told me all the files had been destroyed!'

'They have. But there's something that's impossible to delete – the activity logs.' Seeing Baxter's blank look, he explained: 'Every time a file is created, accessed, edited or deleted on the USIC network, the system notes it in a log – along with the identity of the person who did it, and the terminal they used. It's a security measure: if the same login is used in two different locations at the same time, say, the computer raises an alarm.'

'So how does that prove anything?'

'Because,' growled Harper, 'it shows that I personally accessed and altered the file that was given to Gray to pass on to al-Qaeda – Easton's itinerary.'

They exited the house. Baxter's black Suburban was parked nearby, blue lights flashing. Behind it was the empty Cadillac. 'But the actual file was deleted, wasn't it?' said Baxter.

'It doesn't matter. The logs establish a chain of contact between me and Gray immediately prior to his mission in Islamabad. If Gray gets hold of them and passes them on to the wrong person, we're finished. Even without the files, the logs provide enough evidence to start an investigation. And there are plenty of hard-nosed little bastards who've been waiting for the chance to attack me.'

'People like Sternberg?'

'He's top of the list, yes.' Harper spotted someone in the SUV. 'Who's your driver?'

'Reed.'

'Is he trustworthy?'

'You can trust all my men, sir.'

'Good. You drive my car, and tell him to clear the way for us. Oh, and I need a phone.' Baxter went to the Suburban and issued instructions, returning with Reed's cell phone and giving it to Harper. The two men got into the Cadillac, the DNI taking the back seat. The vehicles set off. 'Are your teams still in the field?'

'Yes, sir.'

'Get them there too. I want Gray and Childs dead before the cops or anyone else get involved.'

'On it.' Baxter took out his phone, and was about to dial a number when it rang. He answered it. 'Baxter. Yes? Okay, hold on. The Admiral's here with me.' He put it on speaker. 'Sir, you should hear this.'

'We got a hit on Dr Childs' credit card,' said the man at the other end of the line. 'It was used at a hardware superstore in Brentwood.'

'How long ago?' Harper demanded. Brentwood was in eastern DC, some five miles north-west of Suitland. If Gray was going there, he had a considerable head start.

'About fifteen minutes.'

'Why wasn't I told immediately?' asked Baxter.

'You ordered us to get a list of anything Dr Childs or Agent Gray bought. The manager was uncooperative and wouldn't give it to us without a warrant. We had to wait for a FISC judge to issue one.'

'Well?' said Harper impatiently. 'What did they buy?'

'I've got the list here, sir. It's, uh . . . odd.'

'Just read it out!'

'Yes, sir. The card was used to buy a compressed air cylinder, a pressure relief valve, an inner tube, a six-foot length of PVC pipe, a hundred feet of rope, a light fitting, five pounds of lead shot, some air hose, a bicycle pump, a roll of duct tape and, ah . . . two footballs.'

Harper and Baxter exchanged bewildered looks in the mirror. 'Footballs?' the latter asked.

'Yes, sir. American footballs, not soccer.'

'Okay,' said Harper in acknowledgement. 'If there's any further activity on their cards, inform us immediately.'

'*Footballs?*' echoed Baxter as he closed the line. 'What the hell do they want with two footballs?'

46

Information Retrieval

Suitland, Maryland

Adam surveyed the large, windowless building from the rooftop of its darkened neighbour. The blocky structure's sole relief from anonymity was an unassuming plaque reading WALTER J. GORMAN FEDERAL DATA REPOSITORY; beyond that, the only signage consisted of warnings against trespass. The presence of a US government facility here would draw no comment – the town of Suitland, a short distance outside the south-eastern boundary of the District of Columbia, was home to several minor agencies including the Census Bureau, and not far from the sprawling Andrews Air Force Base.

Even by bureaucratic standards, he knew, the Gorman Building was dull. It was in essence a glorified digital boxroom, one of several around the country built to store tape and disk backups of the gigabytes of information churned out by the American governmental machine every day. Most of the data it contained was humdrum, barely of interest even to the people who created it.

But one file had now become extremely important.

'So how are we supposed to get in there?' said Bianca. A high fence topped with razor wire surrounded the entire site. She put down a bag containing some of the items the pair had bought. 'And what does Levon's puzzle have to do with anything?'

'You'll see,' Adam replied, making mental calculations. The gap between the two rooftops was about sixty feet over the Gorman Building's parking lot, but he needed something secure on the far side . . .

There was a cluster of boxy air-conditioning units set back from the roof's edge. He squinted, trying to make out more detail in the low spill of light from the street lamps. Lines of shadow became visible: a slatted grille covering an air inlet.

'Pass me the duct tape,' he said, picking up the yellow plastic pipe and propping it on his rooftop's air-con ductwork. As Bianca opened the bag, he lined the pipe up with the distant grille. Harper had many years earlier served as a gunnery officer aboard a destroyer; Adam now used that experience to bolster his own military training. It was a straightforward matter of judging distance and angles of arc to hit the target – the complicating factor was the nature of his 'gun'.

Bianca watched as he set to work, securing the pipe in position with the strong adhesive binding before starting to connect together the cylinder of compressed air, the deflated inner tube and the valve with lengths of hose and more tape. 'Oh, I get it!' she exclaimed as the purpose of the random assemblage suddenly became clear. 'You're making a sort of air cannon.'

'That's right. It fills the inner tube with compressed air from the tank, then when it reaches a certain pressure the relief valve,' he tapped the brass device, 'blows and lets it all out in one go.'

'Firing the footballs?'

'Yeah. I'll put the lead shot in them to give them some weight, then use the pump to inflate them just enough to fill the pipe without sticking in it. Then I attach the rope and the grappling hook.'

'The *hideous* grappling hook,' said Bianca, eyeing the ornate three-armed chandelier. 'Will it be strong enough?'

'It'll do what I need it to do,' he assured her. 'When the pressure valve opens, it'll shoot the ball across to the other roof, and pull the rope with it.'

'Then you climb across to the roof?'

'I climb across, yeah.' His oddly smug smile told her that there was more to his plan than he was going to tell her for now. 'Go back to the car. We'll need to move fast.'

'Do you know what you're looking for inside?'

'More or less. There's a WORM disk—'

'A what?'

'WORM – Write Once, Read Many. Like a bigger and more durable recordable CD. It's got the logs that prove Harper switched the fake itinerary for the real one.'

Bianca looked across at the Gorman Building. 'When you say "more or less" . . . does that mean you don't know exactly where it is? How many disks do they have in there?'

'A couple of million.' Her face fell. 'Don't worry – Harper knows how to get it.'

'I hope they haven't changed the filing system,' she said. 'Okay, I'll be in the car. How long will you be?'

'I don't know. Keep watch – you'll know what to do when you see me.' He turned back to his improvised cannon as Bianca reluctantly headed for the ladder.

Harper's eyes suddenly flicked wide open. 'An air cannon.'

'Sir?' said Baxter.

'That's what he's making, it has to be! The pipe's the barrel –

and the football's like the cork in a popgun.' There was a laptop in the Cadillac's rear; Harper opened it.

'Why would he need to build an air cannon?'

'To fire the rope he bought over the perimeter fence, would be my guess.' He hurriedly tapped at the keyboard, logging on to the secure USIC network via the car's wireless link and bringing up a global map of high-resolution satellite imagery. He typed in the address of the Gorman Building, then waited for the results to download. 'Yeah,' he said when the picture appeared. 'If he got on to the roof of the next building, he could easily shoot a line over from there. How far out are your teams?'

'Spence's team are right behind us. Fallon's is a few minutes away.'

'Tell Spence's unit to send someone up to check the neigh-bouring roof. Childs might be waiting for him there. Everyone else searches the repository.' Baxter nodded and took out his phone, while the Admiral called his office on Reed's. Security checks completed, he barked: 'I need to talk to whoever's in charge at the federal data repository in Suitland. It's a matter of extreme urgency.' He waited impatiently for the connection to be made.

Finally, he heard a timorous voice. 'Hello?'

'This is Admiral Gordon Harper, Director of National Intelligence,' Harper announced imperiously. 'Who am I talking to?'

'I'm, ah, I'm Jerome Butterworth, sir. Night-shift duty officer at the Walter J. Gorman facility. What can I do for you, sir?'

'What you can do, Butterworth, is put your facility on full security alert, right now. Someone is trying to steal classified data from your repository – he may be there already. He'll probably be trying to gain entry via the roof.' When there was no immediate response, he barked: '*Now*, Butterworth!'

'Uh, yes, sir!' The official's voice was muffled as he covered the phone with one hand to shout orders. An alarm bell rang in the background. 'We've gone to full alert, sir. I've put the facility on lockdown.'

'Good. I'm on my way to you with a tac team. The intruder is to be considered armed and *extremely* dangerous. If your people find him, I want them to contain him until I arrive. Do not attempt to engage him – just make sure that he doesn't get away.'

'Understood, sir,' said Butterworth nervously.

Harper disconnected and pocketed the phone. Baxter finished issuing instructions to the other members of his team. 'We're all set, sir.'

'Good.' Harper sat back, watching other cars pull out of the way as the Cadillac sped towards Suitland behind the Suburban, the SUV's lights flashing and siren blaring.

Bianca waited anxiously, checking her watch for the third time in under a minute. Something had just happened at the Gorman Building, more exterior lights snapping on and an alarm ringing. Had Adam been caught? She didn't know. From the Mustang's position a little way down the street from the offices, she hadn't even been able to see him make the crossing.

How long should she wait for him? He'd seemed confident that he could get what he needed, but confidence alone was no guarantor of success. At what point should she cut and run? Ten minutes? Five?

Maybe sooner than that. The wail of an approaching siren reached her. She hunched lower and peered down the road. A large SUV came into view, horn blaring as it bullied its way through traffic. An expensive-looking car was right behind it. They reached the government facility's main entrance and squealed to a halt at the gates. The driver waved furiously for the guard inside the little gatehouse to open the barrier. It swung upwards, and the vehicles surged through to stop at the doors of the building.

A man in a shirt and tie hurried out to meet the occupants as they emerged. Even at a distance through the chain-link fence, she recognised two of them: Harper and Baxter. The latter was carrying a sub-machine gun, as was the SUV's driver.

'Oh God, Adam,' she whispered as they hurried inside. Another siren sounded in the distance, drawing nearer. 'Get out of there . . .'

'The man trying to break in here is after one specific disk,' Harper told Butterworth as they marched into the building. 'I want it located and taken to safety before he can get it.'

The duty officer, a pudgy, balding man in his late forties, was sweating at the unexpected turn of events. 'Couldn't we just, uh, put all our security around the section where the disk's stored?'

Harper glared at him. 'This isn't some crack-addict burglar we're talking about, Butterworth! You've got no idea what this man is capable of. I'm not willing to take any chances with people's lives. Get me that disk, right now.'

'Yes, yes. Right away, sir.' They reached Butterworth's office. 'Do you know its ID number?'

'No, but if I give you the criteria, how long will it take you to locate it?'

'Everything's fully archived on the system, sir.' He gestured at a computer. 'If you put in the details, it should find it immediately.'

Harper sat at the terminal. Baxter was still on his phone. 'Spence's team is here,' he reported.

Bianca watched as a second Suburban powered towards the gates . . .

And drove past them.

The blood froze in her heart. They were coming for her! She grabbed the override, about to start the engine—

The Suburban braked hard, stopping outside the offices. Two men dressed in black combat gear and carrying sub-machine guns jumped out and ran towards the building. The SUV reversed, slewing around and powering back to the repository.

Her relief that the men weren't coming for her was immediately overcome by alarm. The pair rounded the rear of the offices and started to climb the ladder to the roof.

Adam's escape route was cut off.

'The first team is on site,' Baxter told Harper as he listened to his phone. 'Two men are going up to the roof – Spence just entered the facility's grounds.'

Harper finished entering the information into the computer. 'Here,' he said, jabbing a finger at the results. 'Is that enough to find the disk?'

Butterworth looked over his shoulder. 'Yes, sir.'

'Good. Then do it!' As Butterworth gave orders to a subordinate, Harper went to Baxter. 'Have they found Gray? Or Childs?'

'No sign yet, but—'

He broke off as a new alarm, a shrill, rapid bleeping, sounded. 'My God!' gasped Butterworth, rushing back to the computer. 'That's – that's the internal alarm. Someone's broken into the building!'

Baxter brought up his gun. 'Where?'

'It looks like, ah . . .' He brought up a schematic of the building, a small area flashing red. 'You were right, Admiral – he's on the roof! One of the vent covers for the HVAC system has been opened. He must be trying to get in through the ducts.'

'Do you know where he'll come out?' said Harper.

Butterworth clicked through to another layer of the schematic, exposing the rectilinear mazework of the inner structure. 'Yes! The only place he can get out is in section K-6.'

Baxter looked round as Spence and another man ran into the room, accompanied by one of the Gorman Building's security personnel. 'With me,' he ordered.

'Take them to K-6,' Butterworth told the guard. 'Quick!' The group of armed men hurried out.

Harper's phone rang. 'Yes?'

'Sir, this is Morrow – Mr Baxter told me to call you,' came the reply. 'I'm on the roof of the next building.'

'Have you found Childs?' demanded Harper. 'Tell me what you can see!'

The two men moved across the rooftop, the tactical lights mounted on their weapons illuminating the dark crannies amongst its ventilation ductwork with pitiless intensity. There was no sign of their target – but they knew he had been there. 'There's a long piece of pipe pointing at the next building,' said Morrow into his headset, shining his beam upon the bizarre apparatus. 'It's hooked up to a gas cylinder of some kind – it's still hissing.' He cautiously prodded the half-inflated inner tube with the muzzle of his gun. Nothing happened.

'There's a rope here,' said his companion, moving past him and aiming his light out across the gap between the buildings. A line of blue nylon ran between them.

'Sir, he's got across to the federal facility.' Both men swept the other roof with their flashlights, but spotted no signs of life. 'He must be inside – we can't see him.'

'What about Childs?' asked Harper. 'Is she up there?'

'No, sir.'

★ ★ ★

'Damn it!' Harper growled. 'All right, keep watch in case he tries to get out that way.' Capturing the Englishwoman would have given him considerable leverage over Gray – although, it occurred to him, if the agent really was thinking like him, would he sacrifice her to achieve his objective?

His musing was interrupted as Butterworth's subordinate ran back into the office. 'I've got the disk, sir,' he gasped.

'Give it to me.' Harper all but snatched it from the man's hand. It was nothing special to look at, a mirror-like optical disk in a protective transparent plastic caddy. A label bore a barcode and a string of numbers. 'Are you absolutely sure this is the right one?'

Butterworth checked the digits against the search results. 'Yes, sir. This is it.'

Harper attempted to conceal his relief. 'Good. I'm taking this to a secure location. And remember,' he added, raising a threatening finger, 'all of this is a matter of national security and is strictly classified. Nobody in this facility is to discuss it without first receiving written authorisation from my office. Is that understood?'

'Yes, Admiral,' said Butterworth, nodding repeatedly.

'Good. Liaise with Mr Baxter – he'll give you further instructions once the situation has been dealt with.' He turned and without another word strode from the office, heading back to the main entrance.

The disk felt bizarrely heavy in his hand. He had to fight the temptation to smash it there and then. That would lead to unwelcome questions, suspicion.

But he already had a plan. He would return to his home, where a fire – some booby trap set by the intruders, or so it would seem – would destroy it. Again, there would be questions, but they would be much easier to handle. In this scenario, he was the *victim*, attacked by a paranoid and unbalanced rogue agent in his own home. The Persona Project would take the blame for the mental breakdown of its operative. A shame to lose a program that had proved its worth as an intelligence-gathering asset, but it was a price he was more than willing to pay.

Harper emerged into the night air and got into the Cadillac. He put the disk on the passenger seat, then started the engine.

A small, gloating smile curled his lips as he set off. He had the logs – and all Gray would find waiting for him when he emerged from the ducts were bullets.

'It's just down here,' said the guard, leading the way as Baxter and his men hurried through the storage facility. The building was divided into blocks allocated to different agencies of the US government, grids of tall shelving racks holding countless disks and tapes. 'On the right.'

Baxter took the lead, raising his MP5. Spence and the others followed suit. 'Okay, we'll handle this,' he told the guard. 'You stay back.' The man obeyed, with evident relief. Baxter rounded the corner, seeing a door ahead marked with a small sign: K-6.

'Cover me,' he said. He pressed his back against the wall beside the door and took hold of the handle as his men aimed their weapons. 'In three, two . . .'

He silently mouthed *one*, then threw open the door.

There was nobody beyond.

Baxter frowned, surveying the room with suspicion. Ranks of gunmetal-grey filing cabinets lined the walls, not enough space for anyone to hide behind them. Giving his men another non-verbal signal, he darted through the entrance and whipped round, finger on the trigger in case his target was lurking behind the door.

No one there.

That only left . . .

'The vent,' he whispered as his team entered, looking up at the ceiling. There was a large grille in its centre. One corner, he realised, was not quite flush, hanging down from the frame. Something was putting weight on it from above.

Gray. It had to be. If he had left the room, he would have been seen on the CCTV cameras.

He gestured to Spence: *open it.*

Spence clambered up on to the cabinets. He reached across and hooked his fingertips over the grille's edge. All the guns were fixed on the vent.

Baxter nodded. Spence pulled—

The grille swung down. Something dropped from the opening and hit the floor with a muffled thud. Shock raced through Baxter: *a grenade!*

But it didn't explode.

It wasn't a grenade. It was . . .

'A football?' said Spence, bewildered.

Baxter signalled for his men to check the vent. They shone their tactical lights into the darkness above, seeing nothing but the bare metal sides of the duct. He crouched and picked up the football. It was only partially inflated, sagging limply in his hands, but was far heavier than he'd expected. He shook it, hearing something rattling dully about inside.

Lead shot, he remembered. Gray and Childs had bought lead shot. Now he knew what they had used it for: to add weight to the football. But *why?*

'Morrow!' he said into his headset. 'Gray's not here – are you *sure* he's not on the roof?'

The two men atop the offices swept their powerful flashlight beams over the Gorman Building's wide, flat rooftop. All they saw was machinery and ductwork. 'No sight of him, sir,' said Morrow.

The frustration in his commander's voice was clear. 'He's not inside the building either. Tell me *exactly* what you see up there.'

Morrow gave the now swollen inner tube a brief glance before turning his attention to the rest of the apparatus. 'Okay, there's a rope tied to the air-con system on this side, and it goes all the way over to the building you're in. The other end . . .' He fixed his light on one particular spot, catching something in the beam. 'There's what looks like a football attached to the end of the rope, and a hook . . .'

His companion added his own light to the search. 'That vent's broken,' he said, illuminating an opening in the ductwork on the far side of the gap. A slatted grille was bent back as if it had taken a powerful kick.

'He must have gone in through the vent, but—'

Whump!

A sudden detonation made them both jump. 'Jesus!' yelped Morrow, spinning and bringing his gun up before realising what had happened.

'Morrow!' shouted Baxter. 'What happened? Report!'

'Sir, the air cannon – it just fired again.'

'What? How?'

'The gas cylinder was still filling a big inner tube. There's a valve taped to it – it must have released when it got to a certain pressure. Like a time-delay system. But there wasn't anything in the pipe, so the air just blew out through it.'

Baxter was silent, trying to make sense of what had happened. Gray had used the first football to fire a rope across the gap. But why would he need to shoot a second one?

He looked at the flaccid leather ovoid in his hand. It was brand new, but the leather at one end was scuffed and torn, scratches on it looking as if they had been made by knives.

No, not knives – but still something metal and sharp-edged . . .

The vent cover on the roof. Its grille would be made of thin sheet steel, intended only to keep out the weather and birds, not to withstand a projectile weighing close to three pounds fired at it with great force.

Gray had rigged the cannon to hit the vent – and set off the alarm. *Why*, though? And where was he? If he hadn't come down the duct, then . . .

The answer hit him like a truck. 'Shit!' he cried. 'This whole thing – it's a *decoy*! It's all some goddamn *Mission: Impossible* crap! Gray never came in here at all!'

Spence jumped down from the cabinets. 'Then where is he?'

Baxter already had a horrible suspicion. He took out his phone. 'What's your number?' he asked Reed. 'Quick, your cell number! I need to reach the Admiral, now!'

47

End Run

Harper turned at a junction, heading back towards Washington. Given favourable traffic, if he took the Suitland Parkway into DC he would reach his home in around twenty-five minutes. Then he could destroy the WORM disk, and the only piece of evidence linking him to the death of Sandra Easton would be gone.

Lights flashed in his mirrors, some impatient idiot in a muscle car wanting to get past. Despite being in a hurry, he allowed the black car to overtake. The last thing he needed was for a highway cop to pull him over for speeding.

The Mustang powered past with a V8 snarl – then cut back in right ahead of him, slowing to the legal limit. 'I gave you the road, asshole,' Harper muttered. He was about to give the other driver a piece of his mind with the horn when Reed's phone rang. He fumbled in his pocket, taking it out—

'Don't answer it,' said a voice right behind him. 'It's dangerous to use the phone while you're driving.'

A shape rose up in the rear-view mirror. 'Gray!'

'Yeah.' Adam pushed the gun he had taken from the Admiral's house against its owner's head. 'Put it down and pull over.'

Harper reluctantly tossed the phone on to the passenger seat beside the disk. He brought the Cadillac to the kerb. The Mustang ahead also stopped, then backed up, its reversing lights turning Adam's reflection a demonic red. 'So are you going to kill me?'

'No. I just want the disk.'

'What for? Blackmail?'

'Justice.'

Harper made a sarcastic sound. 'There's no such thing in this world.'

'I know you think that – but I also know that not everybody else does. So maybe there's hope for us all yet. Get out. Slowly.'

The phone's trill stopped. Harper glowered over his shoulder at Adam, then opened the door.

'Thank God,' said Bianca as she saw Adam emerge from the CTS. He waved, and she got out and ran to him. 'It's a good job I saw you get into this thing, otherwise I'd still be sitting there waiting for you.'

'I made sure you'd see me,' he replied. He had never even reached the Gorman Building's roof, dropping from the rope once he was over the fence and sneaking through the parking lot. 'I just had to make sure the guards didn't.'

'Why didn't you tell me you were going to hide in his car?' She nervously regarded Harper, who stared back in menacing silence.

'Because I didn't know how I was going to play things until they actually happened. Here, hold the gun. Keep him covered.'

She took the pistol. 'But you knew he'd get the disk.'

Adam leaned into the car to collect the item in question, and the phone. 'It was the only thing connecting him to what happened in Islamabad – and I knew he'd want to destroy it, but in some deniable way that wouldn't incriminate him. A house fire, maybe?' he asked Harper, who couldn't conceal his shock at being second-guessed. 'Yeah, I thought it would be something like that.'

'If you really thought like me, you'd have killed me by now,' the DNI rumbled.

Adam fixed him with an icy look. 'I've considered it. Believe me. The only reason you're still alive is that just because I *can* think like you doesn't mean that I *have* to.' He pocketed the phone and disk, then turned back to Bianca. 'I knew I wouldn't be able to go in there and get it myself. I know all his passwords and security codes, but there's no way I'd be able to pass myself off as him.'

'So you got him to get it for you.' She realised what he had meant earlier. 'That's the solution to Levon's puzzle, isn't it? There's no way you can get the diamond out of the vault yourself – so you mug the owner after he's collected it!'

'That's right. Is the override still in the car?'

'Yes.'

'Good. Okay, I've got to go.' He marched past her towards the Mustang.

'What? Adam, wait!' she cried, not daring to take her eyes off Harper. 'Where are you going?'

'I've got to get the disk to someone who can use it to bring this son of a bitch down.'

'Why can't I come with you?'

'Because that phone call was probably Baxter trying to warn him that I threw them a decoy at the repository. I need you to make sure that Harper doesn't tell anyone where I'm going.'

'But you didn't tell him.'

'He knows.' Adam opened the Mustang's door. 'Keep him here for fifteen minutes, then take the car and go.'

'Why fifteen minutes? What happens then?'

'If I haven't delivered the disk by then, I never will. They'll have stopped me.' He started to get into the car – then hesitated. 'Bianca?'

'What?'

He jogged back to her and, to her surprise, kissed her cheek. 'Thank you.'

'For what?'

'For everything. If it hadn't been for you, I wouldn't have known the truth about what happened in Pakistan – or who I really am.'

'And if it hadn't been for me, we wouldn't be on the run from a bunch of people trying to kill us,' she pointed out.

'The glass is always half empty for you Brits, isn't it?' He became more serious. 'I hope I see you again.' With that, he ran back to the car and jumped in, setting off with a skirl of tyres. The throaty roar of its engine quickly faded as it headed for the Parkway.

'You won't,' said Harper. 'He won't make it to where he's going. And you . . . you'll be spending the rest of your life in prison. I guarantee that, Dr Childs.'

'Shut up,' she said, jabbing the gun at him. 'Get over by the car and sit down.'

He didn't move. 'And if I don't?'

'Then I'll shoot you.'

'No. You won't.' He stepped closer to her; only by a foot, but enough to make a point. 'I don't need the PERSONA machine to know how people think. It's how I got to where I am. I know people – and I know you. You're a *carer*, Dr Childs.' The word sounded almost like an insult. 'Your career, helping Gray – you do what you do because you care about other people, on an individual level.'

'Whereas you don't care about anyone except yourself.'

He shook his head firmly. 'I care about people – as in, *we the people of the United States*. My duty is to protect them and their country. And I'll do whatever's necessary to achieve that.'

'Including murder? You let your own Secretary of State be assassinated. In fact, you gave information to terrorists to make sure it happened! You're not some great patriot – you're a criminal and a traitor.' Her face creased with disgust. 'I'm normally opposed to the death penalty, but in your case I'll make an exception. I hope they hang you.'

His eyes flicked briefly away from Bianca towards something in the distance, then locked back on to her with a newly calculating intensity. She didn't miss the change in his attitude, but was unsure how to respond. Was there really something coming along the road behind her – or was it just an attempt at distraction?

She edged away from him, taking a quick look. A vehicle was approaching. She hurriedly tried to shield the gun from the driver's sight with her body.

'You really don't have a clue what you're doing, do you?' said Harper, voice oozing condescension. 'You don't even know how to hold a gun properly.'

'I know which end the bullets come out of,' she countered.

Another flick of his gaze, then he looked back at the gun. 'But you don't know how to take off the safety catch.'

She almost turned the automatic away from him to check it – but stopped herself. 'Nice try. But Adam wouldn't have given me a gun that I couldn't use.'

'Well done, Dr Childs,' he said, with a faint shrug. 'You're not quite as gullible as I thought. It doesn't matter, though, because that gave Baxter time to get you in his sights.'

'And I thought I wasn't gullible,' Bianca scoffed. But then she saw an expectancy in his expression as he glanced behind her once more – and realised that the oncoming car still hadn't passed.

Keeping the gun aimed at him, she looked back . . .

And saw a black Suburban cruising slowly towards them. Baxter leaned from the passenger window, the needle-thin red line of his MP5's laser sight fixed upon her.

'Drop the gun!' he shouted. 'Do it or I shoot!'

Fear froze her, her hand refusing to obey Baxter's order even to save her life. She stared helplessly back along the laser beam as it moved up to her head—

Thudding footsteps – and she was slammed painfully to the ground as Harper charged at her like a bull. He tore the gun from her grasp, twisting her arm up behind her back with such force that her shoulder joint crackled. She screamed. 'Limey bitch,' he growled. 'Baxter! Get over here!'

The Suburban pulled up, Baxter jumping out. Two more SUVs came speeding in from the other direction. 'Are you okay, sir?' Baxter called.

'I'm fine. How did you find me?'

He nodded towards the Cadillac. 'All government vehicles have trackers. When you didn't answer the phone, I realised that Gray must have got you, so we hauled ass to catch up.' He surveyed the area. 'Where *is* Gray?'

'On his way to DC – with the disk,' said Harper, standing. Bianca tried to move, but he shoved her back down with his foot. 'He's in a black Mustang – Maryland plates, registration BAR 643. He went west, towards the Parkway.'

'We'll get him.' Baxter looked down at Bianca. 'What about her?'

'Leave her with me – you need to take out Gray.'

Baxter nodded to his men. 'Okay, you heard him! We catch that son of a bitch and take him down. Let's go!' He hurried back to his vehicle. With a triple roar of big V8s, the Suburbans lunged away.

Bianca looked up at Harper. 'What are you going to do with me?'

He sneered. 'You're going to be my chauffeuse.' He stepped back, keeping the gun on her. 'Get in and drive.'

Adam made a call as the Mustang raced along the Suitland Parkway, entering one of the numbers he had memorised earlier: the office of the National Security Adviser. 'This is Admiral Gordon Harper,' he said, his voice taking on his borrowed persona's bulldog growl. 'I need to speak to Alan Sternberg immediately.'

He knew that calling from a number not on the list of secure lines would invoke extra security precautions, but he was ready for them. 'Please stand by, Admiral,' said the operator. 'Can you give me your G-2 code, please?'

'Four-zero-two-five-baker-delta-seven,' he replied, rattling out the sequence with machine-gun speed.

'And your daily password?'

'Anthracite.'

A short pause while the codes were checked, then: 'Thank you, Admiral. Connecting you to Mr Sternberg.'

Adam waited, guiding the Mustang past slower traffic on the two-lane highway. Finally, he heard a voice. 'Gordon,' said Sternberg, dislike contained beneath a veneer of professional politeness. 'What can I do for you?'

'Sir, this is Adam Gray from the Persona Project at STS,' Adam said, speaking quickly to prevent Sternberg from interrupting. 'I apologise for the deception, but it's of vital importance that I speak to you.' The other man tried to cut in, but he kept talking. 'I have proof that Secretary of State Sandra Easton was killed in Pakistan because a senior US official leaked her route to al-Qaeda.'

It took the startled Sternberg a couple of seconds to reply. 'Agent Gray, as I understand it you're currently on the run after stealing classified data from STS. Why should I believe you?'

'Because I used the PERSONA device to take the memories of the official in question. I know everything he does – and everything he *did*.'

'Who is this person?' asked Sternberg, in a tone that suggested he had already worked out the answer.

'Admiral Harper, sir.'

A pause. 'That's an extremely serious allegation, Gray. And I need more proof than just your say-so, even if you do have Harper's memories.'

'I've got a disk that the Admiral just took from the federal data repository in Suitland. He intended to destroy it. It's a copy of the log files that show he interfered in a joint CIA-SOCOM undercover op to give disinformation to al-Qaeda in Pakistan, by switching the Secretary's fake itinerary that was meant to lead a terrorist cell into a trap for the real one.'

Another moment of shocked silence. 'Now, it's no secret that Harper and I aren't exactly best buddies,' said Sternberg slowly, 'but you're saying that he's a *traitor*? I can't believe that.'

'Nobody would. That's why he thought he'd get away with it. Sir, I'm on my way into Washington right now to give you the disk. When you have it I'll surrender myself and face any charges against me, but you *have* to see the evidence. Harper can't be allowed to get away with what he's done.'

'All right,' said Sternberg after brief deliberation. 'Bring me the disk. But do I have your word that you'll turn yourself in?'

'Absolutely, sir. Once the disk is in your hand, I'll surrender. Where are you?'

'At the Eisenhower Building.'

'I'm ten minutes away. Where will you be?'

'Meet me at the north entrance on 17th Street. I'll make sure that—'

The rear windscreen exploded.

Adam flinched as a bullet hit the back of the passenger seat's headrest, blowing a hole through the leather. He dropped the phone and took the wheel with both hands, eyes darting between the mirrors.

Lights were coming up fast from behind. Three sets, large vehicles.

Baxter's team had found him.

48

No Limit

Headlight flare from a car on the other side of the median strip gave Adam a glimpse of Baxter leaning out of the lead SUV. Red laser light lanced from his MP5. Adam swerved. Muzzle flash blossomed in the mirror, the gun's rattle accompanied by harsh clanks as rounds hit the trunk lid.

He heard Sternberg's tinny voice from the fallen phone. 'Sir, I'm under fire!' was all he could spare the mental resources to shout before diverting his attention entirely to evasion and escape. The Mustang was on paper much faster than the SUVs, but with their upgraded engines and suspensions the Suburbans were no slouches.

He dropped down a gear and accelerated, the rev counter jumping up into the red. The speedometer reached one hundred and kept climbing. He checked the mirror. His pursuers were falling back . . .

Not fast enough. He was opening a gap, but now the other drivers had their feet hard to the floor.

Adam changed up. One-twenty. Mirror. The lead Suburban was a couple of hundred yards back, out of the sub-machine gun's effective range – but it was now maintaining the distance, its companions right behind it.

He looked ahead—

Red tail lights filled both lanes.

Fear sent an adrenalin shot through his system. He braked, sloughing off speed and swinging the Mustang right to avoid a collision. A vicious *thump-thump* as the wheels mounted the kerb, then the entire car shuddered with earthquake force as it rode along the bumpy grass verge.

It was like driving on ice. Adam grappled with the steering wheel, needing all his skill to hold the car in line as its tail threatened to snap out and send him into a spin. He overtook the obstructing cars, but now saw green rushing at him in his headlamp beams, shrubs and trees directly ahead—

A twitch of the wheel. The Mustang swung back to the left, kicking up dust and shredded grass before crashing on to the blacktop. The jolt as the suspension hit its limits felt like a kick to his spine.

He ignored the pain and straightened out, dropping back through the gears to accelerate again. The lead SUV switched on its strobes, unearthly blue pulses silhouetting the cars he had just overtaken. The one in the inside lane slowed, the other ducking aside to let the faster vehicles through.

The Parkway passed under a bridge. A sign at the roadside told Adam that the chase had just entered the District of Columbia. He was about six miles from his destination.

Six miles. Half of them on the highway. The other half would take him through the busy streets of Washington.

And he would be under attack the whole way.

He kept accelerating, back up to a hundred. This section of the road was a long, sweeping curve through woodland – with a speed limit of only fifty. More traffic ahead. His gaze flicked between the rapidly approaching tail lights and the blue strobes in the mirror. The cars ahead were reasonably spaced out . . .

Adam steeled himself – then pushed the pedal down, committing himself to the run.

He pulled into the right-hand lane, whipping past a car on the inside before swinging sharply back to the left to round another vehicle. No sooner was he past than he dived back to the right, barely a foot ahead of the car he had just overtaken. A horn sounded in anger.

Faster. More red lights rushed at him. Back to the left, foot dabbing the brake before he veered sharply across to the inside lane once more. Mirror. The cars behind were responding to the emergency lights, pulling over to leave the outside lane clear.

The lead SUV closed again, his slalom costing him precious momentum. Gear down, foot down. The rev counter wavered in the red zone. He swung past another couple of vehicles, cutting his turns as close as he dared. Another horn blast, a car weaving as its driver was frightened out of his highway trance.

He looked back. The gap was staying constant—

A pickup truck ahead suddenly pulled across to the outside lane, speeding up to draw alongside a Chevrolet Cruze – then cutting speed to match it. The pickup's driver had seen the strobes behind and decided to make the automotive equivalent of a citizen's arrest, blocking the Mustang's path so that what he thought was law enforcement could catch the speeder.

Adam had no choice but to brake hard, the Ford snaking. He looked frantically to each side of the rolling roadblock. There was no crash barrier along the grassy median strip to his left, but the number of approaching headlights warned him that crossing into the oncoming traffic would be suicide.

A paved cycle lane ran parallel to the highway on his right. But it was too narrow to fit the Mustang . . .

No choice.

He braced himself and swerved over the kerb with another tooth-shaking crash from the suspension. Then the Mustang was straddling it, right wheels all the way over at the cycle lane's far side while the left rattled in the Parkway's gutter.

Foot down. The black car accelerated, drawing level with the Cruze occupying the inside lane – and making contact. The flanks of the two vehicles ground together as the Mustang passed. The door mirror on Adam's side was sheared off with a crack.

The Cruze's driver panicked, instinctively turning away – and sideswiped the pickup.

Adam accelerated and dropped back on to the highway. The Chevrolet swung across the road behind him, just missing the Mustang's rear bumper. The weaving pickup braked hard. Its tail end slewed around, bringing it broadside on across the lane—

A collision was unavoidable for the lead SUV. Reed, driving, took the less damaging option, veering right to hit the smaller Cruze rather than the big 4x4. With two men and their gear aboard, the Suburban was more than twice the weight of the compact car. The result was inevitable. The Cruze was swatted aside, spinning on to the cycle lane with its flank caved in.

But the SUV also took damage. The impact shattered its right headlamp cluster and tore off the front bumper, Reed battling to keep control as the Suburban reeled over the kerb. It ripped through bushes at the roadside before finally slowing.

One down, if only temporarily – but still two to go. The other Suburbans also swerved to avoid the pickup, narrowly missing the wrecked Cruze before overtaking Baxter and sweeping back into pursuit of the Mustang.

The Parkway curved round in a long sweep to head north. Adam was a mile from the Frederick Douglass Bridge, which led across the Anacostia River into the heart of the capital. From there it was about three miles to his destination.

The traffic ahead was more spaced out. He shoved his foot to the floor. The Mustang surged forward. A hundred and ten, one-twenty. The wind noise through the broken rear window sounded like a jet taking off. At this speed the steering felt hypersensitive – the smallest mistake would throw him wildly off course. He gripped the wheel more tightly.

The strobes receded in the mirror. The upgraded Suburbans could probably match his speed in the long run, but he had superior acceleration.

The highway curved back to the north-west. Just seconds had passed, but he had already devoured half a mile, gliding back and forth between the two lanes to flash past other vehicles. Glaring lights to his right, buses lined up beneath them at the Anacostia Metro station.

Traffic lights ahead.

They turned red—

The road widened into four lanes at an intersection. All were filled.

Brake!

Adam stamped on the pedal. The Mustang's tyres shrieked in smoking protest as the speedometer needle plunged. But he wasn't slowing quickly enough, the back of a container truck looming directly ahead like a steel wall . . .

He jerked the wheel to the left. There was a narrow paved dividing strip separating the northbound and southbound sides of the Parkway. The Mustang rode over it with a bang, briefly airborne before slamming back down – heading straight into the oncoming traffic. He pulled hard at the wheel. His car fishtailed, the rear wheels shrilling again as they regained traction and flicked him back on to the right side of the road.

Metal crunched as a car braking to avoid him was hit from

behind, but he was already past the collision. The road ahead was clear. Where were his pursuers?

The strobes of the lead Suburban were visible only as reflections off the sides of the vehicles at the lights. It had been forced to stop. The second—

Its driver was braver – or crazier. It leapt over the divider, following Adam's path through the intersection to swing back in behind him.

The Mustang's thunderous engine note briefly echoed back at Adam as he tore through a concrete underpass. He was coming up to the bridge approach, the two sides of the divided highway splitting apart.

Brake lights flared ahead, a chain reaction rippling back towards him. Traffic was slowing for some reason.

All three lanes were blocked.

Another intersection was rapidly approaching. He looked past it, spying the bridge's street lights as it arched over the river. A glinting ruby line ran beneath them, more tail lights glowing.

The bridge was jammed with vehicles. No way to get across.

Not on *this* side, at least . . .

He threw the Mustang hard to the left, swerving on to a single-lane access ramp.

Lights ahead – a car coming the other way. He rode up on the grass to avoid it. The Ford wriggled like a fish, trying to break out of his grip. The other car whipped past, but now the Mustang's tail was slipping out again, sending him slewing towards a tree.

If he braked, he would spin out—

Mud sprayed up behind him as he feathered the throttle, holding his car on the very limit of control to make a powered drift around the curve. He sawed at the wheel to keep it on course.

Green gave way to grey in the headlights. The Mustang

dropped back on to the road with a chirp from the tyres. He yanked the wheel back in line, heading for the bridge.

The wrong way. He was now driving head-on into traffic coming out of central Washington – and there were only two lanes, concrete barriers hemming them in.

Blue pulses in the mirror. The Suburban was catching up.

Adam flashed the Mustang's headlights, jerking the wheel left and right to weave through the oncoming vehicles. Left into a gap, then sharply back to the right—

Two cars side by side dead ahead. Not enough room on either side to get round them.

All he could do was aim directly between them and pray they had enough sense of self-preservation to get out of his way . . .

The car on the left did, swerving and braking. The driver on the right was either dumbfounded or distracted, continuing straight at him.

Adam jinked to the left. But the gap was still not wide enough—

The second driver finally reacted to the headlights charging at him and jerked away. The Mustang threaded its way through the newly opened gap at sixty miles per hour, clipping the other car and veering to the right. The barrier rushed at Adam . . .

He stamped on the brake, hauling the wheel back to the left. The Mustang slithered around, its back quarter hitting the concrete with a crunch that threw him sideways. He straightened with a pained gasp. The speedometer fell below thirty. He dropped through the gears and accelerated again.

More cars ducked out of his way as he headed into the traffic. Where was the Suburban?

Right behind him—

The SUV rammed the Mustang.

The collision was hard enough to trigger the airbag with a

gunshot *bang* of compressed gas, catching Adam as he was flung against the steering wheel. Even cushioned, it still felt like he had been punched in the face. Dizzied, he sat up. The Mustang was swerving back to the right, towards the divider. He straightened out.

Something sliced through his peripheral vision to the left, very close. The Suburban drew alongside – then sideswiped the smaller vehicle and forced it into the barrier.

Sparks flew from the Mustang's side as it ground against the concrete. Adam tried to steer away, but the SUV was too heavy, pinning him. He looked round. Spence was in the Suburban's front passenger seat, leering down at him.

Raising a gun—

Adam slammed on the brakes.

The Suburban shot past, trim ripping away from its flank as the two vehicles separated. It swerved towards the barrier – then swung sharply to the left as its driver fought to regain control.

The Mustang accelerated again – and hit it.

Adam had deliberately aimed to swipe the SUV's rear quarter. The impact hurled the Suburban into a spin, sending it broadside-on into the left lane—

An oncoming truck smashed into it.

The SUV was thrown into the air like a toy, tumbling over the barrier in a shower of glass and plunging to its doom in the river below.

Adam didn't look back, all his focus on the vehicles ahead. He was over halfway across the bridge, but the accident would cause a concertina effect, backing up the approaching traffic. He flashed his lights again. Startled drivers cleared his path, giving him just enough room to straddle the white line and pass between them.

He squinted through the headlight glare. There was still a steady stream of cars coming out of DC even at this late hour; the capital did not clock off at five. A brief sidelong glance told him the reason for the build-up of northbound traffic, a car's flashing hazard lights marking a breakdown. Beyond the obstruction, the road was clearer. Only a couple of hundred yards more, and he would be off the confines of the bridge . . .

A bus occupied one lane ahead, the driver resolutely refusing to give him extra space. He had no choice but to continue anyway, blasting the horn in warning. The cars alongside the bus opted to let him through, the thought of insurance excesses swaying their drivers' minds. Squeals and shrills of metal against metal as the Mustang rasped along the bus's side, then he was through.

Off the bridge. Clear to navigate. He swung back on to the proper side of the road and accelerated.

Mirror. The tac team's strobe lights were still visible on the bridge, but they had fallen back. This was his chance to lose them, while they were still picking their way through the confusion.

The Nationals' baseball stadium passed on Adam's right as he raced up Capitol Street. He visualised DC's street map. Harper's experience helped him pick out a route, decades of working inside the Beltway as useful as any satnav. Follow Capitol, then cut diagonally across the street grid on Washington Avenue before heading west along the south side of the Mall until he reached 17th Street. The Eisenhower Building was then just a few blocks due north. About three miles. Even though the streets were still busy, he was only minutes from his objective . . .

Pulsing lights in the distance ahead warned him that he would have to change his route. A police car was tearing down Capitol Street towards him.

N Street crossed Capitol at the next intersection. The cops were still a couple of blocks away. He took a left, screeching through the junction. The road was much narrower than the one he had left, but at least this time there was no traffic. Small two-storey houses flicked by. He needed to turn back to the north—

A pickup truck backed out of an alley directly into his path.

Parked cars on each side left him nowhere to turn. He braked hard, the tyres leaving smoking black lines along the asphalt. But they still couldn't stop him in time—

The Mustang was doing about fifteen miles per hour when it hit the pickup. The impact threw Adam forward. With the deflated airbag hanging limply from the steering wheel, there was nothing to stop him from cracking his head against the hub. He slumped back into the seat, dazed by pain.

The engine stalled. He tried to focus, putting a hand to his aching head and feeling dampness. There was a red smear on the flaccid airbag. A paralysing nausea rolled over him as he tried to raise a hand to restart the car.

A middle-aged black man scrambled out of the pickup and stared in dismay at his vehicle's crumpled side before turning to Adam in anger. 'Hey! What the hell? Look what you've done, you asshole!'

Adam took several deep breaths, forcing back the sickening dizziness. His fingers found the override in the ignition. He turned it. Something in the engine bay clattered alarmingly, but then the V8 burbled back to life. He put the gearstick into reverse.

'Oh, *hell* no you don't!' cried the pickup driver, reaching for his door handle. 'You ain't going anywhere!'

Adam reached into his jacket as if about to draw a gun. The other man retreated, worried. 'Sorry, I don't have time to exchange insurance details,' Adam said as he applied power. The Mustang briefly resisted before jerking away from the pickup, leaving a chunk of its radiator grille embedded in the truck's mangled bodywork. One of the headlights was broken.

He reversed until he reached a gap between the parked cars,

then swung up on to the sidewalk to get around the obstacle. The man yelled impotent abuse after him.

A siren behind grew louder. Adam checked the mirror. One of the Suburbans made a slithering turn off Capitol, the blue lights in its grille blazing.

He shoved his foot down, snatching rapidly up through the gears as he powered along the sidewalk and swung back on to the road. The SUV followed, gaining rapidly. The Mustang had suffered mechanical damage – it was only subtle, but Adam could feel that it was less responsive than before.

Another intersection ahead. He threw the car to the right, heading north – realising too late that he was going the wrong way up a one-way street.

Headlights came at him.

He swung the Mustang to the left – then veered sharply back to the right as the other driver panicked and swerved across his path. The two cars missed by inches. He looked back, hoping that the Suburban's route was blocked, but there was just enough room for the SUV to slip by.

Someone leaned from the side window. Fallon. Laser light stabbed from his MP5 as he aimed at the fleeing Mustang.

Adam jerked the wheel left as Fallon fired. Bullets seared past. Another burst as the soldier adjusted his aim, and the Mustang echoed with the hammering hailstone *plunk-plunk-plunk* of rounds tearing through sheet metal. Adam flinched, but the shots didn't hit him.

He was not unhurt, though. His left eye suddenly stung. Blood from the cut on his forehead was running down his face. He wiped it away, but realised from the size of the stain on his hand that the flow was not going to stop.

Traffic ahead. He was approaching the intersection with M Street, cars crossing his path in both directions.

A dazzling red dot fluttered across the dashboard. Adam ducked as Fallon leaned further out and fired again. More sharp thumps of impact – and the right side of the windshield crazed as a hole was punched through it.

The Mustang reached the junction. Left or right?

Neither.

Adam braced himself and ploughed straight across, aiming for what he hoped would remain a gap.

Horns blared, brakes squealed – then the Mustang lurched as a car clipped its back end. A sharp yank at the wheel and he regained control, checking the mirror—

The car that had nicked him spun like a top as Fallon's Suburban slammed into it. The SUV skidded round – then flipped on its side, crushing Fallon beneath it and smearing him over the road before rolling on to its roof. It smashed into a street lamp, practically folding in half around it.

Two down.

But there remained one to go. Baxter was still behind him, the last Suburban refusing to give up its prey.

The Mustang tore past a fire station, men already running out to help the crash victims. He looked ahead. The street ended at a T-junction. He slowed to turn west, feeling a shiver through the steering. The latest collision had added to his ride's woes. Damage to the suspension, or one of the wheels; either way, he couldn't keep going much longer.

But he didn't have to. Only a couple more miles.

If he could survive them.

49

End of the Road

Adam glimpsed a sign: I Street. His mental map of the city warned him that he was in a minor maze of residential roads, with few direct connections to the major arteries he needed to reach. Heading north would only take him deeper into the tangled grid. But if he turned *south* at the western end of I Street, he would emerge on Maine Avenue. From there, he could follow the road north-west past the Washington Monument directly to 17th Street – and then it was a straight run north to the Eisenhower Building.

Where Sternberg was waiting.

The thought galvanised him. He wiped more blood from his eye and accelerated, weaving past trundling traffic. The junction was just ahead.

And Baxter was behind.

Like the Mustang, the last Suburban had lost a headlight. The cyclopean glare in the mirror was briefly lost to view as he made the turn south, then returned, closing in.

Adam swung right and poured on the power to make a sweeping entry on to Maine Avenue. He forced his way into the traffic, leaving a trail of swerving and skidding cars in his wake.

Reed navigated them all, the SUV's siren howling a warning for other drivers to clear the way. Baxter brought up his MP5 again. The laser's dot darted over the surrounding vehicles as Adam wove the Mustang through the shoal.

The speedometer rose – sixty, seventy. But the Suburban was keeping pace – and the shudder through the steering column was getting worse, the Mustang twitching and wavering.

Laser flare in the mirror as the SUV found a gap in the traffic and swung in behind the speeding Ford. There was a car to Adam's left, forcing him to go right to evade – directly across Baxter's line of fire.

The red glare was overpowered by stuttering muzzle flash. More shots struck the Mustang – then the entire windshield imploded, crystalline fragments flying back into Adam's face in the eighty-mile-per-hour slipstream.

He instinctively shut his eyes to protect them from the hard-edged cascade, then forced them open again. He had to squint into the slashing wind – and the first thing he saw was a set of tail lights rushing at him.

He swerved – finding another car already there.

The two vehicles caromed off each other with a crunch of metal, the second car bounding up over the central reservation. Adam hauled the wheel again to slot into its space, missing the slower vehicle ahead by a hair.

The road dropped into a tunnel beneath the Southwest Freeway. He pulled back into the rightmost lane, putting the car he had just passed between the Mustang and the Suburban. That gave him a few seconds' respite.

He would need it. There was a tight turn coming up.

The Mustang emerged from the underpass – and immediately shot through a red light. Adam spun the wheel, bringing the car screaming through the traffic crossing the intersection and down the exit to the left, tearing alongside the monolithic block of the Federal Communications Commission. The road rapidly merged back on to another section of Maine Avenue . . . one leading to 17th Street.

Only a mile to go.

The Suburban reappeared behind him, barging a car aside. Baxter was getting increasingly desperate to stop him, putting civilians at risk. Harper's part of Adam's psyche tried to defend the collateral damage: *the ends justify the means*. Adam didn't accept that, but in this case he had no choice but to do whatever was necessary to reach Sternberg.

The road passed under two bridges. Another red light ahead, cars slowing in all three lanes—

Despite knowing the damage it could cause, Adam swerved up on to the central divider to get past them. The Mustang's suspension protested with a loud bang – then there was another crack of metal as the car hit a street sign, shearing its pole off at the base. He flinched as the sign flew at him, flipping up over the shattered windshield and clanging off the roof.

He veered right to avoid a street light and crashed back on to Maine Avenue. Baxter's SUV followed. The illuminated spire of the Washington Monument pierced the night sky above the trees ahead.

The vibration grew worse. One of the Mustang's wheels was definitely damaged. But he had to keep going. Back up to sixty, weaving through the traffic.

The laser swept through the car—

Pain exploded in his right arm.

Adam screamed. More bullets clattered against the Mustang as it veered out of control and ran up on to the grass. A tree loomed in the headlight beam. He somehow found the strength to over-come the agony and turned the wheel. The trunk whipped past.

Off the road, without street lights, he couldn't see the wound. The bullet had hit his bicep, the muscle on fire. He tried to move his arm. Searing, stinging pain crackled through the nerves – but he still managed to grip the shifter. He changed down, a strained gasp escaping through his gritted teeth. The juddering Mustang found more purchase.

Lights ahead – another road through the park crossing his path. He aimed for a gap in the traffic and braced himself. Another slam came through the tortured suspension as his car hopped the kerb and hit the asphalt before pounding back on to the grass at the far side.

The Washington Monument was an unmissable beacon. Adam turned so that it was off to his right and angled through the park towards another thoroughfare. He swung on to it in front of a startled cab driver.

The pursuing 4x4 had barely been slowed by its off-road excursion as it charged after him. It was still on the grass, Reed running parallel to the road to give Baxter a clear shot. The laser stabbed between the two vehicles. Adam forced another car aside to take cover behind a van.

Baxter fired anyway. Rounds ripped through the van's sides, mangled bullets smacking against the Mustang's battered flank. Adam accelerated. The ex-Marine unleashed another burst as he emerged, but the shots went wide as Reed was forced to turn sharply to avoid a stand of trees. The Suburban bounced back on to the road behind Adam.

The other cars gave him enough illumination to see blood soaking his sleeve. The bullet had gone through his arm, torn flesh around the exit wound. All he could do to staunch the bleeding was to take the wheel with his right hand, clamping his left over the injury.

The burst of pain was so intense that Adam thought he was

going to pass out – but pure adrenalin forced him on. The road ahead forked. He followed it to the right at well over twice the speed limit, at last on 17th Street.

His final destination was dead ahead.

And the man trying to stop him was closing fast from behind. The one-eyed SUV reappeared in the mirror. Baxter leaned out again. His MP5 spat fire. The window beside Adam blew out, more glass showering him.

He cried out again as he let go of the wound, left hand back on the wheel so he could change gear. The Mustang picked up speed. Tail lights rushed at him like meteors. He jinked between them, trying to give himself cover.

No good. He couldn't shake the Suburban. Reed was an expert driver – and his vehicle was only superficially damaged, while Adam's own had taken a severe beating. The Mustang's engine note became rougher. Warning lights flashed on the dash – temperature, oil pressure.

He willed it on. Only half a mile to go. It *had* to make it!

Buildings ahead as he approached the north side of the Mall – and another red light at the intersection with Constitution Avenue. He pulled out into the oncoming lane to pass the waiting cars—

Someone was crossing the road!

Instinctive terror punched at his heart as he braked and swung wide to avoid the pedestrian. The man's look of shock as he shot through the headlight beam burned into Adam's vision like a camera flash. Then he was gone, falling away behind as the Mustang recovered.

The man was silhouetted by the SUV's lights in Adam's mirror—

The Suburban didn't deviate, swatting him aside. The dark figure tumbled along the road like a rag doll.

Horrified, Adam looked ahead – and felt another shot of fear.

Flashing lights ran across 17th Street a few blocks away. A police barricade, multiple cars and vans lined up across his path.

Inevitable, Harper told him smugly. *The Eisenhower Building is right by the White House. Of course they're going to stop you getting anywhere near it.*

But the cops were less of a threat than Baxter. The Suburban drew in, engine snarling. Adam tried to accelerate again, but the crippled Mustang was sluggish. All he could do was keep weaving as he powered up 17th Street, trying to shake off the laser sight.

It was impossible. The SUV loomed ever larger in the mirror – and then Adam's rear view disintegrated as a bullet hit it, more rounds ripping into the roof and seats.

Buildings blurred past on the left. To the right was open parkland, but if he tried to escape that way it would lead him straight into the gunsights of the men guarding the southern perimeter of the White House.

He was out of options. The roadblock was coming up fast, past the intersection with E Street. The only way he could go was left, but that would take him away from Sternberg – and with Baxter right on him and the Mustang almost finished, he wouldn't get far.

Escape, how to escape . . .

No. *Attack.*

A large panel van was waiting on E Street at the intersection, blocking Adam's view of the building behind it.

His view – and Baxter's.

Last chance—

Adam threw the Mustang into what he knew would be its final corner, the wounded vehicle's pain as clear as his own. He passed the van's front – then pulled on the handbrake.

The car went into a spin, its tail flying out wide. He controlled it, feathering the throttle as the Mustang whipped round through a full two hundred and seventy degrees. Its momentum sent it skittering backwards behind the van – then he stamped the pedal all the way to the floor. The rear wheels shrieked, belching out vortices of stinking smoke as they scrabbled for grip.

They found it, arresting the car's rearward motion – and flinging it forwards.

It was the same trick he had used to vanish from Bianca's sight when she had tailed him from STS what felt like a lifetime ago, making a seemingly impossible turn into the warehouse's loading dock just before she rounded the corner and reappearing right behind her.

This time, he wasn't going to give his pursuer a mere nudge.

The Suburban had followed him, Reed and Baxter momentarily confused by his apparent disappearance – before they saw him coming at them from an unexpected direction—

The Mustang rammed the SUV.

Reed's door caved in, not even the airbags enough to save him from injury. The Suburban slewed around – then its right rear wheel struck the kerb. It flipped over, tumbling along the sidewalk before hitting a tree and spinning back into the road in a spray of glass and leaking fluids, ending up on its crushed side.

Adam's car fared no better. The collision flung the Mustang on to the sidewalk. It crashed through the hedges outside an art gallery. He braced himself, grabbing the seat belt – but the force of the collision as it slammed sidelong into the building's wall was enough to dislocate his left shoulder with a hideous crackle of cartilage. He hit the steering wheel again, tearing a deep cut into his cheek.

The engine stalled, the sudden silence almost shocking. He tried to sit upright, only to howl in excruciating pain as nerves scraped in his torn shoulder. He barely heard his own cry through the ringing in his ears. One eye was now blinded by the blood oozing from his forehead. He tried to focus with the other, the cabin swimming into view.

He could still move his right arm, barely. More pain burning through the ripped muscle, he gingerly placed his palm on the centre console and levered himself back into his seat.

A blur resolved into the overturned SUV. Passers-by looked on in astonishment, unsure what to do. A man ran up to the Suburban, peering inside – then jumped back as someone crawled out through the broken windscreen.

Baxter.

One side of his face was covered in rivulets of blood from a ragged cut in his scalp. He lay sprawled on the street for a moment, catching his breath, then stood.

The MP5 was in his hand.

The onlookers hurriedly backed away as Baxter staggered towards the wrecked Mustang. Adam reached into his jacket. His fingers found the disk, still in its case – but he remembered too late that he had given Harper's gun to Bianca.

Baxter drew closer, cold anger on his face. He was going to finish the job.

Adam fumbled for the door handle. It moved, but only a little. Jammed. He pulled harder, but the damaged mechanism still refused to give. He looked up. Baxter continued to limp towards him.

The laser sight flicked on, the beam rising towards Adam. He heard someone shouting, but couldn't make out the words. The edges of his vision began to roil, darkness growing. His body was desperate to shut down, to stop the pain.

He couldn't allow it. Not yet. He tugged the handle again, shifting painfully to push at the door with one knee. It still wouldn't open.

Trapped.

Baxter was only a few yards away, the laser dazzling. Somebody shouted again, more urgently, but the words were still distorted.

Baxter's bloodied mouth twisted into a victorious smile—

A dark flower burst open on his chest. The former Marine staggered, the laser line swinging crazily – and a second entry wound erupted beneath the first. Baxter toppled backwards to the ground as blood gushed from the bullet holes.

Adam looked back. Two cops were running towards him, one keeping his smoking gun fixed on the fallen man. The other hurried to the Mustang, pointing his own weapon at its occupant. Words finally resolved through the ringing. 'Hands where I can see them!'

Adam tried to respond, but a wave of dizziness overwhelmed him. He slumped, head lolling. The cop shouted again. 'Get your hands up! *Now!*' The gun's muzzle moved closer, the black hole swelling as if to swallow him . . .

'Don't shoot!'

A new voice. The cop lowered his gun. Adam gathered all his strength to turn his head. Several men were running around the corner from 17th Street. Most were in dark suits – Secret Service agents, guns at the ready. Amongst them was a thinner man, his clothing far more expensively tailored.

Alan Sternberg.

'Call an ambulance!' shouted the National Security Adviser as the agents spread out to contain the scene. He peered through the Mustang's window. 'Jesus,' he said at the sight of the battered man inside. 'Agent Gray? Can you hear me?'

Adam squinted up at him with his one open eye. 'Sir, I've . . . got the disk,' he managed to say, reaching weakly into his jacket to produce it. 'It's got . . . the proof about Harper. Just before the . . . bombing in Islamabad . . .'

Sternberg gently took it from him. 'If the proof's on this, we'll find it.' He looked back at the Secret Service men. 'Where's that damn ambulance?'

Adam's vision began to tunnel again. He peered past Sternberg towards the intersection. The street was crawling with cops, holding back traffic and pedestrians – but one car had come through. A Cadillac CTS. Harper's.

The rear window wound down. A face looked out. Even in his state of fading consciousness, Adam still felt the odd, dislocated sensation of seeing himself, as his borrowed persona reacted to the sight of Harper staring back at him. 'Sir,' he gasped. 'Open the door . . .'

Sternberg pulled at the handle. The catch finally released. 'Someone help me with him!' A pair of agents rushed over to give assistance.

Adam barely held in a pained cry as he was lifted out of the car. His injured left arm hung limply at his side, but he managed to bring his right up to point at the Cadillac. 'Harper . . . over there . . .'

Sternberg looked round in surprise. He started to speak, only to freeze as he saw Harper emerge from the car with a gun in his hand.

The Secret Service agents saw it too, moving to shield Sternberg. But Harper had already brought his weapon up.

He fired—

Screams came from the onlookers as the white-haired man collapsed beside the limousine, the fire-blackened hole of a bullet wound at point-blank range in his temple.

Adam watched as Harper fell, a mixture of emotions hitting him. Shock at the sight of someone taking his own life; anger that the architect of so many deaths, including Michael Gray's, had found a cowardly way to escape justice. But he also knew exactly why Harper had done it. His thoughts were clear. *I'm a patriot, right to the end. I'll do whatever it takes to protect America.* There would be no humiliation of a public trial.

There was another feeling in Adam's mind, this one all his own. *Completion.* His mission was accomplished.

He could rest. Perhaps for ever.

The last thing he saw as his perception faded to an all-consuming nothingness was Bianca climbing out of the Cadillac, her eyes locked fearfully on to his.

50

Requiem

Kyle watched gloomily as the Bullpen's video wall was switched off. 'So. We're suspended. Again.'

'Cheer up, man,' said Levon, clapping a hand on his shoulder. 'At least it's a *paid* suspension.'

'Rather than the "thrown in a cell awaiting possible criminal charges" kind,' Holly Jo added. She gave Morgan an embarrassed look. 'Thank you for letting us off with just a reprimand, sir.'

'Don't think I didn't consider taking matters further,' Morgan replied sternly. The three young specialists wilted under his gaze – until he unexpectedly winked at them, a small smile breaking through his stony mask.

'Well, I still think it's an outrage,' said Kiddrick, glaring at him. 'I mean, I was *assaulted* in my own office! I suffered injury and emotional trauma, to say nothing of the—'

'Oh, come now, Nate,' boomed a stentorian voice from the back of the room. Everyone turned to see Albion enter, riding in an electric wheelchair. 'Consider it an injury sustained in the line of duty. It's a badge of honour! I got shot by a terrorist; you got a bump on the head. Practically the same thing.'

The others laughed – with one obvious exception. 'I'm not

going to let this lie,' Kiddrick whined. 'I deserve recompense. I should sue!'

Morgan's unsympathetic eyes turned upon him. 'I would seriously advise against anything that might expose STS's operations in an open court, Dr Kiddrick.'

'Well, I should – I still intend to take this higher,' spluttered the scientist.

'To whom?' said Albion, rolling up alongside him. 'The Deputy DNI? He's got enough on his plate right now, trying to deal with all the fallout. And I don't think trying to sully Adam's name will win you much favour with Alan Sternberg.'

Kiddrick glowered at him, then looked around for support. He found none. Face twitching, he stalked away. 'Don't forget we have a meeting,' Morgan called after him.

Kyle made a rude gesture behind Kiddrick's back, stopping when he caught Morgan's disapproving look. He hurriedly tried to camouflage his hand movement by brushing imaginary fluff from his chest. 'So, Doc! Welcome back!'

'How are you feeling?' Holly Jo asked Albion.

'As good as anyone who can see daylight through their torso can feel,' he replied. 'But I should be up on my own two feet in a few weeks.'

'And until then, you've got that sweet ride,' said Kyle, eyeing the wheelchair. Holly Jo tutted.

Albion grinned. 'No, he's right. It *is* rather cool.' He nudged the joystick, the chair doing a full three-sixty spin in place. 'And it grants me unlimited licence to quote *Dr Strangelove*.' He turned again, more slowly, to survey the Bullpen. 'So. Did I miss anything while I was away?'

Groans and giggles came from his co-workers. 'Nah, nothing worth commenting on,' said Levon. 'We barely noticed you were gone.'

'Mm-hmm,' added Holly Jo. 'Dr Childs filled in for you really well.'

'Some might say, almost too easily,' said Morgan. Albion blinked up at him with an expression of total innocence. 'Speaking of Dr Childs,' he added, looking at his watch, 'I've got a meeting to attend. In the meantime, the Persona Project will be officially placed on administrative suspension until further notice, so if anyone's got any personal effects in the facility, make sure you've removed them by eighteen hundred hours. Otherwise, you won't be able to get at them for some time.'

Levon glanced at the toys cluttering his workstation. 'Any idea how long that's likely to be, sir? Days, weeks?'

'Months?' Kyle said hopefully. 'You know, since we're on paid leave and all . . .'

'I should have an answer shortly. Until then, carry on in here. Roger, are you coming?'

'Let's roll,' Albion said with a chuckle. He and Morgan left the Bullpen and headed to one of the briefing rooms.

Waiting for them were Bianca, Tony . . . and Adam, his left arm in a sling and a bandage around his right bicep bulking out his shirt sleeve. More dressings covered the cuts on his forehead and cheek. Kiddrick was also present, sitting at the opposite end of the table from them and frowning in sullen silence. 'Well, now,' said Morgan, regarding the trio, 'between you you've caused a very complicated situation. I don't know what's going to come of it.'

Adam stood. 'Sir, I accepted all along that there would be consequences for my actions. I'm fully prepared to take them.'

Tony joined him. 'So am I.'

Morgan's gaze turned to the Englishwoman. 'Dr Childs?'

'Well, I . . . yeah, I've got to take responsibility for what I did,' she said unhappily. 'But I'd really rather not go to prison for the rest of my life.'

'That's not up to me.' He gestured for the two men to sit back down, then took his place at the head of the table and made a phone call. 'This is Martin Morgan at STS. Tell Mr Sternberg that we're ready for him.'

There was a delay of a couple of minutes, which did nothing to ease the tension in the room, before the screen on the wall came to life. Alan Sternberg looked down owlishly at them. He didn't bother with small talk. 'I'll get straight to the point – the Persona Project has caused the biggest political nightmare for any administration since Iran–Contra. Agent Gray, Agent Carpenter, Dr Childs: you deliberately engineered a major security breach . . . which in turn exposed a conspiracy to commit an act of outright treason at the highest levels of the US government. It's a catastrophic intelligence failure and a diplomatic disaster, and if the truth got out to the world it would cause immeasurable damage to the United States.' He was silent for a moment, staring down at his uncomfortable audience like Big Brother. 'Which is why it never *will* get out.'

Morgan was first to speak. 'What do you mean, sir?'

'I mean, none of this ever happened.'

'You're going to cover it up?' said Bianca.

'Yes, Dr Childs, we're going to cover it up,' said Sternberg scathingly. 'What, did you really think we're going to proclaim to the world that the Director of National Intelligence personally subverted a black operation in order to supply classified information to al-Qaeda, so that they would assassinate his political rival to promulgate the War on Terror?'

'Well, not when you put it that way,' she mumbled, abashed.

'Damn right. Harper committed a terrible crime that cost hundreds of lives, but exposing it would cost *thousands* more – terrorist groups around the world would be emboldened, and the United States' credibility in fighting them would be shattered.

And there's no telling where the loss of confidence in America's democratic institutions would lead. Harper was approved by Congress, remember. This isn't something either side can make political capital out of; everyone's in it together.'

'How are you going to cover it up?' asked Tony. 'Harper killed himself one block from the White House in front of dozens of witnesses. There's probably a video on YouTube already.'

'NSA can take care of that,' said Sternberg, the statement ambiguous enough to suggest that the intelligence agency might already have done so. 'But we can handle it; it's just a matter of presentation. Harper was divorced, in a high-pressure job, the assassination of the Secretary of State took place on his watch, et cetera. A storyline that ends in a self-inflicted gunshot wound practically writes itself.'

Bianca was appalled. 'So the truth just gets buried?'

'As the saying goes, Dr Childs, the truth hurts.'

'So do lies,' Adam said quietly. 'Harper will get a eulogy that paints him as a patriot and a loyal servant of his country, won't he?' Though his tone was even, the bitterness behind it was unmistakable.

Sternberg at least had the courtesy to look uncomfortable before quickly changing the subject. 'Anyway, that's one side of the matter. The other is you. Only a few people know the full story. The President has made it very clear that he expects that to remain the case. In return for a promise of absolute silence on the subject, he's willing to grant all three of you full pardons.' Kiddrick made a flustered sound, but Morgan's stare muted him before he said a word.

Bianca hesitated before asking: 'And the alternative?'

The National Security Adviser laughed sarcastically. 'I hear it gets very hot in Cuba. Especially at a certain US military facility on the southern coast. Lots of insects carrying tropical diseases.'

She sighed. 'Yeah, I thought it would be something like that.'

'What about the Persona Project?' said Tony. 'Is it being shut down permanently, or is this just a temporary suspension?'

'A lot of that depends on Agent Gray,' replied Sternberg. 'If he's fit to return to duty . . . and if he's willing. I can understand that after what he discovered, he might have certain reservations.'

Everyone turned to Adam. 'I haven't made a decision,' he said softly, not meeting anyone's eyes.

'As for the Persona Project itself, it's definitely proven its worth – even if not in the way anyone expected,' Sternberg continued. 'You stopped the RTG plot – and the whole affair provided a kick in the pants to the Russians that they need to step up their nuclear security, thank God – but al-Rais is still out there somewhere. He won't give up, so we can't afford to either. An intelligence asset like Persona is too valuable to relinquish, so I'm sure it'll be reactivated in one form or another. So, Dr Kiddrick, Dr Albion – good to see that you're recovering, by the way – don't send out any résumés to the private sector just yet.'

'I wouldn't dream of it,' said Albion cheerily.

'I'll send over the paperwork regarding the President's offer,' Sternberg went on. 'The option is open for Agents Gray and Carpenter and Dr Childs to go through it with a USIC-approved lawyer, but,' steel entered his voice, 'I would strongly advise that they just sign it, because the terms are not going to change.'

'I'm sure they'll do that,' said Morgan, giving the three a warning look.

'Good. I'll be in touch.' Sternberg's image vanished from the screen.

Morgan leaned back in his chair. 'Is all that acceptable?' There was general, if in some cases begrudging, agreement from around the table. 'I'm glad to hear it. Now, is there anything else?'

'What about the PERSONA equipment?' asked Bianca. 'Was it recovered?'

'What was left of it,' complained Kiddrick. 'The main unit was badly damaged. I don't even know if it's repairable – we'll probably have to build a new one.'

Albion gave him a wry smile. 'Try to make it lighter this time.'

'And what about the disk?' said Adam.

Morgan and Kiddrick exchanged glances, the former hesitating before answering. 'We found it at Harper's. It had been destroyed.'

'Oh, no,' said Bianca, dismayed. She turned to Adam. 'I'm sorry . . .'

He was stone-faced, at least on the surface. 'It told me what I needed to know.'

'But there was more on it than just—'

'I know. It's okay.'

Unwilling to accept that, she turned to the two other scientists. 'Is there any way Adam might be able to recover his memories without the disk?'

'No,' said Kiddrick firmly. 'Not a chance.'

Albion made a scoffing sound. 'Ah, that renowned can-do spirit! Don't be so quick to write him off, Nathaniel.' He looked at Bianca and Adam. 'There might be a way – a modified version of Hyperthymexine to force recall, maybe. I'd have to put some work into it, but all might not be lost.' Kiddrick still displayed clear antipathy to the mere idea, but said nothing.

'Anything more?' said Morgan. Nobody replied. 'All right. Tony, you and I have a lot of paperwork still to do. Everyone else, I hope to see you again if and when the project's restarted.'

The group left the room. Albion paused outside the door. 'Bianca? I'm sorry I dragged you into all of this.'

'Thanks, Roger,' she replied, letting the others past. 'Although, while I wouldn't exactly say it's been *fun*, it's certainly been an interesting experience. Even if I'm not allowed to tell anyone about it on pain of death.'

'Oh, I'm sure they wouldn't actually *kill* you. Just waterboard you for a couple of decades.'

She cringed. 'You say that as a joke, but . . .'

'What's the situation with Jimmy's company?'

'The sale's still going ahead, but everything's bogged down with legal and financial stuff – just like you said. I wouldn't have been able to do any work even if I'd stayed there.'

'Good, good. So are you going back to England?'

She looked down the corridor at Adam and Tony. 'Yes, but not right away. I want to do something here first.'

'Help Adam through this?'

'Yes.'

He smiled. 'That's another reason why I knew you were the right person to do my job.'

'Don't expect me to make a habit of it, okay? It's far too stressful.' She kissed his cheek. 'I'll see you around.'

'Always a pleasure,' he replied.

She hurried to catch up with the two men. 'Hey.'

'Hi,' said Tony. 'Something up?'

'No, I just wanted to let you both know that I'll be staying in the States for a little while longer.'

'Finally taking up that offer of an apartment?' Tony said, grinning. 'Let me know if you need a hand moving in.'

She smiled. 'I may do that.'

He stopped as they reached an office door. 'Sorry, I've got some bureaucracy to deal with,' he told her. 'That's what happens when you let someone wreck a building. But whenever you need me, just give me a call.'

'I will. Thanks.' Another smile, then he entered the office, leaving Bianca and Adam alone.

'So why are you staying?' Adam asked her. 'The project's suspended, and Roger will probably be able to work again by the time it resumes.'

'I'm staying because of you,' she told him.

He looked surprised. 'Me?'

'Yeah. Adam, I know it'll be difficult for you to talk about what happened with other people – like your mother – because of the whole secrecy thing, but I want you to know that you can come to me. For anything.'

'Thank you,' he said.

She waited for him to expand on that, but he remained silent. 'That's it?' she exclaimed when her patience ran out. 'That's all you've got to say?'

'I don't know what else *to* say. I'm still trying to come to terms with everything. And without the disk . . .' A resigned sadness filled his eyes. 'I had it back, Bianca. I had *everything* back. But now nearly all of it's gone again. Like Michael. I know I *had* a brother, but . . . I don't remember him. Not in the important ways.'

'But at least now you remember enough to mourn him. Don't you?'

He sighed, then managed a faint smile. 'Yeah. I guess I do. That's a start, I suppose. Thanks.'

'I'm here to help.'

He nodded, regarding her thoughtfully – then his smile suddenly widened. 'I know something you *can* do to help me.'

'What's that?'

'My apartment's kinda . . . empty.' She arched an eyebrow. 'No, I didn't mean that to sound suggestive!' he said, amused. 'There's a big space in the corner, so I was thinking maybe you'd help me buy a TV. So I can become a normal American again.'

Bianca laughed. 'I'd love to.'